Knight of Jerusalem

Knight of Jerusalem

A Biographical Novel of Balian d'Ibelin

Helena P. Schrader

Knight of Jerusalem: A Biographical Novel of Balian d'Ibelin

Published by Wheatmark®
2030 East Speedway Boulevard, Suite 106
Tucson, Arizona 85719 USA
www.wheatmark.com

ISBN: 978-1-62787-194-5 (paperback)
ISBN: 978-1-62787-205-8 (ebook)
LCCN: 2014950453

rev201501
rev201702

Contents

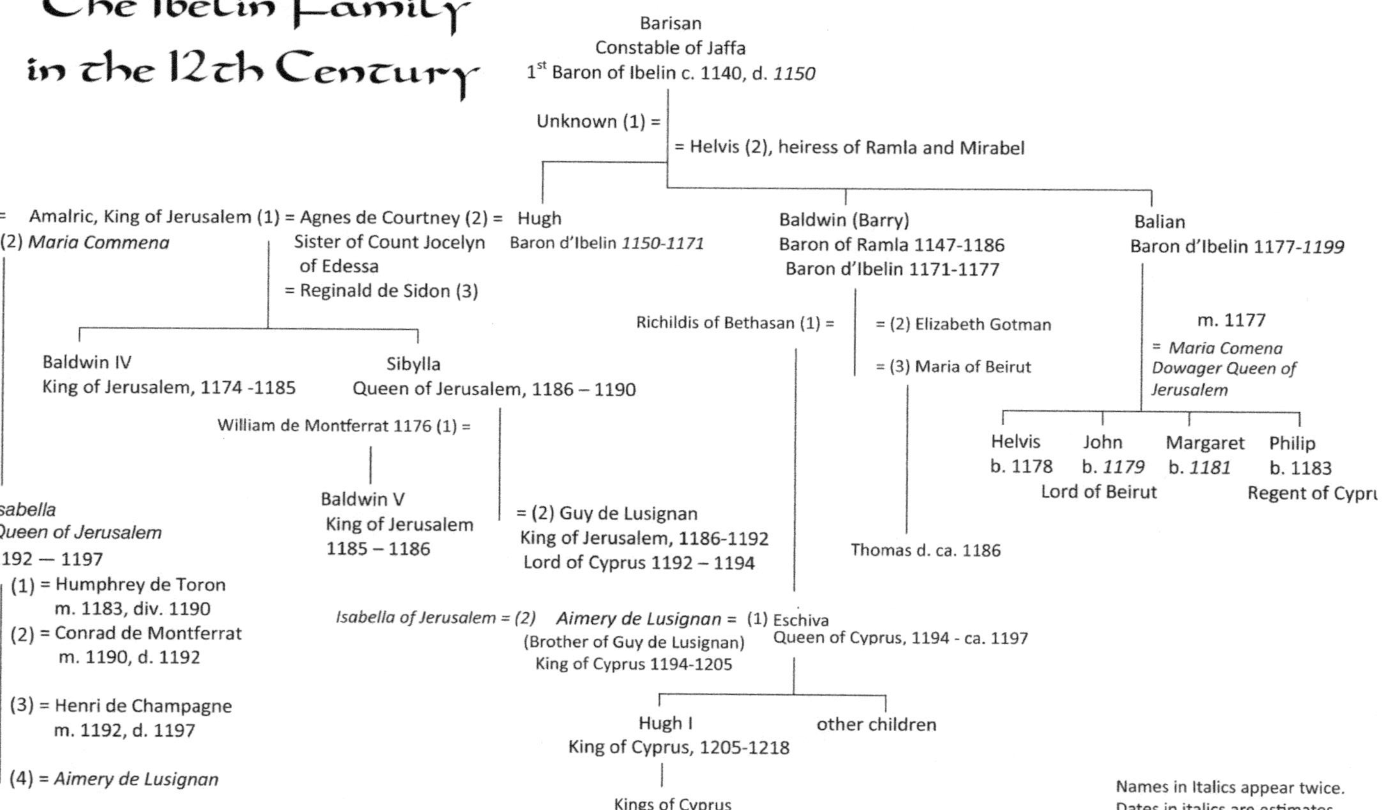

The Ibelin Family in the 12th Century
Barisan
Constable of Jaffa
1st Baron of Ibelin c. 1140, d. 1150
Unknown (1) =
= Helvis (2), heiress of Ramla and Mirabel
= Amalric, King of Jerusalem (1) = Agnes de Courtney (2) =
(2) Maria Commena
Sister of Count Jocelyn of Edessa
= Reginald de Sidon (3)
Hugh
Baron d'Ibelin 1150-1171
Baldwin (Barry)
Baron of Ramla 1147-1186
Baron d'Ibelin 1171-1177
Balian
Baron d'Ibelin 1177-1199
Richildis of Bethasan (1) =
= (2) Elizabeth Gotman
= (3) Maria of Beirut
m. 1177
= Maria Comena
Dowager Queen of Jerusalem
Baldwin IV
King of Jerusalem, 1174 -1185
Sibylla
Queen of Jerusalem, 1186 – 1190
William de Montferrat 1176 (1) =
Helvis
b. 1178
John
b. 1179
Lord of Beirut
Margaret
b. 1181
Philip
b. 1183
Regent of Cypru
Isabella
Queen of Jerusalem
1192 — 1197
Baldwin V
King of Jerusalem
1185 – 1186
= (2) Guy de Lusignan
King of Jerusalem, 1186-1192
Lord of Cyprus 1192 – 1194
Thomas d. ca. 1186
(1) = Humphrey de Toron
m. 1183, div. 1190
(2) = Conrad de Montferrat
m. 1190, d. 1192
(3) = Henri de Champagne
m. 1192, d. 1197
(4) = Aimery de Lusignan
Isabella of Jerusalem = (2) Aimery de Lusignan = (1) Eschiva
(Brother of Guy de Lusignan)
King of Cyprus 1194-1205
Queen of Cyprus, 1194 - ca. 1197
Hugh I
King of Cyprus, 1205-1218
other children
Kings of Cyprus
Names in Italics appear twice.
Dates in italics are estimates

Kings/Queens of Jerusalem 1131 – 1212

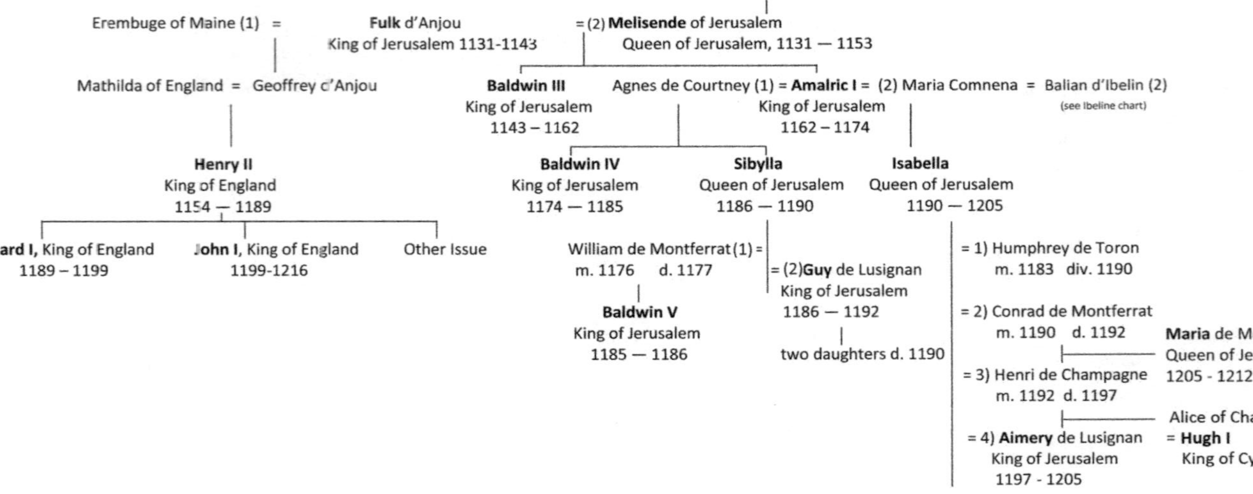

Names in bold are ruling monarchs

The Greek (Byzantine) Emperors in the 12th Century

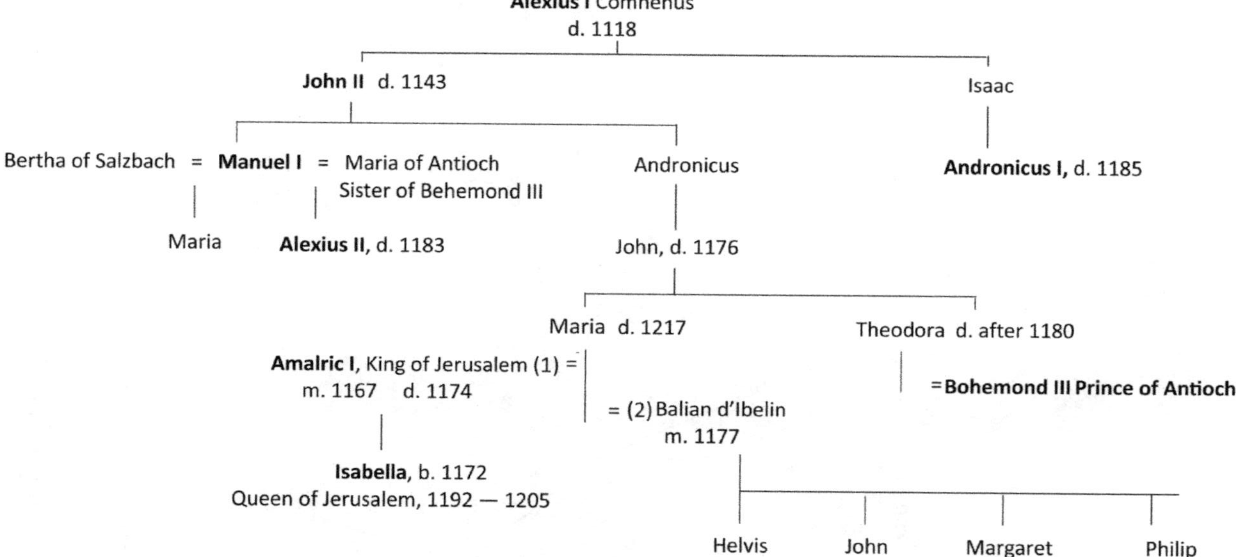

Names in bold are ruling monarchs

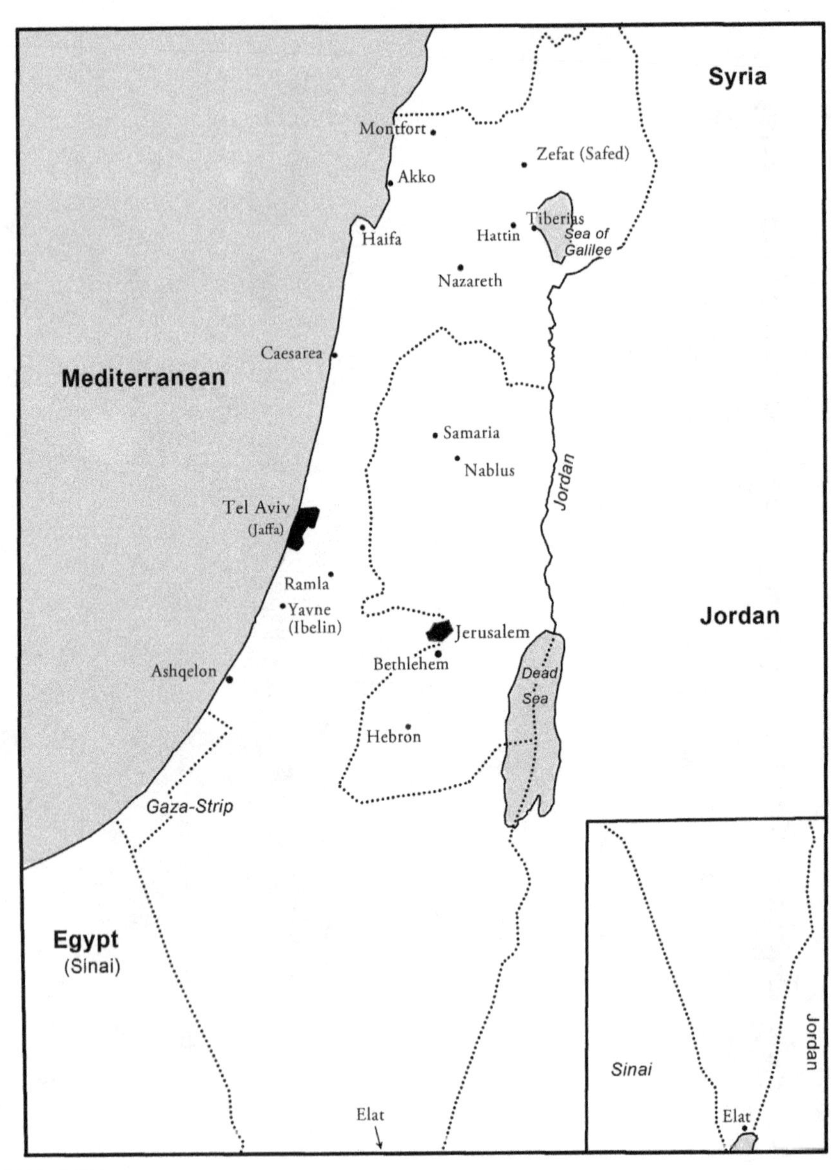

Map of the Holy Land Today (Modern Israel)

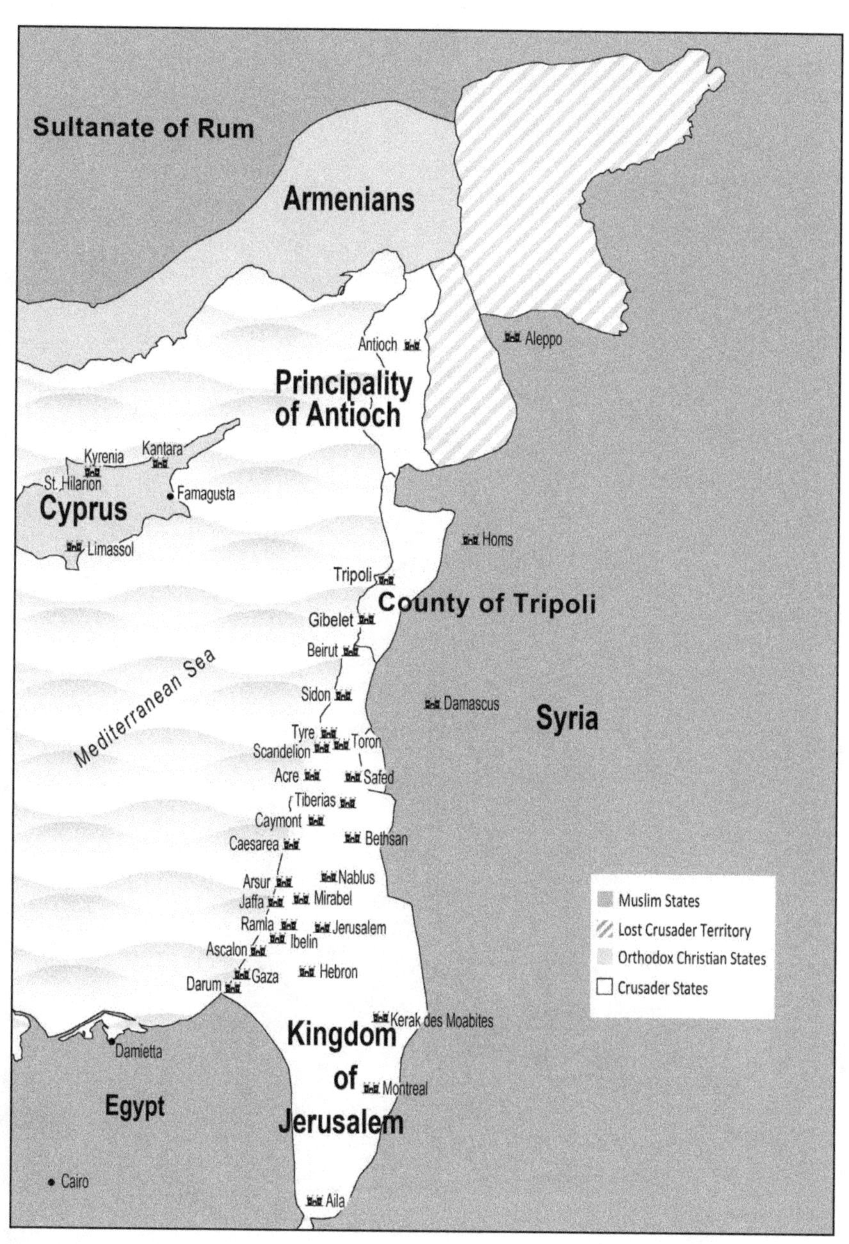

Kingdom of Jerusalem

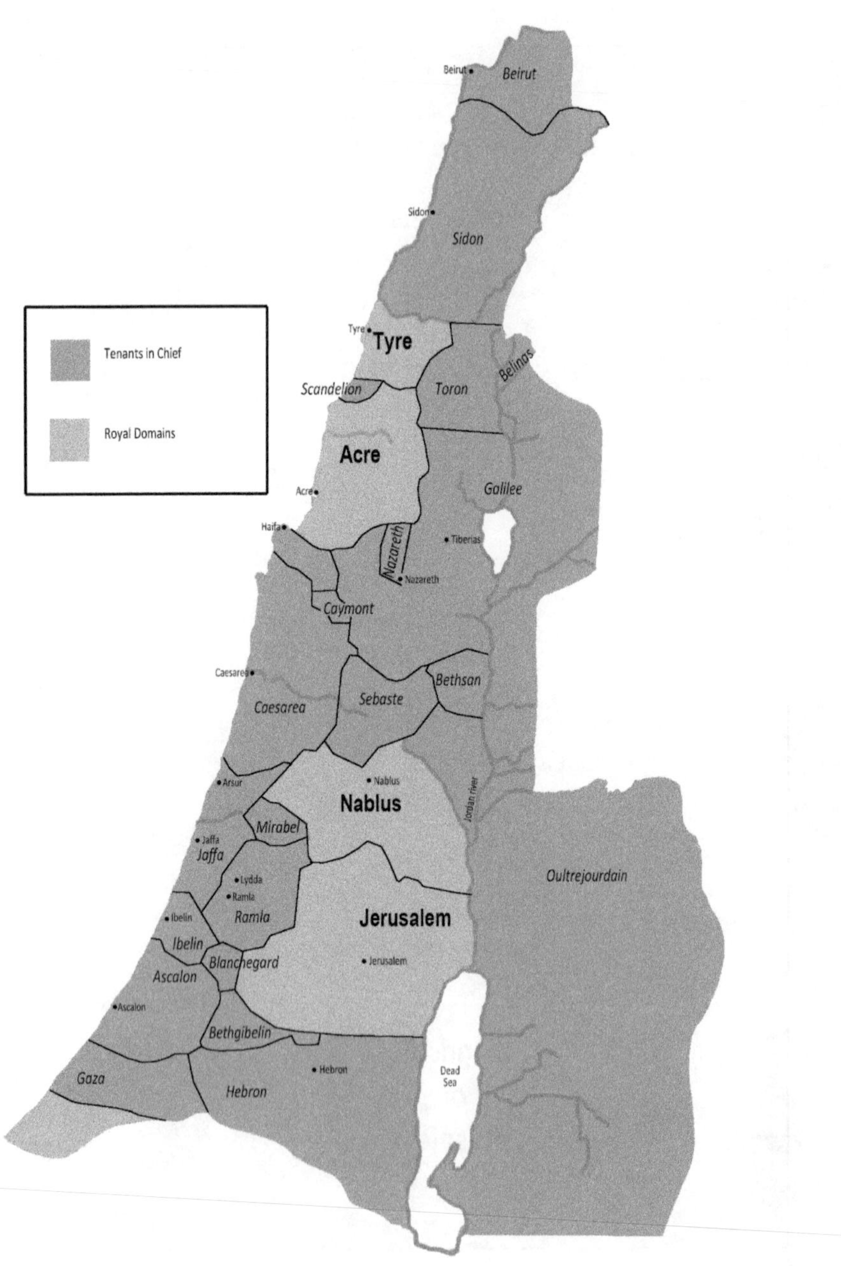

Baronies of Jerusalem

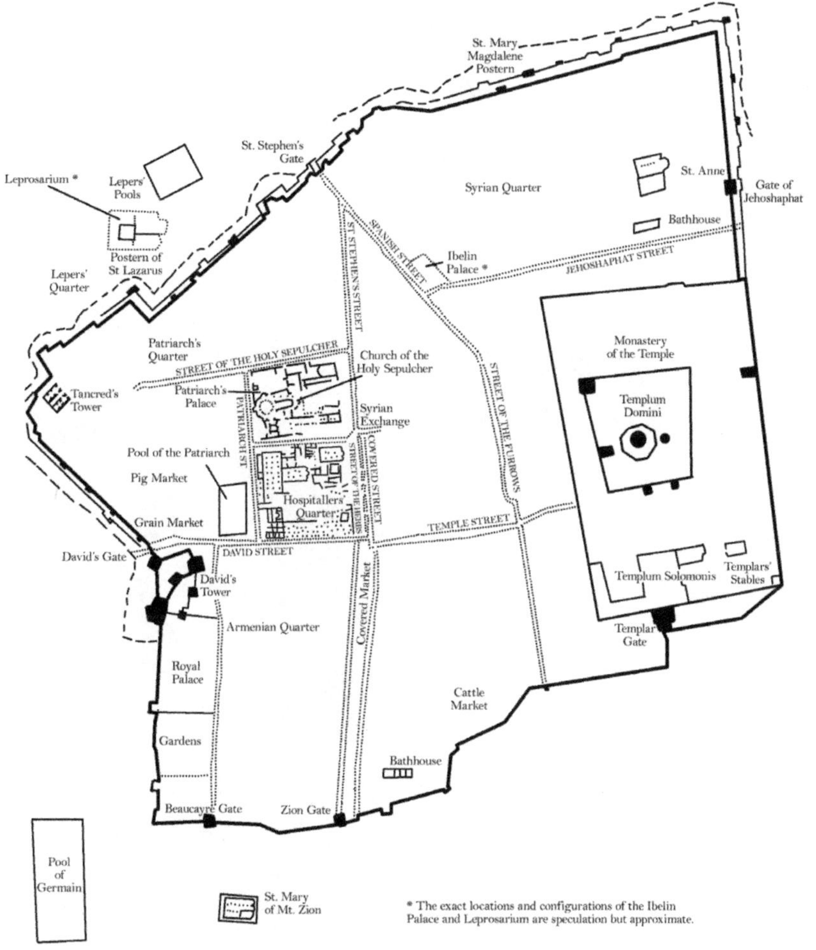

City of Jerusalem in the Twelfth Century

Introduction and Acknowledgments

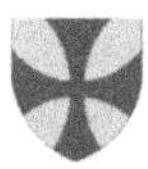

The Kingdom of Heaven, a Twentieth Century Fox film released in 2005 and directed by Ridley Scott, was based—very loosely—on the story of Balian d'Ibelin, a historical figure. Although Scott's film, starring Orlando Bloom as Balian, was a brilliant piece of cinematography, the story of the real Balian d'Ibelin was not only different from but arguably more fascinating than that of the Hollywood hero.

Balian d'Ibelin was a younger son of Barisan d'Ibelin, an adventurer from Western Europe, who first emerged in history when he was named Constable of Jaffa and later granted a fief in the Kingdom of Jerusalem in the mid-1140s. Barisan then did what every self-respecting adventurer did: he married an heiress, the heiress of Ramla and Mirabel. Although the existing sources are ambiguous, it appears that at his death his eldest son Hugh, evidently by an earlier marriage, inherited the paternal title of Ibelin, while Barisan's eldest son by his second and richer wife inherited Ramla and Mirabel. Undisputed is the fact that his third son, Balian, was left empty-handed—a phenomenon unknown in earlier ages but increasingly a problem by the twelfth century.

Despite this handicap, Balian rose to such prominence in the Kingdom of Jerusalem that Arab sources describe him as "like a king." Unusually, and in sharp contrast to his elder brother, he was not merely an outstanding fighting man and knight, effective on the battlefield in offense and defense, but he was also a diplomat and peacemaker. Balian played a decisive mediating role between factions within the Kingdom of Jerusalem and between the Kingdom and its external enemies, including negotiations on two known occasions with Salah ad-Din himself.

Almost equally astonishing for a younger son, he made a brilliant marriage that catapulted him into the royal family—and indeed, his descendants would repeatedly intermarry into the royal houses of both Jerusalem and Cyprus. Furthermore, this marriage was as close to a love match as one can find among the nobility in the twelfth century.

Such a man, it seemed to me, deserved a biography—a biography based on all the known facts, not just those that fit into Ridley Scott's film concept. But while there are many intriguing known facts about Balian, there are many more things we do *not* know, making a traditional biography impossible—just as is the case with Leonidas of Sparta. A biographical novel, on the other hand, is a medium that can turn a name in the history books into a person so vivid, complex, and yet comprehensible that history itself becomes more understandable.

That is my objective with this novel in three parts: to tell Balian's story and to describe the fateful historical events surrounding the collapse of the Christian Kingdom of Jerusalem in the last quarter of the twelfth century, of which Balian was a part. The historical record is the skeleton of this biographical novel, but the flesh and blood—the emotions, dreams, and fears—are extrapolated from those known facts. I hope I have created a tale that my readers will find as fascinating, exciting, and engaging as I do.

I'd like to take this opportunity to thank my test readers Deanna Proach, Anna Clart, and Diana Page for providing invaluable feedback while it was still possible to make changes, and my editor Christina Dickson, who—as always—cleaned up my typos and erratic punctuation and polished the text. Last but not least, I wish to thank Mikhail Greuli for the evocative cover image.

Helena P. Schrader
Addis Ababa
2014

Chapter 1

Ibelin, Kingdom of Jerusalem, March 1171

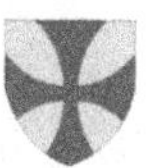

"Sir Balian! Come quick! There's been an accident!" The voice was breathless from the exertion of taking the stone stairs two at a time.

Balian frowned and looked up from the deed he was holding. His elder brother had tasked him with settling a bitter dispute between two of their tenants, which turned on whether a half-dozen acres given as a dower portion could be inherited by sons of a second marriage. Balian was digging through the barony records in search of the land title, and was loath to be interrupted. "What, then?" Balian demanded of the speaker, one of the young grooms, not yet convinced this was something serious.

"My lord's horse has just galloped over the drawbridge without him."

That got Balian's attention: his elder brother was not the kind of man to be unhorsed easily, as he had proved often enough in battle and joust. But he was over fifty now, and his pilgrimage to Santiago de Compostela two years earlier had left him with a chest ailment that gnawed at his health. On the other hand, today's mishap might have been an ambush of some kind. Robber bands and renegades still operated in the mountains to the east, and they might have come down onto the plain because the winter had been harsh and they were short of supplies. It would be just like his brother to try to stop the looting of one of his villages—even if he were alone with no one but a young and inexperienced squire in attendance. Hugh d'Ibelin was nothing if not courageous.

Whatever had happened, Balian was determined to find out. He pounded down the spiral stairs and careened into the castle ward. The stallion had raced home for the safety of his stall, but he felt guilty for leaving his rider behind and so was now tearing around between the keep and the outer walls, trying to avoid the increasing number of grooms and men-at-arms trying to catch him. Balian joined the others, anxious to see if the horse was wounded—or covered in his brother's blood.

They were so focused on catching the horse that they didn't notice the man who came running over the drawbridge and collapsed, panting, just inside the barbican, until he called out: "Lord Balian! Lord Balian! Come quick! The Baron is badly injured."

Balian turned to look at the man in surprise that rapidly turned to horror as the words sunk in. The messenger's long kaftan and sandals marked him as a tenant farmer from one of the Syrian villages, and the wooden cross hanging around his neck marked him as a Christian as well. "What happened?" Balian demanded in Arabic, but then turned to order one of the grooms to saddle his fastest horse before turning back to the breathless farmer.

The farmer shook his head. "I don't know. I wasn't there. It happened near the crossroads." He gestured and spoke in a rush of Arabic too fast for Balian, whose command of the language was limited. Balian grasped intuitively, however, that this man was just the last in a chain of runners. The accident had taken place several miles away, and word had been sent by improvised relays of men passing the message on when they could run no farther. What Balian didn't understand was why his brother's squire had not come with the news himself. Was the squire or his horse also injured?

"Alexis!" Balian called out to his brother's older, more experienced squire, who had been attracted by the commotion in the ward. The young man needed no further orders; he simply nodded and ran toward the stables for his own horse.

Within little more than ten minutes, Balian and Alexis set out for the place where the road to Ibelin crossed the main road from Jaffa to Jerusalem. They were armed and wearing hauberks in case there had been some kind of ambush. They also had fresh horses and set a fast pace, splashing through puddles on the road and cutting across country where they could do so without damaging crops. They skirted around villages of flat-roofed stone houses that stood out white against the lush, green fields. Just short of the main road, they caught sight of a horse tethered near a stand of palm trees beside the main road. There was no sign of any skirmish—no bodies, no lost equipment, not even torn-up turf. Beside the horse, however, Balian made out a figure sitting on the ground. The figure rose to his feet when he spotted the riders and came towards them, waving.

Balian drew up beside the squire. The youth looked up at him, deathly pale, and Balian could read the fear in his eyes. "Sir! Your brother's gravely injured! Come quick!"

"So why didn't you come yourself instead of sending farmers on foot?" Balian asked angrily.

"I—I didn't think—I should leave my lord alone, sir. I'm sorry—"

Balian had already lost interest in the squire. He swung himself down from his stallion, Alexis following his lead, and strode to the imperfect shade of the palms, where Balian could see his brother laid out on his cloak. The sight made him catch his breath. His brother's face was contorted with pain, and although the air was chilly, his skin was drenched in sweat. Balian dropped on one knee beside him. "Hugh! What happened?"

The injured man answered with a gasp, and then opened his eyes and found his younger brother's face. "Thank God! Balian! Fetch me a priest!"

Balian turned around, "Alexis, ride back for a litter!"

When he looked back at his brother, however, the injured man was shaking his head. "No point in that," he gasped. "Find me a priest."

Balian looked up at the two squires, horrified. He wasn't prepared for his brother to die. Hugh, thirty years his senior, had been more a father to him than a brother. Their father had died when Balian was only eighteen months old, and it had fallen to their father's eldest son, Hugh, to raise his three half-brothers, his father's sons by a late second marriage. Balian had no memories of their joint father, but he could remember Hugh carrying him on his shoulders as a toddler, teaching him to say his prayers beside his bed at night, showing him how to ride and play chess, and a thousand other things. Because Hugh had no children of his own, he had lavished attention and affection on his younger brothers, and Balian had returned the affection instinctively at first, then more consciously as he grew up and realized it could have been so different.

His other brothers had not been so lucky. His younger brother Henri was born after their father's death, only weeks before their mother's remarriage. He had lived with his mother until her death and then with her relatives. His older brother Barisan, their father's namesake, had initially been raised with Balian by Hugh at Ibelin, but at sixteen he inherited their mother's barony of Ramla and moved away. For the last eight years, Balian had been treated like Hugh's only son.

"I need a priest, Balian," his brother's voice broke into his thoughts.

"The nearest Latin priest is at Ibelin. I've sent Alexis for a litter—"

"There's an Orthodox church in the next village," Hugh cut him off. "Send for him!" That his devout brother would think of turning to an Orthodox priest made it even more certain that Hugh thought he was dying, but Balian still refused to believe it—even though he dutifully sent the squire for the Syrian priest.

Balian reached for his brother's hand; it was so cold it chilled him. "What happened, Hugh? Were you attacked?"

"No. Nothing so dramatic. My stallion shied. I fell badly. I heard my bones crack. In my neck."

"Can you move your legs?" Balian asked anxiously.

"No. Now you know why I want the priest."

Balian crossed himself and started praying silently. "We'll get you back to Ibelin—" he started to assure his brother, but his brother cut him off.

"No. Just—fetch me—a priest."

"He's on his way, Hugh," Balian assured him, holding his hand.

The cold hand flinched slightly and then closed around Balian's with surprising strength. His brother clamped his teeth together, apparently fighting a wave of pain. As the pain eased somewhat, Hugh started speaking earnestly. "Balian, I'm sorry to leave you like this. I had hoped —" He broke off with a gasp and held his breath until the pain had eased again. "Never forget that our father was a younger son. He came to Outremer with nothing. Nothing but his sword and his courage."

Balian nodded. He had grown up knowing that with two elder brothers, he would inherit nothing. Hugh was still speaking. "He won Ibelin with his service to the King and nothing else."

Balian nodded again; he was intimately familiar with his father's history even if he had never known the man. Hugh had fought alongside their father for a decade and had raised Balian on tales of his father's strength, courage, and wisdom.

"Barry will inherit Ibelin now—since I have no issue." The dying man's regret was audible, and Balian's heart went out to him. Hugh's mind, however, was on the younger brother he had raised like a son. "You'll always have a place in Barry's household—but that will bring you little. Neither honor nor fortune."

Balian had to agree with that. He was only two years younger than their father's namesake and in consequence had always lived in his brother's shadow. Barry was tall, blond, and powerfully built. He cast a big shadow.

"Better to seek honor and wealth elsewhere," Hugh advised, grasping Balian's hand firmly for emphasis. Hugh and Barry had become increasingly estranged ever since Barry came of age and took control of Ramla. Ramla had an income four times that of Ibelin—and Hugh, who'd held Ramla for almost ten years as guardian for his younger brother, naturally felt the loss of both income and prestige. It didn't help that the loss of Ramla had coincided with the "return" of Hugh's lost bride, Agnes de Courtenay. She had done much to poison the atmosphere between the brothers.

"Jerusalem," continued the dying man, drawing Balian's attention back to the present. "Go to Jerusalem."

Balian frowned. He had been at court often enough with his brothers as a child, even attending the coronation and later the marriage of King Amalric, but he had not been to Jerusalem since he was knighted two years earlier and came to live again at Ibelin with Hugh.

"Jerusalem owes me a favor," Hugh remarked, his contorted face twisting into a kind of smile, "and since I cannot call it in, I want you to. Go to Jerusalem and tell him I sent you on my deathbed to collect the debt."

Balian suspected this had to do with his sister-in-law, Agnes. Amalric's succession to the crown of Jerusalem had been controversial at the time and contingent on him setting aside Agnes de Courtenay. Balian speculated that it was only because Hugh had agreed to take Agnes back that it had been possible for Amalric to persuade her, the Patriarch, and her powerful family to accept the dissolution of her marriage to Amalric. Then again, it didn't really matter what debt the King owed Hugh, as long as it helped Balian in a court overflowing with young men who had come to seek their fortunes from all over Christendom. Balian wasn't convinced he had much of a chance of rising among such competition, but he supposed this was as good a place to start as any. "I'll go," he assured his brother.

The pain had its grip on the dying man, and he could only clutch his brother's hand and grind his teeth in answer. When the pain receded, he asked again for the priest.

Balian squinted down the road, straining his eyes until at last he saw motion. He waited until he was sure, then reported: "The priest is coming, Hugh."

Sure enough, Adam was riding beside a Syrian Orthodox priest, who was sitting sideways upon a little donkey. The donkey was trotting as fast as it could, and the Orthodox priest's black robes, white beard, and black hat bobbed comically up and down. Balian got to his feet and approached the priest respectfully. "Father, my brother has broken his back in an accident. He wishes to confess and receive the sacraments."

"I understand, my son," the priest answered, indicating a leather satchel containing the Host and the sacred oil.

The Baron of Ramla and his family arrived at Ibelin in a blinding rainstorm. Thunder grumbled in the distance and flashes of lightning occasionally split the darkness, but the driving rain fell so hard that it drowned out voices and the ringing of church bells. The water rapidly filled the gullies and ran down the streets and alleys of the villages along the way, turning them into muddy streams. The high road, meanwhile, turned to a morass of cream-colored mud and began to wash away in places, slowing progress so much that the Baron's party, although they had left Ramla before Sext, arrived at Ibelin only as dusk was falling.

Balian hastened into the ward to greet his brother's party. In the fading light it was hard to distinguish the Baron from his knights and men-at-arms. The horses were caked in mud right to their knees, their bellies and haunches splattered with it, their tails matted, their manes dripping wet. The riders wore their hooded cloaks pulled as far forward as possible. Balian noticed, however, that a child was sitting in front of one of the riders, and so he went first to that rider and held up his arms. "I'll take Eschiva," he offered.

"Balian! Thank you! I'm so sorry!" It was the voice of his sister-in-law, Richildis. She lifted her daughter up out of the saddle as she spoke, and Balian took the little girl in his own arms. She was shivering and her teeth were chattering, so Balian took her on the crook of his arm and put his own cloak over her to shield her from the rain and cold before turning to help Richildis down. Richildis gratefully turned her bedraggled mare over to one of the grooms, and gave Balian a hug followed by a kiss on both cheeks. "I'm so sorry!" she repeated.

Balian believed her. She had been married to Barry when he was eleven and she only ten, and she had lived with her husband's family and enjoyed Hugh's benevolent guardianship for nearly five years until Barry came of age and set up his own household. "It was such a shock," she exclaimed. "I didn't want to believe it."

"We can talk about this inside," Barry ordered, coming up behind his wife. The Baron of Ramla, and now Ibelin as well, towered over his wife. He was a good six feet tall and broad-shouldered. He wore his blond hair long, and he kept his face clean shaven except for a mustache that drooped to his chin.

Balian didn't contradict him, but led the way out of the ward by the outside stairs, which gave access to a hall running along the inside of the western wall of the castle. Here a fire was blazing and many of the household had gathered to keep warm and dry, but Balian continued through the hall to the solar, located in the chamber beyond the high table. Balian had had the foresight to lay a fire several hours ago. There were now enough embers to give off substantial heat, as well as flames still burning around the log. Balian set his niece down in front of the fire, and turned to take Richildis' and Barry's wet cloaks from them. The rain had soaked through their cloaks and left water stains on their shoulders and chests. Handing off the wet cloaks to Alexis, who was waiting attentively, Balian ordered him to bring warm robes from Hugh's wardrobe for the new arrivals. "I don't really have anything for Eschiva," Balian apologized, looking toward his niece, "except some blankets."

"That's fine. We need to get her to bed as soon as she's had something to eat," Richildis answered.

"Is that bitch Agnes here yet?" Barry asked his younger brother, moving up to hold his hands to the fire after wiping his wet forehead dry with the back of his sleeve.

"Barry! Watch your tongue!" Richildis admonished. "She's your brother's widow—not to mention the mother of the heir to the throne."

"Both of which facts are to be deeply regretted!" Barry countered, unabashed. "The boy she gave the King has turned out to be a leper, and the only babies she gave Hugh were stillborn. I say the woman's cursed!"

Balian and Richildis shared a brief look. It wasn't that they disagreed with Barry's negative opinion of Agnes de Courtenay, but they deplored Barry's tendency to be blunt and uncompromising to a fault.

"Hugh should never have agreed to take her back after she'd jilted him to go to Amalric's bed! It damn near broke his heart to come out of Egyptian captivity to find his fickle 'bride' had up and married someone else!"

"He didn't have any choice," Balian reminded his brother patiently. "He was legally betrothed to her, and could not marry anyone else without a formal annulment. Her marriage to Amalric was not legal—"

"In which case, Amalric's children by her are bastards, including that leper boy," Barry pointed out.

"The High Court agreed to recognize them when he was crowned," Balian reminded his brother unnecessarily; Barry knew this just as well as Balian did.

"And I don't know why we're talking about such things at a time like this!" Richildis told the men. "Your brother is not yet in his grave, and all you can talk about is whether his widow's children by another man are legitimate!"

"There's nothing we can do for Hugh now," Barry countered, "but I don't trust that damned woman not to lay claim to Ibelin. She's as like as not to claim it as her widow's portion, and I'll tell you right now she'll have to *fight* me for it."

"Oh, Barry! Don't say things like that. King Amalric settled a substantial income on her when he set her aside, and she hasn't lived at Ibelin in years."

"She's a covetous bitch!" Barry answered. "And she will try to get her claws on Ibelin any way she can."

"But she has no legal claim," Richildis started, only to fall silent as the solar door opened and Alexis returned laden with robes, blankets, and linen towels. Leaving these, he departed again in answer to Balian's urgings to have the kitchen send up mulled wine and hot food.

Meanwhile, Richildis stripped her six-year-old daughter out of her wet clothes and rubbed her dry before the fire, then wrapped her in one of the soft blankets Alexis had brought. Her husband also stripped and dried himself, pulled a fur-lined robe over his head, and belted it with his own belt, as it was otherwise too wide for him. He took a deep breath. "I suppose I should go pay my respects. Where is Hugh's body laid out?"

"Before the altar of the crypt," Balian answered.

"Let's put Eschiva to bed first," Richildis suggested, but her husband waved the suggestion aside. "You put her to bed. I'm going to pay my respects to my brother."

Richildis seemed to want to protest, but then thought better of it and let her husband stalk out of the solar, by the spiral stairs carved in the thickness of the walls that led both to the bedchamber on the floor above and the family crypt below.

After Barry disappeared down the stairs, there was an awkward moment of silence. Then Balian took hold of a chair and placed it closer to the fire. "Come sit here to warm up and dry off," he urged his sister-in-law. "You must be exhausted."

Richildis took a deep breath and then admitted, "I am." She collected her skirts, weighted down by water and mud, and sank into the chair. Here she removed her ruined shoes and held her feet out toward the fire. Her once-white stockings were so dirty they looked as if she were still wearing shoes. Balian, meanwhile, moved another chair to the fire, sat down in it himself, and pulled Eschiva onto his lap. The six-year-old was so exhausted that she dropped her head on his chest and fell asleep almost immediately.

"You're better with her than Barry is," her mother observed.

"That's because I have the luxury of being her uncle," Balian answered with a laugh. "I can be nice all the time, while Barry has to make sure she grows up into a proper young lady."

"How are you doing, Balian?" Richildis asked next, searching his face.

Balian looked away, into the fire, and did not answer right away. At length he admitted, "I'm still in shock. I knew the day would come when Hugh would be gone, but our father was over sixty when he died. I thought I had another decade—or at least that I'd have more warning, a long, lingering decline." He paused, reflecting on what he'd said, and then remembered his manners and turned to ask his sister-in-law, "And you? How are you doing? It's harder to bury a child than a brother."

His question caught her off guard. Cold and tired as she was, her defenses were weakened. The reference to the daughter she'd buried six months earlier brought tears to her eyes, and she found herself shaking her head and trying to pull herself together. "What woman doesn't bury a child or two?" she asked back, but the tears couldn't be stopped.

Balian wanted to kick himself for raising the issue. He would have reached out to her if Eschiva hadn't been snoring softly in his arms, preventing him from moving.

The moment passed. Richildis wiped the tears away with her hands and turned a twisted smile to Balian. "Don't think you were wrong to ask. It means more to me that you remember my Stephanie, than that you've made me cry. Barry—Barry acts as if he'd never had another daughter. Or as if girls don't matter at all. He wants a son so badly. . . ." She covered her face with her hands.

It was a not a pretty face: Richildis had been endowed with too large a nose in too narrow a face and eyes set too close together. But Balian did not see Richildis as a woman, just as a sister. It hurt him to see her so distressed, and he recognized that the long, wet journey had laid emotions bare that she otherwise concealed. He took his time answering, trying to think how best he might comfort her. "The barons of Jerusalem need sons, Hilde," Balian reminded her gently. "Without sons who can grow up to bear arms, the Kingdom is defenseless. But that doesn't mean we don't value our daughters."

"I know," Richildis answered wearily, dropping her hands to her lap and gazing into the fire. "I know."

Agnes de Courtenay arrived the next day. She was now thirty-six years old and had never been a beauty. Her value lay in the fact that she was the daughter of the Count of Edessa, and although the County of Edessa had been lost in 1144 and her brother held the title only nominally, the family was still well connected and powerful. She had waited out the rain, and arrived escorted by a dozen men-at-arms.

Balian dutifully went to meet her as she emerged from the barbican gate into the ward. "Balian," she greeted him; "always such a good boy. Hugh's darling." Her smile was fake. "Is your older brother here yet?"

"Barry and Hilde arrived last night," Balian answered.

"In the rain? Foolish of them."

Balian didn't answer; he just helped Agnes out of the litter. Unlike Richildis, who had been dressed in mourning, Hugh's widow was wearing a bright-blue cloak over a red gown with elaborate gold embroidery. Her white veils were likewise trimmed with red and gold ribbons. She caught Balian's look of disapproval and snapped at him, "What did you expect? A grieving widow? Hugh was never anything but a nuisance to me! Now at last I'm free of him."

"Why bother to come to the funeral, then?" Balian asked back.

"To gloat, dear boy. To have the triumph of living longer. One day, when you grow up, maybe you'll understand."

"I hope not."

Henri d'Ibelin, the youngest Ibelin brother, was the last to arrive. He was twenty-one, just fifteen months younger than Balian, and had been knighted at Christmas the previous year. He proudly wore his golden spurs and rode the stallion his lord, the Baron of Oultrejourdain, had given him at his knighting. He also carried a shield with Oultrejourdain's arms, for he had chosen to remain in Oultrejourdain's household rather than return to a "home" he hardly knew. He was a slighter, shorter version of Barry: blond like their father, with a nose that hung straight from his forehead like the nosepiece of a Norman helmet, a throwback to his grandfather of Ramla. To his credit, although he had hardly known Hugh, he behaved soberly and respectfully. He was dressed in mourning and knelt at his brother's coffin for half an hour on arrival.

Meanwhile the other guests were arriving for the funeral. The ten knights who owed fealty to Ibelin came from their manors with their entire families to keep a vigil and, of course, swear fealty to the new baron. Many of the freeholders from the villages belonging to the barony also streamed into Ibelin to pay their last respects. These were mostly Latin settlers, men and families, who had come out to the Holy Land after it had been reclaimed for Christianity by the First Crusade. They were free men, not serfs, and many were tradesmen: blacksmiths, carpenters, wheelwrights and tinkers, butchers and brewers, potters and weavers. Some of the tenant farmers from the Ibelin domain also came: native Christians, both Jacobites and Maronites, who had been tenants to Muslim lords before the crusaders came. The few Muslim tenants kept their distance, however, unfamiliar or uncomfortable with Christian burial rites.

The most important guests, however, were the Barons of Bethgibelin, Hebron, Blanchegarde, and Arsur, all of whom came with their wives—while King Amalric sent his seneschal to represent him, along with his "deepest regrets" that the business of the Kingdom prevented him from attending the funeral himself. Everyone knew that the real reason he didn't come was to avoid confronting his discarded wife, Agnes.

Balian was kept busy ensuring that there was accommodation for all these guests and their servants, men-at-arms, and horses, and that there was food and drink for new arrivals and a daily main meal, while Barry accepted the condolences and presided at the high table. Balian didn't mind this division of labor because this was the natural order of things, and being busy helped him to focus on the present rather than grieving for the past or worrying about the future.

He was in the stables, seeing to yet another cavalcade of horses, when Henri sought him out. "So," Henri started, plopping himself down on a bale of straw, his hands on his hips. "Did we get anything?"

"What do you mean?" Balian asked.

"Does it all go to Barry?"

"Of course."

"Ramla, Mirabelle, and Ibelin? That's three baronies, and three of us. They could have been divided between us. I've heard Barry say he doesn't plan to return here anyway. He's going to stay at Ramla because it's more comfortable." Ibelin had been built in 1141, when Ascalon was still in Saracen hands, as a border fortress. It was a defensible castle, but hardly a palace. Ramla had been an Arab city, destroyed in an earthquake centuries before the First Crusade and half buried in sand dunes when the Christians reoccupied it, but it had never been of military importance, and the castle there was more a residence than a fortress.

Balian nodded. "I can understand that."

"If he's going to stay in Ramla, why can't he give one of us Ibelin?"

Balian shrugged. "He could, but he doesn't have to. By right, he inherits all three."

"And you accept that?"

"Of course. Why shouldn't I?"

Henri snorted contemptuously and kicked at some manure that had been dropped in the aisle between the stalls. "Oultrejourdain says that while the Kingdom of Heaven belongs to the meek, the Kingdom of Jerusalem belongs to the bold."

"Bold is not the same thing as covetous. Our father earned his barony with his sword."

"At a time when the Kingdom was expanding. Times have changed."

Balian didn't answer right away. Henri was right. The days when the Kingdom of Jerusalem was pushing back the Saracens, taking city after city, and expanding the territory under Christian control were over. Since the capture of Ascalon almost twenty years ago there had been no more significant territorial acquisitions, and that meant no new fiefdoms that could be awarded to loyal but landless knights. At length he reminded his younger brother, "Greed is a deadly sin, Henri."

"Is it? I don't see other men being punished for it."

"Not in this life."

"I'll repent on my deathbed," Henri declared flippantly, adding, "I honestly don't see why Barry should have it all."

"Then talk to him about it," Balian suggested.

"I will. I just wanted to give you the chance to come with me," Henri countered.

"No."

When the funeral was over and Hugh d'Ibelin sealed in a tomb beside his father, the guests dispersed. To the relief of the Ibelin brothers, Agnes left, too, sarcastically wishing them well as she settled herself in her litter. And then the brothers were alone together. Although Balian didn't witness the confrontation between his brothers, he learned of it when Henri stormed out of the treasury, slamming doors and shouting for his squire to tack and load their horses. Henri almost ran Balian down in the courtyard as he spurred his stallion toward the drawbridge.

Balian sidestepped but reached up and caught his brother's bridle, pulling the surprised stallion to a swirling, protesting standstill.

"Let go of my horse!" Henri demanded.

"Don't leave in anger, Henri," Balian countered. "I know we hardly know each other, but we are brothers."

"Tell that to Barry! He can't expect my support for nothing! Now let me go."

"Wait one day," Balian urged. "Let your temper cool down."

"No! Let me go!"

Balian hesitated—but he realized he didn't have any more arguments, because he knew this brother too little. He released the bridle and stepped back. Henri spurred away, his squire and packhorse in his wake.

That night in the solar, Barry turned on Balian. "Do you know what Henri dared demand of me?"

"No, but I can guess."

Barry snorted. "And what about you? What are your plans now?"

Balian shrugged. "Hugh suggested I go to Jerusalem."

"Don't tell me you still have romantic notions about winning fame and fortune by great deeds?" he asked with contempt. Then he added condescendingly, "It's time you grew up, Balian, and recognized that earning honor with great deeds is for the romances and the songs of troubadours, but not relevant in today's world. Face it," he continued: "nowadays kingdoms and baronies are inherited rather than won by the sword. Look what happened to Reynald de Châtillon when he tried to seize Cyprus by force."

Balian bristled at the suggestion that he was a man like Reynald de Châtillon, a brutal adventurer with no respect for the Church or his feudal overlord. "I have no desire to imitate Reynald de Châtillon!" he snapped at his brother.

Barry laughed, and too late Balian realized his brother had been baiting him. "Even in our father's day, winning a fortune by the sword took longer than the alternatives."

When Balian refused to answer, Barry continued, "Your problem, Balian, is that you're not acquisitive enough. You need to be greedier if you're ever going to make something of yourself."

"Greed is a deadly sin, Barry," Balian answered, echoing what he had said to Henri only a few hours earlier, and adding before Barry could make any snide remarks, "I think I'll go to Jerusalem as Hugh suggested."

"Jerusalem," Barisan countered, "is full of younger sons from every noble house in France, England, and the Holy Roman Empire. You don't have a chance of standing out in that crowd. You should go to Antioch. Prince Bohemond is still young and hasn't been in power very long. He will be in need of men to support him—and the competition isn't as stiff in Antioch."

Balian smiled crookedly. "Thank you for your faith in my abilities, Barry."

"Oh, don't be so thin-skinned! You know I didn't mean it that way. I just want you to be successful. After all, the more successful you are, the more successful we are as a family."

"I'll try my luck with Jerusalem."

Barisan shrugged. "As you wish, but don't come crawling to me if things don't go according to plan."

"No, Barry. Never."

Chapter 2

Jerusalem, Easter 1171

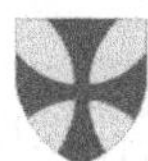

If only jewels could make a woman happy, Maria Zoë Comnena thought as her ladies prepared her for yet another state dinner. Her great-uncle, the Byzantine Emperor Manuel I, had sent her as a bride to the King of Jerusalem, laden with jewels as a way to demonstrate his wealth.

Maria Zoë remembered all too vividly what it had been like when she arrived in Jerusalem at the age of thirteen. The marriage had been celebrated just two days after her arrival, before she had had any chance to recover from the arduous journey. Although she had been given French lessons to prepare her for her marriage to Jerusalem, at the time of her wedding she still needed to concentrate very hard to understand rapidly spoken French. She had been utterly exhausted, from the constant use of a strange tongue and from wearing the heavy, jewel-encrusted gown, long before her husband consummated the marriage.

The next morning she was presented to the court again, this time as a married woman, and she had been so tired she could hardly keep her eyes open—which sparked much jocularity and teasing, and the King had beamed with pride. Amalric had been proud of his little Byzantine bride. She was as pretty as a doll, with curly black hair, big amber eyes, a nubile white body, and the riches of Byzantium draped upon her.

That was five years ago. Now Amalric was also proud of her learning, particularly the fact that she could read and write in Greek, Latin, and French. The King had even been known to brag about the fact that she had read Aristotle and Plato. But such bragging was because he felt her learning, like her bloodlines and her beauty, reflected well on him. These things did not fundamentally alter his attitude towards her. Except in bed, he treated Maria Zoë with the greatest of courtesy, and her authority was never publicly undermined, but he never sought her advice or interacted with her on an intellectual level. She was his Queen, not his companion or friend.

As his Queen, he expected her to be immaculately dressed, coifed, and made up whenever she appeared in public. This started with a daily bath in rose water, followed by skin creams. Her fingernails and toenails were manicured. Then she was dressed in silk undergarments, over which came silk gowns and surcoats embroidered with bright silk, gold, and silver threads. Last but not least, she was laden with jewels: hairpins with pearl or rolled amber heads, earrings that dangled almost to her shoulders, necklaces with multiple strands of gold or beads of precious stones, bracelets as wide as an archer's leather brace, and rings on every finger. A Syrian Christian had been employed for the sole purpose of outlining her eyes, rouging her cheeks and lips, coloring her eyelids, and styling her hair, which was never entirely concealed under the sheer silk veils that she wore.

The result was dazzling to the observer, and utterly stifling to Maria Zoë. She could not move naturally in her clothing, nor sit comfortably, nor relax even for a moment. She was transformed into a doll, her thoughts and feelings completely buried behind the façade.

Amalric also expected her to be punctual. As the time set for him to collect her approached, the ladies attending her became increasingly flustered and agitated. Maria Zoë just sat on her stool while they fluttered around her, completing her toilet with their expert hands. They had just pinned her veils in place when a sharp knocking on the door announced the arrival of the King.

"Come in!" Maria Zoë called, and at once the door was opened by one of the King's squires, who then stepped back so his master could enter.

Amalric of Jerusalem had once been a handsome man. Now, although he was only thirty-five years old, his once powerful body had become flabby to the point of obesity, and his once fine, blond hair was receding. His hazel eyes, however, were hawkish, and they lit up at the sight of his wife. He smiled as he came forward to kiss her on each cheek. "You look lovely, my dear! Absolutely lovely! You'll have all the bachelors swooning at your feet—and my barons as well."

Didn't it ever occur to him that I don't care about that? Maria Zoë wondered. What good are hollow conquests based on attraction to a façade?

The King took her hand through his elbow to lead her out of the chamber. "I swear, my dear, you become more beautiful with each day," he assured her. Evidently he thinks women care only about being beautiful, Maria Zoë concluded with inner resentment.

Because she did not respond with blushing delight at his compliment, Amalric asked, "Is something the matter, my dear? Are you indisposed?" He associated indisposition with pregnancy.

"No, my lord. I am only anxious that the Assassins might take advantage of this gathering of all the important men in the Kingdom."

Amalric's face darkened instantly. He had recently concluded a treaty with the Shiite sect based in the Syrian mountains, who were famous for sending out Assassins to eliminate their enemies. The treaty had been a significant coup for King Amalric, but the Knights Templar had shown their contempt for the King of Jerusalem by striking down the sect's ambassadors during their return journey. The diplomatic consequences were still unforeseeable, but the impudence of the Templars had provoked a domestic crisis. Maria Zoë knew that her husband had tried to seize the Templars responsible for the murders and punish them, but the Templars had met the officers of the King with open defiance, insisting they were subordinate to the Pope alone. In a rage, Amalric had sworn to teach the Templars a lesson. He had even threatened a military confrontation with the mighty Order. In the end, however, cooler heads had prevailed. He had been talked into sending a letter to the Pope demanding that the Templars responsible for the murder of the ambassadors be punished—and demanding that the Order as a whole be chastised and disciplined. Maria Zoë knew all that—but not from her husband.

Her attempt to provoke her husband into discussing the issue, however, failed flatly. Despite his scowl at the mere mention of the incident, he patted her hand and urged her not to "worry her pretty head" about the Assassins. "I promise you, we have everything under control."

Maria Zoë gave up. This was not the time or venue for a renewed attempt to get her husband to view her as a mind, not just a body. They had already reached the great hall, and the assembled nobility raised a cheer for the King and Queen, falling in behind them as they descended to the courtyard of the citadel to walk in procession to the Church of the Holy Sepulchre.

King Amalric's once-bulging muscles might be softening into fat and his blond hair receding, but the intelligence in his eyes was sharper than ever as he critically considered the young knight opposite him. He dealt daily with supplicants for favor, and he considered himself a good judge of character. Aimery de Lusignan, for example, was dangerously ambitious, but he was no fool. Balian was no fool, either, but he wasn't really ambitious enough to make something of himself. He was the type of young man who still thought in terms of honor, and he was devout, too—genuinely devout, unlike the damned Templars! But the fact remained, Balian wasn't ruthless enough to carve out a fortune by force nor cynical enough to seduce an heiress. He was too upright and too idealistic—and that made him just the kind of man Amalric was looking for.

Still, Amalric hesitated for a moment, a twinge of guilt inhibiting him. After all, he did owe Balian's older brother a favor. If Hugh d'Ibelin had not been willing to swear that Agnes de Courtenay had been his betrothed and that he would take her to wife, despite her having lived for six years as Amalric's wife and bearing him two children, neither she nor the Barons of Edessa would have agreed to the divorce.

"Balian, sit down." Amalric indicated an armed chair with a Turkish cushion on the seat.

"My lord." Balian lowered himself reluctantly; he felt better standing up. A man could more readily defend himself if he stood on his own two feet.

"You came here seeking a position at my court," the King opened, stating the obvious.

"Yes, my lord," Balian admitted.

"Well, I have need of a brave man. I presume you consider yourself brave?" he asked with raised eyebrows—knowing that no young knight would ever admit to doubting his own courage.

"I do, my lord," Balian assured him, aware that he was being cornered.

"Yes, well, all young knights think themselves brave," Amalric continued, admitting the pointlessness of his question, "and most think that a few daring tricks at a tournament are proof of it!" he scoffed. "I have need of a household knight who has more courage than most men—old and young and tournament champions included. I can't tell you how many men have already failed the test of courage I have set them." He exaggerated; only two men had in fact rejected his offer to date.

Balian frowned, trying to imagine what test of courage could have daunted so many contemporaries. Less intelligent men, Amalric noted, would have jumped up and down and demanded to be put to the test.

"If you accept the position I offer," the King continued, "you will earn my enduring gratitude, and when the time comes, I will reward you richly." Amalric found the promise easy to give, because he did not believe Balian would live long enough to collect the promised reward. "What say you?" he prompted Balian.

"Let me hear what the position entails first," Balian countered. Amalric's offer struck him as far too generous to be true. He smelled a rat.

Amalric immediately switched tack, turning to flattery. "My eye has fallen on you because you are a remarkable horseman. All noblemen can ride, of course. Your brother was the last man I would have expected to be killed in a riding accident. Yet you still stand out." Amalric studied his victim for a reaction and was gratified to see he had struck the mark.

Balian was proud of his horsemanship; it was one of the few

skills he thought he excelled at more than Barry. But he saw through Amalric nevertheless, and shook his head, noting, "You flatter me, my liege."

Amalric was forced to deny it: "Not at all. Not at all. I saw you the other day, during the hunt, using your bow the way the Turks do, guiding your horse with your knees alone." This was true enough. He had been struck by Balian's grace as he galloped with the reins dropped on the horse's neck and the bow raised in both hands. He had been bareheaded and his silky black hair had blown out in the wind, his surcoat billowing out behind him, drawn tight by his sword belt at his slender waist. In that moment he had looked as beautiful as a Greek statue of Castor.

"I had a good instructor," Balian answered.

"A Turk, I presume?"

"He was a captive who converted to Christianity and served in my brother's garrison."

"You are a good pupil, then," Amalric concluded, adding sharply, "but are you also a good teacher?"

"I don't know," Balian admitted. "I've never tried to teach anyone."

Amalric nodded. "The task I have in mind for you will require that you demonstrate both great courage and an aptitude to teach." Balian looked surprised, but before he could respond, the King moved in for the kill. "You know my son by my first wife, Baldwin, has fallen ill."

Now Balian understood which way the wind was blowing, and he held his breath in alarm: the rumors were that the Prince had leprosy. No one said it out loud, of course, but the Prince had not been seen in public for almost a year. The less people saw of him, the more they suspected the worst. The trap yawned ahead of him, but he saw no escape.

Amalric pressed ahead. "He is now ten, and while the good Archdeacon of Tyre tutors him in all subjects necessary for the intellect, the Archdeacon cannot teach him horsemanship. I need a knight to do that. I think you would be ideal."

If the boy has leprosy, Balian thought, that's little short of a death sentence. He wanted to jump to his feet and tell the King to go to hell. But he did not dare, so the King kept spinning his web, saying in a reasonable tone of voice, "Of course, if you don't have the courage,

I won't blame you. As I said earlier, others have already rejected the job, and I truly won't hold a rejection against you. I'm sure I'll find someone eventually. This Aimery de Lusignan, the young man from Poitou who arrived this spring, might be brave enough to take on this task."

Bastard! Balian thought to himself, conscious that the King was a master of manipulation. He must have noted that Aimery de Lusignan and Barry were almost inseparable. He must guess that Balian resented that—especially the fact that Barry kept holding Aimery up as an example of what a man had to be like to get ahead in the world as a younger son. Aimery and Balian were both third sons.

The King continued, "Then again, I really don't know why you hesitate," letting a touch of annoyance creep into his voice. "It's not as if, as a riding instructor, you would have much physical contact with my son. There's no reason you can't teach from a distance, so there's no reason to assume you will catch the illness he has—whatever it is. I still visit my son daily, you know, and I'm as healthy as ever."

Yes, Balian thought, but you have prohibited your precious young wife and daughter from visiting him. Indeed, the boy was kept sequestered in the Jaffa Tower, away from everyone but his servants and the Archdeacon of Tyre.

Yet the King was right, too: he could teach riding from a distance. Maybe it *was* pure cowardice to refuse this opportunity for reward—or worse, a sin. Besides, the King was offering him no alternative: it was this or nothing.

Balian drew a deep breath. He believed deeply in God, and that meant he believed unexpected developments were often the work of the Lord. He lifted his head and looked the King in the eye. "I will accept this position, my lord."

Amalric broke into a broad smile. "Well done!" he exclaimed, clapping Balian on the back with his powerful hand. "I knew I'd taken the measure of you correctly!" Turning practical, he added in an ordinary tone, "As a knight of the household, you're entitled to food, lodging, a new mantle each year, and an annual salary of one hundred dinar. I'll have my clerks enter you on the rolls right away." The King got to his feet, the audience over, and Balian stood and bowed to him. He felt no sense of exuberance or accomplishment, only dread and uncertainty, but he was resolved to take this chance nevertheless.

William, Archdeacon of Tyre, led Balian along the interior gallery toward the Jaffa Tower. The Archdeacon was not yet an old man, but he was no longer young, either; Balian had heard that he'd spent sixteen years studying in the West before returning to the city of his birth to serve the King. Balian judged he was roughly half a century old. He wore long ecclesiastical robes and soft doeskin slippers, so his feet were silent on the checkerboard of light and dark marble paving stones. "He is a very bright boy," the Archdeacon told the young knight. "He is exceptionally quick to pick up on things, and he has a sharp analytic capability that often surprises me. More than once he has made observations that would honor a grown man. If it weren't for his illness, I would rejoice that the Kingdom of Jerusalem had been blessed by such an intelligent boy as its heir."

Balian nodded, and the Archdeacon looked at him sidelong. "You fear contagion," he concluded.

Balian took a deep breath. "Shouldn't I?"

"You should, for despite what the King says, the boy is almost certainly struck by leprosy. The King does not want to believe that, and as long as we can pretend it might be something else, we do. But in your shoes, I would assume it is leprosy. That said, the danger of contagion is far less than many people believe—especially under the circumstances. You see, the son of a king can afford what commoners cannot: to be bathed morning and night, and to have fresh bandages and fresh clothes each day. The bandages and clothes removed at night are boiled in large vats with salts that sterilize them. I personally wear cotton gloves when I am near Baldwin, and I change my gloves each day, sending the dirty gloves to be sterilized in the same way. I would strongly recommend you bathe nightly as well. I make no promises—after all, none of us know how Prince

Baldwin became infected—but there is no reason to see this assignment as a death sentence."

Balian glanced at the churchman with a wan smile. "Am I so easy to read?"

The Archdeacon laughed. "In this case, yes—but mostly because it is what everyone thinks. Only slaves attend Baldwin, because—I am ashamed to admit—none of the Christian servants were willing to take on the duties of looking after him."

"The Prince of Jerusalem is surrounded by Muslim slaves?" Balian asked, shocked.

"And you and me," the Archdeacon reminded him with a smile, but then he grew serious and halted. They were still a good ten paces from the entrance to the Prince's suite of rooms, guarded by men-at-arms in the livery of Jerusalem. The Archdeacon lowered his voice and looked Balian in the eye. "You and I will be working closely together in the months, maybe even years, ahead. I wish to know more about you."

"I am the third son of the first Baron d'Ibelin, the younger brother of Barisan de Ramla—"

The Archdeacon cut him off with a shake of his head. "I know who you were born, Sir Balian. I am not interested in your bloodlines and estate, but rather in your character. I would like to know why you accepted this position—since evidently you consider it a death sentence."

Balian looked down, embarrassed.

"Would you feel more comfortable in a chapel?" the Archdeacon asked, leaning past Balian to open the doors to a room immediately off the gallery. It was hardly more than an oratory, really, with room for no more than two or three people to kneel before the altar. But Christ was here, the Eucharist candle hanging by silver chains above the altar. The Archdeacon closed the door behind them, and Balian was cornered. This was a confession, only facing the priest.

"There is nothing wrong with admitting you took this position for the rewards the King offered, for I'm sure he offered you something valuable," the Archdeacon told Balian with a smile, as if trying to make this easier for him.

"No, I didn't take it for rewards, since I question whether I will live long enough to collect," Balian answered honestly.

"Then why did you take this position?"

Balian fixed his eyes on the Eucharist rather than the churchman. "Because I thought that if God had seen fit to make the Prince of Jerusalem a leper, then who was I to think I was too good to serve him?"

This answer took even the Archdeacon by surprise. In a spontaneous gesture that was very rare for the learned cleric, he embraced Balian and murmured, "My son!" Then, as if embarrassed by his own gesture, he stepped back and held Balian at arm's length, looking him in the eye. "Do you know what the Byzantines call leprosy? They call it "the holy disease." Lepers are not punished for the blackness of their souls! You will understand that better when you meet Baldwin. Rather, leprosy is a sign of His grace. Lepers have been singled out to suffer as He did—and to give other Christian men an opportunity to demonstrate their faith through service to these poor souls. I see that you understand that, and I am certain the Lord has blessed you, young man. But remember, he who is blessed by the Lord is not guaranteed health or prosperity in this life, but surely in the next. He will be with you always!"

"May I do nothing to offend Him, my lord."

"Amen!"

The Archdeacon opened the door to the chapel and let them out again. They continued down the gallery until they stood before the guards at the entrance to the Jaffa Tower. The Archdeacon announced to the guards that Balian was assigned to the Prince's household and should be granted access whenever he wished. Then they passed into the first-floor chamber of the tower that served as classroom and dayroom of the Prince's apartment.

Unlike the Tower of David, which—as the name implied—dated back to Biblical times, the Jaffa Tower had been built by Fulk d'Anjou only a quarter-century ago. It had fine double-light windows on three walls, and sunlight poured through the western pair onto floors paved with beautiful, brightly glazed mosaics. The furnishings were of Byzantine origin, with elaborate carvings inlaid with mother-of-pearl or ivory.

The Prince, who had been reading in the far window niche, turned and then got respectfully to his feet at the sight of the Archdeacon. Balian had his first shock. Baldwin was a beautiful boy. He had fair hair and a well-formed face. Even his skin was flawless, albeit pale as a result of living confined to these rooms. Balian was completely baffled.

"Did you expect a boy covered with ulcers and lacking limbs?" the Archdeacon remarked with an amused glance at Balian. "As I told you, the symptoms have not yet become unequivocal. Baldwin suffers from a lack of feeling in his right hand and lower arm. That is all for now. The time may come when Baldwin is as unsightly as the beggars in our streets, but that time is not yet." As he spoke he smiled at Baldwin, adding, "Baldwin, this is Sir Balian d'Ibelin; he has agreed to teach you how to ride."

Balian was looking at the boy when the Archdeacon spoke. He saw Baldwin's look of excitement, saw the light ignite—and then extinguish—in his wide blue eyes. He saw the boy's face and shoulders fall as he admitted manfully, "I—I don't have any feeling in my right hand. How can I ride if I can't control my right hand?"

Balian had expected Baldwin to be more than ulcerous and crippled; he had expected him to be embittered and sullen. The boy's unexpected politeness and calm captured Balian's heart. Balian went down on one knee before the Prince and smiled at him. "You can, my lord. It will be more difficult, of course, but it is possible. It is possible to ride a horse completely without the use of your hands, if you will let me show you."

The light was back in Baldwin's eyes. "I love horses!" he exclaimed eagerly. "There is nothing I loved doing so much *before* as riding. I told my father that just the other day—" He cut himself off and looked sharply at his tutor. "That is why he has sent Sir Balian, isn't it?"

The Archdeacon nodded, and Balian revised his opinion of the King, impressed that the King had been moved by his son's longing.

Baldwin was looking at Balian again with wide, serious eyes. "And you aren't afraid of catching my illness?" he asked bluntly.

"I am afraid, my lord, but the good Archdeacon says we can take precautions to prevent it. Have any of your servants taken ill?"

"Not yet," Baldwin admitted, but he still looked skeptical. Turning to the Archdeacon, he asked, "If it is not so dangerous, why don't my stepmother and sister visit me anymore?"

"That is the wish of your father the King," his tutor told him sternly. "He cannot take even a small chance with the future of the Kingdom. Now, it seems to me you should stop complaining about what you *don't* have and rejoice in Sir Balian's presence instead."

Baldwin looked duly chastened, biting down on his lip as he looked at his feet for a moment, and then he turned to Balian. "I'm sorry, sir. I did not mean to be discourteous. Tell me more. I have never seen men ride without using their hands."

"Perhaps not, but you know as well as anyone that the Turks have mounted archers, and they use their bows while charging. They guide their horses with their knees, calves, and the weight of their bodies, to ensure they go exactly where they want them; otherwise it would be impossible for them to take aim."

"That's true!" Baldwin exclaimed, his eyes lighting up again as he started to believe what Balian said. "And you can do that?" he asked eagerly.

"Yes—although not as well as the Turks."

"When can we start?" Baldwin asked, turning instinctively to the Archdeacon.

Balian laughed at his enthusiasm, and then tried to curb it. "My lord, this is going to take a very long time, and the first step is finding a suitable mount. Not all horses are sensitive or intelligent or devoted enough. We must find you a mount that has the potential to understand you, and then one that *wants* to do so. Do you understand me?"

Baldwin looked earnestly at Balian. "Yes," he decided. "And please get up off your knees and come sit with me here in the window seat." He returned to the southern window seat and patted the place beside him. Balian had to overcome a surge of panic at the prospect of such close proximity. Yet he couldn't rebuff the Prince, either. His gesture was innocent and meant only as a courtesy.

Balian joined Baldwin in the window seat, but tried to keep his distance while explaining the plan. "We need to find a horse that accepts you as his master and wants to please you so completely that he seems to read your mind."

The Archdeacon raised his eyebrows skeptically, but Baldwin asked eagerly, "How do we do that?"

"Well, your father says we may use any horse in his stables. I propose that I first select horses that are intelligent enough for what we intend—and then tomorrow, very early, we go together to the stables and you see if one of these horses pleases you particularly. If so, we will start your lessons on that horse, but if the lessons don't go well, we will find another horse. Does that sound reasonable?"

"Oh, yes! Do we have to wait until tomorrow morning?"

"Yes," Balian replied firmly. "You do not want to be observed by idle knights and men-at-arms, do you? Besides, the morning is a good time to get the measure of a horse."

Baldwin seemed to accept this explanation, nodding his head, but then he looked up at Balian again and asked candidly, "You will be my friend, won't you, sir? I'm so very lonely here with just the Archdeacon for company. Even if you can't teach me to ride, you'll still be my friend, won't you?"

Balian was so moved that he put his arm around Baldwin's shoulders and drew him close in a spontaneous gesture of comfort and confirmation. "Yes, Baldwin," he assured the boy, "I'll be your friend no matter what kind of progress we make with the riding."

Baldwin was so overwhelmed by the sudden gesture—by the warmth he had felt from no one in over a year—that tears welled into his eyes. Not even William had ever held him like this, and he found himself looking at the churchman almost reproachfully.

"Now," Balian declared without taking his arm away. "You must get back to your lessons, and I will go down to the stables to select the most suitable mounts for you to choose from tomorrow. But tomorrow morning before the crack of dawn I will be back, so be ready for me." He smiled at the leper Prince.

Baldwin found he couldn't speak, so he just nodded solemnly. He wanted very much to throw his arms around this knight who did not shun him and rest his head on his chest, but he already liked him too much to put him in greater danger, feeling guilty as well as grateful for the arm over his shoulders. “I will be ready,” he promised, adding ruefully with a timid smile, “In fact, I doubt I’ll sleep at all in anticipation. But that doesn’t matter.”

Balian gently withdrew his arm and got to his feet. He smiled down at the little boy. “Until tomorrow, then.”

“Until tomorrow!” Baldwin answered, smiling back brightly.

Chapter 3

Jerusalem, July 1172

THE ACTUAL BIRTH HAD NOT BEEN particularly difficult, the midwife claimed, but a fever came afterwards. It raged so violently that the Queen's sheets became drenched, and by the third day the priests were hovering over her, offering her the last rites.

Maria Zoë was only sporadically conscious. She knew she had given birth to a girl—disappointing her husband, her great-uncle, and the entire Kingdom. She knew that Amalric had not once come to her chamber, although she could not know if the women kept him away or if he simply had no interest in seeing her like this: filthy, stinking, and undignified. A woman suffering from milk fever was not a pretty sight.

She could sometimes hear the wagging tongues of her ladies, unsure whether they thought her senseless or if they thought she would die anyway and have no means to punish them. She heard the way they dismissed her for being so cold and arrogant and vain. "Yet for all her fine airs," they concluded, "she could not produce a male heir! First the miscarriage two years ago, and now this."

"Beauty isn't everything!"

"Much less her fancy learning! Reading Greek philosophers! What nonsense!"

"Do you think the King will remarry?"

"He has to—and he can't wait two years for the Byzantine

Emperor to send him a new child bride. Not with Prince Baldwin dying limb by limb. He'll look for someone closer to home."

"And someone mature—ready and able to bear an heir within a nine-month. Maybe even a widow who's proven she can produce sons. . . ." The voices of her ladies faded, and in their place was the soft pleading of the Egyptian woman, Rahel.

"Don't fret, madame. They are just jealous of you. The Good Lord knows what is in your heart." Rahel was sitting on the floor beside her bed, holding and stroking her hand. She spoke in Greek, which no one else in the room understood.

Rahel had not been with Maria Zoë very long. Rahel had been traveling on pilgrimage to Jerusalem from Alexandria with her brother's family when they had been seized by Bedouins crossing Sinai. Sold in the slave market of Damascus, she had the good fortune to be recognized as a fellow Christian by an Armenian trader from the Principality of Antioch, who bought her as a gift for King Amalric, from whom he hoped for trading concessions. Rahel was a striking woman in her tall, dark, dignified way, and the merchant apparently thought the King would want the Egyptian woman as an exotic bedmate.

The Latin Church, however, did not recognize the right of Christians to hold other Christians as slaves. Amalric accepted the gift, but freed Rahel. He told her there was a Coptic community in Jerusalem and offered to have his servants take her there—but because she spoke Greek and was a widow who had borne four children, he offered her the alternative of serving in his wife's household. Rahel had accepted the position, on the condition that she first be allowed to pray at the Church of the Holy Sepulchre. Amalric had readily granted her wish.

The fact that she spoke Greek, as none of the Queen's other ladies did, had given Rahel an instant advantage in the Queen's household—an advantage that the other women resented. But that was not the only reason Maria Zoë favored Rahel. From the start, Rahel had simply accepted Maria Zoë for what she was: a pregnant teenager facing her first childbirth. She had reassured her that all would go well, speaking matter-of-factly of her own four pregnancies. She had lost all her children, she admitted, before her husband, a merchant, was lost at sea. She was grateful her brother had taken her into his family, and was overjoyed when he allowed her to accompany him on pilgrimage. She had wanted nothing more than to come to Jerusalem, she told Maria Zoë. Now, after many misadventures, she was here, and she had prayed in the very place where Christ was crucified and where He had risen from the grave. She did not speak about her capture, her separation from her brother's family, or the indignity of slavery. That was in the past; it was God's will.

Rahel spoke Greek with an accent, but she soothed Maria Zoë as no one else could. "Christ is very near," she assured Maria Zoë, as if He would cure all ills. Rationally Maria Zoë knew how many people suffered and died in Jerusalem every day, but Rahel made her believe that she would be saved.

The day the fever broke, no one was with Maria Zoë except Rahel. The others had already abandoned her. Rahel single-handedly prepared a bath for her and washed out her tangled hair, massaging her head and her neck with strong, wiry fingers. "When you are strong enough," Rahel promised, "we will go to the Holy Grave to thank Him for your recovery."

"What has happened to my child?" Maria Zoë asked anxiously. "Is she still alive?"

"Yes, she is with a wet nurse. She is healthy and strong and will grow up pretty like you, but with lighter hair. She has been christened Isabella."

"And my husband? Has he forgiven me for giving him a daughter rather than the son he needs?"

Rahel shook her head sadly. "Who can understand the minds of men, madame? Do they think we *decide* the sex of our children? God makes children, madame, and God makes both men and women. You are not to blame, madame," Rahel assured her, making it very clear that her husband took a different stand.

When the King still had not come to her more than a fortnight after her recovery, Maria Zoë took things into her own hands. She knew that Amalric, a conscientious monarch, met with his Privy Council every day at noon in the Tower of David. She ordered her ladies to dress her in her wedding gown with its extravagance of jewels, and she set the crown of Jerusalem upon sheer silk veils that shimmered gold and white over her dark hair. Then she sent for the herald. "Announce me to the King," she ordered the astonished herald.

"But, your grace—" He broke off as she rose to her feet and met him in the eye.

"I am going to the Tower of David to see my husband. Go and announce me."

The herald backed out of her chamber, bowing, and then Maria Zoë could hear his boots as he ran along the gallery leading from the modern palace back to the ancient citadel. Maria Zoë moved slowly to give the herald time to warn her husband, but not so slowly that Amalric could escape her altogether. By the time she reached the exterior stairs leading up to the great audience chamber in the ancient tower, the Patriarch of Jerusalem and the Constable, Humphrey de Toron, were exiting the grand chamber in apparent haste. Both men bowed their heads to their Queen, and Maria Zoë could feel their eyes boring into her back.

As she entered the grand chamber with the throne and a table for the council, two clerks were falling over themselves in their haste to put away their quills and inkpots and clear out. They, too, bowed deeply to Maria Zoë and beat a hasty retreat.

Amalric awaited her seated, his face impassive, his eyes following her alertly. Maria Zoë approached the throne and went down in a formal curtsy. "My lord," she murmured as she righted herself. "Since you have avoided my presence these last two weeks, I thought it was time I sought you out."

"Hmm," Amalric remarked. "You are recovered, then?"

"I am recovered. And you, my lord, you are well?"

"As well as a man can be—after being presented with a second daughter at a time when the Kingdom desperately needs a male heir. People may not say it out loud, but Baldwin has leprosy. Very likely it disqualifies him from the throne altogether. A nobleman with leprosy must enter the Order of St. Lazarus. Can the law exempt a prince?"

"My lord, I am as disappointed as you are that my child is a girl," Maria Zoë answered steadily. "But I cannot decide the sex of my child."

"No, so I'm told," Amalric admitted grudgingly.

"The only solution is for us to try again." Maria Zoë had practiced this line in her head a hundred times and she tried to sound bold, but her voice quavered a little nevertheless.

"Oh, really?" Amalric asked sarcastically, making Maria Zoë blush. "Somehow, I never had the impression you were very enthusiastic about sexual intimacy—at least not with me."

Maria Zoë gasped. "You cannot think I have been unfaithful to you!"

Amalric considered his bride and smiled cynically. He had always preferred married women to girls, precisely because virgins were rarely enthusiastic partners in bed. Maria Zoë's beauty had seduced him at first, but her unresponsiveness—often with a twisted face and gasps of pain—had soon dulled his appetite. She seemed to dislike physical intimacy so intensely that he truly found it hard to imagine her risking her crown, her head, and her soul for the sake of carnal pleasures—unlike Agnes de Courtenay, who was always eager for variety in fornication. Nevertheless, he reasoned that it didn't hurt to let his wife think he doubted her, so that she would be frightened as well as disinclined. In answer to her reply, he merely weighed his head from side to side and remarked, "You're a beautiful young woman—and as such, weak and easily seduced."

"Never!" she declared indignantly, her cheeks flushed. "And how should another man have a chance if you are there?"

"Where? You mean in your bed? Ah, well, believe me, it's quite possible to make love in other venues—but that is a topic best saved for another time, and not exactly the reason you are here, is it?"

"My lord, as you said, the Kingdom of Jerusalem needs a male heir, and only you can sire him."

"Indeed, but not necessarily with you."

So the rumors were true, Maria Zoë registered, and he was considering setting her aside.

"I am your wife—"

"Perhaps not. If my marriage to Agnes was valid, then my marriage to you is bigamous, and you are nothing more than my concubine." He let this sink in, enjoying the look of horror on Maria Zoë's face. Like all Greeks, she considered herself fundamentally superior to other races, and Amalric took a certain pleasure in pointing out the weakness of her position. "I'm sure I could find a priest—even a bishop—who would argue the case. Should I so desire…" Amalric threatened with a mild, unfriendly smile.

"I'm sure you could, too, my lord," Maria Zoë answered steadily, having recovered from the insult of being called a concubine. She wasn't, after all, entirely unprepared for his line of attack. She was no fool, and she had given much thought to where this conversation might lead. Since he had played this trump, however, she drew hers. "And I'm just as certain that my great-uncle would see such a move as an insult incompatible with his status as your overlord."

"The Greek Emperor is *not* my overlord," Amalric retorted sharply.

"No? I thought that was the purpose of your trip to Constantinople last year—to renew your lapsed oaths of homage," Maria Zoë pointed out coolly. Although Amalric had not seen fit to include her in his meetings with her great-uncle, her father had been present, and he had assured her that Amalric had dutifully acknowledged that he held Jerusalem as a vassal of Constantinople.

"The Greek Emperor generously offered me his protection, and I assured him of my goodwill—no more than that," Amalric insisted, frowning sidelong at his beautiful doll-wife, who had never dared talk to him like this before.

Maria Zoë recognized that she could not argue this point, and changed her tactic. "Whether my great-uncle is your overlord or not, neither he nor my brother-in-law of Antioch will allow me to be set aside without consequences for Jerusalem."

Amalric snorted in exasperation—because she was right. The Emperor in Constantinople had made it very clear that he considered himself the center of the universe and would take any slight to his prestige as lèse majesté, while Antioch had tied himself to Constantinople because he needed Greek support to keep the Seljuks at bay. This dependency was reflected in his marriage politics: Prince Bohemond's sister Mary was the Emperor's current wife, while Bohemond himself was married to Maria Zoë's sister. In short, Amalric's two most powerful allies would both side with his wife in any public dispute, and Jerusalem could not afford to fall out with both Constantinople and Antioch.

Amalric considered his wife again through narrowed eyes, registering that she was not as fragile, weak, or docile as he had taken her to be. She was clearly growing up. He grunted a second time. He was stuck with this wife for political reasons—and truth to tell, it was not such a difficult duty to get her pregnant again. "I'll tell you what," Amalric suggested, leaning closer to Maria Zoë and lowering his voice. "You make me feel *welcome* in your bed, and I'll think about spending as much time there as we need to make a son together."

Maria Zoë had fled from her ladies, even Rahel. They knew far too much about what the King expected of her and were too ready with advice. She did not want their advice. She knew what she had to do, but she hated it nevertheless. If only his seed would quicken in her womb again, then the ordeal would be over—at least for a while.

She had first sought the walled garden below the Tower of David, but had only succeeded in stumbling over one of the kitchen clerks making love to one of the laundresses. She had then fled to the stables to seek comfort from her mare, but that plan was ruined when she found half the household there, preparing to accompany her husband on a lion hunt he had organized for the Sicilian ambassador. So she fled toward the mews.

She was still a half-dozen steps away when she was startled by voices coming out of the mews, indicating there were people already there.

"You see, there are some advantages to not having any feeling in your arm," a young male voice declared with a laugh. Maria Zoë gasped in shock, knowing that the speaker could only be addressing her afflicted stepson. Before she could step into the mews to rebuke the speaker for so much callousness, however, the boy started laughing.

The sound of the man and boy laughing together was so enchanting that Maria Zoë followed the sound on soft feet, anxious not to shatter the mood by her intrusion. As she reached the doorway and looked inside, she was startled by how much Baldwin had grown since she had last seen him, but to her relief he was still the beautiful boy she remembered. He was dressed for riding in hose and boots under a practical surcoat and his fine blond hair was covered by a tight-fitting, blue hood that framed his handsome face and brought out the blue of his large eyes. Standing beside him was a vaguely familiar young knight in leather hose, soft leather knee-high boots, and a leather gambeson, but no chain mail. Baldwin had a big falcon on his bare arm, and the talons of the bird dug into his soft, lifeless flesh, drawing blood. Even as she watched, the knight coaxed the bird back onto his own protected arm and hooded the bird expertly.

"He came to me!" Baldwin insisted in a breathless, excited voice, and the bird lifted and flapped his wings as if making a statement.

"Not exactly at the right time," the knight commented, adding, "Let me see that arm."

Baldwin held his arm out to the knight, propping up the right forearm with his left hand while the knight inspected it critically and concluded, "You should have it bandaged."

"Oh no, Balian! What's the point? It's useless anyway. Dead! Please, let's go hawking."

"We can't risk it yet. If we lose one of your father's precious birds, he'll dock my pay from now to doomsday."

"Then take one of mine," the Queen of Jerusalem offered spontaneously, stepping into the mews courtyard.

Both Baldwin and Balian spun about, startled. Balian at once bowed deeply to his Queen, but Baldwin let out a shout of joy and started to run forward—only to remember himself and stop in his tracks, an expression of pain on his face.

"Baldwin!" Maria Zoë reached out her arms to him.

"My lady, no!" Balian lunged forward and pulled Baldwin back, holding him fast in his own arms to stop him taking another step.

Maria Zoë turned on the young knight. "You do not fear to hold him, sir! Why should I?"

"My death is meaningless, my lady. You hold the future of Jerusalem in your hands."

"You mean my womb," Maria Zoë snapped back. "And it is empty at the moment," she added bitterly before ordering, "Let go of my stepson and do not presume to stand between us, Balian d'Ibelin." She had remembered his name at last.

"No. My lady." Sir Balian stood his ground and they stared at one another.

"Don't you know that *our* holy men kiss and wash the feet of lepers?" she told him sharply.

"What holy men do is not necessarily for queens," Balian countered. "After all, holy men may actually seek the mark of the 'holy disease.'"

He could see that she was surprised he knew the term, and he was grateful to the Archdeacon of Tyre for teaching it to him.

Before Maria Zoë could think of a response, Baldwin himself broke into the debate. "Sir Balian's right, Tante Marie. My father has forbidden us to even see each other. You would not want Sir Balian punished." Looking up at Balian, he added, "You can let go of me. I'm not going to go any closer. Do you think I want Tante Marie to get this disease—no matter what you call it? I would not wish it even on my worst enemy!" Turning back to his stepmother, who for five years had been like an older sister to him, he added, "But I am so pleased to *see* you, and there's no risk if you keep distance between us. *Please* stay and talk to me—just a little. Have you seen Sibylla? Is it true I have a little sister now, too?"

Maria Zoë was overwhelmed by Baldwin's pleas and by his calm and maturity. He was so poised and yet so fragile. She wanted more than ever to embrace him as she had before he was sick. Baldwin had been the only one in the whole strange court who had *not* been in awe of her—the only person she had dared be herself with. Even his sister Sibylla, although only a year older, had been more reserved, almost resentful, as if she knew her mother had been sent away to make room for Maria Zoë. But Baldwin had been only two when his mother was sent away, and he had been raised by a wet nurse. He had accepted Maria Zoë without reservation. They had played together, laughed together, sung songs together, and comforted each other.

"We have so much to say to one another, Baldwin, but we must find a more suitable place!" She glanced around at the mews, which stank of birds and the raw meat fed to them.

"My lady, the King has expressly—" Balian started nervously.

"Do not presume to tell me what to do, Sir Balian." Maria Zoë cut him off sharply again, her tone of voice reminding him she was his Queen and had been born into the royal house of the greatest empire on earth. "I know perfectly well what the King has ordered—no less than Prince Baldwin does. And we are both prepared to defy him, aren't we, Baldwin?" she asked her stepson, smiling.

The Prince broke into a broad smile. "Yes! Oh, yes! Balian! I have an idea. Let's go riding. Tante Maria has not seen how well I ride now." He turned back to Maria Zoë. "Sir Balian has taught me how to ride even though I can't use my right hand. I have a wonderful gelding, Misty, who understands everything—well, almost. He's just learning, you see, and so am I, but you'll be amazed by what we can do already. Please! Let's go for a ride together," he begged, looking back and forth between the adults.

Balian, stung by Maria Zoë's earlier rebuke, waited to see what she would say.

"That is a good idea, Baldwin, but we must be clever, or we might be caught by someone who would betray us just to ingratiate himself with your father. I think we should proceed separately, but meet up somewhere outside the city. What do you think, sir?" She turned to Balian, no longer feeling defensive, and all her earlier haughtiness was gone. Indeed, she was gazing at him with eyes almost as big as Baldwin's. She seemed to be pleading for his approval of her plan.

Balian hesitated. Although the knowledge that Baldwin was here in the mews kept most people away, the longer they lingered, the greater was the risk that someone might find them here. It would indeed be better to ride out as he usually did at this time. So he nodded once. "I will take Prince Baldwin to Bethlehem and back, my lady."

"Excellent!" Maria Zoë agreed with a dazzling smile of approval for Balian. He could not have picked a route more suited to the alibi of a chance meeting. What could be more natural for a woman, just recently recovered from childbed yet desperate for another child, than a pilgrimage to the Church of the Nativity in Bethlehem? "We will rendezvous tomorrow," she announced.

"Why not today?" Baldwin started to protest.

Balian shook his head at the boy. "Queen Maria will have her reasons, Baldwin. Besides, we are late for our ride already. To ride so far after a late start would irritate Archdeacon William. Tomorrow is wiser." He nodded to Maria Zoë and she smiled back at him.

"Until tomorrow, then," she declared, and turned so suddenly that her silk skirts billowed out in a swirl of color. And then she was gone.

Baldwin's excitement at meeting with his stepmother transmitted itself immediately to his young gelding. No sooner had they crossed the drawbridge from the citadel into the city than his horse started shying at every little thing, from the barking of dogs to the pigeons landing in the street ahead. With his brother's accident yet so vivid in his memory, Balian became alarmed, and he ordered the Arab groom Abdul, assigned to the Prince because he was a slave and had no say in the matter, to take the boy before him on his own horse. Abdul always rode out with them just in case this might be necessary, but the Prince protested furiously. He wanted to show his stepmother he could ride, not arrive at the rendezvous sitting in front of a groom like a baby. "I can manage by myself! I can manage!" he insisted stubbornly.

"If you're thrown, my lord, your father will hang me!" Balian shot back—not entirely truthfully, but he knew Baldwin's concern for his safety was one of his few weapons.

"No, he won't!" Baldwin shot back, seeing through Balian. "He understands about horses! Just proceed! Misty will follow your stallion!"

"I could take Misty on a lead," Abdul offered.

Balian was skeptical about whether putting Misty on a lead would calm him, since his nervousness stemmed from Baldwin's own excitement, but he could think of no alternative. "We could try that," he replied cautiously.

Abdul removed a lead from his saddlebag and maneuvered his horse beside Baldwin's so he could click the shackle on the ring on Misty's noseband intended for this purpose. Then, holding the line short so that he rode just a few feet ahead of Misty, he nodded to Balian to proceed.

Ten minutes later they had left the crowded, noisy streets behind, passed through the Zion Gate, and started down the steep slope against the stream of pilgrims, hawkers, and beggars trudging towards the walled city. As they started up the far slope the crowds thinned, and Misty calmed down enough for Balian to consent to Abdul removing the lead. Baldwin was still angry, however, so he refused to even look at Balian. Instead he focused only on Abdul, thanking him with a smile.

Balian tried to bridge the hostility by untying his canteen and holding it out to Baldwin. "Would you like something to drink?"

"No!" Baldwin replied stubbornly.

They continued their journey for a half-hour, and then on the outskirts of Bethlehem, paused to water the horses. Here Baldwin turned Misty away from the others and started toward the drinking trough not on a straight line, but making him move laterally first to the left and then the right, in a display of horsemanship he had worked on for weeks and weeks. Misty, as if feeling guilty for misbehaving earlier, performed perfectly.

"Well done!" Balian called out after his charge, but Baldwin only lifted his chin in response. At the trough he tried to make Misty back up before drinking, but the horse was thirsty and ignored him. He thrust his head toward the trough and sucked the water up, slurping loudly.

A pilgrim in long white cotton veils trimmed with blue embroidery emerged from the old Byzantine chapel to their right. The veils were pulled up over her head and wound around her shoulders, covering everything but a foot of shirt below the edge of the veil, almost like the way the Arab women wore their veils—only white instead of black. Baldwin automatically kept his eye on her. She went over to a native woman holding two native horses. One of the horses was little more than a nag, very bony with long ears, but the other mare had a beautiful coat that gleamed in the sun, and she arched her neck and pricked up her ears as the pilgrim went to mount. The saddle was covered in red velvet and decorated with silver, and the bridle had red tassels on it. Baldwin guessed it was the Queen even before she swung herself easily into the saddle and turned to ride towards them.

He rode to meet her, bowing his head as they drew up opposite each other. "My lady! What a coincidence!"

She flung the veils back over her head to expose her face and smiled at him. "Indeed, sir. What brings you so far from Jerusalem?" Balian was struck by what a truly beautiful woman she was. It wasn't just all the jewels and silks that made her beautiful, he noted; on the contrary, these things distracted from her natural beauty. Wearing nothing now but white cotton veils and a gown with a woven blue border, she seemed far more radiant. Had he been an artist, Balian thought blasphemously, this was the woman he would have used as a model of the Virgin Mary.

At last Baldwin noticed her and let out a shout: "Tante Marie!" He trotted over, beaming with pride, and Maria Zoë turned her attention to her stepson. "You ride better than anyone I have ever seen!" she told him. "Or is that a circus horse, that he does such tricks?"

"No, of course not!" Baldwin protested. "I taught him everything myself—with a little help from Sir Balian," he conceded, with a smile at Balian to indicate he had been forgiven.

"Shall we ride a ways together, then?" Maria Zoë asked. She indicated the road that coiled its way up the hill toward the cluster of white buildings surrounding the imposing dome over the Church of the Nativity.

Baldwin nodded eagerly, and with concentration directed his horse to fall in beside his stepmother's. Her woman fell in behind them and Balian gestured for Abdul to ride beside the waiting woman, while he rode past the rest of the party to clear the way for the Queen and Prince. Although he kept a sharp lookout, Balian did not think they encountered anyone who recognized who they were. Their party looked far too ordinary: a knight on pilgrimage with his wife, his son, and their servants. Before they reached the Church of the Nativity, however, he led them off the main road and halted. Turning back, he approached the Queen.

"My lady, the crowds are getting thicker, and the risk of recognition increases. I strongly advise against proceeding any further together."

To his relief, Maria Zoë nodded. "You are right, sir." Turning to Baldwin, she explained, "If no one learns of this, we can repeat it, but if your father finds out, he will take measures to prevent it happening again. Maybe he would even forbid you—or me—from going anywhere without his company or at least his guards. You wouldn't want that, would you?"

"No, of course not," Baldwin agreed solemnly, but he looked very disappointed nevertheless.

"Baldwin." Maria Zoë reached out a hand, and Balian audibly caught his breath. She looked him straight in the eye and held up her hand to show she was wearing thick leather gloves. Then she put her hand on Baldwin's shoulder and looked the boy in the eye. "I *will* find ways to see you again. You must trust me. Sir Balian and I will conspire together and find ways for us to meet. But now, go back to Jerusalem with Sir Balian, and I will continue with my pilgrimage."

The summons to the Queen did not come unexpectedly after this exchange, and Balian went prepared with several suggestions of where they might rendezvous on future rides. Nor was he surprised that the Queen dismissed all her ladies except the Egyptian so they could speak in private; her other ladies were all noblewomen from the Kingdom and might have seen an advantage in betraying her. What surprised him was the cordial tone Queen Maria adopted as soon as the other women had withdrawn. It was as if one minute he had been facing a haughty queen, so cold the very temperature of the room was chilled by her presence, and the next he was being asked by a pretty young woman to make himself comfortable.

Balian reacted with wariness, suspecting she might be trying to manipulate him. "I am quite comfortable standing, my lady," he responded to her invitation to make himself comfortable in the armchair opposite her own.

Maria Zoë caught her breath, wounded. The encounter with Baldwin had been the first ray of sunshine in her life since the birth of Isabella. She could not remember enjoying anything in her whole life as much as she had enjoyed planning and executing the secret rendezvous with her stepson, and plotting new meetings had enlivened her days and distracted her from her sorrows. But she needed Sir Balian's cooperation if her plans were to be realized. No, she corrected herself, she *wanted* his cooperation.

But he was standing in front of her looking as tense and wary as a caged cat, and abruptly she realized he felt trapped and misused. She cringed as she remembered her tone of voice in the mews, and remembered how her ladies called her haughty and cold. That was how Sir Balian saw her, too, she realized with a shock. "Forgive me, sir," she stammered out. "Baldwin and I have put you in an impossible situation, forcing you to disobey the King and risk your future. We should not have done that. I'm sorry. I—I just—I so wanted to see him again!" she admitted rather helplessly. Without her façade, she felt very weak and lost.

Maria Zoë's tone was so sincere and her expression so distressed that Balian's defenses collapsed. "Baldwin wanted it as much as you did, and I did not have the heart to say no to him," Balian conceded with a shrug.

"You truly care for him," Maria Zoë observed. "I could tell that from the very first moment. You were laughing together. I fear he has had little cause for laughter since his illness was discovered and people started whispering it might be leprosy. You have no idea how hard it was: one minute he was heir apparent to the throne, surrounded by his family, faithful servants, and fawners of every class, age, and sex. The next minute he was a pariah, isolated from everyone he loved and trusted, locked in a golden cage and surrounded by slaves. We were not even given a chance to say goodbye to one another. Nor was he allowed to take leave of his sister Sibylla, whom he loves more than anyone in the world."

Balian nodded, but added, "The Archdeacon of Tyre has tried to be a surrogate father to him, my lady, and he seeks to distract Baldwin from his situation with many lessons that expand his horizons."

"Baldwin told me you are learning Arabic with him," Maria Zoë noted cautiously. She had so looked forward to meeting Balian in private, but already the conversation had deviated from her initial script, and she was finding it both more exciting and more confusing. Baldwin was one thing, but quite inexplicably she found herself almost as interested in Balian as in her stepson.

"That was the Archdeacon's doing. For some reason Baldwin balked at learning Arabic, and Archdeacon William thought I might have more luck in persuading him. I told Baldwin that a man was always at a disadvantage when he did not understand what was being said around—or about—him. I said the disadvantage was greater still if that man was a king. I pointed out that he must speak the language of his foes better than they his, if he did not want to be tricked and deceived and outmaneuvered. He protested he would have translators, and I told him that if he relied on translators, he would become their tool rather than the reverse. 'But *you* will be my translator,' he announced with one of his trusting smiles—and I had to admit that for all my fine talk, my knowledge of Arabic was rudimentary. At which point, of course, I was trapped, because Baldwin triumphantly declared that then we would learn Arabic together." Balian laughed at himself and Maria Zoë found herself joining in.

As the laughter died, she asked him: "And do you find that onerous?" She was thinking of how difficult she had found her French lessons. French was such an illogical language!

"No, just difficult!" Balian declared emphatically.

Maria Zoë laughed again, with a feeling of lightheartedness she could not remember since her marriage. She begged again, "*Please* sit down, sir. I want you to tell me more about Baldwin and how I can help make his life more tolerable. I will try to meet him again, of course, but we need to be very, very careful. The worst thing that could happen to him would be for you to be dismissed from his service. We cannot risk that."

Balian felt flattered, but even more, he was impressed that the Queen cared enough for her stepson to want to do what was best for *him.* He showed his revised opinion of her by at last taking the seat offered. Then he suggested, "One thing you could certainly do, ma dame, is *write* to Baldwin. Send him letters about all that is happening at court and in the Kingdom. His father and the Archdeacon William tell him what they *want* him to hear, but I think he would benefit from hearing things from your perspective."

Maria Zoë caught her breath and looked at Balian, startled. "You seem to be the only one in the Kingdom of Jerusalem who thinks I have an opinion at all—let alone one worth hearing."

Balian flinched, realizing he had just blundered. He had automatically assumed the King consulted with his Queen, if only because of her powerful connections. It had not occurred to him that Queen Maria felt she was ignored. Publicly, after all, she always appeared at the King's side, very much his consort.

As he floundered about for an answer, Maria Zoë bridged the awkwardness by declaring, "I would be delighted to write Baldwin my observations about developments in the Kingdom." Then she paused and considered Sir Balian carefully. At first she had been attracted to him because he so clearly loved Baldwin, and now in a few short minutes he had made her laugh twice *and* shown more respect for her intellect than her husband had in five years of marriage. She was getting dangerously close to liking this man more than any other she had met in Jerusalem.

This is risky, she told herself, and deflected her thoughts with a question. "What do you think of this man calling himself Salah ad-Din? He seems most audacious—setting aside the Fatimid Caliphate just like that! Declaring himself Sultan of Egypt without, as far as I can see, even a 'by your leave' from his lord Nur-ad-Din."

"I do not consider myself an expert on Egypt, my lady," Balian began cautiously, "although my brother campaigned with your husband there. Still, it is obvious that the situation had become increasingly chaotic. And if the fear of a Sunni invasion induced the Fatimids to request our aid a decade ago, five invasions have left the people war-weary and hating us as much as the Damascenes."

Maria Zoë heard the implicit criticism of her husband's policies, particularly his recent attempts to seize control of Cairo, but she felt no need to defend her husband. Besides, Sir Balian was in good company: the Templars, too, had refused to take part in the fourth expedition to Egypt, saying that since it was in violation of an agreement, it would only bring God's wrath upon the Kingdom, a prediction that the results seemed to bear out. Meanwhile, Maria Zoë knew from her parents that the Greek Emperor and court were furious about the lack of coordination during the campaigns, and that there was mounting resentment of the alliance with Jerusalem. She chose instead to remark, "But how can a Sunni Muslim from Syria simply declare himself Sultan of the Shiite Caliphate of Egypt?"

"By first pretending to serve the Shiite Caliph, and only turning on him after he had established firm control over the city. But there is nothing to say Salah ad-Din will hold on to power for long. He is very vulnerable. He has given the Shiites a rallying cause. At the same time, he has made his master Nur-ad-Din suspicious of his ambitions. And he is of neither Arab nor Turkish blood, but a Kurd."

"Yes, I had heard that," Maria Zoë agreed, nodding, "and many Arabs and certainly the Seljuks undoubtedly look down on him for it, but the Kurds are fierce fighters. It would be foolish to underestimate them." Maria Zoë had been raised on stories of the Greek Empire's many campaigns against this intransigent people.

Rahel, who had been standing by the door, cleared her throat and gently signaled that it was time to terminate the interview. It would be dangerous for Maria Zoë's reputation for her to be alone too long with a bachelor knight, even in Rahel's presence. Already the women of the household must be gossiping about what she wanted with Sir Balian.

And they were right to be suspicious! Maria Zoë admitted to herself, with a sense of guilt for her feelings toward this landless knight. So she brought the conversation to a close. Standing, she thanked Sir Balian, and assured him she would write to Baldwin often. She offered him her hand. He bowed deeply over it, nodded once, and departed.

No sooner had the door closed behind him than Maria Zoë was overwhelmed by a sense of emptiness. From the moment she decided to meet with Sir Balian, it had buoyed her up, and now it was already over. The rendezvous had been so very short, and yet it had been far more than she had dared expect. Indeed, it had been more than she had imagined it could be. She had expected a man who cared for Baldwin, and she had found a man who made her laugh and talked to her like she was an intelligent human being.

It was cruel that someone as attractive and sympathetic as Sir Balian was right here in her husband's household—and she dared not meet with him again anytime soon. She was so very lonely in this strange court, and letters—whether to her parents or to Baldwin—could not substitute for the warmth of a smile or a candid conversation as if among equals. Maria Zoë felt tears welling up in her throat. It was one thing to barricade herself inside her façade against people she hated like her ladies or, increasingly, Amalric himself, but she didn't want to hide from Sir Balian! And yet she must....

The interview also unsettled Balian. After standing indecisively in the corridor for several moments, he made his way to the spiral stairwell leading to the ramparts of the large southwest tower. From here he had a view along the western wall of Jerusalem with its rows of square towers.

Balian admitted to himself that he had never in his life been so attracted to a woman, high or low, as he was to Queen Maria. She was beautiful, of course, but her public face was so perfect it was intimidating. Today, as during the ride to Bethlehem, he had seen behind the façade to the real flesh-and-blood woman, and she was... tantalizing.

Damn it! Balian beat his fist on the stone balustrade. Leave it to him to be attracted to a woman so utterly inaccessible it was ludicrous.

Then again, all women had become inaccessible since he had taken the position with Baldwin. Ladies never sat near him at meals, nor would they dance with him, and even the serving girls gave him a wide berth. Balian supposed he might have been able to pay a whore enough to risk infection with a man presumed to be carrying leprosy, but Balian had never gone to whores and had no intention of starting. Yet the reaction of women to his position had been an unexpected shock. He might never have been a ladies' man like Barry, but he had enjoyed the company of ladies; he liked music, dancing, and flirting. Now he was excluded from all of it.

All he had was the confidence of the most beautiful and exalted woman at court....

He would have liked to think that today's interview would be repeated, but that was unreasonable. She would not risk it again. She dared not. Her position at court had already been weakened by giving birth to a girl child. She dared not give the King an excuse to set her aside by appearing to dally with a bachelor knight.

And why would she want to? Balian tried to rein in his fantasies. She had been gracious to him and her interest in Baldwin was sincere, but he would be a fool to make more of her kindness than was intended. She was his Queen.

And you are her man, a voice from his heart whispered.

Barry would laugh himself sick! What do you take yourself for? Some modern-day Lancelot? Show me all your deeds-at-arms! When was the last time you even broke a lance? Valorous knight, indeed! Playing nursemaid to a leper prince!

But the Queen respects me for exactly that: for playing nursemaid to an innocent boy, struck down by an illness that terrifies even the bravest. You're terrified of it, too, Barry! Otherwise you wouldn't be avoiding me.

Balian remembered the way the Queen leaned forward when she got excited about something she was saying, the way she frowned a little when she listened intently. She was a worthy object of admiration—and he had nothing else.

Nodding to himself, he turned his back on the view he had not been looking at and left the ramparts of the citadel. It might be an illusion, but he felt stronger and prouder for pledging himself to his Queen.

Chapter 4

Jerusalem, July 1174

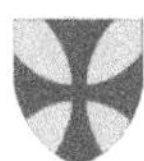

THE PATRIARCH OF JERUSALEM DROPPED ON his knees and began praying so intently that his knuckles turned white. He banged his head against his clasped hands in distress. It could not be! It simply could not be true!

But the corpse was stretched out on the large, sumptuous bed before him. He had himself heard the gasped confession and administered the last rites. Amalric, King of Jerusalem, only thirty-seven years old and until a week ago apparently in the best of health, was dead.

How could he be stricken down like this? Just when Nur-ad-Din was dead and the Syrians were in disarray. When things had looked so promising for the Kingdom. It was bad enough that the attempt to seize Banias had failed; why must the King then drink dirty water on the return journey and become stricken with dysentery? And if he were to be struck down in his prime, why must it be before he had sired another son? Even an infant son would have been better than a leper!

Or why hadn't the leper died first? Then, at least, they could have married the elder girl off to a powerful and vigorous nobleman, a fighting man capable of stepping into Amalric's shoes.

But a leper? Were they really going to place the crown of Jerusalem on the head of a leper? Didn't that besmirch the Crown itself?

The nobles would never accept such an abomination—much less the Templars and Hospitallers.

Jerusalem had from the start been an elected kingship. They would elect a man from among their own ranks—Raymond de Tripoli, perhaps, or Humphrey de Toron, or Miles de Oultrejourdain. The leper would be bypassed, set aside, put away in a mountain monastery, where everyone could soon forget the shame of a leper prince of Jerusalem.

But then the Patriarch caught his breath, reminded of a conversation he had had with the Archdeacon of Tyre. Tyre had argued that God had made the heir to Jerusalem a leper to teach humility to the haughty and vain nobles and bishops of the Holy Land.

Was it possible, the Patriarch asked himself now, that God was angry that the nobles of Outremer had dared to create a king in his city at all? After all, the good Godfrey de Bouillon had refused to "wear a cross of gold where Christ had worn a cross of thorn." His brother and his brother's successors had not been so scrupulous. But the Patriarch dismissed this notion almost as soon as he thought of it. Too much time had elapsed since the coronation of Baldwin I.

But those early kings had been more devout and God-fearing than his contemporaries, the Patriarch reflected, and maybe God felt it was necessary to teach this self-indulgent and impious generation—men like Heraclius, who openly lived with his concubine, and Reynald de Châtillon, who dared humiliate the honest and aging Patriarch of Antioch—a lesson in humility. Weren't all lepers sent to sift the holy from the unholy? For the service to lepers was recognized as near to saintly, and those that served lepers demonstrated their devotion to God. Maybe God had a wise purpose, after all, in sending a leper boy to rule over His Holy City and all the Holy Land.

There were noises on the far side of the door, and the Patriarch realized that the barons were getting restless. Most of them had been with Amalric on the campaign, and they had brought him home to Jerusalem to die. Those few members of the High Court of Jerusalem who had not been on the campaign had been summoned at once, while the Grand Masters of the Templars and Hospitallers had been all but living in the anteroom for days.

From the far side of the door a deep voice boomed, "Just how long does it take for a man to confess?" That was the blustering Lord of Oultrejourdain, a rude and violent man, but a wily one as well. He held the rough, semi-arid lands to the south and beyond the Jordan, one of the most vulnerable parts of the Kingdom. It took a hard, courageous man to hold such lands, threatened from both Syria and Egypt, for Christendom, the Patriarch reasoned—but he disliked the Baron of Oultrejourdain nevertheless.

The men on the other side of the door were laughing now, apparently at a joke the Patriarch had not heard. That irritated him. Here they were on the brink of a catastrophe, and the barons could find nothing better to do than joke—probably about how many sins they had to confess. Damn them all!

The Patriarch pulled himself off his knees with an unconscious groan. His limbs were very stiff. He was nearly fifty, after all, and all his joints hurt. He brushed the dust off the front of his robes, adjusted his crown, and then with measured steps approached the door. He pulled both wings of the door open in a single gesture and had the pleasure of seeing the men-at-arms at the door jump in surprise. The crowd in front of him went deathly still, and they all stared at him.

"The King, my lords, is dead," the Patriarch intoned, consciously refraining from adding, "Long live the King." He saw his own horror reflected on the faces of the men before him. The Grand Master of the Hospitallers dropped his head and crossed himself, his lips moving as he prayed. The Grand Master of the Knights Templar scowled and crossed himself perfunctorily; one could see the wheels spinning in his head already, scheming as he looked about the room at the barons. The Constable of the Kingdom, the aging Lord of Toron, sank down onto a chest in despair. The Lord of Caesarea looked stunned, as if he had never imagined this could happen. The others were sober, deathly sober.

The Comte de Tripoli recovered first. A handsome man with long, curling black hair and a black mustache, he crossed himself and murmured, "God have pity on Jerusalem." The men in the room echoed him—with the exception of Oultrejourdain, who growled instead, "God help *us*; are we to bend our knee to a leper boy or a chit of a girl?" Miles of Oultrejourdain was as dark as Tripoli, but stocky with a piggish face—or so it seemed to the Patriarch.

"This is no time to speak of the succession!" the Patriarch admonished. "Let us join in prayer for the sake of the dead man's soul. Pater Noster…"

Every man in the room joined the Patriarch in the Lord's Prayer, but no sooner had he said "Amen" than they were at it again.

"We need to call the High Court together."

"Damn it, man! Look around you! Every baron on the High Court is right here in this room!"

"Except Beirut and Hebron," the Hospitaller Master pointed out.

"They have been summoned and will be here any moment," the Patriarch assured the assembled nobles.

"Then I say we convene the Court immediately—here and now, before the news gets out of this room. Hebron and Beirut either arrive in time to vote or count as abstentions," the Comte de Tripoli proposed forcefully, and the others nodded with varying degrees of enthusiasm.

"Amalric is dead," he continued, "and he left us just three choices: his son, who is probably suffering from leprosy; his daughter by that whore Agnes; or his daughter by the Byzantine Princess, Maria Zoë Comnena. I say we don't have much choice: we take the girl related to the Byzantine Emperor."

"She's only two years old, Tripoli!" Sidon protested.

"So?" Tripoli countered. "We name a regent until she's of an age to marry, and then select the best man to rule at her side."

"No doubt you presume you'll be Regent!" Oultrejourdain snorted.

"Whoever this High Court thinks best," Tripoli replied coolly.

"There's no precedent for a girl that young being crowned Queen," the Templar Master pointed out.

"Much less for passing over two older children! Amalric's children by Agnes de Courtenay were explicitly recognized as legitimate before he took the crown," Humphrey de Toron reminded his fellow barons.

Oultrejourdain rolled his eyes in disgust, but Barisan de Ramla seconded Toron. "My lord of Toron is right. We all recognized Amalric's children by Agnes de Courtenay as his legitimate offspring."

"Just because your little brother has been playing nursemaid to the leper these past three years is no reason to assume *you'll* have influence at his court, Ramla!" Oultrejourdain growled at him.

"There's been no certain diagnosis," Ramla insisted disingenuously, provoking Tripoli to declare, "Only because his father wouldn't allow it; we all know what it is."

Before Ramla could protest, however, the conversation was interrupted by the arrival of Guillaume de Hebron. He was covered in dust and smelled of sweat. No sooner did he step into the room than he recognized what had happened and crossed himself. He looked as shaken as the rest had felt moments earlier.

"The High Court of Jerusalem is in session," Tripoli told the newcomer brusquely, adding that they were discussing the succession, and continued as if they had not been interrupted: "When we recognized Amalric's children by his first marriage, no one knew the boy had leprosy. Things have changed."

There was a grumble of apparent approval for this remark, and someone asked, "How old is the elder girl now, Agnes' daughter?"

"Sibylla? She must be thirteen or fourteen."

The collected barons looked dubious. Without exception they were all married men, which excluded them from contention to be Sibylla's consort, though some had sons of a suitable age. It fell to the Hospitaller Grand Master to articulate the thoughts of all. "She too would need a regent until a suitable husband can be found."

"Quite," Tripoli agreed, "so why not take the better filly in the first place? Emperor Manuel is our most powerful ally, and he will be far more disposed to support his great-niece than the children of a notorious harlot! For all we know, Sibylla will take after her mother."

Tripoli's insinuations set off a wave of protest, with the Patriarch pointing out that Sibylla had been in a convent since the age of eight.

Someone thought to ask the Patriarch, "Did Amalric say anything about the succession in his last hours?"

The Patriarch looked embarrassed, and unconsciously fidgeted with the large, gem-studded cross that hung around his neck on a thick chain. "King Amalric talked a great deal about his son, saying he was intelligent and wise beyond his years. He doted on the boy."

"As a father should," the Hospitaller Master reminded them sternly, "especially a son stricken with a mark of Divine favor!"

"That has nothing to do with our decision here!" Oultrejourdain countered. "Amalric may have loved his leper son, but the idea of a leper king is preposterous!"

"Why so?" the Hospitaller Master asked. "Christ showed great favor to lepers. Did he not cure the lepers and raise them out of their ritual expulsion from Jewish society to show that the Jews were wrong to reject them? Indeed, He has been known on more than one occasion to take the form of a leper himself! It is a well-recorded fact that He appeared as a leper to St. Martyrios of Lyconia in the lifetime of Pope Gregory I. Clearly, Christ has sent us a leper to be our king so that we might learn the humility that St. Martyrios showed, and bow down before the most miserable of the afflicted."

"Well, that's not what the Saracens believe!" the Templar Grand Master snapped back. "The Saracens will mock us from Aleppo to Cairo!"

"It is sometimes useful to be underestimated by one's foes...." Hebron remarked almost as an aside, but everyone turned to stare at him. He felt compelled to continue. "A leper king with a strong regent would not be such a bad combination."

"If the boy really does have leprosy, he won't last long. How long can lepers live?" Oultrejourdain asked. "Then what happens?"

"Three years from now, Sibylla will be seventeen, and we'll have had time to send to the Kings of France and England for a great prince to be her husband," Humphrey de Toron pointed out.

"And in six years, Isabella will be eight, over the age of consent, and we can just as easily find a husband for her," Tripoli countered.

The Patriarch scowled, "The Church frowns upon marriage among minors."

"Quite right, my lord," Tripoli agreed with a gracious bow in the direction of the Patriarch; but as he righted himself he declared forcefully, "but the defense of Jerusalem may force us to take actions that are less than perfect."

"If the leper lives only two more years, he'll have lived long enough to come of age!" Oultrejourdain reminded them with a growl, "and that's the worst of all possible scenarios."

"Does anyone know how healthy he is?" Hebron asked, and all eyes turned on the Baron of Ramla. He had never laid eyes on his brother's young charge, however, and could only report: "Balian says he's losing the feeling in his left hand now."

The men in the room groaned or shook their heads in collective distress, most of them still unable to grasp how it had come to this. The Bishop of Acre crossed himself and closed his eyes, his lips moving in apparent prayer.

"Crowning the boy is, nevertheless, the simplest solution," Humphrey de Toron announced into the stillness. "Anything else raises legal questions, which could be used to tear the Kingdom apart. Crowning Baldwin king also buys us time to find husbands for *both* his sisters. And should the Saracens think us weak, they will find out otherwise—so long as we are united behind a strong, capable regent."

Toron was astonished by the silence that greeted his words, for he had expected more bickering. As he looked around the room, however, he realized that distasteful as the thought of a leper king was, it was the lowest common denominator. Even the majority of the barons seemed to accept this, although someone muttered sadly but resignedly, "Jerusalem in the hands of a leper."

Only one man remained obdurate: Miles de Plancy, Baron of Oultrejourdain. "You can't be serious! You would pay homage to a leper? Put your hands between his foul and disintegrating fingers?" he asked, outraged. "Kiss his stinking hands? Not I!" he declared.

"In that case, Oultrejourdain, I would say you have disqualified yourself from the post of regent," Tripoli concluded calmly, trying to keep the note of triumph from his voice as he stepped towards the center of the room.

Amalric's closest male relatives on his father's side were the Prince of Antioch—whom no one in Jerusalem wanted to see take control in Jerusalem—and Tripoli. His closest male relative on his mother's side was Joscelin, Comte d'Edessa, whose county and person were in Saracen hands. In terms of administrative experience, however, Toron and Oultrejourdain were the most credible candidates for the regency, as both had served under Amalric, the former as constable and the latter as seneschal.

"Not so fast, Tripoli!" The Templar Grand Master tried to stop the turning tide. "Your qualifications for regent are hardly immaculate—not after the debacle at Antioch. Six years in a Turkish prison hardly qualifies you to be Regent of Jerusalem, either."

Tripoli flushed a violent shade of red. He, along with Prince Thoros of Armenia and a Byzantine army under Constantine Coloman, had rushed to lift a Syrian siege of Antioch ten years ago. Nur-ad-Din had been forced to retreat when confronted by the combined Christian forces, but the Christians had then made the fatal mistake of pursuing too hard, and had been lured into an ambush. Tripoli did not like to be reminded of either his capture or the ensuing six years in a Syrian prison. "At least I'm not a common thief like our friend Oultrejourdain!" he retorted, referring to the latter's reputation for attacking convoys of Egyptian and Syrian merchants traveling through his lands—despite safe conducts issued by the King of Jerusalem.

"Enough!" The Patriarch of Jerusalem managed to raise his voice above the clamor. "My lords! The King of Jerusalem is dead. His heir is a thirteen-year-old boy, possibly suffering from leprosy and likely not to live long enough to achieve his majority. His sisters are unmarried and so disqualified from the crown until such time as they are wed. We *must* unite behind a strong regent."

"Amen!" The Grand Master of the Hospitallers seconded his statement.

"Don't look at me!" Toron protested, holding up both hands. "I'll gladly remain constable, but I will not take on the burden of the regency. I'm too old for that. It would probably kill me, and then you'd need to find a younger man anyway."

There was a moment of silence and then Ramla, with a flush revealing that he was conscious of his own daring, announced: "I give my vote to Raymond de Tripoli."

"And I," followed the highly respected Guillaume de Hebron.

"Me, too," Caymont echoed, followed by Bethsan, Nazareth, Sidon, Blanchegarde, and Bethgibelin.

"The Hospital stands behind Tripoli," the Hospitaller Master intoned next, turning to glare at his counterpart from the Knights Templar.

"You don't need my vote," the Templar growled. "You have a majority already."

They all stared at Oultrejourdain. He stood with his arms crossed and his legs apart. "*You* kiss his ulcerous hands and grovel at his foul feet! I will not pay homage to a leper—nor take orders from you, Tripoli!" Then he turned and stalked out of the room.

"Give me five minutes to prepare him!" Balian begged his brother, who had come with the news that the High Court had agreed to crown Baldwin and had named Tripoli Regent.

"Of course," Barisan answered, glancing over his shoulder at his fellow barons, who were approaching from the far end of the gallery in a gaggle. "Of course. Try to cover up the worst of the ulcers, will you? You can put gloves on his hands, can't you? So we don't have to kiss his diseased hands?" Barisan's face was twisted with revulsion at the mere thought of kissing a leper's hands.

Balian nodded wearily. "I'll do my best," he told his brother, and passed through the heavy doors into the lower chamber of the Prince's apartments. Here he stopped to collect himself. Barisan might be worried about having to kiss a leper's hands when he gave the oath of fealty, but Balian had a different worry: Baldwin loved his father.

William of Tyre had heard the knocking on the door that Balian had answered. He stood in the stairway from the Prince's bedchamber on the floor above and asked anxiously, "It's over?"

Balian nodded.

William crossed himself. "And the High Court? Have the barons recognized Baldwin or passed him over?"

"They have recognized him, and will be here in just a few minutes to pay homage."

"Well, thank God for that, at least." The churchman paused. "Can you keep them here while I break the news to him?"

Balian sighed. "I will try, but I doubt it."

"Do what you can."

William of Tyre turned and climbed up the stairs. Balian held his breath, listening. He heard the Archdeacon murmur, "Baldwin, I am afraid I have some very bad news."

"My father? Is his condition getting worse?" Baldwin's voice at thirteen was beginning to break, but it quavered now, like a boy's.

"No, Baldwin, your father is beyond pain and misery. He is with Christ."

There was dead silence. Then a very tentative, "He—he's dead?"

The Archdeacon must have nodded, because Balian heard no answer.

After a long silence, Baldwin caught the echoes of a strained voice, "And he didn't even send for me. . . ."

Hearing the pain in Baldwin's voice, Balian mentally cursed the dead King for neglecting to take leave of the boy who loved him so much. But Archdeacon William countered firmly, "Your father named you his heir, my lord. You are now King of Jerusalem. The barons are coming to pay you homage."

It was at that moment that Baldwin broke down and started sobbing. Balian ordered the guards to admit no one until he gave them permission to do so, and took the stairs two at a time to go to Baldwin. Through his tears, the boy looked up at him with pleading blue eyes. "Balian, how can I—how can I—I don't want to be King! I don't want—everyone staring at me—I can't move the fingers on either of my hands!"

"My lord, this is God's will!" the Archdeacon admonished him. "You have no choice."

Baldwin ignored his tutor to focus on his friend. "Balian! Help me!"

Balian reached up and brushed away the King's tears. Then he took him by the shoulders and looked him in the eye. "My lord, you do not need the use of your hands to be King of Jerusalem, any more than you need them to ride. You will be King by the force of your mind and the courage of your heart."

"They'll scorn me! They'll revile me—" Baldwin's face was crumpling up again, all the memories suddenly vivid of his first months after the rumors started to spread about his leprosy.

Balian gripped him more firmly. "No, they won't! They will not dare—"

A loud pounding on the door below interrupted them. "My lord!" one of the guards called out, alarmed. "The High Court of Jerusalem and the Regent of the Kingdom demand admittance!" The guard sounded intimidated.

"I'll hold them!" the Archdeacon volunteered, sweeping down the stairs.

Balian turned back to Baldwin. "Your grace—"

"Don't call me that! We're friends, remember?"

"Yes, but you are *also* now my King," Balian insisted.

"And you can accept that?" Baldwin asked, frowning.

"I do—and so will they. Believe me, they will be astonished when they see you, for you look healthy still. More than that: you are a handsome youth. Your face is utterly untouched, and we will hide your discolored hands in the embroidered gloves Queen Maria Zoë gave you."

Baldwin swallowed. "You'll stand behind me, Balian? Right behind me?"

Archdeacon William could be heard loudly scolding the barons for their impatience. "The King has just lost his father. Give him time to compose himself!"

"Yes, your grace," Balian answered Baldwin. "I will be behind you when the barons come. But before that, let me be the first to take the oath of fealty." Balian went down on his knees and held up his folded hands.

Baldwin caught his breath. Then he placed his hands on either side of Balian's and enclosed Balian's hands between lifeless fingers encased in cotton gloves.

"I, Sir Balian d'Ibelin, pledge my oath as knight to you, my liege lord, King of Jerusalem, to serve you with my honor and my life so long as we both do live."

"I accept your oath, Sir Balian, and promise to be a good lord to you so long as you keep your faith with me, so help me God!"

Balian rose to his feet and went to fetch the beautiful kid gloves, embroidered with the arms of Jerusalem, which had been a gift from Queen Maria Zoë. He brought them to Baldwin and, finger by lifeless finger, pulled these over the thin cotton gloves Baldwin was already wearing. Then he went to fetch a comb from the bedchamber on the far side of the wooden partition, but here he was met by the old Arab slave, Ibrahim, who had served Baldwin ever since he had fallen ill. The old man shooed Balian away and called to a colleague. They had been lurking in the background and understood perfectly what had happened. They emerged with a magnificent surcoat, also embroidered with the arms of Jerusalem, with doeskin boots and silk hose. In five minutes Baldwin was dressed like a king, and Balian led him down the stairs to the room below. When William of Tyre saw them, he told the guards to admit the High Court of Jerusalem.

The barons burst in, led by Raymond de Tripoli, and then came to a stunned halt as they caught sight of Baldwin. Balian hung back in the shadows of the stair behind the King. He could not suppress a smile when he saw the amazed faces of the barons, as they found themselves confronted by a fair youth standing straight and with great dignity before them in the splendor of royal robes.

Raymond de Tripoli reacted first. He dropped to one knee and the other barons followed his lead, the last to kneel being Barisan, who was giving Balian a curious look.

"Your grace, your father is dead. We have come to offer homage as your vassals."

"Where is the Lord of Oultrejourdain?" Baldwin answered, and Balian wanted to laugh out loud as the barons gaped at one another in amazement. His eyes met those of William of Tyre across the room, and they shared a moment of pride; Baldwin had immediately and effectively demonstrated that his body might be crippled, but his mind was not.

"Your grace," Tripoli stammered, "Oultrejourdain was—misinformed. I'm sure he will rethink his decision. May I?" Tripoli held up his folded hands.

King Amalric was buried in the Church of the Holy Sepulchre, and Baldwin was crowned King Baldwin IV by the Patriarch of Jerusalem in the Church of the Nativity in Bethlehem. Baldwin rode all the way to Bethlehem from Jerusalem on his magnificently caparisoned white gelding, over which was draped a long trapper stitched with the arms of Jerusalem in gold. Misty pranced and arched his neck so proudly that the crowd mistook him for a stallion.

Baldwin was followed by his sister Sibylla, dressed in cloth of gold and shimmering silk veils, and his stepmother, shrouded in solid black as befitted a widow. The long procession was led by the highest clergy of the realm, including the Patriarch of Jerusalem, the Archbishops of Tyre, Nazareth, and Caesarea, and other bishops of the realm. They were followed by the barons of the Kingdom (except Oultrejourdain), nearly a thousand knights, many with their ladies, and then the merchant companies and guilds, all in their finest. The crowds lining the streets cheered exuberantly, waving banners and scarves and palm leaves.

In his cloth-of-gold cloak, his silk surcoat trimmed with jewels, and his embroidered gloves, Baldwin IV looked splendid. His fair hair was as bright as gold in the sunshine. His return ride, with the crown of Jerusalem on his brow, was if anything more brilliant. The crowds went wild, and the rumor spread that the leper Prince had been healed miraculously the moment he was anointed with oil and had kissed the True Cross.

Back at the royal palace, however, there were no such illusions. Raymond de Tripoli moved into the royal apartments, leaving Baldwin where he had been in the Jaffa Tower. After all, the business of government fell to Tripoli, and there was no point in exposing more people than necessary to the risk of contagion. Raymond ruled Jerusalem, while Baldwin was a puppet to be trotted out for ceremonial purposes only. At the palace, everyone understood that.

Balian d'Ibelin was summoned to the King's audience chamber in the Tower of David the day after the coronation. The chamber was full of supplicants, household officials, hangers-on, clerks, and men-at-arms. Everyone was milling about, apparently anxious to be the first to curry favor with the new power—or to assess it.

As he entered, Balian warily swept the room with his eyes. To his surprise, it seemed that most of the members of the High Court were still here. The Patriarch of Jerusalem stood directly behind Tripoli, listening attentively to all that he was saying, while Hebron was engaged in an apparently earnest conversation with the Archbishop of Nazareth. Beirut, who had arrived too late for the fateful meeting of the High Court but appeared all the more anxious to show his support for Tripoli, was inattentively following their conversation while keeping a weather eye on Tripoli. Although the Masters of the militant orders were absent, they had each sent deputies to keep an eye on what was happening, the Grand Hospitaller and the Marshal of the Temple respectively. These armed monks kept to opposite sides of the room, eyeing each other suspiciously—as always, Balian thought with a sigh; the rivalry between the militant orders weakened both of them and the Kingdom.

More surprising was the presence of the Princess Sibylla. She had been brought out of her convent for her father's funeral and her brother's coronation, but showed no inclination to return now that both events were over. At fourteen she was still more girl than woman, but by the look of things she was nubile, pretty, and very flirtatious. She had ensconced herself in one of the window seats, her long blond hair confined only by a crown-like roll of twisted silk at her brow, and her gown was a splash of vivid red embroidered with gold lotus blossoms. No less than three men were lounging about at her feet as if enthralled. One was the son of the Lord of Tiberius, a legitimate suitor for the Princess' hand, but another was Balian's brother Barry, and the third was Aimery de Lusignan. Although Balian knew that Barry's relationship with Richildis had become increasingly strained since the birth of a stillborn son the year before, he still took offense at his brother's behavior. As for Aimery de Lusignan, he was far too lowborn for the heiress of Jerusalem.

"Ah, Sir Balian," Tripoli called out, catching sight of him in the doorway and gesturing for Balian to come forward.

Balian obeyed, bowing before the count. "My lord."

"First, let me express my thanks for all you have done for the King. I understand the impressive horsemanship he displayed on his way to and from his coronation is all thanks to your tutelage." Balian inclined his head in a gesture of restrained thanks. Teaching a boy to ride was something a good Arab slave could do, and Balian judged that Tripoli saw his service in exactly that light.

"More important, I know you have been a manly influence on him—something he desperately needed. You have shown a rare kind of courage, one I greatly respect." Tripoli paused to lend his remarks weight, and Balian again inclined his head, this time more sincerely than before. Not everyone acknowledged that the role he played had indeed taken courage.

"Naturally, you will be retained at the same rate as heretofore," Tripoli continued in a more businesslike tone, adding, "and for the foreseeable future, there is no need to change your daily routine with the King. Be mindful of his dignity, however. Be sure that he is never seen in public without appropriate attire, and never ride out without a large escort—at least a score of knights and twice that many men-at-arms. Appearances must be maintained," Tripoli admonished. Balian nodded, although he thought the King, not Tripoli, should decide the size of his escort.

"I will be consulting with his physicians regularly, of course, but am counting on you to report to me anything you observe about the King's health that might be relevant. Also, I want you to report to me any remarks he makes about the governing of the Kingdom. If he complains to you about anything I am doing, I want to know about it immediately. Anything else?" he turned to ask the Patriarch, unintentionally giving Balian time to compose himself. Balian was furious about being asked to spy on Baldwin and had no intention of complying, but he knew better than to openly defy Tripoli.

Tripoli turned back to Balian. "I understand King Amalric saw his son daily. I doubt I will have time for that, but I will try to see him once a week at least. Be sure he keeps his distance at these meetings. I recognize that you and the Archdeacon of Tyre have so far avoided contagion, but I intend to take no chances."

"Of course not, my lord," Balian agreed with a cynical smile.

"And one more thing—" Tripoli was interrupted by an outburst of loud giggling from Sibylla. He cut himself off to frown across the room at the Princess. "My God! Does the girl have no sense of propriety? Someone needs to teach her how to behave! I can't have her giggling all day long while I deal with affairs of state! Why doesn't she go back to the convent, or at least keep to her quarters?"

"And who, my lord, is to tell her to do so? You have ordered the Dowager Queen to withdraw to a convent with her infant daughter, and the girl's own mother is the last person on earth who could lecture a maiden on virtue and propriety," the Patriarch pointed out.

Balian caught his breath. No one had told him the Dowager Queen had left court. More distressing: she had not told him herself. She had not taken leave of him at all. That hurt. So much for being her knight, his brain mocked his heart. For two years, it said, you have been living an illusion, a self-serving, childish illusion.... But this was no time to think about that.

A commotion at the door distracted everyone's attention. There were loud voices and stomping feet, the guards stood back respectfully rather than stopping the intruders, and Oultrejourdain stormed into the room with a bevy of knights in his wake. He was dressed in mail, the coif over his head but the aventail dangling open. His surcoat was canvas rather than silk, as if he had just ridden in from somewhere far away, although Balian knew he had remained in his city residence throughout the week despite not taking part in yesterday's coronation.

"You wanted to speak to me, Tripoli?" Oultrejourdain called from halfway across the room, his left hand on his hilt. Balian now understood why the members of the High Court and representatives of the Military Orders were lurking here.

Raymond de Tripoli rose to his feet. He was a tall man, at least a head taller than Oultrejourdain, so that even if standing might seem like an act of respect, it also should have put him at a slight advantage. Oultrejourdain, however, seemed insensitive to it. He stopped a good six feet in front of Tripoli and propped his left foot on a footstool, hastily vacated by a clerk who had been taking notes of Tripoli's orders. Oultrejourdain's legs were clad in mail. He leaned his left elbow on his bent thigh and stood thus, casually and disrespectfully, before the Regent. "So, Tripoli?"

"My lord of Oultrejourdain," Tripoli spoke with blistering politeness, "it has been noticed with deep regret that of all the barons of the realm, you alone have not paid homage to King Baldwin IV."

"You may put the Crown of Jerusalem on an ape for all I care, Tripoli, but that leper boy is no king to me!"

"The King, my lord, has charged me to remind you that you hold the barony of Oultrejourdain from him, and if you do not feel disposed to pay homage to him for it, you forfeit the barony to the crown."

"Tell your jackass leper *king*," Oultrejourdain sneered, "that he is *welcome to come and take* my barony from me." Oultrejourdain let this challenge hang in the air a moment. Then he laughed and his knights joined in, imagining a leper (which they pictured like the belled beggars in the streets) trying to fight Miles de Plancy and his knights. "Tell him," Oultrejourdain added, "I'll be waiting for him at Kerak." Kerak was Oultrejourdain's most formidable castle. Kerak had also come to Oultrejourdain through his wife, and Balian strongly suspected that her rights to it were not impinged even if her husband's titles were forfeit.

Balian looked back at Tripoli, and was relieved that Tripoli appeared not in the least surprised by Oultrejourdain's reaction. Instead he asked calmly, "Is that your final word, Sir Miles?"

"It is, Sir Raymond."

"Then I suggest you withdraw to Kerak at once so you have time to prepare your wife for the indignity of poverty."

Oultrejordain dropped his foot from the stool with a loud clunk and stood upright, glaring directly at the Regent. "If you think I'm frightened of a fop like you, Tripoli, you have even more to learn than I thought." He turned his back and started to leave. Then he stopped and turned again to say: "Oh, and if you thought the dungeon in Damascus was unpleasant, wait until you see the one I have in Kerak."

Balian thought he heard more than one man suck in his breath, but Tripoli was clearly determined not to be provoked. "There is more than one lord who has ended his days in his *own* dungeon," Tripoli answered slowly, "and for lesser insolence to their king than you have demonstrated this day."

"Ah, but I don't have a king," Oultrejourdain countered. "*You* may have kissed the leper's paws, but *I* have not." With these words he continued striding out of the room with his knights in his wake.

No sooner had the door crashed shut than everyone started talking at once. "You can't allow him to withdraw to Kerak!" Blanchegarde gasped. "Kerak is all but invincible!"

"No castle is invincible," Hebron countered sensibly.

"Either Miles de Plancy is a vassal of the King of Jerusalem, or he is no one at all!" Tripoli declared coldly.

"That may be legally correct, but Miles de Plancy has the loyalty of sixty knights and three times that many men-at-arms. Kerak may not be invincible, but it will take a large army and a long siege to subdue it," Bethgibelin warned.

"If we start fighting each other, how long do you think it will be before the Saracen is gobbling up the scraps?" the Grand Hospitaller reminded them all, clearly alarmed. "You must seek reconciliation with Oultrejourdain, my lord," he urged Tripoli.

"You heard the man!" Tripoli retorted. "He mocked his anointed king and refused yet again—for the third time—to do homage to him. If we let him get away with this, we undermine King Baldwin's rule irreparably—practically before it has started. Indeed, we make a mockery of King Baldwin! That, my lord, can be in no one's interest either!"

"Of course not," the Templar Marshal agreed. "But there are other ways to bring a man to heel besides outright warfare!"

"Indeed," Tripoli agreed. "I'll remember that." Then, gesturing toward the open windows through which the rolling bells of a dozen churches were calling to Vespers, he announced, "I will pray for guidance."

The other men could only stand in confusion as Raymond de Tripoli turned and exited the audience chamber.

Balian was still gazing after him when Barry grabbed his arm. "We've got to get word to Henri!" Barry hissed under his breath.

"What do you mean?" Balian asked.

"Don't be dense! We have to warn Henri that Tripoli is serious."

"I doubt he needs us to tell him that," Balian observed.

"Let me be the judge of that! Get word to him. Ask him to meet with us at home tomorrow." By home, Barry meant the Ibelin town residence, a house that took up a city block.

Watching his brothers fight, Balian was struck by how similar they were. They both took after his fair-haired father, and Henri at twenty-four was as muscular and tall as the three-years-older Barry, so they stood eye to eye and jaw to jaw, shouting at one another.

Balian took no part in the fight. Barry was right, of course, to insist that Baldwin IV was king, and the Ibelin family had nothing to gain by denying that fact or undermining the King's authority. He was relieved to find his older brother, who had taken no interest in Baldwin before, was so vehement in his support of the young King. But Balian had sympathy for his brother Henri because of the *way* Barry had handled the entire meeting. He had treated Hugh like a schoolboy, dressing him down and dismissing his objections without even hearing him out. Given the fact that they had parted in anger after their brother's funeral, this was hardly the best way to mend fences.

Henri was now shouting all the insults he'd picked up from Oultrejourdain about the King, and Barry was calling him an idiot and ordering him to quit Oultrejourdain's service.

"You can't make me!" Henri countered.

"Yes, I can!" Barry insisted. "I'll send word to Sir Miles myself—and see how fast he kicks you out!"

Henri's eyes betrayed how much he feared Oultrejourdain would do exactly that, even as he shouted, "He'd never do that! Never!"

Balian nodded to himself, knowing that Oultrejourdain would dismiss Henri—probably without any urging from Barry. If Oultrejourdain had decided on a confrontation with the Crown, he could not afford to have an Ibelin in his household, certainly not as a household knight, knowing how close Balian was to the King.

Balian spoke up for the first time. "There are other lords, Henri. We could probably talk Hebron—"

Henri responded by cursing Balian and the Baron of Hebron, then declaring vehemently: "I'm Oultrejourdain's man! There's no one else in the whole Kingdom half as good as he! The rest of you put together are not his equal!"

"We'll see about that, but you'll see it from the dungeon of Ibelin if you don't obey me!"

"Try to put me there!" Henri screamed and ran for the door.

Barry and Balian both sprang up to follow him, but Henri flung the door shut behind him, gaining precious seconds. He took the back stairs two at a time, and by the time his older brothers reached the kitchen courtyard he was already tearing out of the gate, leaving alarmed packhorses and fluttering chickens in his wake.

"I'll chain him in the dungeon! He won't see the light of day for the next year! Bread and water! He'll beg me to forgive him! He'll grovel at my feet!" Barry blustered furiously.

Balian said nothing and just let Barry blow himself out. Barry finally stopped threatening the brother who was no longer within hearing and glowered at the one who was. "Say something!"

"Oultrejourdain—"

"Sir Miles," Barry corrected him, denying him his forfeit title.

"Sir Miles will throw Henri out of his household in his own self-interest, and Henri will be back, contrite and humiliated."

This was exactly what Henri feared as he fled across Jerusalem. It wasn't just that Henri idolized his lord—he had vowed three years ago never to forgive Barry for cutting him out of their father's inheritance. He could not bear the thought of being dependent on him.

Henri, steaming inwardly, plunged into the covered market, famous for stalls selling swords, daggers, scimitars, and knives from all over the world. There were ornamental weapons with handles inlaid with ivory from Constantinople, Syrian swords with magnificently engraved silver sheaths, and the finest of German broadswords. The merchants were as diverse as their wares: Armenians, Coptic and Syrian Christians, Arabs, Turks, and Kurds.

Henri was so angry he was all but running, despite the upward incline, which left him panting as he took the irregular steps. He dodged overeager shopkeepers who tried to block his way, and elbowed customers aside. He took several right-angled turns as he navigated the warren of vaulted tunnels that housed Jerusalem's market, heading for Oultrejourdain's residence near the Zion Gate. In his mind, he was preparing the impassioned speech he would make to declare his undying loyalty and beg the baron not to dismiss him. He was too focused on his own crisis to take much note of his surroundings until a man almost collided with him, running in the opposite direction. The Turk shoved Henri roughly out of his way with a curse; outraged, Henri turned to shout an insult after the man. The man was tearing his turban from his head as he ran. Why would he do that? Henri asked himself without really caring.

The next instant, however, he was nearly trampled by three Franks shouting frantic orders: "Stop him! Stop him! Murderer!" Because they were shouting in French, most of the people in the market ducked back into their stalls, fearing trouble.

Henri not only understood their words, however, he recognized their livery: these were some of Oultrejourdain's men-at-arms. He spun on his heel and joined in their pursuit of the fleeing criminal.

But the man had already disappeared.

His pursuers stopped, panting, at the intersection of two of the covered alleys and looked around. The culprit had melted away in the welter of stands, shopkeepers, and customers. No matter which way they looked, there was the usual bustle of a busy market, but nothing more. The fugitive had submerged into the market like a stone dropped in a rushing stream.

"What happened?" Henri asked the men in his lord's livery.

"An assassin!" one gasped out breathlessly, but said no more.

They turned and made their way back through the crowded market, to emerge from the arcade just a hundred feet from the entrance to the Oultrejourdain residence. Here a large crowd had gathered around men hovering over something on the steps leading up to the residence.

Henri recognized several of his fellow knights from Oultrejourdain's household. "No!" he screamed and rushed forward, pushing his way through the others with the sheer intensity of his desperation.

Oultrejourdain was stretched out on the first two steps, his face white and wet with sweat and his stomach and abdomen soaked in bright blood.

Two days later Sir Miles de Plancy was dead. King Baldwin IV insisted that he be buried with full honors as a baron of Jerusalem, his loss of titles negated by his death. Baldwin also explicitly recognized the reversion of his lands and titles to his widow, by whose right he had held them in the first place. "We will not punish the innocent widow for the misdeeds of her husband," King Baldwin told his Regent firmly.

Tripoli hesitated, but then bowed to his King and agreed. "Stephanie de Milly is a courageous woman, my liege, and I agree she should not be punished for Miles de Plancy's intransigence. But Oultrejourdain is an exposed and vulnerable barony. The widow will, my liege, need a fighting man to hold her inheritance for her."

"Do you have someone in mind, my lord?" Baldwin asked.

"Not at the moment, but..."

"But what, my lord?"

"I only wanted to draw your attention to the risks we take by returning Oultrejourdain to Stephanie de Milly so long as she is unwed."

"What do you propose we do to reduce those risks, my lord?" Baldwin pressed his Regent, looking at him with large blue eyes that seemed to understand so much more than a thirteen-year-old should.

"We could send royal constables to hold the castles of Kerak and Montreal for her until such time as she remarries."

"Yes, that sounds reasonable," Baldwin agreed. "You will take care of that, my lord?"

"I will," Raymond assured his King.

Kerak, Oultrejourdain

Stephanie de Milly was not an attractive woman, and she had no illusions about why Miles de Plancy had sought her hand in marriage. In that he was no different than her first husband, the younger Humphrey de Toron, to whom her father had given her at a tender age. She was the heiress to a valuable barony, and her father had chosen not the man most pleasing to his immature daughter, but the man most likely to hold on to what he'd gained and held. With young Humphrey it had not been the boy himself, but rather his formidable father, Humphrey II, Baron de Toron and Constable of the Kingdom, who had pleased her father. But the young Humphrey had died in a stupid accident, leaving her a teenage widow with a infant son—who was instantly snatched away by her father-in-law, who wanted the boy (another Humphrey) raised in his own castle.

Meanwhile her father had chosen a second husband for her, Miles de Plancy. Miles had been twenty-three years her senior when he married her, and she had been sixteen. But Miles had been a good husband to her. He had not coddled her or courted her or treated her like a fragile doll. Instead he had recognized that she was as tough as he was, and as fiercely dedicated to holding her father's barony as he was. She had been his ally, his partner, his trusted lieutenant....

It had been a stormy marriage at times. They had fought—even thrown things at one another, when their wills clashed—but they had respected one another. Stephanie had thrived in that marriage, gratified that her word was obeyed as alacritously as her husband's, exhilarated by being entrusted with the defense of her castles when her husband was away, and proud to be called a "she-devil" and other insulting names by their enemies. The Saracens hated a woman who could fight more than anything else on earth, she thought with pride.

At twenty-six, Stephanie de Milly was taller and stronger than many men. She had flesh on her bones, and her detractors accused her of having hair on her chest as well, but nothing had prepared her for the news that her husband had been cut down by an assassin on the streets of Jerusalem. She flatly refused to believe the first messenger. "This is a trick!" she protested, jumping to her feet. "Tripoli thinks he can trick me into surrendering my castles!"

The second messenger fared no better. "Get out of my sight!" she screamed at her husband's squire, sent to fetch her to Jerusalem for her husband's interment. "You are a traitor!"

It was not until Sir Henri d'Ibelin showed her her husband's wedding ring that she understood he was truly dead. Henri knelt before her in the solar of Montreal and simply held up the ring, tears streaming down his face.

Most men did not wear wedding rings, but Stephanie had given Miles this ring with the crest of the Millys on it to remind him that he held Oultrejourdain through her. She'd underestimated the size of his fingers, and he had been unable to jam it over his knuckle at the wedding ceremony, but he'd pocketed it and had it enlarged shortly afterwards. From the day he put it on, he never took it off again.

Stephanie had stared at the ring proffered by the young knight, and felt as if a violent earthquake had brought the castle walls tumbling down around her. Miles dead? "How?" she gasped out, reaching for the ring. "How?"

"It was an assassin, madame," Henri told her, relating how a merchant from the weapons market had stepped into Oultrejourdain's path as he started up the steps into his townhouse, and held him back.

"My husband would never allow that!" Stephanie de Milly protested.

"He was annoyed and turned to hit him with his free hand. In that instant the merchant took the very knife he had been selling and stabbed him. Four times. He was a professional, madame," Henri told the widow, who stared at him with wide eyes and open mouth. "Any of the wounds would have been fatal on their own. The assassin went for the stomach, the liver, and the kidney."

Oultrejourdan's widow was clutching her husband's ring, cutting her fingers on the rough edges where his men had cut the ring from her husband's finger to bring it to her. She did not notice that blood was smearing the front of her dress. "Why?" she asked. "Miles had no quarrel with the Assassins. Miles has even given them safe passage on occasion. . . ."

Henri swallowed and took a deep breath. "My lady."

The widow did not hear him; she was gazing, dazed, at her bloody hands and the ring in them.

"My lady."

She looked up at him, her eyes blank.

"My lady, I don't think it was the Assassins."

She frowned. "What are you babbling about? You said yourself it was a professional. Who else uses such methods?"

"Assassins usually die, madame. They sacrifice their own lives, confident that in killing—and dying—they go to paradise. But this man ran away, and—and—" The intensity with which she stared at him made Henri nervous. He had told the others, but they had not taken what he said seriously. Stephanie de Milly, however, was staring at him as if he were the Archangel Gabriel.

"Madame, he tore off his turban as he ran. In the open street."

Stephanie de Milly started. She understood. "A disguise!"

"Yes, madame! I think it was a disguise. The man was an assassin, but not an Assassin. He was a hired killer, not an adherent of Hassan. I do not think the Old Man of the Mountain sent him, madame."

"Who, then?" Stephanie demanded, horrified and fascinated by what Henri was saying.

"Who had the most to gain by your husband's death, madame?" Henri asked, and when she did not answer him, he provided the answer. "Raymond de Tripoli, madame."

Stephanie de Milly sprang to her feet with a stifled cry, but Henri could see that she believed him. She stood clutching her husband's ring as she thought it all through for herself, and then she nodded and said almost inaudibly, but all the more forcefully: "Tripoli."

She spun away from Henri and started pacing so furiously that he began to fear he had miscalculated. Maybe she would not reward him for bringing her this message.

Abruptly Stephanie de Milly stopped. She turned back on Henri. "I will have my revenge. Wait and see. Miles will not go unavenged."

Henri nodded, convinced by the sheer intensity of her voice, even if he could not imagine how a widow could take revenge on the Regent of Jerusalem.

"Will you help me, Sir Henri?" she asked, leaning closer to him—her eyes boring into his own so sharply that he wanted to squirm as if in physical pain.

"Yes, yes," Henri stammered. "Of course, my lady!"

Still the eyes bore into him, searching his heart and his soul. "Do you mean that, Sir Henri?" she asked him in a low, ominous voice.

"Yes, my lady," he assured her again, sweating from fear that she might not believe him.

But she did. She straightened and drew back a little, keeping her eyes fixed on the household knight she had hardly noticed before. Then she said slowly and deliberately, "You will be my knight, then? . . . *My* knight?"

"Yes, my lady; always!" Henri vowed, crossing himself, to seal his oath by calling on the Holy Trinity as his witness.

Chapter 5

Kingdom of Jerusalem, August 1174

"WHY ARE YOU HERE, MADAME?" THE Mother Superior asked in a cold voice. She was not an old woman. Maria Zoë guessed her age at no more than thirty-five—although nuns usually aged well, spared as they were the cares and hardships of husbands and children. So perhaps this woman was forty. Regardless of her age, she had a lovely, regular face that was well set off by the tight-fitting white wimple of her habit. Her lips were thin, however, and her eyes dark, intelligent, and hostile.

"I have just lost my husband, madame," Maria Zoë returned, astonished by this reception. She had expected the Carmelite nuns at this remote, impoverished convent to welcome a prominent (and wealthy) boarder with open arms. "I wish to withdraw from the world so I may have time to grieve in private."

"Truly, madame?" the Mother Superior asked, with raised eyebrows that underlined her disbelief.

"Of course that is what I wish!" Maria Zoë insisted, starting to get angry. It had been a long and unpleasant journey. Twice they had been caught in unseasonable rain showers and drenched through. With sunset, the temperatures had dropped dramatically here in the mountains. She was cold, damp, and weary, while little Isabella had a running nose and appeared to be coming down with a cold. "Do you think I would have come all this way with my poor child if I did not wish to retreat from the world?" she asked back sharply.

"You have a very strong escort, madame," the Mother Superior countered. "The Comte de Tripoli seems to think there are people in your stepson's Kingdom who wish you harm—or that you are not quite so keen to come here as you claim." Her eyes were searching Maria Zoë's face.

Thinking that the Mother Superior was concerned about whether she had been brought here against her will, Maria Zoë curbed her temper and explained, "The Comte de Tripoli feared that my infant daughter might be seized by men who resent being ruled by a leper—men who would raise her up as the rightful heir and use her for their own purposes."

The older woman nodded, but she still did not smile or offer a welcome. She simply stood and rang a bell on her desk. At once a nun appeared and bobbed her knee to the Mother Superior, her head bowed. "Sister, show the Queen and her attendant to our best guest chambers. Be sure they have sufficient firewood and water to wash with. Arrange for a light meal to be brought to them there, along with hot spiced wine. Send Sister Alys to me at once." The nun dipped her knee again and gestured for Maria Zoë to follow her, but remained dutifully silent.

The guest quarters were not palatial, but they were comfortable, with a large fire that, after some coaxing by the lay sisters who brought wood and coals, started to take the chill off the damp air. Isabella was soon fast asleep in the small bed the sisters brought. Rahel, meanwhile, stripped Maria Zoë's wet clothes off her, sponged her down with the warm water provided by the nuns, and dressed her in a velvet dressing gown trimmed with wolf fur, a gift from her great-uncle. Lastly, Maria Zoë slipped her feet into sealskin slippers, and by the time the hot spiced wine arrived, she was beginning to warm up and relax. Even more than that, she began to feel safe.

Surely no one would look for her here. The place was too obscure, too far off the beaten track, too insignificant for a queen, even a dowager queen. Tripoli was a clever man, if also a calculating and self-serving one, she thought, leaning her head against the high back of the chair, and holding the wine goblet close to her chest so she could breathe in the spicy steam.

It was good to get away from Jerusalem, the court, even her ladies. Her only regret was not having the opportunity to take her leave of either her stepson or Sir Balian d'Ibelin. The thought of the latter gave her an ache in her heart. Not that he wouldn't understand her departure. Sir Balian was an intelligent man. He would surely grasp the advantages of taking Isabella someplace like this in secrecy. Yet the thought of not seeing him again—perhaps for years—hurt.

For two years they had been friends. Not ordinary friends. She had not dared invite him to her apartment after that first interview. She had never spoken to him alone again. When they spoke, it was before the entire court, often with her husband on her arm. However, she had often stopped in public to ask him about Baldwin. Her concern for her stepson was widely praised, and people approved of the way she consulted with the knight who looked after him.

Only Sir Balian and she knew that these frequent and public conversations had had little to do with Baldwin. Her private correspondence with Baldwin had given her all the information she needed about her stepson. When she stopped to talk to Sir Balian, she was seeking only an excuse to talk to *him*. Sir Balian invariably asked if she had anything she wished him to report back to his charge, which gave her the chance to tell Sir Balian what was on her mind.

Oh, dear God, forgive me! She closed her eyes and prayed. "All I really cared about was the expression on his face, the melodic sound of his voice, the sense of being near to him...." Was that such a terrible sin?

No. Perhaps it was not a sin at all. But sin or not, it was over.

Maria Zoë took a sip of the wine and savored the tangy taste of the local red grapes mixed with nutmeg, cloves, and slices of orange. There was better wine in Constantinople, she thought wistfully, and when she first came to Jerusalem she had missed it. But with time she had developed a taste for this wine, which tasted of limestone and desert rather than the sweet, blooming valleys of Greece.

She started as she realized that going home to Constantinople was theoretically an option open to her—but only if she were willing to abandon Isabella. She turned and looked over at the little bed where her daughter lay. She was too weary to get up and go to her, but she did not need to. Even without looking at the child, with her red-brown curls and cherubic face, she knew she would never abandon Isabella—not even to a man as honorable as Tripoli.

Tripoli wanted Isabella safe because he saw her as the true heir to Jerusalem. Furthermore, Tripoli wanted a closer connection to the Eastern Empire. For both reasons, Tripoli intended to keep tight control of Isabella until he could wed her to the man of his choice. But Tripoli was only a man, albeit a powerful one, and no man's life was certain. Tripoli, too, could die of dysentery as Amalric had, or malaria as Nur-ad-Din had done, or fall from his horse as the Baron d'Ibelin had, or... there were so many ways to die.

No, Maria Zoë thought, she could not entrust Isabella to anyone, because no one else would fight for her the way her mother would. Tired as she was, Maria Zoë still sensed the strength that lurked in her. If anyone tried to take Isabella away, or tried to force her into an unsuitable marriage, she would bring down the wrath of God—and the Eastern Empire—upon their head. She crossed herself as she made this vow silently before God.

The knocking on the door startled her and she sat upright, instantly alarmed. Rahel muttered something and went to the door, but did not open it. "Who is there?" she asked.

"The Mother Superior!" came the firm answer.

Rahel looked over her shoulder at her mistress. Maria Zoë nodded and pulled herself together. When the Mother Superior entered she saw a Queen seated stiffly, with her feet perfectly aligned, her back straight, her head high.

"I came to see if you were comfortable, my lady," the Mother Superior declared, coming deeper into the room, her eye taking in every detail, from the fire to the little rugs Rahel had unpacked and the goblet in Maria Zoë's hand—which certainly didn't belong to the convent inventory. Her gaze fell briefly on the sleeping child, and her smile twisted. Then she turned and looked Queen Maria in the eye.

Maria Zoë met her gaze. "Thank you, madame. The rooms are very comfortable."

The Mother Superior stood for a moment with her hands on the tall back of the chair opposite, apparently waiting for Queen Maria to invite her to sit down. When she did not, the nun walked around to the front of the chair and slowly sank down into it anyway. "Then we should talk."

Maria Zoë did not agree. She was tired, only slowly warming up, and in no mood to talk to anyone, but she bit her tongue.

"First, I would like to know just how long you intend to stay here," the Mother Superior asked.

"I don't know."

"A week? A month? A year? A lifetime? Surely you can make an estimate," the Mother Superior countered impatiently.

"More than a month, certainly, and just as certainly not a lifetime," Maria Zoë answered. "Isabella will reach the age of consent at seven and be marriageable at twelve. I think that is the longest I would stay," Maria Zoë answered, realizing that, glad as she was to be here for the moment, she truly could not imagine spending the rest of her life here. But then, did she really know her own mind? All her life, other people had told her what she was supposed to do. She had never had the freedom to decide her own fate. And precisely because freedom was such a new, unexpected state, she had not begun to think through all the possibilities it offered. Aside from protecting Isabella, Maria Zoë realized she did not know what she wanted.

"I see," the Mother Superior answered, obviously displeased. After a moment, she announced: "No one told me you were coming, and no one asked me if I wanted important guests. You will find that life here is not like anything you have known before. This is a silent order, madame. We live in individual cells and do not socialize. We see each other only at Mass and at chapter meetings. We speak only at allotted times, only as necessary—or in circumstances like these, where we are compelled by the outside world to speak. If you think it is cold now, imagine what it is like in the winter. We can have snow up here, but freezing rain is more common. The food is simple, the wine local, and the only music you will hear is the chanting of plainsong. We do not dance or hawk or play games of chess or chance; indeed, even bathing is a luxury we can afford only for special occasions. We bathe in cold water without scents of any kind."

Maria Zoë was too tired to dissemble. "Why don't you want me here, madame?"

"I did not say I did not want you."

"No, but you are doing everything in your power to convince me I do not want to stay."

"No, I simply want you to know what you will find here."

"No sympathy from you, that is certain."

"Did you come here for sympathy?"

"No; for peace and safety. I'm tired of being on display all the time. Tired of being stared at by everyone, criticized for what I do, say, and wear—even the tilt of my head or the way I hold my hands. I'm tired of being a puppet!" The wine on her empty stomach had loosened her tongue.

"Now *that* I can believe," the Mother Superior declared with a slight smile as she leaned back in her chair. "Much better than the 'grieving widow' pose."

Maria Zoë started. Was it that obvious that she did not grieve for Amalric—no matter how much she regretted that he was dead?

"Madame, let me be honest with you," the Mother Superior began.

Maria Zoë could not stifle a sarcastic, "By all means, drop this façade of delighted hospitality."

The Mother Superior acknowledged her quip by lifting the corners of her lips, but her eyes remained as hard as before. "We are a very small community here. Newcomers always disrupt the harmony. Jealousies, rivalries, antagonisms, and disappointments ensue. The presence of a queen—not to mention a small child—will cause trouble. You say you have come here for peace, but you have no idea how little peace there can be among two score women with too much time on their hands."

Without giving Queen Maria a chance to speak, the Mother Superior continued. "One of my charges, madame, was brought here by her brothers after she was discovered with a lover below her station. She did not want to be here, and she made escape attempts; when those failed, she tried to kill herself. Another of my charges had been discarded by a husband interested in a wealthier wife; he found churchmen willing to annul his first marriage, and no one in her family was powerful enough to stop him. She was so full of wrath that she poisoned the very air we breathed. Another of my charges came here after she lost her eighth child. She could not bear the thought of conceiving, bearing, and then burying another—but even here, she grieved so intensely we could not sleep at night for her weeping." She paused and looked at her new guest.

Maria Zoë looked back at her, the goblet of wine held in both hands. "You will find me far less disruptive, madame. I am here of my own free will, and my family is hardly powerless to help me, if I request it. So long as Isabella is well, I have no reason for untoward grief."

"No, I can see that," the Mother Superior agreed with a wan smile, "but you are still a young woman, and your daughter is second in line to the throne. I have already been informed that five men-at-arms and one knight are to remain here at all times to protect you. The men will rotate in and out, but there will always be six men in the hostel just beyond the walls awaiting your orders—and the Regent's, of course. That *alone* is disruptive, madame. I have charges here who were pledged as children; they know nothing of the outside world. Some are frightened of it, and others are attracted to it because it is forbidden fruit."

"It is not easy to have responsibility for others, madame," Maria Zoë answered. "That is the hardest burden of nobility, is it not?"

The Mother Superior nodded her head slowly, smiling without mirth. The Dowager Queen was not going to withdraw. She clearly intended to stay here as long as she pleased, regardless of the impact she had on the forty-three other women living here. The Mother Superior got to her feet. "Good. Then we understand each other," she announced.

"Yes, we do," Maria Zoë answered. "Good night, madame, and thank you for your warm welcome!" She held out her hand for the Mother Superior to kiss, and the older woman had no choice but to bend and kiss the long white fingers of her Queen, with the ring of Jerusalem on her right ring finger.

Jerusalem, September 1174

Walter, Balian's squire, was diligently using a metal brush to remove the rust from the rings of Balian's hauberk. He sat on a chest in Balian's small chamber with the heavy hauberk across his knees, and the wire teeth of the brush made a distinctive soft scraping sound as he worked it back and forth. His tongue played around his lips as he concentrated on the task.

The youth was sixteen and he had been with Balian for three years, ever since Balian's first squire refused to continue in his service after he started serving the leper Prince. Walter was the younger son of one of his brother's knights, a youth with even fewer prospects than Balian himself. After all, his father owned only a new-built manor in a settler town outside of Ramla and had eight children to feed. The fact that Walter was not very adept at arms, despite Balian's best efforts to train him, did not improve his prospects.

"Walter, did you ever think about going into the Church?" Balian asked casually as he watched his squire work.

"Who, me?" Walter looked up alarmed, a shock of dark hair falling into his face, and he jerked his head to try to shake it out again. His mother was a native woman, a Maronite Christian, who had bequeathed him dark hair and skin.

"I don't see anyone else in the room," Balian remarked dryly.

"The Church?" Walter asked back. "Me in the Church?"

"Well, you certainly aren't going to make your fortune with your sword," Balian pointed out.

"Ah, well, true," Walter admitted candidly with a sheepish grin, "but I have other talents."

"Such as?" Balian pressed him out of idle curiosity.

"I'm very discreet, keep secrets well, have a discerning nose for fine wine and food, can bargain exceptionally well—especially with fishmongers and butchers—"

Balian interrupted his catalogue of virtues with a laugh, pointing out, "All talents that would be well suited to a secular clerk!"

"But I can hardly read and write in French, let alone Latin, and—well—I like the ladies far too much." His smile was both shy and proud, making Balian throw back his head and laugh, because it was too true. Walter clearly enjoyed considerable success among the younger ladies of the court. But before Balian could retort, they were interrupted by a knock on the door.

Here in the small chamber allotted him as the King's knight,

Balian rarely had visitors, and he assumed this was a summons from the King. "Come in," he called casually.

The door opened, and a bedraggled street urchin peered into the room with big eyes under a mop of unkempt hair. He was crouching slightly, and his shoulders were hunched as if expecting a blow. He seemed poised for flight even as he inquired, "Sir Balian d'Ibelin?" His eyes darted from knight to squire and settled quickly on Balian.

"Yes?"

"I was promised a dinar if I brought you this." The boy held out a package wrapped in burlap and tied with twine.

Balian frowned, but made no move to take the strange package. "Who told you that?" he wanted to know.

The boy shrugged. "A lady."

"A lady?"

The boy nodded solemnly, but tensed, ready to dodge a blow.

"What sort of lady?" Balian asked skeptically, taking the package from the boy at last and weighing it in his hand before handing it over to Walter.

The boy held out his dirty hand. "She *promised* you'd give me a dinar, sir. I come all the way from Nazareth, sir. She said you'd give me a *dinar*."

Walter cut the twine with his eating knife and unrolled the contents from the burlap, gasping when he saw what he held in his hand. "Sir! It's a book! Look at this! It's beautiful!"

Balian turned to look at the bound book his squire held out to him, and he too caught his breath. Based only on its size and exterior, the book looked like it was worth as much as a destrier or a suit of mail. It was a gift fit for a king. Suddenly Balian's pulse was racing. "The lady who gave you this?" he asked the boy urgently. "Was she young?"

The boy nodded vigorously.

"And pretty?"

"Very pretty, and she smelled good—like roses."

"Maria Zoë Comnena," Balian grasped, turning to look at the book again.

Walter grinned confirmation, holding out the book opened to the text on the first page: it was in beautiful Greek calligraphy and illustrated with vivid pictures.

"Holy Cross! This book is worth a fortune!" Balian declared, and hastily went to get his purse to pay off the boy. In his amazement over the gift, he gave the boy two dinar instead of one, and then stopped the boy as he turned to scamper away down the stairs. "Wait!" He'd had a second thought. "Did she say the book was meant for the King?" He was waking from his dream: a book like this had to be for the King.

"No, sir. She said I was to give it *only* to Sir *Balian* d'Ibelin and no one else, not even the King or the Regent or the Archdeacon of Tyre."

Balian nodded absently and closed the door, the boy forgotten.

Walter was eagerly leafing through the book page by page, his face lighting up as he discovered one witty and lifelike illustration after another. "This is beautiful!" he exclaimed again, smiling up at his still-stunned master. "Maria Zoë Comnena must think highly of you indeed!"

"What sort of book is it?"

"Not a clue, sir, since I can't read Greek, but I don't think it matters. Look at this!" He opened the book to the page with the satin ribbon marker placed in it and held it out to his master. There were no illustrations on either page, but a dried pressed flower lay fragilely upon the parchment.

Balian looked at the flower and up at his squire, more confused than ever.

"Don't you recognize it, sir?" the squire asked, amused. "It's a forget-me-not."

Jerusalem, November 1174

Balian's chain mail gleamed in the morning sun, from the toes of his chausses to his coif. His helmet, which he held under his arm, had also been burnished until it reflected the sunlight. His surcoat, composed of the cross of Ibelin quartered with the crosses of Jerusalem, was made of freshly dyed Ethiopian cotton, bright and vivid, and he'd invested in a new belt for his sword as well. Balian looked his very best.

"You look splendid, Balian!" the young King exclaimed at the sight of his friend in martial finery. "Oh, I wish I were riding with you! Why shouldn't I lead my army? Why can't I?"

"Your grace." Balian kept his voice calm, understanding the boy's frustration all too keenly. "You know we cannot risk our King in a campaign like this inside enemy territory."

"And so I have to stay here? Locked in these rooms? I'm no better off than a canary!"

"By the sound of that growl, I'd call you a caged lion at least," Balian retorted with a smile, and managed to make Baldwin laugh.

But then the King grew serious again. "I know it's not your fault, Balian. I know it is Tripoli who will not let me out of my cage. But I'm serious. I'm thirteen. That's the age other boys start to earn their spurs and learn about warfare. How can you expect me to be King if I know nothing of war?"

"You know a great deal about war," Balian countered. "You've read the *Iliad*, Thucydides, *De Re Militari*—"

"That's all secondhand! I want to go to war! I could dress as your squire," he proposed.

"Dress *like* my squire, yes, but not perform a squire's duties," Balian reminded the leper softly. Baldwin's illness had progressed to the point that he could use neither hand effectively; the fingers were limp and useless, making it impossible for him to grip things. The lack of feeling had also started to creep up his left forearm.

Baldwin looked down, hurt because it was rare for Balian to remind him of his disability. After a moment he admitted, "I know," adding, "But there ought to be some way I could come as an observer. People know about my illness. People know I can't fight, but there is no reason I cannot go along, just as many priests and women do."

Balian saw the logic in that, but it was not his decision to make, so he asked instead: "Have you raised this proposal with Tripoli?"

"Not exactly," Baldwin admitted, not meeting Balian's eye. "I mentioned it to William, but he was not supportive."

"No. I don't expect he was," Balian agreed. Baldwin's former tutor had been appointed Chancellor by the Comte de Tripoli, but William of Tyre was truly a man of peace. Balian suspected the principal reason he had taken the cloth was to avoid having to shed blood.

He respected the Archdeacon for that, but it did not make him the best adviser to young Baldwin in this situation.

"You want me to raise this with Tripoli, don't you?" Balian asked.

"Will you?" Baldwin asked hopefully.

Balian hesitated, but then spoke candidly. "I can raise the issue with Tripoli, but I doubt he will heed me."

"Why shouldn't he heed you?"

"Because I am a twenty-five-year-old landless knight with no experience of war myself. I am neither a powerful baron nor a proven knight."

"But you are the King's man," Baldwin told him softly, with great sadness in his eyes.

"Yes, your grace, I am your knight," Balian assured him.

"Then in the name of God, Sir Balian, be the man I would have been if I had *not* been struck down by this cruel disease! Be a lion! For I have a lion's heart, Balian. Really I do!" Baldwin was on the brink of tears.

Balian reached out and gripped Baldwin's shoulder so firmly it hurt him—for the sickness had not reached his shoulders. "I know you do, Baldwin. Believe me, I know you do."

Baldwin pulled himself together. He looked Balian in the eye and took a deep breath. "I want to know everything that happens. I'm counting on you to remember and tell me everything when you return."

"I promise, your grace," Balian assured him.

"Wait! I almost forgot!" Baldwin sprang up and ran up the stairs to his bedchamber. Balian heard him murmuring with Ibrahim, and then he returned carrying a little casket laid in his cupped hands, the only way he could carry anything these days. "Please take what is inside of this with you, Balian."

Balian frowned warily. "What is it, Baldwin?"

"Open it up and find out!"

Reluctantly, Balian took the beautifully carved ivory casket out of the King's hands, and opened it. A heavy, somewhat battered and misshapen ring lay inside.

"It was the ring Godfrey de Bouillon wore when he took Jerusalem seventy-five years ago."

"Your grace! I can't take this!"

"Just to wear and bring back," Baldwin explained. "To remind you I am with you, in spirit if not in body."

"I am honored, your grace, but it is not necessary. I could never forget that your heart is with us, your army."

"Wear it anyway, Balian. With God's grace, it will bring you luck."

Reverently, Balian took the signet ring out of the box and slipped it on his ring finger. It was too large, so he moved it to his middle finger and formed a fist. "My liege," he murmured, and bowed deeply to the leper.

"We're running out of fodder," Tripoli declared, a grim expression on his tanned face. "Ibelin! Take some of those Turcopoles over there and see what you can collect."

"My lord," Balian acknowledged, trying to suppress his disappointment and resentment. Tripoli was employing him more as a squire than a knight. Both his brothers were with the van of the army, Barry as Baron of Ramla and Henri in the entourage of Oultrejourdain—but Tripoli had assigned Balian to his own staff, and at best he let him carry messages. More often he used him like this: to forage. Balian had not once had occasion to mount his destrier, and Godfrey de Bouillon's ring seemed heavy on his hand, a reminder of his promise to Baldwin to fight like a lion. How could he fight like a lion if he didn't get a chance to fight at all? And what was he going to tell Baldwin when he returned? How important it was to have enough water and fodder for the horses while on campaign?

He swung his palfrey around to trot over to the troop of Turcopoles Tripoli had indicated. The Turcopoles were dismounted, their horses listlessly trying to tear up tufts of dried-out grass and scrub brush. The men themselves were sprawled around in bored inaction since, to be fair, the entire army was in position but had not yet engaged the enemy. At Balian's approach, the Turcopoles got to their feet.

Balian looked them over, trying to decide who was their commander. They were a motley crew, with mismatched armor and round shields of differing sizes, ages, and repair. Most wore leather jerkins of some sort, some had captured chain-mail hauberks, and the poorest had only quilted linen aketons. Most wore woolen hoods of some sort to protect their heads—as much from the cold as from enemy action—although those with captured armor had coifs over these. They were armed with short swords and the reed lances carried by Sarcen horsemen. Balian addressed them in Arabic: "Who's in command here?"

A tall, dark man with bushy black eyebrows and a black mustache at once indicated himself and, flinging the reins over his horse's head, swung himself up into the saddle. He wore scaled leather Turkish armor and a turban, and his horse was sturdy and lively. The horse pricked up his ears and looked at Balian with intelligent eyes as his rider guided him alongside Balian's larger mount. "Sir?" the Turcopole commander asked.

"How many men do you command?"

"Seventeen, sir."

"And you know them well?" Balian asked skeptically. The quality of Turcopole troops was very uneven. Some were highly effective and motivated, others of almost no use at all.

"We are all men from the domains of the Canons of the Holy Sepulchre," came the answer. "We are Maronite Christians, except for Athanasius there, who is Greek."

That was good, as the Maronite Church was in negotiations with the Pope about accepting the supremacy of Rome, and—quite regardless of religious dogma—most Maronite Christians were exceptionally loyal to the current regime. These were men whose fathers or grandfathers still remembered what it was like to live under Turkish rule—and had no desire to return to it.

"You've campaigned together before?" Balian asked hopefully.

"Yes, sir, except for Athanasius and Ezekiel." The commander nodded his head toward two young men, neither of whom looked more than fifteen or sixteen.

"And your name?"

"Amos, sir."

"Amos, we have been ordered to find fodder for the horses. Have you sacks or the like to carry hay?"

"Yes, sir." He indicated a roll of linen tied behind his saddle. "And we have donkeys as well." He pointed a little farther away to a small herd of donkeys waiting docilely.

With an inner sigh, Balian nodded and signaled for the Turcopoles to mount and follow him.

The Christian army had surrounded the city of Homs, which was controlled by troops loyal to the Sultan of Egypt, Salah ad-Din, but the citadel was still in the hands of troops loyal to as-Salih, the young heir of Nur-ad-Din. Salah ad-Din had taken his army north to try to seize Aleppo, where the young as-Salih was protected by the local lord, Gumustekin. The garrison in Homs had requested help from the Christians to raise the siege of the citadel, and Tripoli had responded by moving the Christian army up and surrounding Homs. He was refusing to actually launch an assault on the city to relieve the garrison, however, until the commander at Homs promised to release prominent Christian prisoners he held. However, Balian judged that Tripoli was less concerned with the release of prisoners than with using the Christian "siege" at Homs to relieve the pressure on Aleppo. If Aleppo fell and as-Salih with it, Salah ad-Din would be in a position to take control of Nur-ad-Din's complete Syrian empire. He would then effectively surround the Christian states, as well as more than double the manpower at his disposal—a highly threatening prospect. By threatening Homs, Tripoli hoped to force Salah ad-Din to abandon his attack on Aleppo, and so ensure that Nur-ad-Din's territories remained divided and fought over.

After two weeks in position, however, the Christian army had already consumed all the feed and fodder from the countryside immediately surrounding Homs. It didn't help that the winter so far had been exceptionally dry, so that everything was still brown, with no hint of new growth yet. Most foraging, therefore, followed the Orontes River, but Balian already knew how far he had to ride to reach anything irrigated from the Orontes. On an impulse, he struck out to the east. Tripoli had not charged him with reconnaissance, but Balian decided that if he had to spend his time foraging, he might as well do it where he might also see something relevant to their siege. After all, Salah ad-Din needed to keep in close contact with the forces he'd left in Damascus.

Behind him he could hear the Turcopoles muttering among themselves, and Walter spurred his horse so he could ride beside Balian. "Wouldn't there be more forage along the Orontes?"

Balian shrugged. "Everyone goes there. Let's see what we can find east of here."

Walter made a face and demonstratively pulled the hood of his woolen surcoat up over his coif. The wind across the plain was bitterly cold, and Balian glanced up at the white sky: a mixture of thin cloud and dust that reflected in pastel the brownish-yellow color of the countryside. It was not the kind of sky that promised precipitation, just the kind of sky that blocked out the sun and made the whole landscape bleak.

They rode in silence, each man lost in his own thoughts, past abandoned and partially ruined villages. That was the way the Christians had found them, for the villagers had sought refuge in Homs as soon as Salah ad-Din's army appeared, and it was his troops that had broken down the doors and forced the windows in search of plunder. Balian did not doubt that their own troops had also scavenged through the houses and barns, but by then there would have been only slim pickings.

After about half an hour, they finally came to the first village that had not been sacked. They saw people running out into the orchard, carrying or chasing their children and their goats before them in an attempt to escape the Christian soldiers. Balian halted his troops to look into the crude mud-and-wattle barns, and was surprised to find some twenty bales of hay. These they loaded onto the donkeys, which they then sent back to Tripoli with the youngest of the Turcopoles as escort.

Roughly a quarter-hour further along the road they came upon an abandoned caravansary, and here they found not only hay but some barrels of barley and a broken barrel of rye that mice had gotten into. While the Turcopoles loaded these things into their sacks, Balian went outside and stared into the distance. The horizon was blurred and indistinct—whether from dust or moisture in the air was impossible to tell, but probably dust, as it was clearly thicker at one point.

Balian started and stood up straighter. This was what he had been looking for all day. "Walter! Amos! Come quick!"

His squire emerged out of the caravansary storeroom with straw sticking to his surcoat, the Turcopole commander on his heels. "Sir?"

"Look there! That smudge on the horizon. What do you think?"

It was Amos who answered. "Riders, probably a body of fifty or more."

"Leave the fodder! Have your men mount up at once!"

Amos and Walter gaped at him, and then Amos ducked inside to give the order and Walter protested, "But they must be Saracen. None of our troops would be this far east."

"Exactly."

"Shouldn't we lie low, then? Maybe they won't see us."

"And if they do, do you want to be on foot when they attack?" Balian countered.

Walter ran for their horses without another word.

Within less than five minutes they were all mounted in the courtyard of the caravansary, out of sight of the Saracen riders. Balian ordered them to check their girths, and then took a lance from Walter and ordered him to prepare to use the other one himself. "But you're riding Jupiter!" Walter protested.

"I've trained on him often enough for him to know the drill. Besides, he's still bigger and stronger than most of the native horses."

"You're going to attack?" Amos asked uncertainly in Arabic, for Balian had been speaking to Walter in French.

"Yes, that's exactly what we're going to do," he answered in the same tongue.

Amos's face split into a wide grin, and he hooted in triumph. "Boys! We're going to attack! We're going to attack!"

"Hold your lances upright until I give the order," Balian turned to address the excited troop of Turcopoles. "From a distance, they may take you for Turks and not immediately sense the danger."

The men nodded vigorously, and Amos suggested, "Maybe I should ride in front until you want to launch the attack?"

Balian hesitated. It seemed cowardly, but Amos in his turban and leather armor, carrying a round shield, certainly looked Saracen. Balian nodded curtly, adding, "When I give the order, break left and let Walter and me through, then stay as close to us as possible." He turned and addressed the still-eager troop of Turcopoles, looking into each face. Although one or two of the men looked dubious, the majority seemed genuinely pleased by the prospect of action. "Success will depend on momentum and a compact formation. Stay stirrup to stirrup. Four abreast, no more. Only spread out to swing around us as we engage the enemy—not before!"

They nodded at him, and one was bold enough to say, "We've watched you Franks do it. We can do it."

Balian wasn't so sure, but he *was* sure that he was going to attack. As they filed out of the courtyard they could now clearly see the fast-moving body of horsemen, riding hard across the fallow fields, heading southwest. Banners fluttered from their lance tips. Just as Amos had guessed from the start, the Saracen cavalry was a fairly small troop, no more than fifty riders, and they had their bows and shields slung on their backs. They were going someplace, not attacking.

"Those are Kurdish riders, sir!" Amos informed Balian. "Look at their banners!"

Balian looked, but he was not yet familiar with the heraldry of his enemies. Amos insisted, however: "Those are Kurdish Mamlukes."

"Salah ad-Din's men?" Balian questioned him. "You're sure they are not followers of Gumustekin or Saif-ad-Din?"

"No, sir. Those are some of Salah ad-Din's elite cavalry. See their yellow turbans and the yellow vests!" Amos pointed.

"Then may Christ, St. George, and the Holy Cross be with us all!" Balian gestured for Amos to take the lead, and the little troop set off at once on a course to intercept the Saracen horsemen at an oblique angle.

With each stride they closed the distance, trying not to appear threatening until shouts reached them from the other column of riders. The Mamlukes slowed their horses and turned slightly toward them, trying to assess who these riders were. Salah ad-Din had many enemies, and most of them were Turks. His men were wary. There seemed no point in disguise anymore. Balian ordered Amos out of the way and lowered his lance as he spurred Jupiter forward with a shout of "Jerusalem!"

Walter lagged on his right but Amos, despite having a weaker lance, was pacing him so perfectly that they crashed almost simultaneously into a still-confused enemy. The Mamlukes had been caught by surprise. Only a few managed to pull their shields or bows off their backs, and Balian aimed his lance tip at a man without a shield, pierced him, shook the lance free as he continued forward, Jupiter still at a gallop, and took a second man down as he tried to draw his bow. This time the lance broke, but Balian was also already out at the far side of the column of riders. He drew his sword as he turned Jupiter around and rode back into the enemy, holding it high over his head at the ready.

Meanwhile the rest of his little troop of Turcopoles was among the Mamlukes, shouting their own battle cries as they made their attack. The Turcopoles' lighter lances all broke on the first impact, while Walter appeared to have lost his altogether. Nevertheless, the attackers appeared to have unseated at least one rider apiece, or at least to have drawn blood.

By now dust was starting to obscure the overall picture. Horses were screaming along with their masters, and Balian was focused simply on parrying the blows directed at him while striking back every chance he got. Once he almost attacked one of his own men, unfamiliar as they were—but he recognized the mistake in time, held his hand, and then dropped his sword on the man behind him.

The bodies of the fallen were starting to get in the way of the horses, and Jupiter tripped and then shied sharply, almost unseating Balian. A moment later he sensed a volley of arrows coming at him, and he ducked below his shield. Several arrows thudded into the wooden surface of the shield, one embedded itself into his saddle, and another hit Jupiter in the shoulder. The stallion whinnied in pain and threw up his head, but Balian could see it was not a mortal wound, and he was more concerned about how the enemy could risk a volley when they were in such close combat.

As he spun Jupiter around on his haunches, looking for the source of the volley of arrows, he realized that around him only his own men were still mounted. The bulk of the enemy were drawing away to the south at a gallop, the rear riders firing backwards over their shoulders to discourage pursuit.

There was no point in following. The enemy horses were faster and their numbers still greater than Balian's little troop. He had achieved what he could for the moment; most important, he had proved to himself he was not a coward.

"How can a man have so much luck!" Barisan d'Ibelin complained indignantly to his friend Aimery de Lusignan. "It was nothing but a routine foraging patrol! He was looking after our stomachs, not our honor!"

Aimery wasn't so sure it was luck. The entire strategy of this campaign was to attack the city of Homs in order to relieve the pressure on Aleppo. If the strategy was to work, Salah ad-Din had to be forced to withdraw troops from the assault on Aleppo and send them to reinforce Homs. Balian d'Ibelin's "foraging patrol" had swung far to the east, putting itself across the path of any forces sent by Salah ad-Din from Aleppo to Homs. Aimery strongly suspected that Balian had known exactly what he was doing, but if Barry didn't see it that way, Aimery saw no point in arguing with him. Instead he remarked, "In fairness, that doesn't detract from what he did. With only his squire and fifteen Turcopoles, he attacked some threescore of Salah ad-Din's elite cavalry, spearing no fewer than two men personally and killing another three men with his sword, before capturing four prisoners and putting the rest to flight."

"And what might you and I have done if we'd had the good fortune to encounter Salah ad-Din's cavalry!" Barisan countered. "There's nothing so remarkable about killing five Saracens in the open! It's trying to kill them when they're secure behind high walls that is difficult!"

This was true enough in its way, but Aimery thought it was ungracious of Barry to belittle Balian's achievement. For a young, unproven knight to attack a more numerous force and scatter it after a short engagement was remarkable, and he thought the praise given Balian by Tripoli was both deserved and commensurate. It wasn't as if Tripoli were lavishing him with rewards; he'd simply said "well done" and immediately made him a banneret over five royal knights.

"If we'd had the luck to encounter Salah ad-Din's cavalry, we would have done twice as well," Barisan insisted stubbornly.

"We might have killed more Saracens," Aimery conceded, "but I would not have been able to understand enough to know they were Salah ad-Din's troops and not someone else's," Aimery admitted. "It was that intelligence, far more than the casualties inflicted, that was valuable to us. We now know Salah ad-Din has taken the bait and is indeed trying to reinforce Homs. Tripoli has given your brother more knights not to kill more Saracens, but rather to find out more about Salah ad-Din's intentions. Tripoli rightly wants to know whether Salah ad-Din is withdrawing from the siege of Aleppo."

Barry shrugged, but this incident made Aimery revise his opinion of the younger Ibelin. Barisan, as Baron of Ramla, Ibelin, and Mirabel, might be the more useful friend in the short run, but Balian would bear watching.

Krak de Chevaliers, County of Tripoli

Reynald de Châtillon was having more trouble getting his bearings than he was prepared to admit. He abhorred weakness in anyone, especially himself—and so he could not admit to it, but things were happening too fast even for him. Fifteen years in a dungeon had taken from him much of the flesh on his bones and some of his vision as well. He still could not stand naked sunlight, and he instinctively sought shadows or shaded his eyes with a broad straw hat tied over his coif. He might look ridiculous, but Reynald had left vanity behind in the dungeon at Aleppo.

The Wheel of Fortune, he thought to himself, ought to be on his coat of arms. Born to a family of no consequence, he had come out to Outremer in the train of Louis VII of France, but rather than returning humiliated like his master, he had risen to become Prince of Antioch by seducing a sex-starved and stupid widow. Knowing he'd have nothing after her son came of age, he'd tried to take the Island of Cyprus from the Greeks—and he'd succeeded! But then the Emperor sent a fleet and robbed him of the fruits of his labors. After that he'd groveled in the dirt at the Greek Emperor's feet in a display of abject submission, but the lesson Reynald took away from the incident was only that it was foolish to attack an island without control of the sea. So in subsequent years he'd turned eastward for new conquests—only unfortunately, through no fault of his own, he'd been captured by the Emir of Aleppo and thrown into a dungeon.

The dungeon was deep underground, with no windows to let in daylight. Air came, dank and foul, smelling of death and decay, from long, dark tunnels that led to other cellars, or possibly beyond the walls. Reynald never knew where all the tunnels led, because they were barred to him by iron grilles anchored in bedrock. Only one had seemed important: the one by which he'd entered and—fifteen years later—departed.

In the intervening years, he had lived like the rats in that dungeon: drinking the water that seeped from the walls and collected in dank pools on the stone floor, fighting over the bread and other scraps thrown to them, and shitting where he pleased. He'd seen more than one prisoner die in that dungeon, and he'd contributed to the death of others to be sure that rations never got too short—or when their ravings got on his nerves. Many men went mad in that dungeon; Reynald just became harder.

When he emerged from the dungeon, the Arabs had covered their noses and mouths at the stench of him, and even the bath slaves had made faces when ordered to clean him up. They had shaven off his filthy, matted hair, oiled him, and then scraped and scrubbed him until his white, sun-starved skin was as pink as a boiled crab. They had clipped and filed his toenails and fingernails, and then dressed him in a fine white robe with a turban and returned him to the King of Jerusalem.

It was only after he had been delivered to the Hospitaller castle of Krak des Chevaliers that he learned Baldwin III was dead; that was a bad shock. The second shock was hearing that Amalric, his brother and heir, was also dead. But the third shock had been the worst: learning that Amalric's heir, Baldwin IV, was a boy suffering from leprosy. "So who the hell's in charge?" Reynald demanded, already wondering if there were a widow to be seduced here as well.

"Tripoli."

"Raymond?" Reynald asked, incredulous. Then he sniffed in contempt.

The feelings were mutual.

In a gesture of gratitude, the Emir of Aleppo had freed all the Christian prisoners in thanks for the Christian attack on Homs that had forced Salah ad-Din to lift the seige of Aleppo. The gesture was a generous one, but to the end of his days Tripoli wondered if the Emir of Aleppo had known what he was doing when he released Reynald de Châtillon along with the others. Reynald was to be a thorn in his side until they both died.

Meanwhile, Reynald might have been released from the dungeon in Aleppo, but he was welcome nowhere. The Greek Emperor had accepted his groveling years before, but he had not forgiven the ravaging of Cyprus. Reynald thought the Emperor might concoct some justification for a new arrest—or just poison him. In Antioch, now that his wife was dead and his stepson was in control, he was even less welcome; Bohemond was bitter about the alleged "misrule" of his kingdom and the "plundering" of his coffers by his mother's second husband. Tripoli, meanwhile, had banned Châtillon outright from his own territories, so he was only safe here as long as he was in the care of the Hospitallers. To go to Jerusalem, however, meant doing homage to a leper! Châtillon spat.

But here was this young knight, begging him to leave Krak des Chevaliers for Kerak in Oultrejourdain and attend upon the widow of his old friend Miles de Plancy. "Sylvia's her name, isn't it? Or, no," he snapped his fingers in irritation at his poor memory, "not Sylvia, something with "ie" on the end. Melanie? No, Stephanie, that was her name! No?" Henri d'Ibelin nodded, and Châtillon scratched deeper in the dark corners of his benumbed memory. "She wasn't much to look at, if I recall rightly."

"She is not a conventional beauty, my lord," Henri conceded. "But she has many other qualities."

"I'm beginning to remember now. Miles said she could curse like a sailor, scream like a fishwife, and scratch like a cat—sometimes in fury and sometimes out of ecstasy when he rode her." Châtillon laughed to see the young knight blush at his bluntness. "You're not one of those fools who pledges yourself to a lady and vows chaste love, are you, boy? Let me tell you, chastity will get you nowhere. Rutting in the right place at the right time will."

Henri flushed a darker shade of red, but replied stolidly: "My lady requests that you attend on her at Kerak, my lord. I have been asked to escort you. I know no more."

"The hell you don't!"

By the time they reached Kerak, Henri d'Ibelin was completely under Châtillon's spell. He had never met a man so irreverent of everyone and everything Henri had been raised to think of as holy. Compared to Châtillon, Plancy had been a saint. Châtillon had no respect for secular authority, and even less for the Church. "I'd as soon piss on a holy relic as kiss one," he told Henri as they rode past the holy sites on the Sea of Galilee and down the Jordan, making for the fortress of Kerak east of the Dead Sea. "And I'd as soon kill a priest as dine with one. Ever hear about what I did to the Patriarch of Antioch when he refused to contribute to my Cypriot campaign? I had him flogged and tied to a stake in the middle of the exercise ground where there wasn't a slice of shade. Then I smeared honey all over his tonsured head and left him there until he *begged* me to strip him of his last obol, just to stop the flies from swarming into his eyes, ears, nose, and mouth—not to mention the open wounds on his back! They were so thick by afternoon, he nearly gagged on them!" Reynald laughed heartily at the memory. "In fact, there were so many flies he didn't even get a sunburn on his skull, although he held out most of the day. Stupid man!" Reynald shook his head in disgust, and Henri was awed beyond comprehension.

At Kerak, Henri was ordered to escort Châtillon to the spacious and well-furnished suite once used by Miles de Plancy. He had been instructed to make sure Châtillon *knew* these rooms belonged to the Lord of Oultrejourdain, just as he had been instructed to point out all the lands that belonged to the barony as they rode through them. Stephanie wanted Châtillon to understand just how rich she was, even if she didn't bring him a princely title.

On arrival at Kerak, Henri organized a bath for Châtillon and provided him with fresh clothes from Miles de Plancy's own wardrobe. They hung on Châtillon, who had grown thin in captivity, but they were finely woven with golden borders. Châtillon looked down at them and nodded in satisfaction. He had survived living like a rat for fifteen years, but he preferred this. He took a deep breath of air scented with crushed rosemary and thyme, considered the finely carved chests and cabinets, the wall tapestries, and the thick rugs, and nodded. Yes, this was definitely better.

He demanded a mirror and considered his face critically. He had been a handsome youth, handsome enough to seduce a princess. Now his face was like a ravaged desert, cut deep with dry gullies. His eyes were sunken, glittering pools of burning ambition under a jutting forehead filled still with plans. As a youth he'd worn his hair shoulder length, but after the initial shock of seeing his reflection with a shaved head, he decided bald suited him better. "Henri! Send me a barber to shave off this fuzz! I'm not going to grow my hair back. Too much trouble to keep it clean, and bald is cooler in the summer heat."

At last Châtillon was ready for his interview, but to his annoyance he was not admitted. "My lady will send for you when she's ready, my lord," Henri informed him.

"I thought she already had!" Châtillon snapped back. "We've been riding nigh on a fortnight *because* she sent for me. Take me to her now!" he ordered.

Although Henri admired Châtillon's spirit, he had pledged himself to Stephanie. "When she's ready, my lord."

Châtillon raised his hand to strike Henri or shove him out of the way, but then their eyes locked, and he changed his mind. "Right," Châtillon agreed. "When she's ready, she can send again—but tell her I might not be here if she waits too long."

Henri withdrew, and Châtillon was left to stew in his own impatience. He paced the wide chamber as if measuring it. He stepped into the windows to look out across the wide, arid valley dominated by Kerak—but the sun had set, and with it any hope of seeing anything beyond the uncertain points of light that marked villages or Bedouin camps.

Oultrejourdain was a frontier, Châtillon reminded himself. A borderland without a border. The richest caravans in the world passed along just out there—in the darkness beyond the last flickering light. The caravans carrying all the riches of Arabia, the Red Sea, Egypt, and the very source of the Nile. If Miles' widow was too stupid to take him to her bed, he'd just go out there and make his own fortune!

But he needed horses, armor, and weapons for that. And at least a half-dozen men as desperate as himself. The Holy Land was filled with such men, and weapons and armor, too. Why, there were probably enough weapons and armor buried in the sands of the desert to fit out a host ten thousand strong! Horses would be the hardest thing to come by, but not impossible.

"Are you drawn to the darkness, my lord?" a voice asked, startling him from his thoughts, and Châtillon spun around.

She was standing by the fireplace, and for the life of him Châtillon could not see how she had crossed the room without his hearing her—for if his eyes had dimmed, his hearing had sharpened in the darkness of the dungeon. He guessed there was a disguised door beside the fireplace—a secret passageway by which the lady could come to her lord, or vice versa. She had planned this well, he thought appreciatively, and his opinion of her increased.

"I have come from the darkness, my lady," he answered her cautiously. "Let us say, I have grown accustomed to it."

"And to having nothing but your naked life, I believe." It was not a question.

Châtillon could not deny what she said, but he did not like admitting it, either, so he remained silent, considering the woman opposite him. She was indeed no beauty. She was hefty as a cow as well, but to her credit she made no pretense of being what she was not. She had not adorned herself in some futile attempt to make herself appealing. Her dress was black, her wimple as tight and heavy as a nun's, her face unrouged. She wore no jewelry except her wedding band and a signet ring that looked like one Miles had worn. No doubt it *was* the one he had worn.

"Why do you think I sent for you, my lord?"

Châtillon was not a man who liked dissembling unless he knew it was to his advantage. Seduction could be very advantageous; but how do you seduce a woman built like a battle-ax, dressed like a nun, and as welcoming as the Sinai Desert? He took a chance on flippancy. "Because you can't wait to get my cock up your lap?"

Stephanie did not even flinch. "I can be a lot cruder than that, so don't try to shock me. I sent for you because I have been told you are the most ruthless, godless, and brutally ambitious man the Kingdom of Jerusalem has ever seen—and it's seen more than its share of ruthless and godless men."

"You flatter me, my lady." Châtillon mimicked a courtly bow.

"You are also a penniless adventurer."

"That's the way I started out in life," he pointed out with a shrug.

"But you'd rather be rich."

"Who wouldn't?"

"I'm willing to cut a deal with you, Reynald de Châtillon."

"Indeed. Why—if it's not for my famous and *very hungry* cock?" Fifteen years was a long time to go without a woman, and to his own surprise, he found himself increasingly attracted by the idea of bedding this formidable female. Mounting a woman like her would be so much more exciting than mounting some simpering girl or jaded whore. It would be like winning a joust.

"It's because I want a man who is not afraid of anyone."

"Who on earth should I be afraid of, madame?" Reynald held out his arms in a wide, sweeping gesture.

Stephanie de Milly moved toward him slowly and deliberately. She did not smile, and her feet made no sound on the carpet. She glided forward until they stood only a foot apart. She was not much shorter than Reynald, and they looked eye to eye. "I am offering you the Barony of Oultrejourdain and all its wealth in exchange for one thing only."

The look in her eyes at this range banished all banter and jesting. Châtillon found himself asking, "What?"

"Revenge," Stephanie told him, her eyes locked on his, watching for the slightest hesitation, shock, or discomfort. "Revenge for my husband."

Châtillon was not shocked. He could understand such a wish. "On whom, and how?"

"How is for you to decide, my lord; as for whom, I want you to destroy Raymond de Tripoli."

That surprised Châtillon. "Tripoli? Why Tripoli?"

"Because he was behind my husband's murder."

Châtillon looked skeptical. He did not think Tripoli was the type of man to hire an assassin. Then again, he didn't care if Tripoli were really to blame or not. If the price of Oultrejourdain was killing Tripoli, it was a small price. Châtillon shrugged, and stepped back so he could bow again. "At your service, madame. Do you want me to kill him before or after the nuptials?"

"Don't mock me, Châtillon. I know killing a man like Tripoli will not be easy. I know it will take time, and murdering a man's reputation can sometimes be better than murdering his mortal body. This is not a topic I take lightly, and it is not one *you* should take lightly—unless you intend to walk away from my offer."

Châtillon considered the widow again. At this range he could smell the sweat and wood smoke clinging to the wool of her gown. No perfumes for this woman; but her very manliness aroused him—as did her passion for revenge. "You and I would make an invincible pair, my lady," Châtillon told her slowly.

"We will see," she answered practically. But then, for the first time, she gave him a fleeting echo of a smile when she added, "But I think we very well might."

Chapter 6

Jerusalem, July 1176

The Privy Council of the King was collecting as usual on the first floor of the Tower of David. The clerks were fussing with their ink pots and scrolls of paper, trying to get ready for any dictation they might have to take. One servant was wiping off the oak table, while another shooed away Tripoli's dogs, which for some reason liked to lounge in this room more than any other in the palace. The Chancellor, now installed in the recently vacant Archiepiscopal See of Tyre, had pulled Tripoli into the window niche and was earnestly talking to him, while the lesser members of the Council took their usual seats.

Most chatted casually with one another in easy familiarity. Only the titular count of Edessa, Jocelyn de Courtenay, sat apart from the others. Edessa no longer existed as an independent county (having been overrun by the Saracens more than thirty years ago), but Jocelyn de Courtenay had been one of the many prisoners released by the Emir of Aleppo in thanks for Jerusalem's support against Salah ad-Din. Unlike Oultrejourdan, who had earned the Emir of Aleppo's hatred for preying on Muslim pilgrims, the Count of Edessa had been treated courteously during his captivity. He was confined to a tower chamber rather than a dungeon; he had been well fed and even allowed books to read and servants and female slaves to look after his bodily needs. Nevertheless, the years away from court and the emptiness of his hereditary title set him apart from the others on the Privy Council. Most of all, there was unspoken mistrust between Tripoli and the men he'd appointed and the Count of Edessa. Edessa did not owe his place on the Council to Tripoli's favor, but rather to the fact that he was the King's closest surviving male relative: Baldwin's maternal uncle.

A short but firm knock was followed by the stentorian announcement: "His Grace, King Baldwin IV of Jerusalem!" With this announcement, the man-at-arms at the door brought the Council to their feet—but did not stop the various conversations from continuing as the men stood up.

The King paused in the doorway, taking in the scene. Had any of his councilmen been looking at him, they would have seen his lips pull back in controlled anger—but no one stopped to watch their King advance to his large, armed chair, covered by a baldachin of satin bearing the arms of Jerusalem. Baldwin took his seat and waited, his inner anger simmering. He allowed himself only one glance at his uncle, who winked at him, but otherwise retained his impassive pose.

At length the Regent nodded to the Chancellor, and together they stepped down from the window niche to take their places on either side of the King. This signaled to the others that the meeting of the Privy Council was about to begin. The other members broke off their own conversations, while the clerks squirmed themselves comfortable and waited expectantly.

"The most important item of business today is, of course, the marriage of—"

"My lord." Baldwin had to speak out loud to stop the Regent's flow of words, because the Count had ignored his raised hand.

Tripoli looked over, startled and annoyed. "What is it, your grace?" he asked, obviously irritated by the interruption.

"Before we take up the agenda, can anyone in this room tell me what day it is?"

The men around the table looked blankly at one another—except for Jocelyn de Courtenay, who looked down at his hands with a smirk playing around his lips.

"It's the Feast of St. Alexis of Edessa—" the Patriarch began automatically, and the Chancellor caught his breath so loudly that they all turned to stare at William of Tyre.

Only Baldwin remained cool, remarking, "I believe the good Archbishop has grasped the significance of the date—at last." There was a well of bitterness in those last two words, and the Archbishop of Tyre flushed as he bowed deeply to his King.

"Your grace does well to admonish me. I can only beg indulgence that negotiations over the marriage of your sister to William of Montferrat..." He fell silent, conscious that no excuse was good enough.

Baldwin offered the Archbishop no respite from his embarrassment, staring at him in his discomfort for several seconds before enlightening the rest of the baffled Council. "Exactly fifteen years ago, on the Feast of St. Alexis of Edessa in the Year of Our Lord 1161, I was born. In consequence, according to the laws and customs of the Kingdom of Jerusalem, my lords, I am no longer a minor." The meaning of his words had dawned on all the Privy Council members long before he finished speaking. No one replied, however. They just gazed at him, wondering what would come next—except for Edessa, of course, who was grinning triumphantly.

King Baldwin turned to the Count of Tripoli and spoke slowly and deliberately. "I wish to thank you, my lord, for the great service you have rendered the Kingdom by so ably governing during the years of my minority. I appreciate the great sacrifices you have made in my service, and I wish to state explicitly that I am most pleased with your stewardship." Baldwin paused and looked directly at the clerks. "Note down that King Baldwin IV thanks the Count of Tripoli warmly and sincerely for his stewardship, and wishes as a token of his gratitude to bestow upon him the right to marry the widow Eschiva of Galilee." That brought a gasp from some of the men in the room, because Galilee was one of the richest baronies in the Kingdom, owing one hundred knights. To join this with Tripoli made Raymond the richest and most powerful baron in the Kingdom. The gesture was also well calculated to silence any protest from the recipient of the favor—and any suggestions that Baldwin was not pleased with Tripoli's stewardship. "Now, let us turn to the agenda. You were saying, my lord of Tripoli?"

Tripoli recovered quickly from his initial surprise. Two years earlier he had believed that Baldwin might die before he came of age, but frequent contact with the King had convinced him otherwise. While Baldwin's leprosy was irreversible, it appeared to have been arrested. Baldwin's increased activity after his coronation had given his face a healthy complexion without a trace of corruption. His riding had improved to the point where ordinary men compared him to a centaur, and he walked without apparent difficulty or impediment. His hands and forearms, to be sure, were discolored and lifeless, but they were not covered with ulcers, and none of his limbs had actually become deformed, much less fallen off. Tripoli had long since accepted that Baldwin would reach his maturity and take power for himself; it was just that he had hoped to conclude a few items of business first. For some reason, he'd thought Baldwin's birthday was not until the end of the month. Now Tripoli bowed his head to Baldwin and thanked him for his "kind words and generosity." He added, "I have always served you, your grace, with the utmost conscientiousness and with all the facilities in my power."

"Thank you," Baldwin replied simply. "Now, to the first order of business: the marriage of my sister Sibylla."

"Yes, your grace. The Marquis of Montferrat has agreed to all our terms with only minor alterations, and is prepared to sail before the autumn storms. He expects to arrive no later than the end of October."

"What alterations?" Baldwin wanted to know.

"They were—" The Chancellor had been about to say they were of no consequence; but reading Baldwin's mood correctly, he cut himself off, turned to one of the clerks, and set him scampering for a copy of the revised marriage contract.

"You are certain that the Marquis will sail before the winter?" Baldwin asked the Chancellor after the clerk had departed.

"Quite certain, your grace."

"Then we need to start making plans for the wedding. I want it to be very splendid—almost like a coronation. And my sister has asked that she be attended by our mother on the occasion."

The consternation in the room was tangible but unspoken. All eyes turned instantly on her brother, the Count of Edessa, whose smug expression seemed to confirm all suspicions that he was behind this surprise move.

"I will ask Queen Maria Zoë to return to court as well," Baldwin continued, as if seeking to mollify his obviously outraged Council. "I want my little sister Isabella to grow up at court." It sounded innocent enough, but Tripoli's face revealed just how much he disapproved. He opened his mouth to protest, but then snapped it shut again, unable to think of a way to word his objections that would not sound self-serving.

The King beamed at his Uncle Jocelyn and declared, "We can all be together. A family at last!"

"Maybe it is understandable that the King has come to resent me," the Archbishop of Tyre conceded in a tone of voice that suggested he thought the opposite, "but how, in the name of our ever-loving Savior, could he turn on *you*? You! The only man to befriend him when he was *treated* like a leper! The man who gave him the courage to train the healthy parts of his body, who taught him to ride, who—more than anyone in the entire court—gave him back his smile! How can he just push you aside for that worthless man!"

"My lord," Balian tried to calm the Archbishop, "I don't think the King intended any offense. He has come of age and wants to demonstrate his independence—"

"Independence that consists of doing everything that weasel whispers into his ear!" Tyre protested.

Balian sighed, "I admit he is rather taken with his uncle of Edessa at the moment, but I really don't think he meant to insult either of us. Baldwin has long felt caged. It may have been a gilded cage, but it was a cage all the same, and he felt locked inside. Now he's broken out, and the last people he wants around him are his former jailers. I can understand that."

"Well. Good for you." The Archbishop looked at him with cold eyes and narrow lips. "That is, undoubtedly, very Christian of you," he conceded. "But whether you can 'understand' or not, the consequences are catastrophic! After tutoring that boy for years, I can honestly say I never thought he would prove so—not just ungrateful—but foolish! He's not stupid! He's wise beyond his years! How can he not see what his mother and her brother are doing to him?"

"Perhaps we are to blame for that, too, my lord."

"Just what is that supposed to mean?" Tyre demanded, looking at Balian with an expression of complete incomprehension.

Balian shrugged. "We sheltered him, my lord. We surrounded him with genuine respect and affection. How should he now be able to distinguish between respect and flattery—between sincere affection and the pretense of it? How can we expect him to see through the likes of Edessa, when we have spent the better part of the last five years making sure he didn't have anything to do with such men?"

"Damn it! No one wanted anything to do with him until he became King!"

"Edessa says he wanted to be here—but he was in a Saracen prison. And his mother has filled his ears with tales of suffering *agony* 'not for losing a crown, but for being separated from my sweet babies.'" Balian could not keep the sarcasm out of his voice as he quoted his sister-in-law. The whole time she had been married to his brother, he couldn't remember her once referring to her children by Amalric.

"Ha! So you are more angry than you let on," Tyre remarked, relieved that Balian was not as saintly as he'd sounded a moment earlier.

"If I could find a way to remove Agnes de Courtenay from the face of the earth without committing a mortal sin, I would spirit her away in an instant. I do not dispute your assessment of the Queen Mother or the Count of Edessa, my lord; I simply don't think Baldwin is to blame for falling under their spell. He has been starved of affection, especially after his father died."

"And *you* were the one to give it to him!" Tyre returned to his original argument. "He should love you more than the others, for being there when he needed it most!"

"That's not the point. After being starved of affection for so long, he finds it intoxicating to have it given lavishly by two people who can honestly claim they were *prevented* from showing him their love before. *They* may be hypocrites, but Baldwin is not to blame for believing them."

The Archbishop of Tyre sighed and looked at Balian with an annoyed expression of resignation. "I begin to doubt if the King *deserves* the loyalty you give him, but I stand humbled before you, Sir Balian."

Balian shook his head with a wry smile. "No, my lord, that would be inappropriate. It is true that I love Baldwin, and if he wanted me to remain his closest advisor, I would be honored. But after five years in nearly as much isolation as the King himself, I cannot pretend I do not welcome more freedom. I'm twenty-seven years old, and I have nothing to show for it."

"What are you talking about?" Tyre was astonished by this self-assessment. "You covered yourself with glory in the campaign against Homs. Tripoli calls you the ablest of his bannerets and said he would—" Tyre cut himself off, as he remembered that Tripoli no longer named the royal bannerets; the Count of Edessa had been appointed seneschal of Jerusalem, with the power to make all appointments. He gazed at Balian with understanding now, and asked, "Where will you go? Your brother—"

"I'm not *that* desperate!" Balian cut him off decisively.

The Archbishop was surprised by Balian's vehemence, but accepted his sentiments; he was not the only younger son who was uncomfortable serving an older brother. Moreover, he had a higher opinion of Balian than of the Baron of Ramla, and inwardly applauded Balian's stance. "I know service to a prince of the Church is not considered particularly prestigious or exciting, but it can be lucrative and rewarding nevertheless. I would be happy to offer you service in my household," he proposed next.

Balian smiled at that, a little crooked smile that was somehow sad, even as he answered the Archbishop. "Thank you, your grace. I may take you up on it, but I'm not making any decisions today. It's not as though Baldwin has stopped my pay and thrown me out of his household or banned me from court. I have—and need—time to think."

"Of course. That is very wise of you. And my offer will not evaporate in the summer sun. I would be honored to have you in my service. You would be a banneret, of course."

Balian thanked the Archbishop again and the churchman continued on his way, leaving Balian by the courtyard fountain of the royal palace where he had found him.

Walter, who had discreetly removed himself to the shadows of the surrounding arcade as soon as the Archbishop stopped to talk to his master, re-emerged to stand beside Balian. The sun was already hot although it was still early morning, and it glittered on the gently tumbling water.

"How do you feel about going home to Ramla, Walter?"

"Ramla?" The squire sounded astonished. His father held a knight's fee in the barony of Ramla, but Walter's father wasn't a rich man, and he had recently taken a new wife. Walter's face betrayed how much he dreaded going home, even as he dutifully answered, "I'll go wherever you do, sir." But he couldn't help from adding, "I just wonder where Queen Maria Zoë is. I thought the King had sent for her, too."

Balian laughed bitterly. "Don't bark up that tree, Walter. Except for a book and a dusty flower, we've had nothing from that quarter—ever."

Walter was startled by the bitterness in his master's voice. He had not heard it there before, and it worried him.

Jerusalem, August 1176

Was it really two years since she had left Jerusalem by the dark of night? The memory of wrapping herself in a dusky cloak, putting Isabella to sleep with wine laced with poppy seed, taking the service stairs down to the postern gate, and mounting up outside the city walls was still vivid. And the city itself did not seem to have changed very much: it still gleamed white in the sunlight from miles away, its proud ring of square towers enclosing it like a crown of stone. After entering through St. Stephen's Gate, the maze of narrow, paved streets, pungent with odors pleasant and vile, and the crowded covered markets with their haggling vendors and customers seemed as familiar as the words of the Ave Maria. The cacophony of different languages and the hordes of pilgrims toiling their way along the Via Dolorosa were no different from the day she'd left.

Yet so much *had* changed. The court Maria Zoë had left had been in mourning for a dead King and in shock over the accession of a leper boy. Even prior to that, the court she had known for her seven years as Jerusalem's Queen had been a sober court, dominated by a man renowned for his military competence and his diplomatic successes, but not for his patronage of the arts or his flamboyance. Amalric had put a great deal of emphasis on displays of wealth and power as tools to enhance the standing and dignity of his Crown, but he did not much care for frivolous entertainment or wanton extravagance. Agnes de Courtenay evidently saw things differently, and Agnes de Courtenay and her inconsequential brother were setting the tone at court now.

Maria Zoë came full of prejudice against the pair. She was perfectly aware that she owed her crown to the fact that Agnes had been unacceptable as Queen, and she had been imbued with the notion that she, as a Comnena and a pure virgin bride, was immeasurably superior to her husband's discarded wife. As for the Comte d'Edessa, he had been characterized to her as a shallow man, content to wear an empty title, a man of ready wit but no wisdom.

Two years with the Carmelites had no doubt left their mark as well, Maria Zoë admitted to herself. She had not lived as part of their community, but *had* lived beside it. She had not been governed by their strict rule, but had been surrounded by it. Her cook had ensured she did not suffer the monotony of convent fare, but her isolation had reduced the menu to modest, wholesome foods. The only music she had heard was what they could make themselves: Rahel singing, Maria Zoë playing the cittern, and Abel, the groom, playing his flute. They had taught Isabella her letters with the only book in Latin script that they had with them, a Bible.

It had been liberating to have no duties, no ceremony, no state banquets, no state processions—and no husband to answer to. It had been a relief to wear comfortable clothes that were not weighed down with jewels, nor cut to reveal or conceal the state of her belly. It had been delightful to walk barefoot on the sun-warmed tiles of the courtyard, and refreshing to cool off by splashing water onto her face and neck at the fountain.

Simple life had its pleasures. Maria Zoë knew that now. She knew that she could always go back to it, and it gave her strength to know that she could be content without either the trappings or the substance of wealth and power. She would never be like Agnes de Courtenay, so desperate for power that she was enslaved by her own desires.

But that was not the same thing as being *without* desires. Maria Zoë was twenty-two years old, and two years with the Carmelites had, if anything, sharpened her awareness of her own senses. She came to crave the bright colors disdained by the sisters, and had taken an interest in stitching merely for the sake of working with the bright threads. She learned to love the taste of each spice and herb because her cook could only use them sparingly, not all mixed together. She learned to love the feel of all things soft—fur and silk and sunlight—because so much of the convent environment had been hard. And she had learned that she did not want to spend her life among women.

Men were much more interesting. They were interesting because they could go places women dare not go, and they could do things women were incapable of or prohibited from doing. These experiences gave them more to talk about. Men had traveled to the ends of the earth, seen strange lands and exotic peoples; they had conquered the seas by harnessing the wind, fought wild beasts, and vanquished countless foes. What did women have to talk about that compared to such deeds?

But mostly men were more interesting because they held the reins of power, and so what they did was important. After the initial novelty of her flight and isolation had worn off, Maria Zoë realized that what she missed most was not the luxuries of the court, but simply knowing what was going on in the world. It was not long before she was wondering how Baldwin was doing, whether Salah ad-Din had defeated his rivals, whether her great-uncle had pushed back the Seljuks—and everything else that might be happening out there in the wide world.

After two years with the nuns, Maria Zoë was also prepared to admit to herself, if not out loud, that she was not keen on celibacy, either. It was true she had never found pleasure in her husband's bed—and by the end of her marriage had abhorred it. But she was also acutely aware that Amalric, fat and shapeless as he had been, was not representative of all men. She remembered how much pleasure she had felt whenever she saw Balian d'Ibelin, and with each passing month in seclusion her eagerness for the weekly meeting with her escort increased. Each time the knight in command of her escort was replaced, she went to the meeting hoping the new commander would be Balian. And when it was not, she was disappointed, but she still enjoyed talking with whomever was "condemned" to spend two months providing her "protection" and a means of communicating with the Comte de Tripoli. Most of the knights had been bachelors, and she had liked more than one of them, returning flushed and excited from her weekly meetings. How much more exciting would it be if she were not in retreat from the world, but openly returning to it?

Returning to the world, she found Jerusalem and the court *exciting* after two years with the Carmelites. Maria Zoë found pleasure she could not remember in the polished marble flooring on the gallery and the potted palms and blooming hibiscus in the courtyard; she noted the mosaics and the tapestries and the rugs with appreciation. She sighed deeply as she sank onto the large, soft bed of the chamber put at her disposal. (She was no longer housed in the apartments of the Queen—those were occupied by Agnes de Courtenay.) Although Maria Zoë thought it was a disgrace that so unworthy a woman was housed in the royal apartments, she did not personally aspire to return there. She did not want to sleep in the bed she had shared with Amalric. She was happier here.

She was happy, too, to put on a new gown with long inner sleeves of sheer silk the color of turquoise, and outer sleeves so long that the points brushed the floor when she let her arms hang. She happily retrieved a belt from her chest with strings of pearls edging it. Gems on a belt were an accent and garnish, but they did not weigh her down or restrict her movements. The gown itself was closely fitted at the bust and then flared slowly until it trailed behind her, two layers of silk that floated and billowed when she moved. The lightness of it all made her want to twirl and spin and dance, and Rahel laughed at her, while Isabella clapped her hands, catching her mother's excitement.

And yet, when the moment came to be presented to the King, Maria Zoë discovered she felt more insecure and frightened than she had nine years ago. As a thirteen-year-old bride she had still been her great-uncle's puppet, schooled so incessantly to play her role that she had no room to be afraid. She had been Maria Zoë Comnena, the Greek Princess sent to marry the King of Jerusalem. She knew how to walk, how to stand, how to sit, how to smile, how to look pleased without smiling and look displeased without frowning. She had practiced everything again and again and again....

But what was she now? No longer a virgin bride who enchanted everyone who saw her by her nubile beauty and her staggering wealth and pedigree. Nor the Queen of Jerusalem and consort of the King. She was not even the Queen Mother. That position was taken and fiercely guarded by the woman who now glowered from the throne beside King Baldwin, the throne where once Maria Zoë had sat.

Agnes de Courtenay was no longer beautiful, if she ever had been. Maria Zoë suspected that she had not, because Maria Zoë had noticed that a lack of beauty often drove women to offer sex. A beautiful woman could afford to say no, and men would still desire her; a less attractive woman had to bait her snares. Agnes had certainly baited hers!

If Agnes' hair had ever been naturally blond, that was long ago; now she obviously used some kind of bleach on it. Her lips were painted on, and she'd applied so much kohl to her eyes that they were ghoulish, or so Maria Zoë thought. Her mouth was twisted into the mockery of a smile as she watched Maria Zoë approach. Maria Zoë could not decide what made that smile so bitter. After all, Agnes was sitting on the very throne that the High Court of Jerusalem had denied her thirteen years ago. She ought to be feeling triumphant.

With a start, Maria Zoë realized it was Baldwin's smile that so displeased his mother. Worse, Baldwin stood and came down the two steps from his throne to meet his stepmother on equal footing. He looked so radiant with happiness that it brought tears to Maria Zoë's eyes.

"At last! We can be together openly!" Baldwin greeted Maria Zoë enthusiastically.

Maria Zoë sank down into a deep curtsy as she had been taught, her forehead touching her knee—but as she rose up, she spontaneously grasped the King's gloved hands in both of hers and raised them to her lips. It had not been planned, but in that moment—remembering that Baldwin could no longer use his hands, and therefore could not raise her up or kiss her hand as he otherwise might have done—she had felt the need to make the gesture for him.

The look in his eyes as she returned his hands was worth all the gasps and the muttering of those around them. "Thank you, Tante Marie! I will never forget how you were my friend when everyone else scorned me, nor that you defied my father to meet with me and correspond with me. I will never forget that! You will always have a place at my court—and in my heart."

"My, my!" Agnes tutted in the background, but Baldwin either didn't hear or didn't care. In that moment he had eyes only for Maria Zoë.

"Your grace, the greatest pleasure I can have is seeing you so well and so happy."

"But where is my sister Isabella?" Baldwin answered. "I have longed to set eyes on her ever since she was born!"

Maria Zoë looked up, startled. "I didn't think—a child in such a formal setting—" Children were never presented at court.

"You are right. I am only impatient to welcome Isabella. I want her to feel at home here. You will bring her to my apartments this afternoon? After dinner?"

"We will come before Vespers, your grace."

"Excellent. Now, let me introduce my lady mother, Agnes de Courtenay," the women exchanged venomous smiles, "and my Uncle Jocelyn, whom you also had no chance to meet before." The Comte d'Edessa's smile was considerably more sincere; in fact, it bordered on the importunate. "And here is someone you'll also not know: my lord of Oultrejourdain, formerly Prince of Antioch." Baldwin indicated Reynald de Châtillon, standing with Stephanie de Milly at his side.

Maria Zoë had been told through Tripoli's knights that Reynald de Châtillon had married Plancy's widow, but she had not been prepared to meet this barbarous man at court. Châtillon had invaded Cyprus without warning or cause, burning, plundering, desecrating churches, and raping nuns. There was no one in Christendom that Maria Zoë considered more abhorrent than Reynald de Châtillon. She recoiled instinctively, taking a step backwards and refusing to offer him her hand. Châtillon only laughed. "Can't forgive me Cyprus, eh?"

Baldwin looked embarrassed, and Agnes at once hissed to her brother loud enough for all to hear, "You can see where *her* loyalties are: back in Constantinople."

"The sack of Cyprus, madame," the Patriarch reminded the Queen Mother pointedly, "was condemned by the King of Jerusalem *and* his Holiness the Pope, no less than by the Greek Emperor."

Baldwin tried to divert attention from his mother by continuing with the introductions, saying, "Here's someone you *will* remember: Aimery de Lusignan."

Lusignan bowed deeply to Maria Zoë and came up smiling. "I would not blame you if you don't remember me, madame. I was and remain most insignificant."

"But an honest and honorable man," Maria Zoë hastened to assure him with a gracious smile, to underline her words and contrast her behavior toward Châtillon.

Later, when others had the attention of the King and Maria Zoë was left to fend for herself, she found herself straying about the hall, a little lost. It was strange to be just one person in a crowd. Strange not to have everyone staring at her. And strange, too, how many strangers there seemed to be here. Where had they all come from? And where were the people she knew? Tripoli, the Archbishop of Tyre, and Balian …

"Madame!" The voice caught her somewhat by surprise, as Aimery de Lusignan bowed gallantly at her side. "Might I offer you a little company? You seem most unjustly neglected."

"No, no. I was just looking for—where are the Comte de Tripoli, the Archbishop of Tyre, and your good friend the Baron of Ramla?"

"Ah, the good Comte de Tripoli, naturally, felt it was time to return to his own lands, which he was forced to neglect while acting as Regent. Likewise the Chancellor asked leave to look after ecclesiastical affairs for a change, and Ramla is somewhere around." Aimery scanned the room hastily, but then returned his gaze to Maria

Zoë. "But I hope you do not take it amiss that I do not miss him." Lusignan had moved a fraction closer to her and leaned down slightly to murmur, "I don't want any competition for your attention."

No one had ever flirted with Maria Zoë before. The knights sent to wait on her at the convent had been too junior to risk this kind of open flirting. She realized in retrospect that in trying to stress that her treatment of Oultrejourdain was exceptional and justified, she had unintentionally given Lusignan encouragement as well. But it was not as if she wanted him to go away, exactly. On the contrary, she found his presence stimulating. He was a handsome man.

"You have my attention, sir," she answered him uncertainly, acutely aware of her inexperience. Most women her age, she thought, would know much better how to handle this. "I am most curious about all the changes that have taken place in my absence. Perhaps you could be so kind as to tell me what has happened?"

"It would be my pleasure, madame. Shall we sit?" He indicated a window niche that had just been vacated.

Maria Zoë was alarmed; a window seat, by its nature, tended to crush people together. Window niches were for lovers and conspirators. But how could she say no? It would seem rude. She nodded, and Aimery took her by the elbow and guided her to the window, gallantly helping her up the step. She seated herself carefully, spreading her skirts around her to indicate he should not sit too close. Aimery took the hint without appearing to notice. He smiled and asked, "Where shall I begin?"

"First, how is it that for years everyone was afraid to even lay eyes upon Baldwin, much less be close to him, and now they flutter around him like moths around a flame?"

"An apt analogy, my lady, because they flutter around but treat touching as the kiss of death. If you watch closely, you will see that even Edessa and the Queen Mother do not actually touch Baldwin, as you just did. The fear of contagion is still there, but it is overpowered by their greater need to be near the font of all patronage."

Maria Zoë nodded, her eyes following the crowd surrounding the King as he moved across the room toward two people who had just entered. Tracking her gaze, he exclaimed: "Ah, the Princess Sibylla, whom you will remember—"

"As a silly girl!" Maria Zoë told him bluntly, stunned by the transformation that had taken place. "She's grown up!" Sibylla's features were too like her mother's to be called beautiful, but she had also inherited her mother's voluptuous figure, which was very top-heavy. She dressed to display her advantages, and like her mother was heavily rouged, with outlined eyes and a display of wealth Maria Zoë remembered all too well.

"Um," Aimery agreed, his eyes on her, "ripe for her wedding, it seems."

"Indeed," Maria Zoë agreed, thinking that sixteen was indeed a riper age than thirteen, as she had been. "And the man with her?"

"Reginald de Sidon's youngest son. She seems rather taken with him at the moment, but last week it was the Caesarea boy, and the week before that, Tiberius' son." Aimery concluded guardedly, "She seems intent on enjoying her last months of freedom before the arrival of her husband this fall." He changed the subject. "Do you see that bishop hovering near Edessa?"

"Ye-es," Maria Zoë confirmed, as she searched and finally found a remarkably young-looking man in ecclesiastical robes. He was as handsome as an archangel, with beautiful chestnut curls and perfect, regular features in a smooth-cheeked face.

"He calls himself Heraclius. He is a native of these parts, illegitimate I believe; certainly obscure, albeit well educated."

"And already a bishop!" Maria Zoë remarked, stunned by his youth.

"Exactly," Aimery agreed, his lips tight and his eyes hard.

"He must have some exceptional qualities," Maria Zoë insisted, although her remark sounded naive even to her own ears.

"Indeed, the willingness to service the Queen Mother; but if he looks nervous, it is because the Queen Mother appears to be tiring of him."

"But—" Maria Zoë was shocked. Of course, clerics were men. Of course, there were priests and monks who broke their vows. But an anointed bishop? And one who looked as innocent as an archangel?

"The Queen Mother favors youth and beauty—even if it is found under a cassock, madame," Lusignan noted acidly.

"Surely you are not jealous of such a man!" Maria Zoë challenged Lusignan.

"No, of course not," Lusignan answered hastily, then tipped his head to one side and added, "but I cannot deny I am jealous of his rapid rise to wealth and influence. It would seem I have been employing the wrong tactics."

"But I heard you have been married, my lord. Is that not true?" Maria Zoë was sure one of Tripoli's messengers had mentioned something about Lusignan "getting an heiress at last."

"Married, yes, but my bride is only eleven—and even I'm not so jaded as to bed the girl. I've promised to wait until she's fourteen. And in any case, I'll only inherit Ramla when her father dies—and if he has no sons in the meantime."

"She's the Lord of Ramla's daughter?" Maria Zoë asked, surprised and excited. This at last gave her the opportunity to ask the question she had been burning to ask all evening. "And Sir Balian? The Baron's younger brother. What has become of him? I would have expected him to rise high in King Baldwin's court after his years of loyal service."

"Yes, one *would* have expected that, but he does not enjoy the favor of Edessa or the Queen Mother. She was his sister-in-law, you know, and apparently her marriage to his brother was quite acrimonious. At any rate, she doesn't like Balian, and both she and Edessa are jealous of the affection the King still bears him."

"Has he left court?"

"I'm not sure. There were rumors he had taken service with the Archbishop of Tyre, but I don't believe he's left Jerusalem yet. Why?"

Maria Zoë felt guilty, because her interest was far from innocent, but she had years of experience disguising her feelings and found an indifferent tone of voice in which to continue. "I just remember how well he looked after Baldwin when no one else would go near him. He seemed a good man."

"Yes," Aimery agreed, his eyes watching her closely. "But as his brother pointed out, he bet on the wrong horse. Five years nursing a leper, and he hasn't been given so much as a cast-off cup in reward. Such is the gratitude of princes."

Maria Zoë looked from the bitter smile on Lusignan's face to the man he was staring at across the room, King Baldwin. The King was surrounded by his family: his mother, his uncle, and his sister, with his mother's lover hanging in the background and anxiously trying to become part of the circle.

"There appears to be only one way into that circle, my lord," Maria Zoë found herself observing.

"Yes, I noticed," Aimery answered, looking down at her with a wistful smile. "And it would have been so much more pleasurable seducing *you*." Was there the slightest hint of a question at the end? Maria Zoë wasn't sure, but she was sure what her answer was.

"No, my lord, don't waste your time on me. I have nothing to give you." She held out her empty hands. She had, of course, her widow's portion—notably the castle, town and lordship of Nablus, which ensured she had sufficient income to support a suitable lifestyle—but the terms of the entailment prohibited her portion from being passed on; it reverted to the Crown at her death. This meant she had nothing in her *gift*—no titles to bestow upon a husband, much less a lover.

"A pity," Aimery whispered wistfully, and their eyes met.

Maria Zoë felt her pulse racing. Why not? some part of her brain said. Why not let this handsome young man teach her what love was? The romances were full of illicit lovers, and it was not as if she would have been betraying anyone. Not even Aimery's eleven-year-old bride could object to her husband taking his pleasure elsewhere while waiting for her to grow up.

Aimery seemed to be contemplating the same thing. He moved his head just a shade closer, watching for her response. Maria Zoë raised her face and held her breath. If he kissed her …

He drew back, raising her hand to his lips instead. "Farewell, ma dame," he murmured and then withdrew, leaving Maria Zoë alone and confused in the window niche.

Maria Zoë pulled the embroidered cap down over Isabella's reddish-brown curls and tied it under the chin, so that only a few wisps escaped around her soft, clear face. "There you go, Princess!" she told her daughter with a smile. Isabella chortled, then broke away to run to her mother's dresser, grab the hand mirror, and look at herself. Maria Zoë could not remember being so interested in her own reflection at that age, and she hoped it was not indicative of excessive vanity. Isabella turned her head from side to side, inspecting herself critically, and then put the mirror down and smiled at her mother. "Shoes?" she asked. "Can I wear my new shoes?"

"Yes, sweetheart. You are going to see the King, and you must look your very best."

Isabella at once sat down and stuck her feet out at her mother, but it was Rahel who came with the pair of embroidered slippers that matched the cap on Isabella's head, while Maria Zoë fetched the embroidered surcoat. She and Rahel had done all the stitching themselves after learning that Maria Zoë had been summoned to court. A critical eye would have noticed that the professional needlewomen made more regular stitches and produced more symmetrical patterns, but Isabella would grow out of these things long before she was old enough to care.

"Now, sweetheart," Maria Zoë began as she helped Isabella put her arms into the sleeves. "You have to understand that the King—"

"My brother!" Isabella remembered.

"Yes, your brother the King is very, very sick. He doesn't *look* sick when he's dressed up as he will be, but underneath his beautiful silk gloves his hands are dead."

"Dead?" Isabella looked shocked.

"Yes. Dead and slowly rotting away. He cannot use his fingers—cannot move or feel them anymore. And that means he cannot reach out and take your hands in his or otherwise stroke and pat you like adults usually do. Nor should you be impertinent and reach out to him," Maria Zoë warned.

Isabella's expression suggested she was not at all tempted to try to touch something "dead." Maria Zoë reached out and stroked her daughter's shoulder. "You mustn't be afraid, either. Your brother Baldwin is a very good man, and he is your guardian."

This did not appear to mollify Isabella, and she abruptly buried her face in her mother's skirts and asked, "Do we have to go? Do we have to go see a man with dead hands?"

"Yes, we do," her mother told her firmly. "Straighten up and behave yourself." Her tone of voice was one that broached no contradiction or disobedience. Isabella sighed deeply, stood upright, and took her mother's hand.

Outside the King's apartments, when the men-at-arms announced them, Maria Zoë sank down to Isabella's height, kissed her on the cheek, and murmured in her ear, "Smile, sweetheart."

Isabella turned big brown eyes on her that said silently, "You can command me to behave, but not to smile," and solemnly the little girl walked beside her mother into the royal solar. Her big eyes searched the beautiful room with its glittering mosaic floor, glazed tile facings, and carved and painted furnishings, and stopped when she found a handsome youth with bright blond hair smiling at her. "So you're Isabella!" he said warmly.

Isabella went stock still. "Are you the King?" she asked.

"No, I'm your brother."

Isabella looked up at her mother reproachfully for not telling her she had two brothers.

"Isabella, look what I have here," the youth coaxed her.

Isabella looked back at the beautiful youth. He had raised his arm and gestured with it, the hand limp at the end, toward his lap. Isabella noticed that he had something furry in it—and then it moved, and Isabella gasped with excitement. "Kittens!"

Before her mother could stop her, she rushed forward, halting just short of Baldwin, to look up and ask, "Oh, please, may I pet them?"

"You can do more than that," Baldwin assured her. "You can choose which one you want to keep."

"Oh, Mama! May I? May I have a kitten?" Isabella pleaded, looking anxiously over her shoulder to her mother.

Maria Zoë looked at Baldwin, and he smiled at her. "I have discovered bribery is a most effective means of winning friends—and I so want Isabella and me to be friends," he pleaded with her.

How could she fault him for that? "Yes, darling," she answered Isabella, "you may have a kitten."

Isabella needed no more encouragement. She started petting first one kitten and then the others in turn. "Do they have names?" she asked the King, without taking her eyes off the kittens.

"Not yet," he answered. "That is for you to give them."

"This one is Blondy, and this one is Tiger, and this one is…" Isabella weighed her head from side to side, trying to decide on an appropriate name. "This one is Gluttony, because he wears a white bib so he can eat all the time," Isabella declared solemnly, and frowned when the adults burst out laughing.

"I really don't see why you have to see the King alone," the Comte d'Edessa told Balian. "He'll tell me everything you say to him anyway."

Balian had seldom been so conscious of his utter helplessness. All he wanted to do was say goodbye to the youth he had come to love so well, but he had no desire to show his emotions in front of this man, much less his venomous sister-in-law, the Queen Mother. Yet he could hardly insist on a private interview. He had no right to one, and he couldn't think of a fabricated excuse fast enough, either.

Balian briefly considered going without saying farewell, but he remembered how upset Baldwin had been when Queen Maria Zoë did the same thing two years ago.

But that had been a different Baldwin. Maybe the new Baldwin wouldn't care if he just went away. Maybe it would be the best thing for both of them….

"You can sit there until summoned." Edessa pointed to one of the chests along the wall, which doubled as a bench. It was well worn along the side by the many heels that had swung and rubbed against it in hours of waiting on royalty.

Balian looked at the chest and shook his head. "I'd rather wait standing."

"You may wait a long time," Edessa told him with a shrug. "My sister's in there with her lover, and she's vowed not to leave until the King has made him Marshal of Jerusalem."

Balian started. For the last week the Queen Mother had been flaunting her latest bedmate as if he were a trophy. To his credit, Aimery de Lusignan had the decency to look embarrassed by the flagrant way she favored him, and even tried to maintain a modicum of modesty. But Agnes de Courtenay was not a woman to be trifled with. When Lusignan would not come and stand behind her at the high table, she swept down off the dais and demonstratively took a seat beside him at one of the lower tables. When they sat together, Agnes could not keep her hands off him, and when he came to her apartments, she made sure that the whole household knew about it by calling for wine and snacks and even music while he was with her. It was as if she could only convince herself that she had captured this virile young lover by seeing the shocked expressions on other people's faces. When Balian remembered the indifference she had shown his brother—her husband—it made him boil inwardly and increased the antipathy he felt for her, but he could hardly blame Aimery de Lusignan for exploiting the situation.

Heraclius, meanwhile, had been sent back to Caesarea to "do whatever it is bishops do." It was rumored that Agnes had advised him: "Be a priest for a change." And when rebuked by the Patriarch for her behavior, she had demanded to know why she should make do with a pretty boy when she could have a real man?

The banging of the double doors to the audience chamber interrupted Balian's thoughts, and he was confronted by a beaming Aimery de Lusignan. Lusignan drew up at the sight of Balian, and his smile broadened. "Ah! Sir Balian! You can be the first to hear the good news! I have just been appointed Marshal of Jerusalem!"

"Congratulations, my lord," Balian replied, bowing his head politely. He didn't dislike Aimery de Lusignan as a man; he simply resented the way he had come by this prestigious and important position.

"No need to look so disapproving," Aimery told him, laughing. He was in such a good mood that he flung his arm over Balian's shoulder and added, "I am not the kind of man to forget my wife's relatives, Balian."

"Balian?" the voice called from inside the audience chamber, and it made everyone turn around. "Balian?" the King called again, his voice clearly nearer. "Where are you?"

"Here, your grace."

"Why did no one tell me you were here?" Baldwin reached the doorway and looked pointedly at his uncle. Edessa bowed his head silently without explaining himself.

"Balian, come in, come in!" The King gestured to the audience room behind him, and Balian followed him, with Edessa and Lusignan in his wake. In the middle of the room, the King turned around and faced Balian. "I have heard rumors, Balian," Baldwin told him earnestly. "Rumors that you have quit my service and given your sword to the Archbishop of Tyre."

"Neither rumor is true, your grace," Balian answered steadily. "I came today to request that you release me from your service. Until you have done so, I cannot give my sword to another lord."

"Why do you want to leave my service?" Baldwin asked bluntly.

"Because I am no longer needed here, your grace." Balian looked pointedly at Edessa and Lusignan. "You have other advisers and servants now."

Baldwin looked past Balian to his uncle and his newly appointed marshal, and then back at Balian. "You think I have rewarded you ill for your loyalty, don't you?"

"No, your grace. I simply think it is time I looked after my own interests—now that you and the Kingdom are in such good hands that my services are superfluous."

"And you think your interests are safer with the Chancellor than with me?"

"The Archbishop of Tyre has promised me a position of responsibility in his household, your grace."

"And what would that be, Balian? Chasing after wayward clerks in the town brothels or guarding the Archbishop's wine cellars from the covetous rabble? What can he offer you that would equal being Constable of Ascalon?"

The Queen Mother gasped, and Balian turned to look at his sister-in-law with narrowed eyes, but Aimery de Lusignan quickly crossed over to her and took her in his arms. He whispered something in her ear, and she dissolved into giggles. Balian turned and looked at Edessa, but the Count had a mask in place. Balian turned back to the King and asked, disbelieving, "Constable of Ascalon?"

"It is near Ibelin," the King remarked, as if by way of explanation.

It was also one of the most exposed, vulnerable, and strategically important cities in the Kingdom of Jerusalem. It had been in Egyptian hands until 1153, and as long as the Egyptians held it, they had used it as a base from which to raid deep into the Kingdom of

Jerusalem. Indeed, the castle at Ibelin had been built as a bulwark against such raids. Balian's father had taken part in several attempts to seize the city, and his brother Hugh had been one of the commanders at the seven-month siege that finally brought the city under Christian control.

The loss of Ascalon had been a serious defeat to the Fatimid Caliphate, and there could be no question that Salah ad-Din would want to take it back—if nothing else, to shore up his weak position with his Egyptian subjects. To be Constable of Ascalon was no luxury and no empty reward. It was a huge responsibility, and a mark of trust. Nor could Balian forget that his father's first step toward a barony of his own had been his appointment as Constable of Jaffa. "I am overwhelmed, your grace," Balian murmured sincerely.

The King smiled. "I thought you might be—but you have been hard to find of late," he replied, in gentle reproach to Balian for avoiding the court in recent weeks.

Balian almost remarked that all Baldwin had needed do was send for him, but he bit his tongue; the recipient of such an honor should not bemoan the manner or timing of the gift. Meanwhile the King had turned to Lusignan. "And what say you, Marshal?"

"Good choice, your grace. I couldn't have thought of a better man for the post—or a better post for the man."

Balian looked sharply at Aimery, but he was still grinning, his arm around the Queen Mother's shoulders, and he seemed completely sincere. His goodwill, furthermore, had clearly silenced any objections from Agnes de Courtenay, who Balian was sure would have begrudged him anything if left to her own counsel. Instead, because of Aimery's support, she was smiling benevolently as if it had all been her idea. Balian looked again at Edessa, who shrugged. "I hear the palace of the Constable is in a poor state of repair."

"Who is *now* the Constable of Ascalon?" Balian asked, frowning, thinking that he was in a bad position to be making powerful enemies, regardless of the King's favor. Such favor was notoriously fickle—as he had experienced over the last several months.

"You!" the King insisted, smiling.

"But who has been up to now?"

"Godfrey de Hebron was the man appointed by my father, but he died of a stomach ailment about six months ago, and Tripoli didn't get around to appointing a replacement."

Balian was comforted by this answer, because it indicated no one was being pushed aside for his sake, and there was a precedent of appointing the younger brothers of Crown vassals to the post. Baldwin appeared to have thought this through, Balian concluded, and he looked again at Aimery de Lusignan. It struck him that Aimery was not such a poor choice for Marshal of Jerusalem, either. He had been in the Kingdom five years, he had married into an established family, he had proved his courage during the attack on Homs, and he certainly had a good head on his shoulders. Balian started to suspect that that appointment, too, was more calculated than it first appeared—and not owing entirely to the Queen Mother's favor.

King Baldwin was choosing his officers from among men he thought were loyal to *him*—not to Tripoli, or Antioch, or anyone else in the Kingdom. Edessa because he was his uncle and had no other base of power, Lusignan because he was a man equally dependent on royal favor, and Balian. The young King, Balian concluded, knew exactly what he was doing.

"Your grace." Balian dropped to one knee and offered his folded hands. "If you see fit to bestow this honor upon me, I will serve you—as I always have—with all my strength and all my mind and all my heart."

Baldwin smiled at him. "I know." He enclosed Balian's hands in his limp, gloved fingers, and then bent and kissed Balian on the forehead. "With the help of God, Balian d'Ibelin, hold Ascalon for me—and for Christ."

Chapter 7

Ascalon, August 1176

Balian and Walter approached Ascalon from the east, riding directly from Jerusalem. Balian had considered a detour to Ramla to tell his brother of his appointment, but his impatience to take command in Ascalon was too great. Barry would hear the news soon enough; it was more important to secure his unexpected reward.

At this time of year, when the heat and dust was at its worst, Balian chose not to exhaust his horses and took two days for the trip, including midday breaks. He and Walter spent the one night en route at Bethgibelin, where they were refreshed and feted by the lord, and had a good discussion with the local Hospitaller commander about the growing threat from Egypt and Salah ad-Din.

As they left the mountains behind, the weather became scorching, as the fields lay fallow after the harvest and the dust blew across them in tiny cyclones. By late afternoon, however, the white walls of Ascalon came into view, beyond a plain green with citrus and pomegranate orchards against the blue backdrop of the glistening Mediterranean. It looked like paradise.

As they drew nearer, a sea breeze reached them, drying the sweat on their horses and fluttering their surcoats and the canvas covering the luggage on the packhorse Walter was leading. The breeze offered them welcome relief from the heat.

The walls of Ascalon were built upon earth mounds that enclosed the rubble from the walls of earlier centuries. As they drew nearer, Balian could see where the Byzantine walls ended short of the top and new, brilliant white masonry, not yet weathered with time, increased their height by as much as ten feet in places. The walls had also been reinforced by massive barbicans before the gates.

They soon found themselves caught in the stream of traffic heading for the gate. In contrast to the traffic into Jerusalem, however, there were hardly any pilgrims. Ascalon had no important pilgrimage sites, and most pilgrims from the west landed farther north, at Jaffa or Acre. Instead of pilgrims, the road was jammed with Egyptian camel caravans, trains of Armenian pack mules, and local farmers with ox-carts. The pace was torturously slow, apparently bottlenecking at the gate.

Unwilling to slow down to the pace of the oxen, mules, and camels, Balian turned off the road and trotted along beside it, ducking low branches and jumping over irrigation ditches with his destrier on the lead behind him, and Walter with the packhorse in his wake. As he cut back onto the road at the gate, it became clear why traffic was backing up: the guards here were actually checking cargoes and questioning each merchant.

Balian drew up beside the guards, who all wore tunics with the five crosses of Jerusalem sewn on their left breast. His palfrey was anxious to find feed and water and flung his head in irritation, splattering the guards with froth, while the destrier was so fractious he tried to bolt. Balian jerked on the lead twice to make him pay attention. The man-at-arms looked up, annoyed. With inner relish, Balian drew his commission from inside his gambeson and handed it to the man. The royal soldier looked at the folded parchment blankly, turned it over, saw the royal seal, and his eyes widened. "Sir?" he asked with a flickering glance at Balian's heels. "You come from the King?"

"I do. Balian d'Ibelin. Constable of Ascalon." Balian liked the sound of that.

"My lord!" the man responded, then turned and started shouting. A moment later a handful of other men, similarly dressed, spilled out of the barbican, and a red-faced man with a bushy beard and eyebrows came over to stand at Balian's stirrup. The guard handed his sergeant the parchment, but the latter was as illiterate as his subordinate and contented himself with the same question: "You are from the King?"

"Yes. I have been appointed Constable of Ascalon."

"My lord!" the sergeant echoed his subordinate. "We had no warning, have made no preparations. Ah, how many are you?" He looked back along the column of caravans and farm wagons, as if expecting to see an escort of dozens of knights and scores of mounted men-at-arms.

"Myself and my squire," Balian answered.

"I'll escort you to the Constable's residence," he concluded, and turned to lead them through the barbican and gate.

The city of Ascalon lay in the basin formed by the semicircle of man-made walls that enclosed it to landward. The sea wall was lower than the land wall; this meant that much of the city had a view to the Mediterranean, and there was almost always a pleasant breeze.

Balian had not remembered Ascalon like this. He had been about eight years old when Hugh took him on a trip to the city. In his memory, the city had been dusty and dry. Thinking back, he realized there had been a lot of construction going on: wagons straining under loads of stone had creaked and waddled through the potholes, tearing up the surface even more, and wooden scaffolding had been slapped up everywhere, while huge wooden cranes blocked the alleys and his brother warned him sharply to keep away from them.

Now the city appeared much more prosperous than Balian remembered. When the Christians captured Ascalon, there had been no massacre as at Jerusalem a half-century earlier; the lives of all residents and the Muslim garrison had been spared. But the terms of surrender also stated that no Muslim inhabitants were to be allowed to remain in the city; instead, they were given forty days to pack up their valuables and depart with everything they could carry. As a result the city had been underpopulated, and parts of it eerily abandoned, when Balian had visited as a child.

Judging by what he saw, Balian concluded that many people had settled here since his boyhood visit, and they had fixed up the buildings. Fresh paint covered the plaster exteriors; bright awnings, new shutters, and balconies marked the houses. The skyline, however, was still dominated by domes and minarets; the domes mostly marked Greek churches that had been here before the Muslims came, while the minarets remained silent reminders to the centuries of Muslim domination.

Shortly inside the Jerusalem Gate was the large, cross-shaped Greek Church of St. Mary, set in a pleasant garden with tall cypress trees, and not far away was a paved square surrounded by an arcade used as a marketplace. Another large, imposing building with Roman columns incorporated into heavy masonry was identified by their guide as the Bishop's palace, and he added, "But some say it was Herod's palace first." Just beyond this structure, Balian's guide turned left and then right again, stopping before a wide two-story structure with a battery of grilled windows on either side of a tall, peaked door reinforced with iron. In front of the door stood a man-at-arms wearing the arms of Jerusalem.

Balian's guide duly announced him to the sentry. The man looked up at Balian, both amazed and alarmed, but then stepped through the doorway and, with considerable clatter and creaking, opened half of the large door to admit Balian and Walter, still mounted, into a cool passageway giving access to a cobbled courtyard. The courtyard was completely surrounded by an arcade on the ground and first floors; a covered octagonal well stood in the center. Weeds were pushing up between the cracks of the cobbles and the well grew grass that swayed slowly in the water, but the four horses plunged their heads down into it and sucked the water up their throats gratefully, stamping on the worn, yellow paving stones as if to ask why it had taken their riders so long to get them here.

A black-haired boy with olive skin came running out from under the arcade, announcing loudly, "I'll take them! I'll take them!"

"No, you won't!" a deeper voice commanded from the shadows, and a moment later a big man with a rough-hewn face, red-brown from the sun, caught the boy in the crook of his arm and held him back in an iron grip. His blue eyes quickly appraised Balian and Walter and their horses, and even before the guards could tell him Balian's identity, he had guessed it. "My lord? You are the new Constable of Ascalon?"

"I am," Balian agreed, swinging down from the saddle. The father at once ordered his boy to "fetch Mathewos and Dawit. Then run for Father Laurence."

"But I can—"

"No! Do as you're told!" The man straightened and bowed his head to Balian. "My name is Roger Shoreham, my lord, and I am the Senior Sergeant of the garrison here in Ascalon, charged with holding the city until a successor to Sir Godfrey would be named."

"A pleasure, Master Shoreham." Balian held out his hand. "The name sounds English," he noted.

"It is, my lord. I came out on pilgrimage, took part in the siege of Ascalon, then married a local girl and decided to settle here."

It was a common enough story, and Balian simply nodded. "I will need your assistance in becoming familiar with Ascalon's defenses and garrison, Master Shoreham—but at the moment I would appreciate a bath, a change of clothes, a meal, and a clean bed. Is there a household steward?"

"I've sent my boy for him, my lord. He is a cleric and chose to live with the Augustines while awaiting a new constable. That way the household could be dispersed and expenses spared. But your chambers are ready, and I will fetch you a hot meal from a nearby tavern. A bath might have to wait for tomorrow, or there is a good public bath not far away," he added tentatively.

A tall, slender black man, and a youth so similar that Balian assumed it was his son, emerged from under the arcade. The man bowed to Balian, while the youth immediately went to untie the lead of Balian's destrier. Balian watched automatically to see that his precious warhorse was properly and competently handled, but the black youth clearly knew what he was doing, and exuded so much calm that the normally fussy stallion was as docile as the palfrey the youth took in his other hand. The older man, meanwhile, took Walter's horse and the packhorse.

Sergeant Shoreham led Balian under the arcade to a broad, shallow stairway, and at the top of the stairs proceeded along the upper gallery to the central room at the far side of the court from the street. Here he opened the door and stood back so that Balian could enter first. Balian found himself in a large rectangular chamber with a marble floor in a black-and-white checkerboard pattern, tiled walls, and a vaulted ceiling. In front of him were three eight-foot-tall arches closed by shutters, which Shoreham hastened to open. Beyond was a rooftop terrace with a magnificent view across a second courtyard to the Mediterranean.

Balian was drawn to the terrace like a moth to light. He stepped out onto an imperfect mosaic floor and crossed the terrace. Although immediately below him was a working courtyard that housed stables, kitchen, and warehouses, his eyes automatically sought the sea, turquoise near the shore and deep blue in the depths. The waves were crested with white, and the sound of them meeting the shore was clearly audible, although the beach was a couple hundred yards away.

Shoreham was beside him again, anxiously pointing to a door leading off from the main room. "The bedroom is there on the left, my lord."

Somewhat reluctantly Balian left the terrace to cross the room, his spurs making a soft chinking sound on the marble, to open the indicated door. The adjoining room was half the size of the central room and dominated by a raised four-poster bed. It had bedding already and rugs on the floor, all a little dusty. But it was his.

"Is there a hall?" Balian asked Shoreham.

"Not really, my lord. This was a caravansary. It has two courtyards and thirty-two rooms, in addition to kitchens, stables, pantries, and storerooms around the back courtyard, but no hall, I'm afraid." He seemed worried that Balian was displeased, so Balian let him in on the secret and grinned at him.

"I think it will do. Don't you, Walter?" he asked his squire, who was looking as amazed as he felt.

"Yes, sir—I mean, my lord."

By the next morning the whole city knew they had a new Constable, and a crowd began to gather in the street in front of the "palace" to get an audience or at least a glimpse of him. Meanwhile the household, which had been dispersed during the vacancy, returned to take up their duties. From every corner of the caravansary came the sound of sweeping, sloshing, and talking as women with brooms, mops, and pails of water set to cleaning out the unused rooms. From the kitchen courtyard came the sound of someone chopping wood, someone else hauling bucket after bucket from the well on a squeaky pulley, and the cackling of disturbed fowl.

The steward, Father Laurence, had presented himself the previous evening, but only briefly because Balian had been tired. He was a vigorous, healthy man in his early forties who also had charge of the accounts, and he was anxious for Balian to look these over. Very much to the priest's disapproval, Balian turned him over to Walter, opting for a tour of the city with Roger instead.

This morning Roger's face and hands were red from scrubbing. His beard and hair had been trimmed and he was wearing a fresh tunic as well. Balian smiled at him. "You look like you're going to either a wedding or a funeral."

Roger cleared his throat. "Ah, no, sir, it's just my wife, sir. She thinks—ah, she wanted me to make a good impression on you, my lord."

"And so you have, Roger. It started with the guards searching everyone entering the city yesterday. I noticed the number of men on the walls as well. And so far I have not seen a single man-at-arms who looked drunk or disorderly."

"Oh, you'll see plenty of those if you go out the Water Gate to the harbor, my lord; that's where the taverns and brothels are. But I—um—if I catch 'em drunk on duty, I give 'em a kick in the backside they don't forget so easy. Still, we've been too long without a Constable, my lord. With this firebrand Salah ad-Din preaching *jihad*, we're on pins and needles awaiting the next attack."

Balian nodded at that. It was astonishing that Salah ad-Din had bypassed Ascalon on his way to Damascus two years ago. Had he succeeded in taking the city, it would have bolstered his position and might have made it easier for him to lay claim to Damascus. On the other hand, a defeat might have shattered his chances in Damascus, and he had evidently preferred to go for the jugular by taking Damascus directly. This left Christian Ascalon a thorn in his side, however, constantly threatening his lines of communication between Damascus and his power base in Egypt. Balian mused that the Kingdom of Jerusalem was lucky Salah ad-Din had faced so many internal revolts and plots against him that he had no time or troops to focus on his *jihad.*

"Come, Roger. I want to walk all the way around the city while you tell me everything I need to know."

"Yes, my lord. Let's slip out the back, then, so we won't get caught by the crowd outside."

Balian agreed and followed Roger through the kitchen courtyard, past the stables, and out into the street by a service entry. Roger led him through a series of narrow alleys to a stone stairway that led up the back of the wall to the wall walk, and here Roger paused to point out the major landmarks of the city spread out at their feet.

"As you can see, the walls are essentially a semicircle on the landward side and straight here along the shore. There are just four gates to the city. The Sea Gate that gives access to the harbor and shore is there." He pointed to a tall, modern gatehouse with the typical peaked arches of the region, and Balian nodded—although he couldn't see much of the harbor itself, since it was hidden behind the wall.

"If you follow the wall past the harbor you see the Gaza Gate, leading south to Gaza and Egypt." Roger pointed to the massive square gate that loomed over the wall to the south. It was crenelated and windowless, sporting only narrow slits at strategic places.

Roger continued. "Then, over there, on the far side of the city, is the Jerusalem Gate by which you entered—and finally, way over there is the Jaffa Gate, leading north along the coast." The gates were relatively easy to find, because the barbicans reared up above the walls themselves, and Balian's eye turned inward to the city itself. From here Balian could see how green the city was, with countless inner courtyards filled with palm trees, cypress, and lemons.

"The Muslim population of the town was expelled when we took the city," Roger explained.

"I know. My brother Hugh was there," Balian told the Sergeant.

"Ah, good." Roger seemed to digest this fact and then remarked,

"Then you know that there was a large Coptic Christian population that remained when their Muslim masters left. They lived mostly in the northern quarters, but after we had control of the city, many Copts moved here from Egypt. They took over many of the areas vacated by the Muslims." He pointed as he spoke.

"How much of the population is Coptic today?" Balian wanted to know.

Roger weighed his head from side to side and then made a guess. "Fifty per cent, my lord. There are also remnants of a Greek community that survived the centuries of Arab domination—maybe 15 per cent of the population now. They have three churches. Then there's the Ethiopian community with a church, and the Jewish quarter is up there." He pointed toward the Jaffa Gate. "It is quite small. About two hundred souls, I'm told.

"Near the Gaza Gate there is one mosque that is allowed to operate for visitors, and there are also four caravansaries run by Arabs who have been allowed to resettle here. The largest Latin church is St. Paul's Cathedral—that large, domed building there. It was built on Greek foundations, but was almost completely rebuilt by Baldwin III because the roof had caved in and the Arabs had used it as a quarry. St. Mary's by the Sea is also a Latin church, and the Venetians have their own church, of course, St. Mark." He pointed. "St. Mary's gets lots of donations from seafarers who make it safely to Ascalon after a difficult voyage, and from pilgrims blown off course heading for Jaffa."

Balian nodded, taking it all in. Roger waited but then prompted, "Shall we continue?"

"Yes," Balian agreed.

Roger led first to the Sea Gate, where they had a splendid view of the harbor, enclosed by a man-made sea wall.

"The port is not particularly busy," Roger admitted. "Mostly coastal traffic. Some wood and iron from Cyprus. Almost no pilgrims, unless they get blown off course, as I mentioned. There's good fish, however, especially octopus and squid, in the dockside taverns, and a daily fish market where your cook gets the best of the daily catch." Balian nodded, satisfied, and Roger continued with the tour.

On the Gaza Gate Roger explained, "This is where the wealth of the city is made. Through this gate pass some of the most valuable caravans in the world. They bring gold all the way from the source of the Nile, along with incense, ivory, rock salt, papyrus, scents, and spices. All the cargoes from the Nile and many from the Red Sea funnel up through here on their way to Damascus, Aleppo, Antioch, Constantinople, and beyond. The traffic going the other way includes sugar, grain, olives, horses, silks, jade, other gemstones, and silver—a lot of silver."

Balian nodded. This was what made Ascalon so important to whoever controlled it—and was also what made it vulnerable.

"Tell me about the garrison. For a start, how large is it?"

"We are just 114 men at the moment, my lord, mostly men-at-arms and eight sergeants. But really, we are many more." Roger paused again and turned toward the city. "I wasn't the only crusader who chose to stay here after the siege ended, my lord. See there, that smithy: the smith's an old comrade-in-arms, an Englishman like myself. And there, that fine house with the bright red shutters—that belongs to Joachim, a German crusader, now owner of the best carpentry shop in Ascalon, with five or six journeymen and twice that many apprentices. He's made half the furnishings in your palace, but he's just as skilled at building siege engines. I can't name all the crusaders still here, my lord, but in an emergency we can reinforce the garrison with another hundred men at least—good, experienced men. Add their sons and sons-in-law, and we can mount a defense three hundred strong."

"How many knights?"

"Ah," Roger licked his lips. "Ah, is the young man who rode in with you yesterday a knight?"

"Not yet," Balian admitted.

"Then I think you are the only knight in Ascalon, my lord."

Balian laughed, unsure whether the King was unaware of this, or if the joke was on him. "My predecessor—how many knights did he command?"

"None, that I know of, my lord," Roger confessed, adding, "Ascalon controls almost no land, my lord, no knight's fiefs."

"And the militant orders? The Templars and Hospitallers are not here?"

"The Templar castle of Gaza is less than twenty miles south of here, my lord. It has a very strong garrison: I think over a hundred knights and three times that number of sergeants and Turcopoles. The Hospitallers maintain that large hospice over there," he continued, pointing to a large square building with a tall tower. "There are at least five priests and a score of lay brothers, but no fighting men."

Balian didn't like the sound of that, but he nodded and kept his opinion to himself. They continued with the tour.

It was midmorning before they returned to the governor's residence by the same route they had left it. The crowd in front was greater now, and Balian was glad to avoid it by entering at the back. Here the smells from the kitchen were mouth-watering, and Balian decided to stop and meet his kitchen staff.

There were a dozen men and boys engaged in a variety of activities: dicing carrots, slicing onions, gutting chickens, stirring steaming pots, feeding wood to the fireplace, or pumping the bellows to fan the embers. One fat man covered in flour was pounding dough with massive fists, sweat dripping from his brow, and another man was pounding meat with a wooden hammer. Gradually, as the boys and men caught sight of Roger followed by a knight in a bright red-and-yellow surcoat, they stopped whatever they were doing to gape at the knight.

Roger stopped in front of a dark, wiry man who was frowning as he measured out wine into a saucepan. The rolling silence caught his attention at last and he glanced over his shoulder. His eyes widened, and—flustered—he spilled wine as he tried to set the jug down and dry his hands on his apron before going down on one knee before Balian.

"This is Demetrius, my lord," Roger introduced the cook. "He's Syrian Christian."

"My lord," Demetrius concurred humbly.

"And the best cook for a hundred miles—if not more," Roger added, winning a grateful smile from Demetrius, who remained on his knee.

Balian gestured him to his feet. "I was always told to beware a thin cook," Balian jested, but the look of fear on the man's face made him realize it was too soon for jesting. He corrected his tone and announced, "Dinner smells delicious. I am looking forward to it." The cook looked relieved at that, and again his eyes darted to Roger.

"Demetrius learned to cook in the household of the Caliph of Damascus," Roger explained.

"Only as a boy, my lord," Demetrius hastened to assure Balian, afraid this would be held against him.

"Better than not at all," Balian returned. "I understand the Caliph maintains some of the largest and best-appointed kitchens in the world."

Demetrius nodded vigorously, adding, "I was given as a gift to an imam here when I was still a youth. I was here when the city fell to King Baldwin III, and your generous predecessor allowed me to prove my worth, my lord."

"And I will do the same," Balian assured him, then nodded and retreated. As soon as they were out in the courtyard again, Balian asked Roger, "Why is he so afraid?"

Roger shrugged. "Lord Godfrey died suddenly of a stomach ailment. The King suspected poison—or Tripoli did—and ordered Demetrius arrested. He was imprisoned for several weeks before Lord Godfrey's physician convinced Tripoli your predecessor died of the flux, not poison."

"He said he was given as a gift. He was a slave?"

Roger nodded. "Yes, from childhood." He paused and added, "Demetrius is also a eunuch, my lord."

Balian winced inwardly. It was one thing to know about eunuchs in the abstract; it was something else to meet one face to face.

Roger continued, "I don't know why, but gelding horses makes them calmer, and gelding men makes them timid."

Balian looked sidelong at the hardened sergeant and raised his eyebrows slightly; the remark suggested that Roger had more experience with eunuchs than he had had, but he did not pursue the topic. Instead he allowed himself to be distracted by the sight of his horses being groomed in front of the stables opposite the kitchens.

While a little boy was busy removing stable stains from the packhorse with a currycomb, the black-skinned youth of the evening before was vigorously brushing the hooves of Balian's destrier with a stiff, wet brush that removed every clump of mud and manure, leaving the hooves glistening. Behind him, the older man was combing out his palfrey's tail with long, gentle fingers, separating the hairs just a few at a time. Balian paused to watch the two Ethiopians work until, feeling his eyes on them, they stopped and bowed to him shyly.

Balian had rarely seen grooms take so much time or show so much gentleness toward high-strung horses. It was more common for grooms to try to show who was master by smacking and shoving and yanking on their leads. He went closer. "I did not catch your names yesterday."

The older man nodded and bowed again. "I am Mathewos, my lord, and this is my son Dawit."

"Are you from Ascalon?"

"We are Ethiopians, my lord, although my son was born here in Ascalon eight years after the city was liberated."

"Where did you learn about horses?"

"I learned from my father, and he from his father before him. My grandfather served the Emperors of Ethiopia, but my father came on pilgrimage. He settled in Ascalon because of the horse market here, but in the siege, all his horses were killed and eaten by the garrison. That broke his heart and he died of grief—but I was young, and I found work with the new lord of Ascalon."

Balian nodded and went to stand beside his destrier. The youth backed away deferentially, his hands still wet and dirty from the work. "This," Balian clapped the stallion on his thick neck, "is Gladiator. And that," he pointed to his chestnut palfrey, "is Jupiter." The youth smiled shyly at him.

"You are sixteen, your father says," Balian addressed the youth.

The youth nodded vigorously.

"And you are your father's oldest son?"

He nodded again.

"So you want to follow in his footsteps?"

The youth nodded.

Balian turned to Gladiator and combed his fingers through the horse's bushy forelock while he considered carefully. Since learning he was the only knight in Ascalon, he had decided that Walter had to be knighted sooner rather than later. He was nineteen already, and while he was not particularly adept with either lance or sword, no amount of further training was going to make him significantly better. Knighting him would increase his stature and enable Balian to employ him more flexibly. But that meant he needed one or, preferably, two youths to look after his horses, his equipment, and himself. Since there were no other knights or noblemen in Ascalon, he could not look among their sons for squires.

He turned back to the Ethiopians. "I need a youth to serve as my squire, Mathewos. Would you be willing to lend me Dawit for a few years? Two or three at the most?"

Mathewos looked astonished; then he bowed very low and came up smiling. "I would be honored, my lord!"

"And you?" Balian turned to look at the Ethiopian youth, but his grin was so broad he didn't need to verbalize his answer.

"Good," Balian nodded, satisfied. "I will have Walter teach you your duties over the next several weeks." That settled, Balian started to turn away and continue into the main building, but his eyes fell on the little boy, who was standing on tiptoe and straining to reach, imperfectly, the back of the packhorse with his currycomb. Balian smiled at him and announced, "That is Job, and he loves carrots."

The little boy turned around and considered Balian curiously. "What horse doesn't?" he wanted to know.

"Mind your manners!" his father bellowed, shocked by such impudence, but Balian laughed and asked Roger Shoreham, "What's your son's name?"

"That jackanapes is Gabriel," Roger answered, with a frown at the boy but pride in his voice. "And he's as mad about horses as a healthy journeyman is for women of easy virtue. I expect I'll have to 'prentice him to a stablemaster." He shook his head as if in disgust, but Balian heard the pride that seeped through.

"You have other sons?"

"Aye. Four altogether."

"Tell me about them," Balian urged.

"The oldest was 'prenticed to Joachim Zimmermann, the carpenter I was telling you about. He's a master carpenter now, and married to one of Joachim's daughters. He hopes to take over the carpentry when the time comes, but he has rivals in his brothers-in-law, so I'm not so sure. The second boy took the cloth and was ordained last year." Shoreham was clearly proud of this, adding in obvious amazement, "He can read and write!"

Balian nodded approvingly. "That leaves one more?"

"Yes, Daniel." Roger didn't elaborate.

"How old is Daniel?"

"Fifteen now, my lord."

"Apprenticed?"

"Of course, but he's a bit of a troublemaker, Daniel is. A good boy!" Roger hastened to add. "Sharp as they come and full of spirit and daring, but he's still a bit wild. He'd make a good soldier, my lord, but my wife won't hear of it."

Balian nodded, storing the information away, and they continued into the main part of the palace. Under the arcade Roger stopped. "Ah, my lord, if you no longer need my services, I—with your permission—would like to attend to my duties. I mean, my *other* duties. I mean—"

"Of course," Balian agreed. "Report back to me at Vespers."

"Yes, my lord." Roger bowed and withdrew toward the stables again, while Balian continued under the arcade to the corner room used by Father Laurence as an office and archive. As he entered, Walter glanced up with a look of relief. "I was beginning to worry something had happened, s— my lord."

"Ascalon is not small," Balian answered, sitting down on the bench beside Walter and looking at the priest, who occupied the head of the table.

Father Laurence had been piqued that Balian had not taken time for him the night before, and even more annoyed to be given second place to Roger this morning. His intelligent face was easy to read, and it was disapproving as he remarked almost sourly, "Nor is Ascalon poor, my lord."

"Tell me."

"There are a variety of dues and fees owed to you, but the main sources of revenue are the rents that every household in the city owes you and the fees every guild that holds a market must pay. Of course, you also collect the taxes on goods imported into the Kingdom through the port and, more important, the Gaza Gate."

"The taxes belong to the King," Balian noted, watching the priest carefully. There were many men who were happy to cheat a distant king in favor of helping their immediate lord make more money. They expected rewards for their corruption from the man who paid their annuity. But King Baldwin IV was not a distant crown to Balian, and he did not intend to cheat him.

"Indeed, but you are entitled to one-twelfth of the revenues generated—to cover expenses."

"Of course. And just how high are my expenses?"

"That depends on you, my lord. Do you have a lady?"

"Not yet."

"Then I presume, like your predecessor, you will not do so much entertaining. Lord Godfrey was, however, very generous to the Church."

"No doubt," Balian replied with a mirthless smile. He considered himself a good son of the Church, but he did not like churchmen putting pressure on him to give away income he had not yet collected, let alone enjoyed. "How many households are there in Ascalon?"

"Roughly four thousand, my lord. The total population is somewhere between twenty-one and twenty-two thousand, not counting transients, of course. At any one time there are usually about twenty-five thousand people in the city. During the important markets at Easter and Ramadan, there can be as many as thirty thousand."

"And the Constable's average annual income?"

"Close to twenty-five thousand dinar."

Walter caught his breath, suitably impressed, but Balian kept his own expression impassive. The Constable also paid the garrison and was responsible for their equipment and the upkeep of the walls—huge expenses. "And the average expenses of my predecessor?"

"A little over twenty-two thousand dinar."

"Without entertaining or building?"

"Correct, my lord—but there are certainly a variety of means to increase revenues, if you find these inadequate."

"For example?"

"Rents are very low because there were so many vacant houses initially that to encourage settlement, rents were set low. Now that the population is roughly what it was before the Egyptians were driven out, you could afford to raise the rents."

Balian did not like the idea; it was the kind of thing that made common people feel they had been betrayed. People had been known to riot for less cause. Besides, he remembered what Roger said about many of the residents being either former crusaders who would help defend the city, or refugees from Egypt. Both kinds of residents made good defenders, and he would not want to see them leave to be replaced with the type who could pay more but would also be quicker to make terms with the enemy to save their property.

"I think the guilds and passing merchants a better milk-cow, Father, but for the moment the discussion is purely theoretical. The walls are in excellent condition, and I see no need for major building projects or lavish entertaining. We will work with what we have—for now."

"As you wish, my lord." Father Laurence bowed his head graciously, but Balian sensed continued disapproval.

"How large is my household?" Balian asked next.

"Twenty-eight." That sounded reasonable.

"What else do I need to know?"

"Since this is a Crown domain, as Constable you are the King's representative and hold court in his name. There has been no court here since your predecessor's death—which explains the large crowd out in front." Father Laurence gestured toward the window facing the street; although narrow and glazed with thick, milky glass, it still let in a dull rumble of voices.

Balian nodded. "I will hold court after dinner. I will need clerks to record the names of the people seeking audience, and someone to take notes of the proceedings as well. Are there household clerks available for these tasks?"

"Yes, there are two clerks."

Balian nodded and got to his feet. "I think that is enough for now. I will—no, there is one thing more: I want a hall of some kind. You can arrange that?"

"Yes, my lord, of course." The two men exchanged a look that suggested that for the first time, Father Laurence approved of something Balian had decided. That was a start, Balian concluded.

As he walked out of the room, he glanced up at the clear sky over his courtyard, and still could not believe it. He was master of twenty-two thousand souls with an income of three thousand dinar! It might not be hereditary, and he might hold it only at the whim and in the name of the King, but it was a success that even Barry could not belittle. And it was only a beginning, he vowed.

Chapter 8

Ascalon, September 1176

THE PACE OF THE MUSIC (IF not the quality) was increasing as the musicians and their audience became more and more inebriated. The bride's garland of flowers was slipping farther and farther off her head as she spun on the arm of first her bridegroom and then all his guild brothers. Despite the canvas stretched across the cobbled courtyard of the smithy, the late afternoon sun was so hot that she was the color of boiled crab under her bright, blond curls, free of covering veils for the last time in her life. Most of all, her laughter was contagious.

Chuckling as he left the floor to make way for younger dancers, George Smith thumped himself down on a bench beside his old friend and companion-in-arms, Sergeant Roger Shoreham. Smith, too, was beet red from the heat and the exertion of dancing, and he used the back of his arm to wipe away the sweat dripping down his brow. Then he grabbed a tankard of ale from the tray of a passing servant and declared, "I'll be damned if she ain't the prettiest bride I've ever seen. Good housekeeper, too, or so my boy says."

"Oh, I think you can count on that," Roger agreed, clunking his large pottery tankard with that of the father of the groom. "All Joachim's girls have been well trained by their mother to keep a proper house." Roger could speak with authority since his eldest boy, Edwin, was married to the second Zimmermann girl, the bride's older sister.

"I guess we're kin now," Smith declared, nodding smugly, before gulping down half the ale in his tankard to quench his thirst.

"Indeed," Roger agreed, clunking tankards again. "Which I didn't expect, seeing as we both have only boys."

"Speaking of which, what's this I hear about Daniel running away from his apprenticeship?"

Roger frowned. It was a subject he would have preferred not to discuss on a happy occasion such as this, but it was the scandal of the town, and he could hardly expect Smith to ignore it. "The boy's a disgrace! He was late to work, impudent, and then when Fulk thrashed him—as he well deserved—he ran away. Fulk says he won't have him back, not for anything," Roger admitted glumly, shaking his head.

Smith nodded sympathetically, noting, "Daniel always had a wild streak in him. He got into all kinds of scrapes as a boy."

Roger growled. "Well, at fifteen he's not a boy anymore! And who'll take him on after this? No master worth his salt will hire an apprentice with Daniel's reputation. His mother is in despair and thinks he should be given to a monastery to learn discipline."

Smith grunted, expressing eloquently—if nonverbally—Roger's own doubts. He felt *almost* obligated to offer Daniel an apprenticeship in his smithy, but was reluctant to do so. Even if he'd known the boy all his life, he didn't need an apprentice who wasn't punctual, much less talked back. He decided to change the subject before Roger thought to ask him outright for the favor, since it would have been hard to deny him when they'd just become kin. "What's your opinion of the new Constable, now that he's been here three weeks?"

"Sir Balian?" Roger asked, surprised but relieved to change the subject from his troublesome son. "I like him. He's not the kind of lord to lord it over you, if you know what I mean. He always talks to me man to man. But he's clever, too. Father Laurence didn't want to like him. I don't know why, just snobby as he is, I guess. But then this Coptic shopkeeper brought a complaint against an Arab merchant and Father Laurence wanted an interpreter, only to have Sir Balian put him in his place! It seems Sir Balian speaks fluent Arabic and proceeded to prove it. And did you hear he's talked the Hospitallers into stationing ten knights in Ascalon?"

"How did he manage that?" Smith asked in amazement, his hands resting on his knees, the tankard still in his right fist.

"He invited the Hospitaller Marshal to Ascalon and then wined him and dined him, and talked so long and hard about the importance of Ascalon and the fragile state of its defenses that the Marshal finally broke down and promised to send ten knights." Roger laughed at the memory of the harassed Hospitaller. "Ten!" he'd repeated several times, "and not one more! Ten knights and ten sergeants—to be maintained at *your* expense, not that of the Hospital." Roger chuckled to himself at his lord's triumph, then lifted his tankard and took a long gulp before turning to Smith and asking, "What do you hear from customers?"

"Oh, they like him, for the most part. Some of the older men grumble that he's too young, wet behind the ears, and never taken part in a siege—on either side—but most people like him. I'm out of ale. Shall I fetch us each a tankard?"

Roger drained his tankard and handed the empty to Smith with a nod. He didn't notice his second son, Michael, slipping out the back with a full tankard in each hand.

Michael hastened down the narrow alley between the courtyards and ducked into his father's house by the back gate. He had to be careful not to trip over his cassock as he stepped over the wooden doorstep into the kitchen garden with both hands full. Beside the outhouse a wooden door gave access to the cellar, and here he set down one of the tankards to release the wooden bolt that kept the door closed from the outside. The door squeaked as he opened it, and he had to kick it when it tried to fall shut again after he'd picked up the second tankard. He then descended the wooden steps carefully, his eyes adjusting slowly to the darkness.

At the foot of the stairs he stopped and looked around bewildered for a moment, until he finally spotted his younger brother Daniel curled up in the far corner on a pile of hides. He looked like he was asleep and Michael approached cautiously, unsure about disturbing him. The streaks of blood on his brother's back, however, made him gasp. He went down on his heels, setting the tankards on the floor, and reached to shake his brother's shoulder.

Daniel woke with a start, reared up as if frightened, and then recognized his brother. "What are you doing here?" he demanded sullenly, from a face misshapen with an ugly bruise that had discolored his entire left cheek and all but closed his left eye.

"I brought you some ale," Michael answered, gesturing toward the tankards, "but first tell me what happened to your face."

"What do you think? Dad hit me!" Daniel spat at him.

Michael raised his eyebrows. He had never known his father's fists. Roger was not a brutal man, certainly not with his children, and Michael had been a good boy.

"You don't have to say it!" Daniel retorted, deflecting the expected criticism. "I deserved it! I'm a worthless piece of shit! A disgrace to the family! A—"

"God loves you, Daniel, and so does our father," Michael replied, cutting off his brother's tirade of self-loathing. "Now let me look at your back."

Daniel didn't seem to know how to react. His jaw was set as defiantly as his aching teeth would allow, but something stung his eyes. He hadn't expected any sympathy, not even from Michael.

Taking advantage of his confusion, Michael took hold of Daniel's shirttails and shoved the cloth upwards. Although he tried to be careful, the cotton of the shirt stuck in the coagulated blood, and Daniel cried out in pain. The bleeding started afresh in several places, and Michael drew in his breath. "Did Dad do this, too?" he asked, unable to believe it.

"Of course not. That was Fulk. For being thirteen minutes late!" Daniel's resentment started to swell up again. "Thirteen goddamned minutes!" He cursed to provoke his clerical brother, but Michael was too wise to take the bait, so Daniel had no choice but to continue raging. "Thirteen goddamned minutes on one day of three hundred sixty-five, and do you know what time it was? Four o'clock in the morning—or four-thirteen. For a whole year I'd been there on time, and just once I'm late! And it wasn't even my fault, but no one bothered to ask why I was late. No, just beat the shit out of him! Kick him around until I just had to run away! I had to! Do you know what? Fulk wanted to humiliate me from the day I started, because he's always resented that Dad got promoted over him when they were taking part in the siege. All that blood on my back was meant to be Dad's!"

Michael had only been half listening to his brother, thinking it best to let Daniel get the rage out of his system, but this remark made him lift his head and look more sharply at him.

"Dad's so naive!" Daniel continued. "He thinks everyone who fought with him a quarter-century ago is his friend. Well, they're not."

"But most of them are," Michael insisted, thinking it was time to counter his brother's bitterness.

"How do you know?" Daniel challenged him.

Michael didn't bother answering; he just settled down on the floor and handed Daniel one of the tankards, taking the other for himself. "We need to get that back cleaned up before it starts to fester." He paused and then admitted, "Mom wants to send you to a monastery—preferably one of the ones in Sinai."

Daniel gaped in horror. "They wouldn't—Surely, Dad—Michael! I'd go mad! I'd end up killing someone—myself, if no one else! You've got to stop them from sending me there! I'll run away!"

"Relax. Dad knows it's not right for you—"

"Sure!" Daniel scoffed. "Like he knew I wasn't cut out to be a baker, either! But he can't stand up to Mom when she gets something in her head."

"That isn't what I was going to say. It's just..."

"What?" Daniel demanded, through a mustache of ale foam.

"It's that he doesn't know what else to do with you. It won't be easy to find a master willing to take on an apprentice with your reputation."

"Tell me something I don't know!" Daniel snapped back, and tried to chug down the ale all at once. Instead, he only succeeded in getting some of it down his windpipe. He doubled up, coughing, and when Michael automatically clapped him on his back, Daniel howled in outraged pain.

"Sorry!" Michael pleaded, wincing at his own thoughtlessness. Then as Daniel's coughing subsided and he laid his head on his knees in despair, Michael laid a hand gently on his shoulder and promised, "I'm going to fetch you some of the food now, and later I'll talk to Mom. I'll convince her you don't belong in the Church. She'll accept it from me as she won't from you or Dad."

Daniel nodded without lifting his head. He kept his face buried in his knees—because he wanted to cry and was fighting it with all his strength.

Michael took the empty tankards in one hand, hitched up his cassock in the other, and started back up the stairs, kicking the door open at the top. He thought about leaving the door unbolted but changed his mind, for fear one of the servants fetching something for the wedding feast might notice and raise the alarm. He returned the way he'd come, left the empty tankards on a sideboard where servants collected them for rinsing and reuse, and then pushed his way through the crowd into the forge itself, where two sheep were slowly roasting over the fire. He waited his turn in line for a plate piled high with slices of fatty lamb, and then started back down the alley.

The next instant he collided with his youngest brother Gabriel so hard he was almost knocked over. The plate tipped up and the lamb fell into the mud of the alley. "What's got into you?" Michael demanded angrily, furious about the wasted meat and a little afraid of being caught feeding Daniel, who was supposed to be on bread and water in punishment.

"Dad! We've got to get Dad!" Gabriel answered breathlessly. Gabriel was too young to like dancing, flirting, or even drinking, and he had wandered off from the wedding feast hours ago.

"Why? He's enjoying the day off—"

"But it's Jerusalem!"

"What do you mean, 'It's Jerusalem'?" Michael asked back, scowling.

"The party of riders coming towards us! They're flying the banners of Jerusalem! It must be the King!" Gabriel could hardly breathe from excitement.

Michael was torn between disbelief and the realization that if his brother were right, his father indeed needed to be warned. He glanced in the direction from which his brother had come, hoping to see a more reliable messenger. There was none, he decided. "Take this empty plate back and go tell Dad. Tell him I've gone ahead to the Jerusalem Gate." Not watching to see his orders carried out, Michael grabbed a liberal fistful of cassock and held it up so he could run.

By the time he reached the barbican, he had to pause to catch his breath more than once on the stairs up. At the top, however, he was rewarded by the sight of the guards clustered on the ramparts, gesturing and talking excitedly. Michael did not interrupt them. He just went to the edge and followed their outstretched fingers. The forerider, carrying an upright lance with the banner of Jerusalem fluttering from it, was now only four or five hundred yards from the gate. It was easy to see he was a young man wearing a tunic with the arms of Jerusalem over a chain-mail hauberk. He rode a chestnut stallion with a white blaze and four white socks.

The main party, however, was still some distance behind. Michael thought it looked too small to be the entourage of a king. He counted only eight horses, and the two lead horses appeared to be ridden by women. Women in Outremer rode astride. The terrain was too difficult and the risk of ambush too great to give women the luxury of riding sidesaddle like the Greeks, but it was still obvious that the two leading riders had long skirts and veils that blew out behind them. Would the women of the King's household ride in front of him? Michael asked himself, and heard his answer on the lips of the soldiers. "Take word to Lord Balian that the *Queen* of Jerusalem is approaching the city," one soldier ordered, and at once one of the men clattered down the spiral stairs.

Satisfied that this justified interrupting his father's day off, but relieved it wasn't the burden of a full royal visit, Michael slipped back down the stairs. The Queen was unlikely to want an inspection of the garrison, he reasoned; she was more likely just stopping here on her way somewhere else. Her arrival would distract his father for a while, however, and Michael decided it was a good opportunity to take care of his brother's lacerated back.

No sooner was Michael gone than Roger Shoreham came pounding up the stairs. He strode to the cluster of men still looking out over the ramparts. "What's this about the King?" he demanded, and they answered in a chorus: "The Queen, not the King!"

"What the devil..." Roger asked as he gazed out at the unmistakable sight of a woman, wearing a neat silver circle over her fluttering white veils, cantering on a sweating but far from tired black mare toward the gates. The gates were already open to admit her, and the Queen swept in under him, still at a fast canter.

The news reached Balian when he returned from the lists, where he had been tilting with the quintain because he had no better partner. He was drenched in sweat and the dust of the tiltyard clung to him. He stank of horse and leather, and his hair stood stiff with salt from sweating hard in his helmet.

"*Which* Queen of Jerusalem?" he demanded of the messenger.

"Are there two?" the guard answered, astonished.

"Yes, fool! Agnes de Courtenay and Maria Zoë Comnena." But even as he spoke he knew that Agnes de Courtenay might have moved into the Queen's apartments and might sit beside her son, but she was not entitled to carry the arms of Jerusalem. It had to be Queen Maria Zoë. "God's nails!" Balian cursed, then asked, "Where's Father Laurence? Where's Sir Walter? Tell them to receive the Queen, and make up chambers for her and the rest of her party. They need to warn Demetrius, too. He must prepare a feast. Have them tell the Queen I will receive her as soon as I return."

"But you're here!" the guard protested.

"No, I'm not. I'm at the baths."

Balian had already decided it would be much faster to get himself cleaned up at one of the public baths than to have the servants draw and heat water for his private bath. So he turned Gladiator over to the waiting Dawit and exited by the back.

To save time, Balian did not head for the large and luxurious baths, dating back to the Romans, that he usually used, but instead ducked into the small Turkish bath just around the corner from the palace. It was not just smaller and darker—it catered to a less exalted clientele than the Roman baths. The arrival of the Constable without his squire caused an immediate commotion.

"Just get me cleaned up!" Balian insisted to the flustered attendants.

At last a dark, mustachioed man of indecipherable origins started giving orders and shooing other customers away, while no less than three boys were ordered to help Balian out of his clothes.

Balian tossed his surcoat on the nearest bench, then unlaced the leather ties at the throat of his hauberk and bent over to let gravity help him out of the heavy chain mail as he crossed his arms behind his back and pulled from the shoulders. The hauberk fell to the tiled floor with a rush and a loud metallic hissing. Balian kicked it to one side. "Go to the palace for clean things!" Balian ordered one of the bath boys as he stripped out of his sweat-soaked gambeson, peeling it and his shirt off his body together. His braies were equally sweat-soaked, and he undid the cord to let them drop to his feet, stepping out of them and then tossing them to the boy, who had already picked up his shirt and gambeson. "Get a clean surcoat as well!" he instructed, pointing to the one he'd tossed over a bench.

The boy grabbed it, then looked at him wide-eyed over the disorderly heap of clothes. "But who will give me your clean things?"

"Ask in the stables for Dawit," Balian instructed him, and the boy departed.

Naked, Balian turned to enter the steam baths and was startled to find one of his household clerks, the second son of Roger Shoreham, coming toward him with an unfamiliar youth. Michael caught his breath and drew back as if caught in the act of something shameful—which made Balian look more closely at the youth, rumors of clerical sodomy shooting through his mind.

"This is my brother Daniel," Michael explained before Balian's suspicions could take hold. "I brought him here to clean him up."

Balian noted the boy's bloated, discolored face and drew the right conclusion. "You're the one who just got thrown out of his apprenticeship by his master, aren't you?" Balian answered, showing he knew more about his staff than Michael expected. Before Michael or Daniel could answer, Balian grabbed Daniel and ordered, "Come with me and make yourself useful. I'm in a hurry."

Maria Zoë was not expecting an elaborate reception. Her decision to come to Ascalon had been made in private, and not even her escort had been told her destination until they were on the road. She had forbidden them to send a harbinger as well. "We are not so large a party that we will inconvenience the Constable," she told her escort commander.

"Ascalon is an outpost, my lady," he had countered. "There is no royal palace there and no suitable accommodation for you."

"I lived with the Carmelite nuns quite contentedly for years. I'm sure the Constable of Ascalon will be able to find something at least as comfortable as a Carmelite convent." Her tone of voice brooked no further contradiction, and the commander had not pressed the point.

Now, as they rode through the city of Ascalon, Maria Zoë felt justified in her assessment. It was a pleasant city with many trees and fountains—clearly remnants of its Greek heritage, she concluded. Furthermore, the bishop's palace looked like it could offer more than comfortable accommodation—but, of course, that was not where she wanted to stay. . . .

Her guide stopped before the entrance to a sandstone caravansary with batteries of windows on two stories and canvas shades suggesting a rooftop terrace as well. The lower-story windows were grated and glazed with small, dark roundels of glass set in plaster, but the upper-story windows were gracious and open. The gate creaked open to admit the Queen's party, and Maria Zoë found herself in a pleasant courtyard with a two-story arcade enclosing it. The fountain gurgled and glittered in the sunlight, and large palm plants stood in massive pots at each of the four corners. She lifted her eyes toward the second story, half hoping to see Sir Balian lean over the railing to greet her, but there was no sign of him.

The next moment a priest emerged out of the shadows of the arcade with his robes fluttering about him. "I'll see to her grace," he called out in an irritated tone to a groom approaching from the other direction, and offered Queen Maria a hand dismounting.

Maria Zoë jumped down lightly and stood to face the priest, who was stammering: "Your grace, we were not warned of your impending visit. It will take us some time to prepare suitable accommodation. My Lord Constable is absent, but I will take you up to his private apartments while we see to fixing up some of the empty rooms. Refreshments will be brought to you there. Will you be staying with us long?"

"I'm not sure yet," Maria Zoë answered vaguely, and bit her tongue to stop from asking where her host was. It had not occurred to her that Sir Balian might be absent. How foolish not to check first—but then people would have known why she was here. She retained her façade of dignity and indifference as she followed Father Laurence up to the second story with Rahel in her wake.

She was led to a spacious room with a marble floor and tiled walls. It had three arches open to a terrace spilling bright sunshine in, and it was modestly furnished with two tall carved cabinets, several carved chests, and two chairs beside a small round table in the space between two of the windows. It was a pleasant room—and utterly devoid of personality. It could have been anyone's room. Not one thing hinted at the identity of the Constable, not even a hanging with his coat of arms.

Disappointed, Maria Zoë went to one of the chairs between the arches and slowly sank down onto it. From habit she folded her hands in her lap, and the image she presented to the outside world was one of a patient queen, awaiting the refreshments promised. Behind that façade, however, her emotions were teetering on the brink of panic. She had ridden all this way, mystifying those around her, for a confrontation with what? A ghost from her past? A figment of her imagination?

Just who was Sir Balian d'Ibelin?

In this functional room, shorn of all her dreams and wishful thinking, she realized that she did not know him at all. He had never said one word about himself—about *his* feelings, *his* plans, *his* dreams. He had always spoken of Baldwin. Baldwin had been their shared interest. Nothing more.

There was a knock on the door and she caught her breath, turning toward it expectantly. But the young knight who entered was not Sir Balian. He looked vaguely familiar, but Maria Zoë could not place him. He came toward her, smiling, and bowed deeply from two feet away before announcing, "My lord was out in the lists, but he will return shortly. Meanwhile, is there anything I can do to make you more comfortable, your grace? Sherbet is being prepared even as we speak, but perhaps you would like something more substantial?"

"At the moment, no, aside from learning your name, sir."

"Oh, I'm Sir Walter. You'll remember me as Sir Balian's squire."

"Ah, yes, of course." Now that he said it, she did recognize him, although he had matured significantly; his lean body had filled out and his face looked like it could now grow a beard. "So you've been knighted," she noted politely. Two years was a long time for a youth on the brink of manhood.

Walter grinned at her. "Sir Balian didn't have any choice. He felt the city was inadequately defended, so he doubled the number of knights in Ascalon by knighting me."

Maria Zoë looked suitably shocked, and Walter laughed. "And even so, he'd rather tilt with the quintain than with me. I fall off the horse from just *thinking* about the lance hitting me. Ah! Here's the sherbet." Walter went to open the door wider for a servant carrying a silver tray, laden with two glazed pottery bowls packed with sherbet, a bowl of cashews, and spoons. The servant set the tray down on the table beside Maria Zoë and offloaded it. Rahel motioned to Walter to sit with her lady, but he shook his head, adding graciously to the waiting woman, "Refresh yourself, my lady. You've had a hot ride, while I've been comfortable in the shade. But I will keep you company, if you like?" The question was directed to the Queen.

"By all means," the latter assured him as Rahel sat down, and Walter grabbed a stool to sit astride at Maria Zoë's feet.

Maria Zoë's head was filled with questions that Walter could undoubtedly answer. For example, was Sir Balian looking for a wife? And if so, where? And if not, why not? But she dared not ask.

"Did you come directly from Jerusalem, your grace?" Walter asked in the vacuum left by her own silence.

"Yes, we did."

"Then could you be so kind as to tell us the latest news? Is it true Salah ad-Din has left Damascus?"

"Yes, he has returned to Egypt. Our spies suggest there was a revolt, but Salah ad-Din is said to have ruthlessly suppressed it with terrible bloodshed." Maria Zoë had been with the King when this word was brought to him by a Syrian Christian who traded in ivory between Cairo and Damascus. "Our source says that he sealed off the quarter of the city in which the rebels lived and sent his men in to slaughter the women and children house by house until none survived." Maria Zoë shook her head in aversion at the story, adding, "And now he is preaching *jihad* and threatening us with the same fate. It is said Salah ad-Din has vowed to drive the Kingdom of Jerusalem into the sea."

"Then this is an odd time to visit Ascalon," Sir Balian remarked softly, coming in the open door.

Maria Zoë started at the sound of his voice and looked up with racing pulse. He was exactly as she remembered him—no, he was much more handsome. Two years ago he had been a knight in her husband's service: young, strong, tanned, and earnest, as befitted the only knight who dared serve a leper. Now he commanded a city, and his new position gave him stature. But the eyes were still the same molten bronze. No, they weren't. They were much bolder. He looked her straight in the eye as he approached, and it took her breath away.

Sir Balian's skin was flushed from the steam bath and glowed with oils, and he smelled of balsam. His hair was still wet and looked almost black, but the drying strands looked as soft and silky as Maria Zoë's own when her hair was freshly cleaned, only straight rather than curly. Sir Balian's chin was slightly darkened with the promise of a beard to come, as he had not taken the time to shave. Maria Zoë heard her heart thundering in her ears—and registered that this must be what the troubadours meant when they sang of a knight making his lady's blood burn.

Sir Balian had crossed the room, and he bowed deeply over her hand. "Welcome to Ascalon, your grace. I regret that without warning, we could not provide you with a more suitable welcome. I hope Sir Walter has been behaving himself and has made you feel at home?"

"Sir Walter is a paragon of chivalry, my lord," Maria Zoë answered smoothly, too conscious of the turmoil of her emotions to realize how cool and aloof she sounded.

Walter had jumped to his feet when Sir Balian arrived, and Rahel had stood, too. She again gestured to the seat she had occupied.

Sir Balian shook his head to Rahel, gesturing for her to resume her seat. He looked over his shoulder and found a smaller chair, which he grabbed and placed before the table. "To what do we owe the honor of your presence in Ascalon, your grace?"

Sir Balian could not have been more formal, and Walter wanted to kick him. That's no way to court a lady, he wanted to shout at his lord, not *any* lady—much less one of the most beautiful creatures on God's earth, with a queen's dower portion on top!

Walter was right, of course. Maria Zoë felt as if she had been burned by ice. Sir Balian had always been meticulously polite to her, of course, but before, it had been a façade. Hadn't it? He had been polite to disguise how much he really felt for her, hadn't he? She had been so sure of it at the time. She had *believed* in his affection for the two years she had been with the Carmelites. It was the conviction that he would be pleased to see her that had brought her here—two days' ride from Jerusalem to the most vulnerable city in the Kingdom.

"The horse market," she answered with immaculate composure. "It is rumored to be the finest not only in the Kingdom, but anywhere between Cairo and Antioch. I am in need of a new mount, and I thought I would come here. Of course, I was also interested in seeing this city, the only one in my late husband's Kingdom that I never had the chance to visit before."

"Mathewos, my head groom, will be able to help you with finding a horse, your grace. He comes from a distinguished line of horse breeders. His grandfather served the Emperors of Ethiopia." Then, indicating the empty bowls, he announced, "You will need a proper meal. I'll go see how the preparations—"

Walter forestalled him. "I'll do that, my lord! If you'll excuse me, my lady?" He bowed to Maria Zoë with a grin.

She had a smile for him and a nod, and then he was gone, leaving Sir Balian no choice but to sit down again.

"You will not be staying long, then," Sir Balian surmised. "The horse market is the day after tomorrow."

"No, probably not," Maria Zoë agreed, thinking that she would freeze to death in this frigid atmosphere more surely than in the snows on Mount Olympus.

Father Laurence appeared in the door, smiling. "Your grace, your accommodations have been prepared for you now. I would be happy to take you there, if you wish. Will you also be requiring a bath?"

"Yes," Maria Zoë agreed, standing. "Yes, I could use a bath."

Sir Balian was also on his feet. "You may ask whatever you wish of my household, madame. We will do all we can to make your short stay with us as pleasant as possible."

"Thank you, Sir Balian. I am much indebted to you." She smiled and held out her hand to him.

He bowed over it.

Maria Zoë swept out of the room with Rahel at her heels, and Father Laurence hastened after her to show her the way.

It took them some time to bring the cork-lined tub up to the corner room and heat water for it. The household servants carried up bucket after bucket of water, while Maria Zoë sat patiently in the window niche, watching the sun sink down the sky. It turned a vivid orange before it was lost from sight behind a bank of clouds. The tall palm in the garden of the house opposite loomed up, sharply silhouetted against the coppery sky.

"Your bath is ready, madame," Rahel said softly, gesturing elegantly to the tub.

Maria Zoë left the window and moved slowly toward the bath, removing the circlet of silver from her brow and unwinding her veils as she came. She felt utterly exhausted and drained of all energy and emotion. The disappointment was over. Sir Balian d'Ibelin was not the man she had imagined him to be. He was indifferent to her. Maybe even hostile, like her former ladies-in-waiting and most of the court, she had concluded.

But Sir Balian had always been different, her heart protested. He had been her friend! Her only friend. Why had he turned against her? Had she offended him in some way? Did he blame her for leaving court two years ago? Or for not writing when she was away? She had written religiously to Baldwin; hadn't he realized those letters were as much for him as for the King? Or was it something else?

She reached out to test the temperature of the water. As she had requested, it was tepid. She nodded absently, and Rahel came to help her out of her clothes. "You are unhappy, madame?" Rahel asked gently.

Maria Zoë nodded, but dared not say why.

Rahel worked deftly, unlacing and unbuttoning, then pulling the material off over Maria Zoë's head, one layer at a time: the loose white surcoat trimmed with bands of bright embroidery, the striped gown, the gauze shift. She unpinned Maria Zoë's thick, curly hair and combed it with her fingers. She gave Maria Zoë her hand as she stepped over the high sides of the tub, and she poured rose oil into the waters as Maria Zoë sank down into the water. She took a sponge, squeezed it under water, and released the pressure so it would soak up the rose-scented water. She removed the sponge and squeezed again, expelling the bulk of the water before gently using it to wipe away Maria Zoë's tears. "Don't cry, madame," she whispered. "Not yet."

Balian was pacing the ramparts of his city. It was completely dark now. The stars were sharp pinpoints in the sky overhead. Even the harbor-side taverns had slowly quieted down, and their torches had all but burned out. Balian just kept walking, annoying the guards, who hated being under the scrutiny of the Constable at this time of night. The breeze off the Mediterranean was fresh, almost chilly, hinting at the change of season in the offing. Soon the rains would come....

Why had *she* come? Certainly not for a horse market that was only marginally better than those at Jaffa, Acre, Tyre, or Beirut, not to mention Antioch. To see this outpost of her husband's Kingdom that she had not seen before? If she was taking a measure of her Kingdom, then why without Isabella? Isabella was second in line to the throne, and it would make sense to start introducing her to her inheritance—in all its breadth, depth, and danger.

Or was she consciously fleeing her maternal duties, in need of a break from them after being confined with the child for two years?

Balian had reached a section of the wall directly over the sea, and he paused to listen to the rhythmic crunch and hiss of the waves, slapping the shore and rolling over the stones as they retreated some two dozen feet below him. He leaned his elbows on the thick stone, still warmed by the heat of the day, and looked out to sea.

He had been surprised by his reaction at the sight of her. He had always known she was a beautiful woman, but since that one private interview she had always been a beautiful *queen*. Today she had been dressed for riding, in the loosely woven cottons of Gaza that gave shade without blocking out the breeze. Her gowns had been loosely fitted to give freedom of movement, and bleached a bright white to reflect rather than absorb the heat. These were the kind of clothes Richildis wore for every day, too. They made Maria Zoë seem more his equal than the bejeweled queen he had encountered, admired, and pledged himself to at court.

That was dangerous, he concluded, because she was too beautiful by half for the man in him. He had been completely discomfited by the sight and proximity of her, and he had tried to put distance between them, ashamed of his tangible physical reaction to her—fortunately hidden under his cotton surcoat. Now in the cool of night, his blood had calmed, but he was still unsettled by his reactions. He was attracted to this woman as he had been to no other. He admired her intelligence, and he sensed that there was a hidden gentleness in her as well. Balian was reminded of that one private interview he'd had with her—and how she had conspired to help ease Baldwin's loneliness. She was not the restrained, haughty princess most people saw. He knew that. He knew that she was capable of strong feelings—loyalty for one, and sympathy for another. He had been told how she had kissed Baldwin's hands when she returned to court. That said a great deal about her. Behind the façade of the perfect queen was a woman of deep—maybe even passionate—emotions. . . .

Balian shook his head to clear it. He was starved of female company, and at last freed of the restraints that had condemned him to a life of celibacy more rigid than any monk's vows. He had already written to Richildis, confiding in her his desire to marry and asking her to make discreet inquiries about suitable maidens. But marriage negotiations could take months or even years. And Queen Maria was here.

She was a widow.

A king's widow.

But a widow, nonetheless. The rules of engagement were different for widows. There was no father or husband who could be offended. A widow, at least a mature woman such as Queen Maria, decided for herself whom to take to her bed. Just as that bitch Agnes de Courtenay did. And Queen Maria was here in Ascalon, under his roof. . . .

When he returned to his rooms, he found both Dawit and Daniel asleep on the chest by the door. The sound of his return roused the boys. Dawit jumped up and came toward him, his hands outstretched to relieve Balian of his sword as he did each night. Balian unbuckled the weapon and handed it to the Ethiopian youth with a nod of thanks. Daniel pulled himself to his feet, using one of the posters of the bed for support, and stood awkwardly in the shadows, stammering, "You didn't dismiss me, my lord, and Dawit said I could sleep here."

"Only if you earn your keep," Balian answered, sinking onto the edge of the bed and thrusting out his feet. "Remove my spurs and help me out of my boots and hose."

"Yes, my lord!" Daniel sprang to obey, instantly awake. After helping Balian at the baths he had followed him to the palace, ostensibly in search of Michael, but really just to avoid going home to face his parents. But Michael was busy helping sort out accommodations for the Queen's escort, and had no time for Daniel. So Daniel loitered around the kitchens until he was kicked out, and found himself in the stables helping fix up stalls for the horses of the Queen's party, then watering and feeding them. By then it was dark, and Dawit went to attend on Sir Balian. Mathewos, however, invited Daniel to share his bread and wine. Daniel hadn't waited to be asked twice; he was famished, not having had a proper meal since his disgrace three days ago.

Mathewos had known Daniel all his life, and he knew he was in disgrace. He shared his evening meal with him, seated side by side on a tack chest in the tack room. Mathewos was a man of few words, and he did not harass Daniel with impertinent questions, just shared his wine glass with him, until Daniel asked, "Couldn't you use extra help here, Mathewos? Now that Dawit is squire to Sir Balian, you must be short-handed with the horses."

Mathewos nodded and looked out the tack-room door to the stables. Even now they were only half full, because they had been built to take caravans and their escorts. But then he dashed Daniel's hopes by saying: "Sir Balian must decide if we hire more men; I cannot do that."

"But I come free—or nearly so," Daniel continued desperately. "I'll work just for a roof over my head and two meals a day," he offered.

Mathewos seemed to consider this, but then shook his head. "You must talk to Sir Balian. I'll have Dawit take you to him."

Not long afterwards, Dawit returned to say good night to his father, and his father told him that Daniel needed to speak to Sir Balian. "He's gone out," Dawit admitted. "But Daniel can wait for him with me."

And so Daniel had gone with Dawit to Balian's chamber and waited with him there for Balian's return. Daniel had never taken much notice of Dawit before, because he had his own circle of friends. Dawit, like his father, and like the horses, was shy. Daniel had not valued that before, but he did now. Dawit, like his father, did not ask him why he had been late for work that fateful morning three days ago, or how he could talk back to his master. He did not ask any questions at all. He just showed Daniel how he turned down Sir Balian's sheets and laid out his nightshirt, how he fetched water in a pitcher and a pottery goblet to set on the table by Sir Balian's bed. He checked that the privy was clean and smelled fresh, and he lit a candle. He spoke very softly about what "Sir Balian likes," and Daniel could see how much he wanted to please. "You like him, don't you?" he asked when all was finished and they sat down to wait.

"Yes. He's a good master."

"Serving a knight is different from being a 'prentice," Daniel defended himself. "A knight *is* someone. If I were in your shoes, I'd never let Sir Balian down, either."

Dawit just nodded. Eventually they fell asleep waiting, only to be woken by Balian's return. Daniel was so eager to assist that he fell over backwards as he pulled off the first of Balian's boots. Balian laughed shortly and then advised, "Take it easy."

"But, but—sir—my lord—did you mean what you said? May I stay?"

Balian dropped his braies and swung his feet onto the bed. "Stay?"

"I mean—"

"Oh, you want a job? Being unemployed at the moment and all."

"Sir, I can explain what happened, if only anyone would listen to me. It wasn't just irresponsibility. I—"

"Shhh! I'm tired. I need to sleep. Put your head down, and we'll see how I feel about taking on a disgraced baker's boy in the morning."

"But—"

Daniel felt Dawit's hand on his arm and looked over angrily. The Ethiopian was shaking his head slowly in warning. Daniel bit his tongue and sank back onto the floor. Dawit signaled for him to come over and share his pallet. Gratefully, Daniel did.

They were alone at a small table, set up in Balian's private chambers. The room was lit only by the four-pronged bronze candelabra on the table, and they were being served by Dawit, who was so silent and discreet he seemed to fade into the shadows in the corners. Maria Zoë did not know exactly how she had ended up here.

The day had started well, however. Rahel had woken her with the news that Sir Balian wished to show her Ascalon, since she had a day of waiting until the horse market. Rahel had been smiling broadly as she announced this, and she had made Maria Zoë dress in the same gown she had worn for her reintroduction at court, only without the jeweled belt.

Maria Zoë still dreaded the confrontation with Sir Balian, but when she walked into the hall to join him for breakfast, his eyes lit up. The ice of the night before seemed to have melted entirely away with the dawn of the new day. Sir Balian bade Maria Zoë sit at the high table while he personally brought her what she wanted from the buffet, and then he sat beside her—although a good two feet away—and explained that he wished to show her Ascalon. "I hope you will then be able to report favorably on my service to King Baldwin."

"Baldwin does not doubt your service, sir."

"All the more reason that I should not misuse his trust," Balian answered.

The tour that followed had been vigorous and comprehensive, from the wall walk to a visit to the major churches of the city, the Roman baths, and the port. Maria Zoë had not walked so much since she'd retired from court, and she was footsore and weary long before Sir Balian brought her to the Bishop's palace for dinner. The Bishop of Ascalon had prepared a sumptuous feast, and he was intent on plying her ear with a catalog of complaints and requests that he expected her to take back to the King and the Patriarch of Jerusalem. Maria Zoë was used to such meals and such appeals, and so endured it graciously, but she was relieved and delighted when Sir Balian returned and spirited her away, with a feeble excuse to the Bishop about her being overdue at the orphanage "of which she is the patroness."

Maria Zoë waited until she had remounted and Sir Balian had

taken up his reins to remark, "I don't believe I *am* the patroness of any orphanage in Ascalon."

"No, but the Hospitaller Sisters would be very honored and delighted if you would accept the patronage of their orphanage, madame."

"I see," Maria Zoë answered carefully, and then could not stop from laughing. The look Sir Balian gave her then was so much like the looks Aimery de Lusignan had given her that she started to feel giddy.

But first they faced the orphanage. Sir Balian explained, "There are more abandoned children in Ascalon than in most cities. That has to do with its history. There are many different peoples here. They live together in harmony for the most part—going to the same markets, the same shops, the same taverns. But men rarely like it when their women stray."

"Stray?" asked Maria Zoë, as if she didn't understand him.

Sir Balian just smiled and continued, "Most of the children in the orphanage are of mixed parentage."

"The entire Kingdom is populated by people of mixed blood," Maria Zoë pointed out, "starting with my own daughter."

"Yes, of course, and the bulk of the crusaders that settled here are like Roger Shoreham, my senior sergeant, who married a Coptic woman. The men who settled and married have raised their children with pride. But Ascalon has too many transients."

Maria Zoë thought that, too, could be said of the entire Kingdom, but she did not want to argue the point; she found it admirable that Sir Balian took such a strong interest in orphans. So they visited the Hospitaller orphanage.

Maria Zoë was led around by a Hospitaller sister who was a plump and cheerful woman from Flanders, thrilled to be receiving a queen. When Maria Zoë asked if she could donate a hundred dinar and take on the role of patroness, the Hospitaller sister almost died of joy.

When Sir Balian suggested they get some fresh air by going down to a seaside tavern outside the city walls, with tables directly on the sandy beach, to watch the sun go down, Maria Zoë started to think she, too, had died and gone to heaven.

The outside tables stood unevenly in the sand, lined with crude benches of bleached wood. The proprietor became so flustered by the presence of the Queen that Sir Walter took him aside and lectured him. After that, the wine and the grilled catch of the day, dripping olive oil, simply appeared on the table, and the rest of the beach was empty—except for the table behind Maria Zoë and Balian, at which Rahel and Walter talked softly, while Dawit and Daniel shared a bowl of squid on the steps of the tavern.

And now this.

Maria Zoë was conscious of being slightly tipsy, but Sir Balian was dead sober. She had the feeling he'd been drinking water while she drank wine. One of the three doors to the rooftop terrace was open, letting in a soft evening breeze and the call of the gulls.

"I hope you had a pleasant day, my lady."

"You know I did, Sir Balian." Maria Zoë leaned her head against the back of her chair and looked at him through half-closed lids. He had never looked more attractive to her than he did right now. He had not worn armor all day, dressing instead in a long parti-colored silk surcoat over suede boots and a long-sleeved silk shirt. The surcoat had short, broad sleeves, and half was a vivid marigold with the red cross of Ibelin scattered liberally across it, while the other half was bright blue with the five crosses of Jerusalem stitched in gold. The candlelight glowed on his dark hair.

He had turned in his chair to stretch out his long legs and had crossed them at the ankles. He looked completely relaxed and content as he smiled at her over the rim of his silver goblet. "Will you grant me the boon of a question?" he asked her, tipping the goblet up to shield his face.

"Of course."

"Why are you really here?"

Maria Zoë started, held her breath, and then answered as she let it out. "Because these past two years I could not get you out of my mind, sir. Because I wanted to meet you again—and see if you were really the perfect knight I pictured you to be."

"Then I have no hope," Sir Balian answered with a small, twisted smile.

"Hope of what?" Maria Zoë asked, puzzled.

"Of winning your favor—since no real man can live up to the ideal of a perfect knight."

"You come very close," she admitted, letting the wine speak.

Sir Balian put his goblet down and came around the table to stand beside her chair. "What do you want of your perfect knight, my lady queen?"

"First, that you call me by my name, not my title. And that is Zoë. There were so many Marias in Constantinople at my great-uncle's court that we all went by our second names."

"Zoë means life," Sir Balian noted, sinking on his heels to be eye to eye with her.

"Yes," she agreed, "but most of my life I have been only a lifeless puppet."

"And tonight?"

"Tonight? Tonight, I would like to be more than that." She met his eyes. Two of the candles had gone out, and the room was very dark, lit only by the light of the stars and a sliver of moon admitted through the open door. Maria Zoë had the impression that Dawit had withdrawn, silent as always. Balian must have given him a signal.

Balian leaned closer, and his lips hovered over hers. She could feel his breath and it made her tingle all over. Please kiss me, she prayed, but she did not make the first move. She couldn't overcome her upbringing.

Balian touched his lips to hers and felt them twitch and open. He put his hand behind her head and held her gently but insistently, his nerves alert for the slightest indication of resistance. But there was none. Maria—Zoë—was wax in his hands, waiting—no, smoldering—with inchoate desire.

Balian sensed that for all that she was a widow, she was innocent, too. King Amalric had not only been twenty years her senior, but by the time Zoë came to Jerusalem he had been a fat man with receding hair. Balian did not like to picture what it must been like for the delicate Greek maiden in his bed. He sensed that she had known only rape up to now—even if it was the sanctioned rape of marriage. She wanted him to show her love.

Christ, he prayed silently, give me the strength and stamina to make the most of this, to drag it out as long as possible, to savor every second, for I may never have this chance again.

"Balian, will you marry me?"

His eyes widened with surprise, reassuring Maria Zoë that he had not done this for material gain, even before he asked, "Are you out of your mind?"

"What is mad about wanting to repeat this?" Maria Zoë wanted to know.

"Nothing. But this," he dropped his head to kiss her gently, "is about love." He kissed her again before drawing back to declare dryly, "Marriage is about politics."

"I know," she retorted with a frown of irritation. "Nothing could have been more political than my first marriage! It took over two years to get the terms right, and I was an exchangeable commodity throughout most of it. I think my great-uncle considered five different female relatives at one time or another, before he finally decided on me. But at thirteen I was my great-uncle's pawn, and now I am a queen."

"And I am the younger son of an adventurer and parvenu. Just what do you think your great-uncle would say if I asked for you to wife?" The question was rhetorical.

"If *you* asked, he'd definitely say 'No' and throw you out of his court—assuming he didn't order your tongue torn out for such impudence." She giggled to indicate this was just a joke.

"What a pleasant prospect!" Balian noted sarcastically, turning over to lie on his back to protest her teasing about such things.

"If," Maria Zoë continued, rising up on one elbow and leaning over to look down on him, her long, thick hair cascading down like a black curtain around them. "If, on the other hand, *I* asked him, his answer would more likely be, "Why?"

"I somehow doubt," Balian reflected, brushing a strand of hair away from her face with the back of his hand to see her more perfectly, "that my love for you would bear much weight with the Emperor of the Eastern Empire."

"Not at all," Maria Zoë agreed readily and matter-of-factly. "But there *are* other reasons."

"Such as?" Balian asked cautiously and curiously.

Maria Zoë smiled and dropped down to rest her head on his naked shoulder, nestling closer to him as she did so. "Baldwin cannot have heirs of his body."

Balian did not answer. It was hardly news to him, and she knew it.

"Princess Sibylla is due to marry at St. Martins and *may* have a litter of healthy little boys with her Italian marquis—or she may not. Life is so uncertain. Meanwhile, my daughter Isabella is second in line to the throne."

"She *has* been for the last four years. What does that have to do with making me a suitable consort for the Dowager Queen of Jerusalem?" Balian's tone was so earnest that Maria Zoë concluded he was seriously considering her proposal.

"Isabella needs a strong protector. As long as Tripoli was Regent, she had one, because he favored her claim to the throne. And Baldwin dotes on her—maybe even more than he doted on Sibylla. But Baldwin—" She hesitated to say it out loud because she knew how much Balian loved the King, but it had to be said—"Baldwin is very much under the influence of his mother and uncle at the moment.... And I'm not so sure *they* have Isabella's best interests at heart."

Balian still did not answer. Again, she was not telling him something new—but until tonight Isabella had been only a name, a fact, the King's second daughter and the second in line to the throne. For the first time he started to see her as something more than that, as the precious child of the woman he loved.

Maria Zoë continued softly, "If—as—Baldwin becomes weaker," Maria Zoë continued softly, "I'm afraid Isabella will need—*I* will need—a man who is strong enough and courageous enough to defy Agnes and Edessa, for they will certainly try to control her—or even eliminate her."

Balian took his time answering, for he could sense that her fears were very real, and in all honesty he could not dismiss them as unfounded. Agnes de Courtenay was not the woman he would like to trust his child's fate to! But he also had to be honest about his own power. "Any baron of the Kingdom—not to mention an Armenian or Greek prince—would be more suitable for the role of protecting Isabella than I, Zoë," Balian answered solemnly. "I owe everything to Baldwin, and when he dies I stand to lose my post here—and my ability to protect you and Isabella."

"Not if you are married to a Byzantine princess and have the ear of the Emperor of the Eastern Empire," Maria Zoë countered triumphantly.

Balian couldn't picture it the way she did. He saw only that he would be brushed aside as a man of no consequence. If he challenged the Queen Mother and Edessa, who would support him? Montferrat, as the future husband of Sibylla, would automatically side with Agnes de Courtenay, and he enjoyed the support of the Holy Roman Emperor. Tripoli, to be sure, favored Isabella's claim to the throne, but his power had been neatly checkmated by Oultrejourdain, who hated Tripoli and so had thrown in his lot with the Courtenays. His brother would support him, of course—Barry had long urged him to "seduce a heiress"—and even Lusignan might line up behind him, but was that enough? Somehow he couldn't shake the conviction that with Montferrat, Agnes de Courtenay, and Oultrejourdain against him, he was far more likely to end up dead or chained in a dungeon for the rest of his life. He shook his head firmly at the thought.

"Then just what was *this* all about?" Maria Zoë reared up and demanded with big, reproachful eyes. "A night's entertainment? Am I just a conquest? A trophy? Something to brag about to other men?" She was naked. All her layers of protection were stripped away—not just the physical ones, but the emotional ones as well. With each question her anger grew, until her eyes were dark with fury.

Balian knew he had been right to imagine she had a passionate inner core and knew, too, that he was playing with fire now that he had laid it bare. He reached up to pull her back down onto his chest, but she resisted him. He could see her anger fueling itself. Like embers caught in a sudden breeze, the fury glinted sharply in her eyes.

"Do you feel conquered?" he asked her, stroking her naked shoulder. "Defeated?"

She met his eyes and the fire died down, but it was not extinguished. Instead, her eyes burned with something more intangible. "No," she admitted honestly, remembering both how humiliating the consummation of her marriage had been and how utterly different and exhilarating it had been to make love to Balian. But that led her back to her dilemma. "But if you will not marry me, what is our future, Balian? Am I just to ride away tomorrow or the day after?"

"I hope not!" Balian answered and pulled her into his arms again.

This time she did not resist. He stroked the back of her head and then nuzzled the hair over her ear until he could reach it with his tongue. "I would that this could go on forever," he whispered into her ear.

She turned her head to look at him. "You mean like Aimery and Agnes de Courtenay?"

Her tone was stinging, and Balian knew he was on the brink of a precipice. Last night he might have been in control of the situation, but this morning he was not. He had to tread very, very carefully if he did not want to destroy what had been born between them. "How could it be like that when you are so utterly unlike Agnes de Courtenay?" he murmured, meeting her eyes.

Maria Zoë considered him solemnly. "That was neatly parried, sir," she admitted, but she did not sound in the least appeased.

"Five years in the service of a king teaches even a country bumpkin some things," he countered.

"But I'm *serious*, Balian," she pleaded, and Balian noticed a sheen of tears over her eyes, which ignited a wave of protectiveness in him.

He covered her eyes with kisses. "Don't cry, Zoë. There's nothing to cry about."

"Yes, there is," she protested, surrendering to her tears, because his sympathy had melted the very last of her defenses. "I love you, Balian. I love you as I think no woman ever loved anyone before. I love you because I've never been *allowed* to love anyone, and you're the first man who ever treated me like I was not just a jewel, a prize, a tool, and a trophy—" she dissolved into heartrending sobs that left Balian utterly helpless.

Part of his mind was laughing at him, noting: "You got more than you bargained for." And another part was preaching to him, saying, "See how you've abused the trust of an innocent child!" But mostly, he just felt desperately protective and wanted to make Zoë happy again. "Zoë, don't cry," he pleaded. "Look! A new day is dawning, and there is no reason why it cannot be as beautiful as yesterday." He parted the striped linen bed curtains, letting the rose-colored sunshine pour in through the eastern window.

"You're telling me to live one day at a time," Maria Zoë answered in a strained voice as she pulled herself together.

"Yes," Balian answered slowly, reflecting on what he had said.

"Yes. Today we are both richer for what we have—for knowing how we feel about one another. Let us make the most of that. God alone knows the future, and God knows that things can change in the most unexpected ways. Who would have thought, four years ago when we first met in the royal mews, that we would ever lie together like this?"

She looked up at him with molten eyes, but said softly, "You are right, Balian. We must be thankful for what He has given us." Then she closed her eyes and offered him her lips instead.

Chapter 9

Ascalon, November 1177

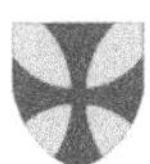

"SALAH AD-DIN!" THE MAN SHOUTED UP to the lookouts on the ramparts of the barbican. "With his whole army!" He gestured wildly to the south with one hand while trying to drag a reluctant overloaded mule toward the closed Gaza Gate with the other. It was nearly midnight and the gates were locked and barred, but the watch peered down at not just one man with a mule, but dozens of people streaming toward the city by the light of the setting moon.

The captain of the watch squinted into the darkness, trying to estimate the number of refugees. Then he turned to the man next to him and said, "Better rouse Sergeant Shoreham. I'm not opening these gates without his orders." He leaned over the ramparts and shouted down to the man with the mule, "Patience! We'll let the lot of you in at once, not piecemeal."

By the time Roger arrived, his hair sticking up in all directions, the crowd at the gate had grown to an angry, milling mob of nearly a half a hundred people, including squalling babies, whimpering children, and pleading women. "Salah ad-Din!" the men kept shouting and gesturing. "He's coming with his whole army!"

Roger gave the order to admit the refugees and, after hesitating a moment, also ordered the sounding of the alarm to call the garrison to the walls. The men stared at him in shock, but then one of them grabbed the bell cord and began vigorously ringing the heavy brass bell on the Gaza barbican with all his might. The sound seemed paltry in the vastness of the night, but it was quickly answered by the bells on the other gates—and slowly, haphazardly, as priests and deacons were roused from their sleep, the bells of the city's churches took up the clangor. Within minutes St. Paul's added its deep, heavy voice to the chorus of bells, and St. Mary's, the main Orthodox church, seemed to be competing for the loudest clang.

The sound brought Balian from his sleep with a start, trying to remember what saint's day it was. Then he registered that it was pitch dark, and he sat bolt upright in his bed as he realized the bells could only be ringing alarm. He had been Constable of Ascalon for fifteen months now, but this was the first time he had heard the bells rung in earnest. He flung off the light covers and jumped out of bed. "Arms! Bring my arms!" he shouted at a bewildered Dawit, just dragging himself out of his own sleep.

Balian flug off his nightshirt and grabbed his braies. He pulled them on and tied the cord, while Daniel stumbled to his feet to bring him his shirt. Balian pulled this over his head and snapped his fingers for his hose, which Daniel brought and helped him draw on and make fast to his braies. Balian was already in his gambeson and stuffing his feet into knee-high suede boots by the time a servant knocked on the door, shouting: "Sir Balian! Sir Balian! Sergeant Shoreham requests your presence at the Gaza Gate!"

"I'm coming!" Balian answered, and bent so Dawit could slip his hauberk over his head. He pushed his arms through the slack chain-mail sleeves while Daniel waited with his surcoat. He pulled this on, grabbed his sword from Dawit's outstretched arms, and selected the lighter, open-faced crevelier rather than the heavy helm Daniel offered him. Finished at last, he ordered his squires to dress themselves, wake Sir Walter, and join him on the Gaza Gate.

By the time Balian reached the Gaza Gate, the number of refugees had swollen to nearly a hundred, and the ten Hospitaller knights had also mustered on foot. "They're saying Salah ad-Din is on the move with his entire army!" one of the Hospitallers called out to Balian as the latter jumped down from Jupiter to mount the stairs onto the barbican.

Balian handed his reins to one of the Hospitallers, asking: "How far away is he supposed to be?"

"Not more than twelve miles, they say. Most of these people fled early in the morning and have been making for Ascalon all day."

"That would mean he's marched past the Templar castle at Gaza," Balian countered.

"These people are reporting one hundred thousand soldiers with Salah ad-Din; the Templars only have five hundred fighting men at Gaza. Even *they* wouldn't be mad enough to attack against those odds."

"These people are panicked refugees. I'll believe this is Salah ad-Din's whole army, and not just a raid, when I have better evidence than the panicked claims of fleeing peasants. How soon can you be ready to ride?" he asked the Hospitaller.

The man glanced back at his troops and then replied, "Ten minutes."

"Good. Make ready," Balian ordered (although he had no right to do so), and then plunged into the darkness of the narrow spiral stairwell leading up to the ramparts of the barbican.

When Balian stepped out of the stairwell onto the roof of the barbican, he quickly counted double the number of men usually stationed there, and recognized George Smith and Joachim Zimmermann among them. They were wearing leather jacks with hoods and had swords at their hips. Just as Roger had promised, it wasn't just the garrison that had responded to the clanging of the bells.

Roger caught sight of Balian and went over to him. "You've seen the refugees, my lord? They're saying Salah ad-Din is on the march with his whole army."

"What makes you think this is an invasion and not a raid?"

"I don't know, sir. I would just rather be safe than sorry."

Balian nodded his approval, but his guts were twisting themselves in knots. Salah ad-Din had assembled his army to counter a threat posed by a Byzantine fleet sent to support the troops of the Count of Flanders and the Army of Jerusalem, but Flanders had quarreled with the Byzantines (ignoring Zoë's advice, she confided in him), and now the Byzantine fleet had withdrawn and the Count of Flanders had gone campaigning in the north. This left Salah ad-Din with his assembled forces on the southern border of the Kingdom at a time when it was virtually denuded of troops. The Saracens would be mad not to take advantage of the situation and attack, Balian thought as he followed Roger to the parapet. And Ascalon made the most tempting target. The Sultan must be itching to take it back and regain a base for his own fleet.

"There! Do you see the pinpoints of light on the horizon?" Roger broke into his thoughts.

Balian had to look very hard, but then he nodded. "Burning villages?"

"That's my guess, my lord."

Balian nodded again. "Roger, I want you to put the city on the defensive."

"Yes, my lord, that's what we've done."

"Yes. What I meant is: I want you to take command of the defense."

"But, my lord—"

Balian held up his hand and turned to Walter, Dawit, and Daniel, who had just arrived together. "Dawit, tack up Gladiator—with battle gear, the chain reins—and bring him here."

"Do you need your lance and helmet, sir?" Daniel asked with breathless excitement.

"Yes."

"You aren't going out there, my lord!" Roger gasped.

"The Hospitallers and I will ride reconnaissance," Balian answered.

"Then I need to mount up, too," Walter declared and turned to fetch his own horse, but Balian stopped him.

"I want you to stay here, but ready to ride to Jerusalem as soon as we have a better estimate of the size of Salah ad-Din's forces. The King knows you, Walter," Balian cut off his protest firmly. "He'll give your word more credence than that of any other messenger I can send."

"Yes, my lord." Walter accepted the decision, part of him relieved to be spared the prospect of battle; he knew his own limitations as a warrior and gave himself only moderate chances of survival in an engagement.

"Take Jupiter; he's faster and in better condition than your stallion. Take plenty of water and food with you and be prepared to ride without halting, just resting at a walk. Which means, try to get some sleep now so you're as rested as possible when I return with instructions."

"Yes, sir." Walter was beginning to grasp the significance of the role Balian had given him, and it filled him with both pride and trepidation. He must not fail to reach Jerusalem in the shortest possible time, nor fail to convince the King of the earnestness of the situation.

Balian turned back to Roger, who looked very grim. "Have Father Laurence see that the refugees are put up in the caravansaries, hospices, and churches, if necessary. Tell him to be sure they have plenty of water, bread, and broth at my expense, but no wine and no meat. We need to keep our reserves until we know what the situation is."

"Yes, my lord," Roger answered, licking his lips uncomfortably. "But do you really think you and ten Hospitallers—"

"Yes, I do. Be sure you keep all the gates manned and men patrolling between them. Also, set up a duty roster for the volunteers as well as the garrison. We don't want everyone up here all night tonight, and then exhausted when Salah ad-Din arrives tomorrow."

"I understand, my lord," Roger nodded. He was confident he could do that; in fact, he had an old roster he could rapidly update.

"Good. If I'm not back by tomorrow night, you have command of the city and should send Walter to Jerusalem with news that Salah ad-Din is advancing with an army. Even if it's not true, it will be the safest thing to do."

"Yes, my lord," Roger answered, but Balian could sense that the English veteran was very unhappy with the situation.

At the foot of the steps Balian found Daniel and Dawit with Gladiator, his helmet, and two lances. The Hospitallers, meanwhile, had also mounted and had brought their squires, so they were twenty men. "Shouldn't one of us go with you, sir?" Daniel asked eagerly.

Balian hesitated, sensing that Dawit would be the greater help with reconnaissance but Daniel better in a skirmish. Then he shook his head. "Neither of you is trained well enough yet. You'd only give me something more to worry about. If you want to make yourself useful, be sure Sir Walter has two water skins, bread, sausage, and cheese, and then help Father Laurence with the refugees."

Daniel's face expressed his disdain for these menial tasks, but Dawit nodded and assured Balian they would "look after Sir Walter."

Balian swung himself up on an agitated Gladiator, whom Dawit held and tried to soothe as Balian took the lances Daniel handed up to him and secured them to his saddle. He took the arming cap Daniel handed him next and made it fast over his crevelier, but laid the helmet across his lap, ready for later use. Finally he turned Gladiator around, signaled for the Hospitallers to follow him, and gestured for the gate to open.

Soldiers directly behind the gate manhandled the heavy beams out of the braces holding them, and Balian rode through the barbican. The sound of hooves echoed in the vaulting overhead as they turned first to the right and then, confronted by a massive wall, turned to the left to come up behind the second gate. The soldiers again lifted the beams bolting the gate shut, and as Balian rode onto the bridge over the dry ditch beyond, he let Gladiator break into a canter just to let off some of his nervous energy.

In front of them the road was bathed in moonlight, and the orchards to the left rustled in a light breeze. To the right, however, between the road and the shore, there was a patchwork of vegetable gardens, chicken coops, and goat pens belonging to residents who sold eggs, milk, cheese, and vegetables in Ascalon's daily markets. People were moving around in these, collecting their cackling chickens, bleating sheep, and whinnying goats to take them to safety inside the city walls. Beyond, the Mediterranean stretched out cool and calm, ruffled by a steady breeze.

Balian reined in beside the Hospitaller commander. "Although I fear the worst, I do not want to send word to the King until we have a more reliable estimate of Salah ad-Din's numbers and some better indication of his intentions," he explained.

"We can do that best by splitting up. Patrols of no more than four men apiece, circling further inland as well as following the coast."

Balian nodded. "Agreed."

The Hospitaller turned and ordered his men to divide up into four troops. One troop was to attempt to reach the Templar castle of Gaza and find out what intelligence the Templars had. The other three troops were told to ride to different outlying villages and see what they could find. His orders were clear and simple: "Stay out of bowshot. Don't allow yourselves to be provoked, no matter how few they appear to be. Don't stop to help refugees, but assure them Ascalon will receive them. Don't stop to bury the dead. Return to Ascalon with whatever information you have."

Balian and the Hospitaller commander rode together along the coastal road with one other Hospitaller knight and two squires. As soon as they had left the irrigated pomegranate plantations that skirted Ascalon, the road led through a bleak landscape of desolate dunes, occasionally dotted by scrub brush or palm groves.

It was daylight before they came across any indication that something was amiss: a dead man with two arrows in his back. He had evidently managed to get away and keep walking for God knew how long before he had been reduced to crawling and then, finally, had bled to death. One of thc Hospitaller squires dismounted and verified that the arrows were of Egyptian origin.

They looked around at the desolate landscape. They were in a depression caused by a now-dry wadi. The dunes had gradually given way to gravel and stone. Except for the Mediterranean on their right, they were surrounded by low but barren hills, and the dawn was creeping up on them. While the sun brought welcome warmth, it also exposed them to the scouts of Salah ad-Din's army. As the Christians looked around at the deserted countryside, they felt naked. Just how far had the dead man managed to travel after he was shot, and how long ago had he died?

Balian and the Hospitallers agreed to ride a little farther up the road to the top of the hill ahead of them, hoping this would give them a better view into the far valley. Balian decided it was time to put his helmet on, and he took one of the lances into his hand as well. It was not entirely rational, but he had the feeling he was not going to like what he saw on the far side of that low hill.

Just before they breasted the hill, Gladiator shied sharply sideways, spun on his haunches, and tried to run back the way he'd come. By the time Balian had him back under control, the Hospitallers were beside him, and the commander was making motions for them to dismount. Balian jumped down and handed a still fretting Gladiator over to one of the Hospitaller squires, so that he and the Hospitaller knights could approach the crest of the hill on foot, keeping their heads down as much as possible. Suddenly the wailing of a muezzin split the early morning air. The sound was like the yowling of a cat, and it made the hair on the back of Balian's neck stand on end. He glanced toward the Hospitaller commander in horror, and saw the older man drop to his belly. Balian followed his example. They pulled themselves forward across the rubble and gravel by their elbows until they could gaze down on the encampment of the Saracen army.

By then Balian was expecting what he saw: rows and rows of bright-colored tents with long banners emblazoned with Arabic writing fluttering in the wind. Between the tents the commoners camped, covering the ground like a carpet of moving moss as far as the eye could see.

The whole camp was slowly coming to life as men roused themselves to pray facing Mecca. On the fringes of the camp the horse lines stirred, too, as the horses anticipated feed and water after this daily ritual of prayer. Balian concentrated on the horses. If he knew the number of horse, he could roughly calculate the size of the whole army: four foot soldiers to each mounted man. There were two clusters of horses, and both were too many to count, so he gave up. He had his answer already. This was no simple raid, nor a reconnaissance in force: this was an invasion.

By noon only the patrol sent to the Templar Castle of Gaza had not returned to Ascalon, and Walter was on his way to Jerusalem. Balian checked over the preparations made by Roger for manning the walls, and found them sound. He then checked in with Father Laurence to be sure the refugees had been given accommodation and water. This was less well organized, if only because the number of refugees was still growing, many of them bringing livestock and household goods piled high on carts and wagons. The latter were starting to clog the streets of the city. Balian called on the Bishop and suggested that he and his staff take over the organization of the refugees. As expected, the Bishop considered this task outside his mandate—but he had a vigorous and competent secretary, who escorted Balian out of the episcopal palace and promised to do what he could.

Balian was exhausted, and decided he would serve the city best by lying down for a few hours and resting, even if he was too agitated to actually sleep. He would need his strength when Salah ad-Din's army actually arrived. So he returned to his residence, fed himself standing up in the kitchen, and let Dawit and Daniel strip his armor and sponge the worst of the day's sweat and dust from him, then lay down naked on his bed. The bells of the churches were already ringing Vespers.

Balian woke to the bells ringing Matins, having fallen into a deep sleep despite himself. He sat up in bed, poured himself some water, and then lay back, listening to the deep breathing of his squires and the regular calls of the night watchmen in the street below.

Staring at the vaulted ceiling over his head, he tried to estimate how long it would take Salah ad-Din to reach Ascalon. Maybe, he decided, another day or even two, given the size of the army he had seen—easily thirty thousand men. In that time, Walter could—would, he told himself—reach Jerusalem. The question was: what response could he expect?

The bulk of the barons, including the most experienced and competent commanders, Tripoli and the Constable Humphrey de Toron, were campaigning north of Beirut with Philip of Flanders. Balian was not absolutely sure who was still in Jerusalem—except Edessa, of course. Neither Edessa nor Agnes de Courtenay was likely to urge the King to relieve Ascalon; they would both undoubtedly care more about their own safety than assisting Balian. As far as he knew, Oultrejourdain was also still in the south of the Kingdom. He had certainly not gone north with Flanders, and whatever else one thought of him, he was a powerful fighting man and commanded fully sixty knights. Aimery de Lusignan too, if he was still in Jerusalem and not with Tripoli and Toron, was intelligent enough to understand they could not afford to lose Ascalon. He would surely urge the King to send troops. Possibly Lusignan would come himself. But how many knights could Jerusalem spare under the circumstances? Lusignan would have to send knights, because foot soldiers would not get here in time.

Knights were, moreover, what Balian needed. The citizens of Ascalon would provide the substance of the defense. Roger was right about that. Today he had seen them: butchers and bakers, tinkers and tailors, coopers and carpenters, masters and journeymen and apprentices. They were all determined to defend Ascalon to their last breath, while their women had organized field kitchens, one behind each gate, dispensing ale, meals, and good cheer.

Balian was acutely aware that these people, with their sober determination to hold out and their practical approach to defense, were a marvelous gift, for he had not made them so. If he were to weather the ordeal facing him, then it would be due to their courage and common sense more than to his own. "So help me, God, for their sake," he prayed to the crucifix hanging inside the door, a gift from Hugh when he went off to serve as a squire. "Don't forget your prayers," Hugh had admonished him, "and don't let the other boys lead you to commit sins of the flesh."

Remembering these words, Balian was also reminded of the nights he had spent with Zoë in this very bed on five different visits over the last year. Had that been so terrible a sin that God would now punish him for it? He did not think so, but he added another prayer nevertheless: "If my sins offend you, Christ, then punish me—not Ascalon."

Father Michael had not slept in two days. It was easy for Father Laurence to give him responsibility for feeding the refugees and then turn his mind to other problems. Father Laurence *did* have other problems, and Michael recognized that. A city under siege (or about to be under siege) needed to have clean water supplies, it needed infirmaries, and it had to have carefully controlled rations. Father Laurence organized members of the household to guard the most important cisterns and wells in the city to prevent them from being contaminated or seized for private use (since no fighting men could be spared for this guard duty). He made sure the bakeries had firewood to keep their ovens heated, because the need for bread in the days to come would be enormous. He set about doing an inventory of the city's reserves of grain, meat, and wine, while the Hospitallers naturally set to work preparing for the expected wounded.

Yet Michael was not someone who could see dehydrated children vomiting, feet lacerated to the bone, or old people so disoriented that they could only rock back and forth singing lullabies, without being moved. "Feeding" the refugees meant going to them, seeing their condition, and hearing their stories. The bulk of the refugees had fled long before their own homes and fields were threatened, responding to the flight of those farther south or the sight of smoke on the horizon, but some of the refugees had escaped only by the grace of God.

One boy, no more than fourteen or fifteen, had been in the outhouse when the Saracen cavalry overran his father's farm. He had seen the mounted Saracens chasing his parents and siblings around in the little farmyard like frightened livestock. He had watched the turbaned cavalrymen laughing and joking with one another while his loved ones screamed in terror and pain as they were hacked to pieces.

A young mother had seen her young son pierced by an arrow as he ran to her for safety in a cellar. He had died in her arms and she held him still, until Michael pried her cramped hands away from the stiffened body and laid the child in a newly dug grave.

Michael had not just fed the refugees—he had listened to them, prayed with them, and tried to comfort them. But he was only nineteen, and he was at the end of his strength. After a young mother died in his arms from the injuries she had sustained falling off a wagon while fleeing over rugged terrain, Michael stumbled out of the caravansary and walked blindly down the street, oblivious to the outraged demands of the woman's husband. "You can't just walk away!" the man shouted. "You have to bury her! And what about the kids? I can't look after two toddlers! The baby's still at breast! What am I supposed to do with an unweaned baby?"

That pierced Michael's consciousness enough for him to turn around. He went back, picked up the squalling baby, and left a second time. The man was still demanding a burial and asking about the other children, but Michael paid him no heed. He had a single mission: to bring the baby to the Hospitaller orphanage.

The sisters at the orphanage took one look at Michael and whisked the baby out of his arms. Then one of the women made Michael sit down, and a moment later he had a jug of ale in his hand. "Drink that," she ordered briskly.

"There are so many refugees," Michael muttered.

"Yes, and many more townsfolk able to look after them," the Hospitaller sister answered firmly. "What you need, father, is to lie down for a wee bit and get your strength back. When was the last time you had a bite to eat yourself?"

Michael shook his head. "I'm not hungry. They hacked people to pieces!" he protested. "Just carved them up while still alive!"

The sister laid her hand on his shoulder. It was a gesture of comfort, yet Michael could feel her fingers were trembling, too, and felt guilty for his outburst. "We have strong walls," he told her, repeating a litany he had said a thousand times already to the refugees. "We have strong walls."

"And strong hearts," the Hospitaller sister answered. "Now come. Lie down right here."

"I haven't heard Mass—except for the dead—in two days," Michael protested. "And I need to confess my sins."

"Certainly, but not at this moment," the sister insisted. "Lie down." She led him to a wooden bed frame filled with straw, apparently the night watchman's bed. Michael fell more than lay down in it, and sleep closed over him instantly.

He was woken by anxious voices in the room next door. "It's certain, then?" a woman asked.

"Sir Balian has ordered the Gaza Gate closed. Anyone seeking admittance now must come around to the Jerusalem Gate."

"The smoke we saw earlier, then?"

"Yes. They're burning everything they can't put on their camels. One of our brothers said the Templars counted over two hundred camels without burdens—brought along just to carry the loot they expect to seize."

"But they bypassed Gaza; maybe they'll bypass Ascalon?"

"Why attack a Templar castle bristling with knights and sergeants ready to find martyrdom, when they can take a rich city with only a handful of knights to defend it? Ascalon is the prize. The Saracens have never been reconciled to her loss."

Michael dragged himself upright, feeling dizzy. He had a splitting headache and all his limbs ached. He was aware of hunger, too. He had to eat and drink something if he was to be of any use to anyone. He struggled to get up over the wooden edge of the box bed and got unsteadily to his feet, looking around the room to orient himself. Just to his left was the door through which the voices came, and to his right—

The door burst open and a Hospitaller sergeant broke in. He did not see Michael but plunged on, tearing open the next door to blurt out, "Horsemen are riding straight for the Jerusalem Gate. Hundreds of them. We've been outflanked and are going to be taken from the east!"

Even as he spoke, Michael heard the alarm bells on the walls take up a wild clamor. In the street men were running, shouting as they went: "Get to the Jerusalem Gate! Reinforce the Jerusalem Gate!"

Ducking out the door to stand in the doorway, Michael lifted his eyes to the wall itself and saw men silhouetted against the orange light of dusk, moving purposefully along the wall walk. It was hard to tell in this light, but the fluttering surcoat of the leading man suggested it was Sir Balian himself, and the figure trailing right behind him seemed so familiar it could only be his brother Daniel.

Michael hesitated, trying to decide where he would be needed most. His brain said: the refugees. They would surely be thrown into panic by this latest news. But his youth drew him toward the scene of the action. He cut between the kitchen gardens and zigzagged through familiar alleyways until he was at the foot of one of the stairways built on the inside of the wall to give access to the wall walk. Taking his cassock in his fist, he mounted the stairs as fast as he could and went immediately to the parapet to look out.

Darkness was settling very rapidly, which was a comfort, since Salah ad-Din surely wouldn't launch an assault on the city at night. They would have at least one night to rest and eat and collect their courage. But even as he thought this, he made out the large column of horses coming inexorably toward the Jerusalem Gate. It was like an evil serpent weaving through the contours of the land as the horsemen followed the road. He stared at the approaching monster, transfixed with a sense of doom—and then jerked himself out of his trance, crossed himself, and began reciting the rosary as he hurried toward the Jerusalem Gate. He was fighting panic, a feeling reinforced by the sense of the earth rumbling under him. It was like a slow earthquake, he thought, and then he realized it was the sound of hundreds and hundreds of hooves on the earth outside. "Oh, Christ, protect us!" he pleaded helplessly.

Wild shouting had broken out ahead of him, but it wasn't curses or shouts of defiance as it should have been. Someone was shouting, "Open the gate! Open the gate!"

Traitor! Surely no one would heed him? But fear that this man had accomplices drove Michael to run faster. Before he could take a dozen steps, the strap on one of his sandals broke. He removed it and continued with one bare foot until the sound of the gates crashing against the interior of the barbican paralyzed him with terror. The next instant the hooves echoed inside the barbican, as the head of that ominous snake of horsemen surged into the city.

Michael did not know what to do. Lamed with horror, he stared down into the streets of the city, expecting to see turbaned horsemen hacking at terrified townsmen—and caught his breath at the sight of knights in helmets and carrying lances. Only now did he think to look at the banner, and almost fell off the wall walk as he dropped to his knees in wonder. It was the crosses of Jerusalem—and below it, on a gray stallion, was a young man with a crown on the brow of his helmet.

"Jerusalem!" Michael gasped, and around him more and more people were shouting it out. "Jerusalem! Jerusalem! Jerusalem has come!"

Demetrius was in a frenzy, trying to put together a meal fit for a king without any warning and after days of preparing for a siege rather than a banquet. Mathewos, meanwhile, was putting two horses in every stall, but still couldn't find places for all the horses of the King's entourage. Dawit and Daniel were running relays with wine and water for the high table, and couldn't believe what had happened to them.

"I thought he was a leper!" Daniel exclaimed to Dawit in the arcade in front of the room Balian had turned into a hall, as he traded an empty pitcher for a full one from his fellow squire. "But he's beautiful!"

"He rides very well," Dawit agreed.

"You have to see him up close!" Daniel urged.

"Do you think they will ever have enough to drink?" Dawit retorted skeptically, peering through the door at the overcrowded room.

"And that's only half of them," Daniel answered in amazement. "More than two hundred knights with the Baron of Oultrajordain were sent to the Bishop's palace."

"I didn't know there were so many knights in the whole Kingdom!" Dawit admitted, letting his eyes linger on the men in chain mail and long swords choking the little improvised hall. All his life he had seen knights only in ones or twos—until the Hospitallers mustered all ten of their knights at one time three days ago. Now there appeared to be hundreds of them here.

He would have been surprised to learn that his lord was nearly as amazed as he was. Not that Balian had not seen so many knights assembled, but he had never thought to see them here—and even less to have his sovereign at his table at a time like this. For even as King Baldwin beamed down from the high table at his assembled knights, Balian knew that Salah ad-Din's campfires were visible from the Gaza Gate—as numerous as the night stars.

King Baldwin was radiant. He sat in the central chair, his gloved hands resting on the arms, and he could not wipe the smile off his face. "We made it, Balian," he insisted triumphantly. "Nobody thought we would. Aimery tried to talk me out of it."

"And well he should have, your grace."

"We cannot afford to lose Ascalon," Baldwin countered. "You did not really think I would leave you in the lurch, did you?"

"Your grace, I did not doubt you would send me aid," Balian reasoned, "and I'm grateful for every man in the room—save you."

"Ha! You mean I should have sent Lusignan at the head of my relief force—or sent my uncle of Edessa and Prince Reynald without me?"

"I do, your grace." It wasn't just that Baldwin's illness rendered him incapable of fighting; it was the fact that the succession was again endangered. The Marquis of Montferrat, who had married Princess Sibylla a year ago, had died of a sudden fever in June. While he lived, Montferrat had ensured that at Baldwin's death the Kingdom would be left in the hands of a man both battle-hardened and well-connected, but Montferrat's death meant that—until they found a new husband for Sibylla—the Kingdom would be without a king should Baldwin be killed. It did not help that Sibylla was pregnant, and any new husband would have to recognize another man's son as his heir.

"Well, my lord," the King told Balian pointedly, "you share that opinion with practically everyone else in Jerusalem, including my mother—but I am no longer a child who can be told, 'No, you cannot do that' or 'Don't touch, that is for adults only.'" Ice had crept into Baldwin's voice, and although he was smiling, he was no longer jubilant. "I have been told far too long what I can*not* do. Now take note of what I *can* do!"

Balian bowed his head to his young king in submission, and then poured for him and held the silver goblet to his lips so he could drink, tipping the cup very carefully as Baldwin sipped. When the King pulled back his head, shaking his head to signal he had had enough, their eyes met. "How many knights did you bring, your grace?" Balian asked him in a low voice.

King Baldwin answered proudly: "Three hundred and sixty-seven!"

Balian's estimate had not been far off this, but it still amazed him to hear the number confirmed. With Tripoli and Antioch engaged in their own campaign against Hama, Jerusalem could call on no troops from those states and was dependent on its own resources. "What did you do? Call on every knight physically present in the city?"

"Exactly," Baldwin agreed. "Sir Walter made it clear that we didn't have time to muster the feudal levies. The only way I could get here before the Saracen siege army closed around you was to take every mounted knight available in Jerusalem—except Aimery, of course, whom I left in command there. I called up every able-bodied knight in Jerusalem, *and they came*!" Even Oultrejourdain! He sounded a little surprised at that, and Balian caught a glimpse of his inner uncertainty—which also explained his elation. Baldwin had issued a command he hadn't really believed would be followed. It surprised and excited him to find that he did indeed command the forces of the Kingdom, despite his handicap.

Balian took his own goblet and raised it to his King. "You have the heart of a lion, your grace—and, I hope, Godfrey de Bouillon's ring to bring us luck."

"I've done better than that, Balian. Didn't you recognize Albert, Bishop of Bethlehem, beneath all his armor? He is carrying a piece of the True Cross in a gold reliquary beneath his gambeson."

Balian looked over, startled, toward the "knight" Baldwin had indicated. He had not recognized the Bishop of Bethlehem, but now that he looked he realized that the man was indeed tonsured, and like all clerics that took to the battlefield, he carried a mace rather than a sword to avoid "shedding blood."

"I am grateful for the Bishop's aid," Balian told his King, and he smiled as he spoke—but it did not escape Baldwin that his eyes were still deep wells of worry.

By midday the city was completely invested by the enemy. They kept out of range of the garrison's crossbows, but they swarmed through the orchards and trampled the vegetable gardens under. The tents of the emirs billowed up brightly, and the howling of the muezzin provoked the garrison into jeers and shouts, until the church bells took up a wild clanging to drown out the Muslim call to prayers.

With the King, Edessa, and Reynald de Châtillon, Baron of Oultrejourdain, the only baron who happened to be in Jerusalem when the King put out his call to arms, Balian walked the walls of the city, taking the measure of the enemy. They counted roughly 120 tents, which put the enemy strength very near the thirty thousand Balian had first estimated. They eventually identified a tent that they thought might belong to the Sultan Salah ad-Din, but it was quite far back, behind many others, and they could not be completely sure. Nor could they make out any siege engines. Still, the Saracen army was clearly digging in and preparing to besiege Ascalon. They dug ditches to protect their own positions from sorties, and also as latrines, draining into the sea to both the north and south.

From what the garrison could see, the vast majority of the troops were black, which meant they were Salah ad-Din's Egyptian infantry. The cavalry, in contrast, were Turkomen or Kurds, Edessa confirmed, and included what looked like one thousand Mamlukes in the bright yellow tunics and turbans of Salah ad-Din's personal bodyguard. The cavalry bivouacked to the north of the city and turned their horses out to pasture on the now-fallow fields along the road to Jaffa.

At the council of war held that afternoon, there was considerable discussion of a sortie. Having pulled nearly four hundred knights together, it seemed a shame to waste them in a purely defensive battle, Oultrejourdain argued persuasively. Four hundred heavy horse packed an almost invincible punch and would undoubtedly cause havoc in the enemy camp—until they got bogged down and surrounded by the sheer weight of numbers. If Salah ad-Din's tent had been closer, it would have been tempting to try to kill or capture the Sultan himself, Oultrejourdain proposed.

But despite the King's patent eagerness to show his mettle, he did not let himself get talked into anything foolish. The sortie idea was put on hold until a clear objective—such as siege engines being brought to bear or sappers being deployed—was at hand. So the defenders of Ascalon went to bed that night uneasy, but not unduly alarmed. Father Laurence had assured them they had enough food for six months, and water was plentiful from four deep wells that tapped into the ground water below sea level. Furthermore, it was the start of the rainy season, of which they were reminded by the rain that set in just before dusk.

The following morning, however, the garrison had the first inkling that something was amiss in the enemy camp. One of the night watchmen complained to Roger Shoreham that the enemy had been "too loud." Another watchman, in contrast, reported smugly that the muezzin "had learned to pipe down a bit"—and that set off Roger's alarm bells. He was damned sure the muezzin of a Saracen army would not "quiet down" just because they stood opposite a Christian city, and he started to suspect the enemy had split their forces. The morning rain had closed down visibility, however, and all he could do was squint fractiously into the drenching rain and try to determine if there were as many tents out there as there had been the day before. All he got was soggier and soggier. It was nearly noon before the rain let up enough for him to see what he needed to report to the Constable.

The rain had kept the knights and squires indoors. Roger, his soft leather ankle books soaked through, squelched his way across the hall, weaving between the clusters of men playing dice, polishing their weapons, or just talking. They cast him irritated glances as he dripped on them, but they recognized a man with a purpose and let him through.

Roger found Balian with the King and several other lords at the high table. Balian and the King were playing chess, with the King verbally identifying which piece to move where, and Balian moving the pieces for both of them. It was apparently a close game, because the others at the table appeared to be watching intently, and Daniel and Dawit hovered behind the players with pitchers ready to refill the goblets on the table.

"Your grace!" Roger bowed stiffly to his young King.

King Baldwin looked over, surprised, but it was Balian who answered. "What is it, Master Shoreham?"

"My lord, your grace," he bowed again to the King, obviously discomfited by the presence of royalty. "The Saracen cavalry is gone."

"What?" The King sat up straighter, instantly alert.

"All the horses, they're gone, and—as best I can see—so is Salah ad-Din's tent and maybe half the army."

King Baldwin sprang to his feet, attracting the attention of the other men in the hall. "Are you sure?"

"No, I'm not sure," Roger admitted honestly, but Balian stepped in. "Sergeant Shoreham would not have come to us on a whim, your grace."

Baldwin looked at Balian, but his expression suggested he still did not want to believe it. Turning sharply to one of the knights who had been following their game, he ordered, "Sir Tancred! Go with this man and see what he is talking about!"

"I'll go myself," Balian offered, but Sir Tancred was not so easily put off. Together they went with Roger to look out from the Jaffa Gate and then walked back along the landward side of the wall, trying to measure the depth of the ranks facing them, before reporting back to the King.

"My guess is that Salah ad-Din has left no more than a third of his army here, your grace," Sir Tancred reported and Balian concurred, adding, "That's still about ten thousand men, but no cavalry."

"He's making for Jerusalem, Baldwin," Edessa declared in alarm. "I warned you this could happen if you denuded Jerusalem of defenses!"

Balian heard the echoes of what must have been a stormy argument before the King's departure for Ascalon. Meanwhile, more and more knights were crowding around the high table, trying to hear what was happening. Some of the bolder men called out, demanding to know what was going on.

Balian and Tancred told them what they had seen, and soon the discussion was swirling around the hall. Men started to argue with one another, while others went out to see for themselves. In the midst of it all, Baldwin sat as if lamed, unmoving and silent, while Edessa harangued him with increasing virulence, until Balian felt compelled to intervene with a sharp, "That's enough, my lord!"

"Well enough for you to say!" Edessa flung back at him, jealously. "For *your* sake, the King left Jerusalem defenseless!"

"Hardly!" Balian countered. "There's a garrison there, too, and many able-bodied pilgrims capable of bearing arms. Furthermore, the Marshal of Jerusalem can call up the rest of the feudal levies—"

"Which will now be short more than 350 knights!"

"What good is Ascalon if Jerusalem falls?" another knight took up the complaint.

"You have thrown away your crown, your grace! For a foolish display of bravado, you have exposed the Holy Sepulchre to ravishment by the Saracen!"

"Christ's teeth! Hold your tongue, fool!" Reynald de Châtillon bellowed even before Balian could come to the King's defense. "We still have plenty of options."

Edessa cut off Oultrejourdain in a voice tinged with rising panic. "Christendom depends on *us* to defend Jerusalem—and we're trapped here in Ascalon like so many rabbits in a hutch!"

"Why?" The question came from the King, who lifted his head and spoke with ringing clarity.

The men around him were stunned into silence, and the silence spread as others sensed the tension at the high table.

"Why are we trapped? Did we not discuss a sortie just yesterday? What goal could be more appropriate than Jerusalem itself?"

"There are ten thousand men drawn up around this city, your grace! You can't just ride out of here!" Edessa dismissed the suggestion.

"Armed and with couched lances, we *can* ride out of here," the King insisted, earning a "Damned right!" from Oultrejourdain.

"To your death, your grace! Even if we could cut through the siege force, the rest of Salah ad-Din's army now lies between us and Jerusalem."

"But they won't expect us to attack them from the rear," the King countered, again earning a growl of support from Oultrejourdain.

But that brought more than one snort and even a laugh from the men in the hall—all of whom, however, now attentively watched their King.

"Even with surprise—and God—on our side, we can't attack twenty thousand men with 370." Edessa argued back

"The Templars have three hundred knights and that many sergeants again at Gaza," Baldwin answered.

Men glanced at one another and shifted uneasily. A thousand knights against twenty thousand might sound ridiculous, but these were fighting men—men who preferred the prospect of a battle to being trapped and helpless. Furthermore, the bulk of those twenty thousand enemy were foot soldiers, and the knights could dismiss them with impunity. Salah ad-Din had between eight and nine thousand cavalry with him—which meant that, with the Templars, the odds were at worst ten to one. Not good, but if the alternative was to risk the loss of Jerusalem, it was worth considering.

"And how do you propose to get word to the Templars that you expect them to sortie? How can you tell them where and when to join forces with us?" Edessa asked into the stillness.

Baldwin looked up at his uncle and declared with great dignity, "We will find a volunteer willing to cross the enemy lines." Then, before anyone could protest, he turned to Balian and added, "My lord, would you be so kind as to bring me to your chapel? I wish to pray."

This ignited a new wave of agitated debate across the hall, but

Balian led the King out the back exit and up a narrow spiral stairway to his chamber on the floor above. As he started to lead out of the chamber, Baldwin stopped him. "I don't need a chapel, Balian—just to speak to you alone."

Balian waited.

"Tell me the truth: is a sortie madness?"

"Not if we can coordinate it with the Templars." Balian hesitated, then asked with trepidation, "Do you want me try to reach them?"

"No! Of course not! I was thinking of Abdul."

"Your groom?"

"Yes. He can pass among the enemy without arousing any suspicion. He is one of them."

Balian did not answer.

"You are not enthusiastic," Baldwin noted with a twisted smile of disappointment.

"Your grace—"

"Don't call me that in private, Balian. I want your advice as my friend."

"As I said below in the hall, there are other feudal levies, a large garrison, and many armed pilgrims that still stand between Salah ad-Din and Jerusalem. Although the Hospitallers are engaged with Philip of Flanders, the Templars can be expected to reinforce Jerusalem from the castles within a fifty-mile radius, or even more. There is no reason to assume that Salah ad-Din will be successful in taking Jerusalem before word can be sent to Flanders, Tripoli, and Antioch to break off their assault on Hama and come to Jerusalem's relief."

"I do not *assume* that Salah ad-Din will capture Jerusalem, but I do not intend to just stay here and watch while my capital—my Kingdom—is threatened, either. I *will* sortie out of here, Balian, and I *will* send word to the Templars ordering them to rendezvous with us at a set place and time. It is only a question of whom to send. Do you have a better suggestion than Abdul?"

Balian wished he did, because he did not trust slaves—or not ones like Abdul, who had been a fighting man before his capture. "Let us talk to him," he equivocated.

The King nodded, and let Balian lead him down to the ground floor again and across the back courtyard. Neither man found anything odd about going to the stables together, because they had done it so often before, but members of Balian's household nearly jumped out of their skins to find the King among them. At the stables the King called out: "Abdul! Come here! I want to speak to you!"

A moment later the slave emerged out of the shadows and bowed deeply. "Abdul," the King started without preamble. "We are trapped here in Ascalon, while the Sultan Salah ad-Din has taken the bulk of his army onward to attack Jerusalem."

Abdul bowed deeply again.

"I wish to give you a message to carry through the Sultan's army to the Knights Templar at Gaza. Would you do that for me?"

"You are my master; you can command me as you wish."

"If you do this for me, Abdul, I will set you free—but only on your return."

"If I do not return, master, I will also be free," Abdul replied, and Baldwin caught his breath, but Balian thanked God for the slave's honesty. It would have been so much easier for him to swear anything, and then take the King's message straight to the enemy.

"I will go, my lord," Mathewos declared, coming out of the shadows.

The King started and asked sharply, "Who are you?"

"He is my marshal—and a Christian," Balian answered for him, adding, "He can be trusted, *and* the Templars are more likely to believe him—but are you sure you can get through the enemy lines, Mathewos?"

"Only God can know if I will be successful, my lord, but I am all but invisible in the night, and I speak the kind of Arabic they expect of a slave. Most of the men out there are Nubians, while the officers are Arabs. The Arabs look down on their own troops, and will take no note of me because to them I am like their men—worthless."

"If you are successful, you will know a king's gratitude," Baldwin promised warmly. "Balian, find me a scribe that I may write my message."

As Constable of Ascalon, Balian had not expected to take part in the sortie. The King had other ideas. "You are my knight," he reminded Balian simply. "You pledged yourself to me first, before all the barons of the realm. You fought for me at Homs. If I am to ride out of Ascalon to face an army at least twenty times as large as ours, then I want you to bear my lance—since I cannot bear it myself."

There is no way to say "no" to such an appeal. Balian bowed his head and went to inform Daniel and Dawit to prepare his armor and Gladiator. The youths were in a state of such excessive excitement that Dawit was making Gladiator nervous and Daniel kept dropping things. Daniel could not take the suspense very long and blurted out, "Which of us are you taking with you?"

"Neither of you," Balian shattered their hopes. "The King has four body squires, and one of them will look after me." He was confident of this because the squires were nominal in any case; their fear of contagion kept them from actually helping Baldwin bathe or dress, services still performed by the loyal Ibrahim.

Balian paused in his own thoughts to note that he considered Ibrahim loyal, despite being a slave and a Muslim, but he would not have entrusted even him with a message to the Templars. Some kinds of temptation are simply too great.

Now as night fell, the knights from Jerusalem, and Balian with them, attended Mass at St. Paul's Cathedral, while their squires groomed and tacked the horses. From beyond the walls the muezzin called the Faithful to prayer, competing with the bells of Vespers, and the watch chased people into their homes to clear the streets—while the garrison pretended to watch the enemy, while instead watching the activities in the streets behind them.

They went from Mass to a stand-up evening meal, washed down with large quantities of watered wine. Then, under orders to maintain silence, they started to mount up. Roger Shoreham paced along beside Balian, taking his final instructions. "Do not—I repeat—*do not* open the gates to let anyone back in. If we don't break out and are forced back to the walls of Ascalon, it is God's will, and we will die there."

"Yes, sir," Roger answered smartly, but they both knew he was lying. He would, when the time came, make his own call about the risks involved.

Balian grabbed his shoulder. "I promise we will do our best not to test your resolve."

Balian turned, gathered up the chain reins clothed in leather, and put his toe in the triangular stirrup. He pulled himself up into the saddle, took a lance from Daniel, and then guided Gladiator through the press of milling knights to the King's side.

Unable to couch a lance, Baldwin agreed that he would not lead the sortie, but rather ride in the very center, surrounded by his knights. It had also been agreed that they would issue forth from the Gaza Gate—the one where the besiegers would least expect it. The idea was to open the gate as quietly as possible and slip out two at time, the knights leading and the squires bringing up the rear. It would take roughly twenty-five minutes for the knights and their squires to slip out at this rate, and no one really expected that they would all make it out before the enemy discovered what was happening and took counter-measures. The plan, therefore, was to fling the gate wide open and allow any remaining knights and squires to ride out as rapidly as possible as soon as the enemy sounded the alarm. Meanwhile the leading knights would form up just beyond the bridge over the surrounding dry ditch. When the last squire of the sortie party was out of Ascalon, the gate would slam shut and the barbican bell would ring, signaling the leading knights to put spurs to their horses and charge.

Success depended on a series of factors: not being seen until enough knights had managed to slip out of the gate to defend the bridgehead beyond the dry moat; maintaining close formation when they started their charge; the absence of walls, ditches, or other barricades to break their charge once they started; and then being able to outrun their pursuers far enough to circle around again to the north and head for the place designated for the rendezvous with the Templars.

Of course, they did not know if the Templars had received their message—or if they would obey the King's orders. Mathewos might have been captured or killed by the Saracens. Or he might have made it through enemy lines only to fall victim to some other form of accident. He might have reached the Templar Castle at Gaza, yet failed to convince the Templars he was not a spy. Or, the worst but most likely scenario, in Balian's opinion: the Templars might read the King's message, but only shrug and choose to pursue a different strategy. The Templars were not vassals of the Kings of Jerusalem, and they had far too often underlined this fact by pursuing independent policies in the past. For all Balian knew, the Templars had intentionally let Salah ad-Din pass by Gaza, or even made a separate truce that entailed a promise not to attack.

A nervous rustle went through the ranks of horsemen as the gate creaked open. Horses fretted, throwing up their heads, sidling, or backing, kicking and lashing out with their teeth because the nervousness of their riders unsettled them. Like water through a narrow sluice, the mass of horseflesh slowly began to ooze forward at the front, but clogged outside the barbican. Still, no one spoke, and they all wore their helmets with nosepieces or full visors covering their faces.

Balian, at the King's side, was almost to the entrance of the barbican, and there was still no indication that the enemy had spotted the open gate. Poor watch, he noted mentally as he and the King entered the darkened barbican, the sound of scores of hooves echoing overhead. Ahead of them a horse whinnied, and then someone cursed.

As they emerged from the barbican, the night was alive with shouting and waving torches. "Form up! Form up!" Reynald de Châtillon shouted; he commanded the van and was on the far side of the dry ditch. Since the alarm had been raised, there was no longer any reason to maintain silence.

The men around Balian and the King started trotting and then cantering, hurrying to cross the bridge and get on firm land before the enemy could launch an attack. Balian was relieved when the hollow clunking of wood beneath his horse's hooves gave way to the higher-pitched chinking of iron horseshoes on packed sand. The horses, pressed together as more and more riders followed them off the bridge, were getting more agitated than ever, and some started to rear up as they tried to break free but were held back.

A shouted warning was followed by the distinctive sound of arrows burying themselves in shields. The King, of course, could no more carry a shield than he could a lance, but Sir Tancred was on his left and charged with his protection. Balian could only pray that no arrow would find its way through the surrounding wall of men.

A moment later, the barbican bell started ringing wildly—almost joyously. The last of the sortie party was out of Ascalon; the gates closed again. Oultrejourdain shouted, "Jerusalem!" and the horses at the front of the pack sprang forward. The riders immediately behind were caught a little by surprise, but soon put spurs to their horses and started forward. Balian, with the King beside him, had no need of spurs. The herd instinct of the horses had taken over, and their mounts started charging with the rest.

Balian focused on keeping beside the King, checking Gladiator just enough not to outdistance the less powerful Misty. He heard shouting around them, and the thudding of arrows still accompanied them, but mostly he was aware of the night being increasingly lit up. The Saracens were lighting fires to enable them to shoot better or to try to frighten the horses—or both—but the King's conroi of heavy armor was increasing in speed and had become all but unstoppable—unless there were spiked ditches ahead of them.

Balian heard the sounds of fighting—the shouts of men engaging, the unmistakable and familiar sound of a lance shattering, the clang of metal on wood. But these noises were on the periphery. In the center of the charge, the dominant sound was the thundering of hooves, the chink of armor, the panting of men and horses. Within minutes the sky was darkening again as the shouting started to recede. Men began to sit back and slow down their chargers. Balian reined in Gladiator to a controlled canter and then let him fall into a trot, as the King likewise sat back, and Misty dropped his head and snorted as if to say: that's enough.

A moment later, the knights ahead parted to let Reynald de Châtillon through. He rode straight to the King, who stopped to wait for him. "Your grace, we are clear of the city. The road ahead is free."

"Then let us make for the rendezvous with the Templars," Baldwin answered, and he sent Misty cantering forward to take his place at the head of his knights.

They reached the rendezvous before dawn, and most men dismounted, stretched out, and tried to catch some sleep, while the squires watered the horses from the well, one creaking bucket at a time. Balian dismounted to give Gladiator some rest, but found it impossible to sleep on the wet ground. Instead he stayed beside Baldwin, who sat staring at the road leading southeast: the road the Templars would take to join them.

Ibrahim was hovering nearby, and once he whispered to Balian, "My master needs his bandages changed and his feet cleaned. It is not good for him to go so long without washing his feet and hands or putting on fresh bandages."

Balian shook his head. "This once, he must." Balian did not want the King's increasingly discolored hands and arms exposed to the knights around him; he feared the sight would dishearten them. Better they saw him only in his beautiful leather gloves and gleaming chain mail.

The sound of Balian and Ibrahim speaking together pierced Baldwin's consciousness, and he spoke in a low voice into the murky grey of dawn: "My sister is due any day now, and the Count of Flanders wants to impose his own candidate as her next husband."

Balian was not surprised. The Count of Flanders had come out to Outremer with several hundred knights and the blessings of the Kings of France and England. When he discovered that the Marquis de Montferrat had died unexpectedly, he immediately started scheming to put someone "suitable" into Princess Sibylla's bed—and onto the throne of Jerusalem. "What does Princess Sibylla say?" Balian asked cautiously.

Baldwin shrugged eloquently, adding, "She does not like Flanders."

That did not surprise Balian. Although he had not met the Count, Zoë had described him as prim, finicky, self-important, and scheming. She claimed he had refused to lead the combined armies of the Kingdom of Jerusalem, the Greek Empire, and his own substantial force of crusaders into Egypt unless he would be made King of Egypt. The Greek Emperor and the King of Jerusalem, however, naturally felt that since they were providing the bulk of the troops and supplies, they, not Flanders, should gain from any new territories conquered in the course of the campaign.

"He's not very good-looking," Baldwin noted, reminding Balian that Sibylla was a very different woman from Zoë—and her reasons for disliking the Count equally different. "And he does not have much respect for me or my Kingdom," Baldwin added, with a depth of dejection that made Balian stiffen with protectiveness. How dare a Count of Flanders look down on a King of Jerusalem?

"The Templars don't have much respect for the Kings of Jerusalem, either," Baldwin continued, in a voice laden with discouragement. "They murdered men to whom my father had given a safe conduct."

"And they have vowed *on the surety of their souls* to defend the Holy Land and all Christians," Balian countered, alarmed by the King's despondency and his doubts about the Templars—particularly since they echoed his own.

An eloquent snort of disgust came from Reynald de Châtillon.

"If they do not come," the King announced, taking a deep breath and pulling himself upright, "we will follow Salah ad-Din's army anyway."

No one contradicted him. They were committed now. There was no going back.

Balian's eyes were falling shut, and he started walking to keep himself awake. He paced around their makeshift camp once, twice.... As the sky lightened, the horizon became a smudge of gray to the north and west. That seemed odd, his tired brain thought, and then he shook himself awake. That was smoke!

"Your grace!" he turned and called over his shoulder, but Baldwin could spare him no attention. The King was standing and looking toward something in the east, shading his eyes against the sun that had come over the horizon like a blazing chariot. Balian followed his gaze and thought he saw it, too, but he wasn't sure. Motion? Dust? The glint of sun on chain mail?

"The Templars!" the King decided, with so much relief in his voice that it made the men around him smile, weary as they were.

The men who had been lying down stirred, dragged themselves to their feet, and shaded their own eyes. After another moment, other men started to nod and grunt agreement. Something was definitely coming toward them on the road, but it was too soon to be sure it was the Templars.

Balian went to stand beside Baldwin and remarked softly, "It will be easy to follow Salah ad-Din's army."

Baldwin looked over at him. "What do you mean?"

"It's burning its way north—and not straight for Jerusalem, either."

Baldwin absorbed the intelligence calmly, but his face tightened as if he were in pain. After a moment he remarked: "Then it will be slower than we are."

"It *is* the Templars, by God's balls." Reynald de Châtillon declared, as if he had not really believed it until this moment.

Balian looked back down the road, and it was now clear: the approaching horsemen were wearing plain white or black surcoats, and the banners fluttering from the raised lances of the bannerets were likewise devoid of color. No Saracen force would have been this sober.

The King gave the order for his knights to mount up, and Balian collected Gladiator from the field where he was grazing hobbled. He untied the hobble, tightened the girth again, and mounted. By the time he returned to the King, it was possible to see that a lone rider was out of formation: Mathewos was riding with the Templars, Balian noted, surprised how glad he was to have the Ethiopian with him again.

Meanwhile the bearded faces of the leading Templar knights were recognizable, and Reynald de Châtillon declared, "God's nails, your grace, that's Odo de St. Amand himself, the Grand Master. He must have taken reinforcements to Gaza."

Balian's encounters with the Grand Master up to now had been brief and not particularly cordial. The Grand Master of the Knights Templar did not think the younger son of a local baron, much less the riding instructor of a leper prince, was a personage of note. St. Amand had always treated Balian as an object, rarely meeting his eyes when they spoke, and dismissing him as he would any other lesser being. But even Balian had to give the Grand Master credit for the immaculate turnout and perfect discipline of the troops he brought to the rendezvous. They trotted forward, four abreast, in perfect blocks of twenty, blocks of knights alternating with blocks of sergeants. Their formation made it easy to count: the Templars had brought two hundred twenty knights and three hundred eighty sergeants, a total of exactly six hundred mounted fighting men. The King now had a force of almost one thousand heavy horse—and, counting the squires, nearly fifteen hundred mounted men-at-arms. Balian felt considerably better about their prospects of survival.

Chapter 10

Ibelin, November 24, 1177

CONTRARY TO EXPECTATIONS, AS BALIAN HAD foretold, Salah ad-Din had not made straight for Jerusalem. Instead his army had continued north, ravaging a wide swath of land as it advanced. By nightfall it was clear that Ibelin was burning. Balian had no idea where his brother was, but he presumed he was at Ramla, so he asked Baldwin for permission to take some knights to relieve his birthplace. Over the objections of St. Amand and Edessa, who argued that Jerusalem's forces were too small to split up, the King detailed fifty knights with their squires to go with Balian and see what they could do.

Halfway there, a short rain shower doused the fires ahead and soaked the relief force to the bone. The rain made the road slippery, and the horses were tired after thirty-six hours without proper feed or rest. Gladiator hung his head and snorted repeatedly to indicate he thought he was being abused.

When they reached the town, the smoldering fires indicated it had been overrun by Saracen troops. This was hardly surprising, since the town was not fortified, only enclosed by low earthworks about ten feet high. These could easily be scaled, since they were not crenelated or supported by flanking towers. It was clear that the enemy had forced the eastern gate, which hung on its hinges, half shattered; beyond this, the eastern portions of the town were smoldering ruins. Deeper into the town, however, the rain had come soon enough for the buildings to remain standing, and from the sounds coming from the city it was evident the Saracens were plundering the houses, dragging furnishings and bedclothes out into the streets, chasing chickens, and smashing barrels, casks, and chests open.

There was no evidence of armed resistance at this point, nor any screams of terror, but Balian could not know if this was because all the inhabitants had already been subdued, or because they had managed to take refuge in the castle.

The castle occupied the northwest corner of the town and had been built on a slight rise that elevated it above the town, which lay on the flat plain at its feet. North and west of the castle the dunes stretched as far as the eye could see except on a very clear day, but east and south of the town lay a fertile valley fed by underground springs. This valley had been turned into a garden by the settlers brought in by Balian's father, and so the town lay surrounded by olive, pomegranate, and citrus orchards that gradually gave way to vineyards and then wheat fields, now laying fallow.

Lacking a natural escarpment on which to locate the castle, the builders had followed a simple, functional design: a dry ditch surrounded a quadrangle with four corner towers and a main gate facing south, reinforced by a barbican. A drawbridge led across the dry ditch to an outer gatehouse that protected the drawbridge landing, while within the outer wall a square keep loomed up fifteen feet higher than the walls themselves. To Balian's relief, the keep was still flying the banners of Ibelin. Furthermore, the tall, square bell tower of the basilica of St. George, beside the main market square, was still crowned by a cross. Either the Saracens hadn't taken the time to tear it down yet or, just possibly, its solid stone exterior and heavy wooden doors were still sheltering those townspeople who had not made it to the castle.

Balian hardly had to give the order. Around him the knights were reaching down to tighten their girths, pulling their helmets over their soggy arming caps, and signaling for their squires to bring up their lances. They had been following Salah ad-Din's army for nearly twenty-four hours, and they might be tired, wet, and hungry, but here at last was a chance to hit the enemy—and hit him at almost no risk to themselves. Even the squires were tightening their girths and donning their helmets.

Balian pulled out ahead of the others and waited until the knights stopped fidgeting with their equipment. When they sat still and attentive, he turned back toward Ibelin and urged Gladiator to a weary jog. When they were roughly five hundred yards from the shattered eastern gate, he took up a slow, comfortable canter. Behind him the others followed, their horses reviving in the pleasure of the run.

While Balian rode straight for the shattered eastern gate, some of the knights and squires peeled off and rode along the southern wall of the town, making for the south gate. Balian rode through the eastern gate, past buildings little more than charred skeletons with macabre twisted forms inside that might or might not be corpses, past the basilica of St. George, standing like a rock amid the wreckage strewn around it, and then on to the intact part of the city without raising a shout.

The surprise was absolute. One moment the Saracen troops were happily squabbling over the spoils, flinging wine down their throats, and stuffing their tunics with stolen goods—and the next instant, straight out of the smoldering and smoking ruins of the eastern town, massive horses bearing armed men rode them down. Before they could run, lances skewered them. The knights killed with such devastating ease that many lances could be reused twice or even three times. When their lances eventually broke, the Frankish knights drew their swords and kept riding, slashing downwards: right, left, and right again.

When the Saracens tried to run out the southern gate, they were met by more mounted Franks with leveled lances. When they tried to seek refuge in the narrow alleys between the houses, thinking the knights would have no room to swing their swords, the Franks' horses trampled them down with malicious intent. When they tried to hide inside the houses they had plundered, they discovered that the squires had dismounted and were ready to hack them to pieces as they cowered on the beds where—so short a time ago—they had taken delight in raping the girls they found. If any of them escaped, it was by slipping silently out of the still-open gates and hiding in the surrounding orchards until there were no more mounted men scouring the town for prey.

Balian left the mopping-up to the others and returned to the basilica of St. George. He jumped down and hammered on the door with his mailed fist, shouting: "This is Balian d'Ibelin. The town is cleared of Saracens."

He was greeted by a loud, inarticulate murmur and then the sound of heavy objects being dragged away from the doors. At last the doors swung open and a priest fell on his knees in front of him. "Christ has heard our prayers! Truly, my lord, you are sent from Heaven!" The priest was staring up at him as if he were an angel.

Embarrassed, Balian pulled him to his feet, shocked by how much the parish priest had aged since the last time he had seen him. The priest, who he remembered being a vigorous forty-something, had gone completely white. Balian could not know that it had happened in the last few hours. "We saw the fires, Father Vitus," he explained simply as the priest embraced him, terror still shaking the older man's bones. Balian tried to calm him with the firmness of his own clasp. "You're safe now," he assured the priest, who had taught him his catechism as a child.

From the interior of the church, townspeople were spilling out into the cool, damp air of the pre-dawn day. The terror of the last hours was still naked on their faces, and one after another they tried to kiss Balian's hands—or if they could not reach them, the hem of his surcoat. Yet even as they thanked him for their rescue, the sight of the shambles of their town made many break out into tears or cries of lament.

Balian was disquieted by how many were here in the church, which at best offered only temporary refuge. The church had solid, sheer stone walls and only very narrow, high windows, but it held neither water nor food, and the Muslims were known for setting churches on fire and burning alive those trapped inside. Pulling gently but firmly away from the Syrian women who were still trying to kiss his hands, Balian directed the townspeople toward the castle. He remounted and guided Gladiator in the same direction, wondering again where his brother Barry was while his town burned. Hugh and his father, he thought, must be clawing at the roofs of their tombs trying to get out!

Although the Ibelin arms were flying from the keep and the drawbridge over the dry ditch was raised, Balian saw no evidence of defenders on the walls as he rode up to the outer gatehouse that protected the drawbridge landing. This gatehouse was a modest stone building with a flat crenelated roof. As Balian drew up in front of it, a head leaned over the parapet to call down to him, "Who goes?"

Balian recognized the voice of the old gatekeeper and looked up. "Arnulf?"

"Lord Balian? Can it be? Is it really you?"

"Yes, Arnulf, it's me."

"Christ be praised! Christ be praised!" The old man at once began waving a torch over his head, and within minutes his signal was answered by the creaking and clanking of the drawbridge being lowered from the barbican opposite. Meanwhile, Arnulf ran down the stairs and came out to grab Balian's stirrup—saying again, as he held the young knight's leg in his hands, "Christ be praised!"

"Are you alone in the gatehouse?" Balian asked.

"Of course," Arnulf answered. "We had to concentrate the men capable of fighting in the castle."

"Where's the garrison?" Balian answered.

"My lord Barisan called most of them to muster at Ramla, sir. He left only ten men here—and they are not the youngest."

Balian frowned. It was true that Ramla was even less defensible than Ibelin, but no castle could be held without an adequate garrison. Even the highest and sheerest walls could be scaled if there was no one on the ramparts pushing the ladders back, hurling missiles and boiling oil on the besiegers, and ready to meet the assailants with sword, ax, and mace if they made it the top.

"Who's commanding?" Balian asked next.

"Well, officially the Lady Richildis, of course—"

"Lady Richildis is here?" Balian couldn't fathom it. His brother had left his wife undefended? He knew Barry and Richildis had become increasingly estranged over the last several years, but it went beyond his comprehension that any nobleman would leave his lady defenseless.

"Yes, my lord—" The drawbridge banged into position, distracting both Balian and the gatekeeper.

Balian leaned down and clasped the old man's shoulder. "I've brought a hundred men and we've cleared the town of Saracens, but much of the town is in ruins. The people will need to take refuge here."

Arnulf nodded. "Of course, my lord. I'll let them in."

Balian refrained from pointing out that they should have been let in *before* the Saracens had destroyed their homes and shops—because whoever had made the decision to raise the drawbridge before the bulk of the townspeople had been given refuge, it was not Arnulf. Balian found it hard to believe that Richildis had given such an order, either....

Balian crossed the drawbridge and rode through the barbican into the ward of Ibelin castle. Here he was met by a crowd of men, many wearing linen aketons and the brimmed metal "kettle" hats of the infantry, although others wore only leather jerkins and were armed with nothing more than clubs and butcher's knives. They were cheering him and holding their weapons triumphantly in the air as if they had just won a great victory. He cast his gaze farther afield and realized that women and children were pouring out of the outbuildings abutting the outer walls to join in the cheering.

So many of the townsfolk had made it to the castle after all, he registered, but they appeared completely disorganized and leaderless. With this many men inside the castle, they should have been manning the walls. There were crossbows in the armory for just that purpose. If Roger Shoreham had been in command here, he thought, the walls would have been bristling with defenders discouraging any attack. Under the circumstances, it was a wonder that the Saracens had turned to plundering the town rather than taking the chance to seize the castle. Balian was ashamed to think that Barry had neglected Ibelin to this extent; clearly he had not even given orders to the townsmen about what to do in an emergency. If Hugh had been alive... The image of his dead brother trying to escape his grave again flitted through his head.

Someone recognized him despite the darkness and started chanting, "Ibelin! Ibelin! It's the young lord." A moment later the crowd pressed in so close that they blocked his way to the keep.

"The town is cleared of Saracens," he called out to calm them.

"Are the Saracens gone for good?" someone asked.

"God alone knows, but the King is pursuing them with a thousand heavy horse."

"Praise be to God!" "God bless him!" "God save Jerusalem!" they exclaimed in chorus. But then someone started shouting, "We were betrayed!" and others echoed him: "Aye, my lord! The Muslims opened the southern gate!"

Although the bulk of the population was composed of Christian settlers, the original village around which the town had grown had been a mixture of Muslims and Orthodox Christians. A mosque, near the southern gate, had been allowed to operate for as long as Balian could remember, and the relations between the townspeople had, at least in Hugh's time, been harmonious.

"If that is true, they will be punished," Balian promised. "Now let me through," he ordered, and the townsfolk parted so he could ride to the foot of the keep.

The entrance was twelve feet over his head, and could only be gained by an external staircase that led to a wooden footbridge in front of the door. This had been raised to cover the door, providing extra protection from arrows, while leaving a six-foot gap between the top of the stairs and the doorstep.

Balian dismounted, turning Gladiator's reins over to one of the men in the ward, and started up the stairs. Even before he reached the top, the footbridge dropped into place and a voice called out: "Christ in Heaven! Lord Balian! Where did you come from? I thought you were trapped in Ascalon, surrounded by ten thousand Saracen!" The speaker was Sir Giles, one of the ten knights that owed homage to the Baron d'Ibelin. He had served Balian's father as squire in his time, and must be nearly seventy years of age by now.

"I was. With the King we sortied out of Ascalon, joined forces with the Templars from Gaza, and are now following in the wake of Salah ad-Din's army and blocking the road to Jerusalem. Where is the garrison, and why weren't more townspeople given refuge in the castle?" Balian answered as he reached the top of the stairs.

"They took us by surprise, my lord. We didn't realize what was happening until they were already in the town—by the southern gate. The gate was either left open by mistake, or someone opened it to them. They cut the whole eastern half of the town off from the castle and we—we were lucky to get the drawbridge up before they swarmed across. I had to think of my lady."

Balian could hear panic in the old man's voice. He believed that if the walls had been adequately defended, the garrison, such as it was, could have provided covering fire to enable many more people to get inside. But he bit off his retort. There was no point in lecturing the old man. Sir Giles should never have been left in command of Ibelin's garrison. Period.

Balian changed the subject. "Our horses have been without feed or rest for two days. They need both. Go down and prepare to receive the rest of my men. We're a hundred strong." Without awaiting an answer, Balian ducked into the great chamber.

The cook and several of the household clerks were just inside the door, manning the footbridge, and they clapped him on the back, thanking and blessing him as he entered. But Balian's eyes were already searching the far side of the room, where the women of the household were gathered together in an agitated bevy. All the shutters had been closed and there were only a couple of torches, so Balian could not at once identify his sister-in-law. He called for her, "Richildis?"

"Balian? Is it really you?" She broke away from the other women and ran to him. "Thank God!" Richildis was in his arms. "And thank *you*! It's twice as far from Ascalon as Ramla!" Richildis was trembling in his embrace, just as Father Vitus had done, but then she gasped and drew back. "My God! Balian! Where are you wounded?" She stared in horror at his drenched surcoat and the smears of blood now down the front of her gown as well.

"None of it's mine," Balian assured her.

But the terror and tension broke out of his sister-in-law in a flood of tears. She wiped at her eyes irritably, but her body was racked with sobs. Balian pulled her back into his arms and held her firmly. "It's all right, Hilde. You're safe now."

"It was horrible!" She broke down completely. "We could hear the girls screaming for help, and there was nothing we could do! Screaming and screaming— And we didn't know when they would get to us, or if help was on the way—"

"Hush. It's all over." Balian rubbed her back with his hand as her waiting woman, Gudrun, came up beside her and joined Balian in cooing comfort. Gudrun had been middle-aged when Richildis married Barry, and she was now old enough to be a grandmother. Richildis had been more a daughter to her than a mistress.

Fortunately the old steward, whom Balian had known all his life, had also emerged out of the shadows, and it was to him that Balian now turned, his arm still around Richildis. "I have a hundred men with me, and we need rest and food—as do our horses. The horses first and foremost. Also, half the town is in ruins, and I've told the townspeople to come here."

"Of course," the steward answered, at once dispensing orders to the cook to prepare a meal for Balian's men, sending a page down to tell the grooms to look after the horses, and ordering the laundry women to set up an infirmary for the injured.

Gudrun leaned closer to Balian and whispered in his ear. "Forgive her, my lord. It's her fear for her daughter that has so distraught her. Let me see to her now, and you can come up later."

"Her daughter?" Balian asked as he let Gudrun gently pull Richildis out of his arms. "You can't mean Eschiva is here?"

Gudrun nodded, pointing to the ceiling. "Just up there."

As daylight broke over Ibelin, the townspeople who still had homes worked to remove the dead Saracens and scratch together their belongings. Those without homes took over the task of burying the enemy dead—after removing any valuables they found on the Saracen corpses, of course. The knights and squires of Balian's party, meanwhile, gathered in the castle for a meal that was still in the making. Their horses milled about in the ward, relieved of their saddles and bridles for the first time in thirty-six hours, while the overwhelmed castle grooms pitched hay out to them by the bale and left them to feed and water themselves. Most of the men had stretched out on the floor of the hall for some needed sleep, while waiting for Ibelin's cooks to produce something edible.

Balian, however, climbed the interior stairs from the great chamber to the second floor of the keep, where Richildis had taken refuge. At the sight of him, Richildis rose up from the chair before the fire, a strained expression on her weary face. "Balian, forgive me! Please! I know I behaved badly—"

"Hush. I'm not here to lecture you. Surely you know that? If anyone deserves a lecture, it is Barry!" he added, too tired to control his tongue. "How could he leave you—not to mention his only child and heir—without an adequate garrison?" Balian meant it as a rhetorical question—or at any rate, one his brother needed to answer.

Richildis reacted with the anguished admission, "We—we are estranged."

"What does that have to do with anything?" Balian snapped back. "You're still his wife, and Eschiva is his heir!" he insisted indignantly.

"And Barry wishes that both were not the case! Surely you know he wants to divorce me?" Richildis answered.

At this news, Balian felt all the weariness of the last sleepless days, the hours in the saddle, the clearing of the town, fall on his shoulders. With a sigh he sank down on the chest near the door. "What grounds can he possibly find for divorcing you? You have always been a faithful and devoted wife to him," he indicated she should sit down beside him on the chest.

"Barry hates being associated with losers, and my brother is bogged in a terrible lawsuit and likely to lose half his property," Richildis answered bitterly. "But mostly he says I can't give him sons. Though how I should, when he scorns my bed for harlots with pretty faces, I don't know!" She flung the last words out furiously. Balian winced at her bitterness, but was at a loss for words. After so many years together, Richildis knew his brother well, and what she said was true. Barry had complained more than once about being "sold cheap," hinting that—as Baron of Ramla, Mirabel, and Ibelin—he deserved a wife with better family connections than Richildis. As for pretty women—bold and blond as Barry was, he'd never had trouble seducing women. For as long as Balian could remember, he'd had his "affairs." Richildis had known about them, and she'd never complained before.

As if reading his thoughts, she added, "He brought her under my roof this time. Had her installed in the chamber next to his, and told me if I didn't like it, I could leave."

"I'm sorry," Balian told her sincerely, and would have put his arm over her shoulders in comfort, but he felt too filthy. "I could use a change of clothes," he observed out loud. "Are Hugh's clothes still in that chest over there, or have you given them away?"

"No, they're still there." Richildis jumped up at once, crossed the room, and flung open the heavy cover. As she started pulling out things that had lain there since his brother's funeral, Balian was given time to digest what he had just learned. Images of Barry "comforting" Princess Sibylla for the loss of Montferrat flashed through his mind. Surely Barry couldn't be that bold? He couldn't seriously imagine that the High Court would let Sibylla marry a local baron? Then again, a local baron with an understanding of warfare in Outremer might be preferable to the men Flanders was suggesting, none of whom had ever set foot in the Kingdom.

Balian stood and unbuckled his sword, while Gudrun came to help him out of his damp surcoat, his sand-filled chain mail, and then the stinking gambeson. When Balian had stripped naked, Gudrun sponged the worst of the mud, blood, and sweat off him with warm water from a cauldron over the fire, while Balian wondered silently if his brother would dare to aim so high. He decided he might. Barry had a high opinion of himself.

Absently Balian put on clean underclothes, while Gudrun shook most of the sand out of his chain mail and then helped him back into it. The longer he thought about it, the more convinced he became that this sudden desire to divorce Richildis had nothing to do with him fancying some serving wench with a pretty face; Barry was grasping for the Crown.

Gudrun announced she would get him something to eat and drink, leaving the Ibelins alone. Richildis brought Balian one of Hugh's surcoats with the arms of Ibelin on it. As she handed it to him, he could see her hands were still trembling. He caught one of them and held it fast, forcing her to look at him. Then he gently pulled her down on the chest beside him again and put his arm over her shoulders. "Barry may like a pretty face, but in the eyes of God you are his wife, and before his peers and his King you are his lady."

"No," she shook her head. "Things have changed in the last year—the last six months, particularly," she said, confirming his worst suspicions: this had all come to a head after the death of William de Montferrat. "He is determined to be rid of me. Maybe he even *wanted* the Saracens to kill us all!" Richildis insisted, tears breaking free and running down her face again.

Balian pulled her closer and kissed the top of her head, murmuring, "I'm sure that's not true. Try to calm yourself," he urged, and they sat in silence together as Richildis tried to absorb strength and peace from her brother-in-law.

Gudrun returned with refreshments, and Balian helped himself to these, ravenous. When he had satisfied his hunger, however, he resisted the temptation to lie down and rest. "I'm going to reorganize the defense under new command," he told Richildis. "Sir Giles is too old."

Richildis looked at him with eyes wide with alarm. "You mean it isn't over? They might be back?"

He drew a deep breath and admitted, "Hilde, until we bring them to bay, they will inflict as much damage as possible." He didn't dare tell her that even if they forced Salah ad-Din to give battle, they might be defeated. If the King were killed and the army destroyed, the entire Kingdom was at risk—because *then* even the return of the Count of Flanders with Tripoli and Antioch would not be enough to stop Salah ad-Din.

Montgisard, November 25, 1177

Balian and his raiding force rejoined the King's army just after noon, to discover that it had been swelled by thousands of infantry. The King had issued the "*arrière ban*"—the royal summons for every able-bodied man—and from towns and villages all across the lowland plain, they were streaming in with whatever arms they could lay their hands on. Even more important, the Barons of Blanchegarde, Hebron, and Ramla had brought up mounted reinforcements. Hebron reported that Salah ad-Din's forces had cut a swath of destruction through Hebron's territories and raided all the way to the outskirts of Bethlehem. Ramla, however, insisted that the main body of Salah ad-Din's army now lay due east of Ibelin. Given these conflicting reports, Templar patrols had been dispatched immediately to try to find out just where Salah ad-Din was.

Balian pulled his brother aside and asked him what he had been thinking when he left Ibelin—and his wife and daughter—virtually undefended. "I was thinking of the Kingdom!" Barry retorted sharply. "We need every knight we can get if we are to crush Salah ad-Din. If we don't, he will certainly crush us!"

Balian would have liked to point out that his brother need not have left knights to defend Ibelin—a well-organized citizen militia could do that—but before he could open his mouth, Barry continued, "Besides, it wasn't *my* idea for Richildis to withdraw to Ibelin. Did she say I'd sent her there? She's lying. She was the one who insisted on removing herself and Eschiva from Ramla! I told her Ibelin didn't have a strong garrison, but she was more concerned about not exposing Eschiva to my 'bad morals' than about her safety. Maybe this will have taught her a lesson."

"Eschiva is your daughter—not to mention your heir!" Balian pointed out, determined not to get into a discussion of who was to blame for Richildis being in Ibelin.

"At the moment, yes," came the icy answer.

"Ibelin is our heritage!" Balian found himself getting angry.

"Oh, is that why you're wearing the Ibelin arms?" Barry demanded. "Have you decided, like Henri, that you are owed a piece of *my* inheritance? That you are the rightful heir of Ibelin?"

"Don't be ridiculous. My surcoat was soaked, bloodied, and stinking. I changed into one of Hugh's just to get out of it. The question is: have *you* forgotten that the people of Ibelin are *your* responsibility? Their fathers left safe homes in France to settle here at our father's invitation! You owe them protection."

"That's what I'm giving them by being here!" Barry insisted, and turned his back on Balian.

Several hours later, one of the Templar reconnaissance patrols returned with word that they had tracked down Salah ad-Din. The Christian army was mustered and Odo de St. Amand declared pompously, "Salah ad-Din is just three miles away with most of his cavalry, but little of his infantry. His host is making itself comfortable in the valley of Tell Jezer."

Tell Jezer was a rugged valley with steep slopes and a usually dry riverbed. But the rains had started and there would be water flowing through that riverbed at this time of year, Balian noted, making it a good place to camp.

"They are watering their horses and appear to be preparing to make camp," Odo echoed his thoughts. "They also appear to have no inkling that we are so near at hand."

The knights and squires were drawn up in a large semicircle around the Grand Master and the King. Balian automatically glanced toward the sun behind him. It was still high in the sky, albeit past its zenith, and he thought it was early to be making camp. Then again, the Sultan might have realized his troops were widely dispersed and that it was wise to call a halt and collect them again—or perhaps they were just stopping to water their horses.

At all events, there were still a good four to five hours of daylight for the King's army to go on the attack. Or they could wait until the morrow and attack at dawn. There were clear advantages to that, too, as they would be more rested—but so would the enemy. If they were lucky and routed the Saracens, then a dawn attack would give them all day to pursue the enemy—but it would also mean they could be mercilessly pursued if they were overwhelmed by the superior numbers of their foe. Balian waited to see what the King would decide.

The King, like the rest of them, had been in the field for three days now. His surcoat was filthy. The bright white-and-gold arms of Jerusalem were smeared with reddish stains from dust soaked by showers and dried again. His chain mail had lost its gleam, and even his crown seemed dulled from exposure to the elements. But he sat straight and looked sharply at the Grand Master. "We do not want Salah ad-Din to slip away in the dark as he did once before. We will attack at once."

The secular knights, Balian included, greeted this announcement with a cheer and turned to get their horses. The Templars, however, disdained such a show of enthusiasm. Instead, Odo ordered his knights to kneel, and together they said the Lord's Prayer before turning to mount up in silence.

Mathewos brought Gladiator and held the off stirrup as Balian mounted. He passed up the last lance they had with them, and then stroked Gladiator's neck affectionately. "May the Lord be with you, my lord."

"And also with you, Mathewos. Were it not for your courage, we would not stand a chance."

"It was a privilege, my lord, to serve Christ in this way. Now, ride with St. George beside you!"

Balian had to canter a few hundred feet to catch up with the body of knights, who were advancing at a purposeful trot. As he caught up with the leaders he found his brother in a furious fight with Oultrejourdain over who had the right to lead the attack. Ramla was arguing that since the battle would be fought in his barony, it was his "right" to lead the vanguard. Oultrejourdain was countering with the argument that he was the senior baron present, calling himself a prince, although his title was empty now that his step-son ruled in Antioch. There was no telling how long or how bitterly they would have contested their points if the King had not intervened with the announcement that the Templars would lead the van. "My lords of Ramla and Oultrejourdain may share the glory of leading the main division." Then without giving either baron a chance to contradict him, he turned and singled out Balian, gesturing him forward with his head.

"On my right, Sir Balian; you are my lance. Sir Tancred is my shield." He nodded to the other knight, whom Balian had met briefly at Ascalon. Tancred was considerably broader, though shorter, than Balian, making him as good a shield as any. He nodded to Balian as the latter took up his position.

It took them almost an hour to reach the shallow valley west of Tell Jezer. Here the Templars halted and dismounted, and Baldwin cursed. "What are they doing? We're losing the light," he snapped irritably.

"We have to let the infantry catch up with us," Balian explained. Baldwin sighed audibly, and Balian knew the King's nerves were reaching the breaking point.

Finally the infantry came up, and the Templars, who had been waiting in disciplined silence beside their grazing horses, remounted and started to form up, preparing for the charge. The Templar knights and sergeants formed up in near-perfect lines, broken or bent only by the contours of the land, gullies and large rocks. Ramla, with the other barons—Edessa, Hebron, Blanchegarde, and Oultrejourdain—formed up directly behind the Templars in a larger and more colorful formation—but one that lacked the Templars' discipline and order, making it look ragged and unruly. Last of all came the King's division. It was the smallest of the mounted divisions, no more than two hundred fighting men, with no barons at all. The royal household knights formed up around the King while the squires were sent to the back.

Although the infantry was still straggling in, Balian was comforted by their presence. After the shock of the charge wore off and the knights were bogged down in hand-to-hand fighting, the risk was always greatest. That was when the enemy's superiority of numbers would tell most. They would be able to swarm around and kill the horses or drag the knights off their backs. The Christian infantry was their best hope of preventing that; they could come between the enemy and the knights' horses with their shields and swords.

The Templars advanced at a walk to the very top of the crest and then, amazingly, over it as well. "Why don't they charge?" Baldwin demanded furiously.

Balian didn't have a clue. Ahead of them, Barry could be heard cursing. Some of the other knights surged forward, but then were forced to draw up and follow the Templar example, until the center also slowly disappeared over the ridge amidst growing plumes of dust.

At last the rear guard crested the ridge and could see both the enemy and the Templars descending at a controlled trot, their formation almost perfect—while the main force, evidently unable to rein in their eagerness, cantered and veered to the left around the Templars, outflanking them, with the apparent intention of falling on the enemy first. The banner of Oultrejourdain pulled even with that of Ramla even as Balian watched, and he guessed that Oultrejourdain (and Henri) were challenging Barry for the lead, forcing him to charge or lose command.

The Saracen camp was in complete disarray, as men and horses ran every which way without apparent purpose. Men were shouting and drums were beating, but the entire host looked to Balian more like ants on a disturbed anthill than an army.

The King's squadron took up a trot on the downward slope, giving their horses long reins to find their own footing and bracing themselves in the stirrups. Meanwhile the Templars had reached the bottom of the ravine, and shouting "Vive Dieu St. Amour!" they sprang forward with lances couched. Beyond them, Ramla and the other barons were already through the shallow stream and starting to roll up the valley from the west with their lances lowered.

It was a beautiful sight—much more satisfying and devastating than his own attack on the plunderers at Ibelin, Balian thought. The barons of Jerusalem just rolled over the confused Saracen army, cutting down anything that got in their way, while the Templars smashed into them from the side, causing greater confusion—particularly as they cut through the horse lines, slicing their tethers, so that panicked horses fleeing wildly across the battlefield soon added their whinnies and the thundering of their hooves to the general chaos.

This left the rear guard little room to maneuver, and the King turned his horse right toward the less glamorous baggage train with its rows of kneeling camels, tents, and field kitchens. Less glamorous, Balian registered, and less dangerous for the crippled King as well; it was an intelligent decision for his lion-hearted King.

The camels took the arrival of hordes of horsemen with equanimity; only one or two even felt compelled to get to its feet, while the others remained kneeling and slowly chewing as the strange horses and riders crashed among the field kitchens. The cooks and slaves scattered in all directions in open terror, some of them screaming out loud as they ran. They were hardly worthy opponents, and Balian let them go, his eyes focused on the bright tents beyond, thinking there might yet be an emir or two over there.

Only because he was focusing on these tents did he see a flurry of commotion around one of them, as several men in glittering armor and brightly-colored silk turbans and sashes emerged, gesticulating decisively. A moment later, drums started beating.

Balian saw a man in a yellow turban run forward with his scimitar drawn; his mouth was wide open as he tried to make himself heard above the chaos engulfing the rest of the camp. For several minutes, it seemed, this man tried to bring some order to the chaos, but then the yellow turban turned and started toward the camel lines, with the other emirs clustered around him. Balian decided the man in the yellow turban must be Salah ad-Din himself.

"There!" He drew the King's attention. "In the yellow turban! It's Salah ad-Din!" And as he spoke, he spurred Gladiator forward in a dash to cut off the Sultan from the camels.

Some of the men around Salah ad-Din spotted the approaching squadron of Christian knights. Shouting furiously and drawing their swords, they sprang forward.

The threat to the Sultan had attracted the attention of the Sultan's bodyguard as well. These men had been camped in front of the Sultan's tent, which was to the left of Jerusalem's squadron. Although they were dismounted, these slaves now hurled themselves as a massed body of men into the flank of Jerusalem's knights.

The desperation of the Sultan's bodyguard made it more effective than footmen usually were. Swinging their swords in great figure eights, they began to bring down the horses of the Franks with sickening efficiency. The bulk of the King's squadron had to turn to bring their lances to bear against the Mamlukes before they could kill any more horses.

This left the King almost alone, with Balian and Tancred still charging to cut off Salah ad-Din's escape. One of Salah ad-Din's emirs reached the closest camel and started kicking it to its feet, to the loud protests of the ornery beast. Tancred, who was closest, spurred forward shouting "Jerusalem!" in one last desperate effort to cut off Salah ad-Din's escape, thereby exposing the King's left, and at once a half-dozen young men on foot raced toward him with raised scimitars shouting "Allahu Akbar!"

Balian cut sharply to the left, crossing in front of his King, who was trailing by a length, and met the attackers. He skewered the first with his lance, but he could not pull it out in time for a second thrust. He grabbed his sword as the other Turks closed around him. Two of them tried to drag him off Gladiator, while the others were getting in each other's way as they wielded their scimitars in a furious attempt to kill him or Gladiator or better yet, both of them.

Balian bent his knees and touched his spurs to Gladiator's belly, and the stallion reared up on his haunches, waving his hooves like weapons. With one powerful kick, he sent one of the attackers backwards with a shattered face. Then he broke the shoulder of a second as he brought his hooves down on top of him and stamped a second time for good measure. By then, Sir Tancred had ridden up and pierced a third with his lance.

"Salah ad-Din!" he shouted as he drew up beside Balian, the immediate danger past. "He's getting away!" He pointed after a man in a magnificent brocade tunic, hunched over the back of a camel he was flaying into a gallop.

Balian turned Gladiator to pursue and felt him lurch. The stallion's hip dropped away, and Balian nearly fell backwards out of the saddle. He looked down and back and saw the horrible gash that had cut open the stallion's flank. Blood was pouring out of the wound, and Gladiator would not put weight on his hip. Tancred and other knights of the King's squadron were flying after the fleeing Sultan, but Balian could not join them. He paused to catch his breath and looked around the battlefield.

The floor of the ravine was littered with Saracen dead, scattered equipment, trampled tents, toppled field kitchens, and panicked horses still running this way and that. Here and there, at the fringes, the Templars were still slaughtering, but there was no organized resistance, only pockets of desperate men determined to sell their lives dearly. Others, however, were on their knees begging the secular knights for mercy, while farther away, the Christian foot soldiers were trying to stop some of the fleeing Muslims.

Ransoms! Balian thought with sudden clarity, now that the danger was past. The young men who had rushed to Salah ad-Din's defense were surely men of quality. If he could take just one or two of them captive, he would be a made man: maybe even rich enough to marry a dowager queen. He flung himself down from Gladiator and strode back to the men Gladiator had so effectively defeated, his sword drawn.

Three survivors were still there. The man who had taken a hoof in the face was sitting cross-legged, holding a blood-soaked cloth to his face and swaying back and forth in pain. Beside him, the man with a broken shoulder was hunched over in pain, while a third man, or youth really, tried to bind it in a sling. They looked up at Balian's approach, their eyes widening in alarm, and the youth who was not wounded leaped to his feet and brandished his sword.

Balian raised his sword over his head and addressed him in Arabic. "I'll kill you if you want, but your army is destroyed, your Sultan has fled. Throw away your sword and surrender to me, and you will live to grow a beard."

The young man hesitated, but the man with the broken shoulder called out between clenched teeth, "Enough widows and orphans of Believers have been made this day. Let be." Turning to Balian, he declared, "We are your prisoners. All of us."

Just then the King trotted up beside Balian. "I think," he declared cautiously, still not daring to believe what he saw, "I think the day is ours."

Chapter 11

Ibelin, December 1177

The fireplace was smoking badly. It had been raining for days, and since the castle was flooded with nearly a thousand homeless, they had already used up their dry wood. They were also going through other supplies at an alarming rate, or so it seemed to Richildis. She looked anxiously at the records her clerk had put in front of her and tried to make sense of the figures. Mathematics had never been her strong point, but today she was also distracted because a fever had broken out among some of the homeless children. With everyone crowded together in too little space and the garrison latrines overflowing, she feared an epidemic, while the stench of so much miserable humanity was starting to penetrate to the solar and chapel.

If only we could rebuild some of the houses, Richildis wished, but she knew the cost of wood was prohibitive. Ibelin, as the steward made clear to her, could not possibly pay for the necessary timber, which would have to be imported from Cyprus, from its own revenues.

"The glass factory was gutted, my lady," the steward reminded her. "The structure is sound enough, but none of the equipment survived."

The potters, too, another important source of revenue, had lost all their wares, senselessly shattered and crushed in willful acts of destruction. The distinctive regional pots, glazed on the inside, were popular with pilgrims and sold well in the markets of Jaffa and Jerusalem—but months of work had been destroyed in a single night, impoverishing twenty families without enriching the men responsible. The little community of weavers, however, had suffered most, because their homes had been near the eastern gate, and it was here that the fire had started. The untreated wool, kept in a central warehouse, had been put to the torch, creating a gigantic fire that rapidly spread, consuming first the bolts of finished cloth and then the looms themselves. In the weavers' quarter the fire had been so intense that the beams of the houses had caught fire and collapsed. Richildis shook her head for the thousandth time; she could not understand senseless destruction, any more than she could understand cruelty.

"Mama! Mama!" The sound of Eschiva's excited voice broke in on her thoughts, replacing her despair over the past with fear for the future. She wished she could keep Eschiva away from the sick children. But how could she teach her Christian charity if she forbade contact with the ill and less fortunate?

Eschiva's clog-shod feet clattered loudly on the dais before she burst into the solar. "Mama! A herald just rode into the outer ward, and he's wearing the arms of Jerusalem!"

"A herald?" Richildis could not remember the last time a herald had come to Ibelin—certainly not since she had lived separate from her husband. "Are you sure?"

"Yes, I saw him! He's from Jerusalem, Mama! Maybe he's from my husband?" All the twelve-year-old's hopes were in those breathless words and her flushed face. Richildis had not approved her husband marrying her daughter to a grown man. She had not approved of Aimery de Lusignan, either, but her word counted for nothing anymore. Eschiva had been married—not just betrothed—to Lusignan before her eighth birthday. To his credit, Lusignan had flattered Eschiva by treating her like a lady at the wedding, kissing her hand and dancing with her, impeccably polite and gallant. Eschiva had fallen madly in love with him, and she lived for some word or letter from him. But it was no surprise to Richildis that Lusignan rarely gave a thought to his child bride—certainly not since he'd been made Marshal of Jerusalem.

Richildis opened her mouth to warn her daughter not to get her hopes up, but then closed it again. Why not let her hope another few minutes? So she tried to smile and took her daughter's hand, saying simply, "Let's go see what it is he wants."

Minutes later the herald bowed deeply before the Lady of Ramla, his wet cap in his hand, and announced, "The Queen of Jerusalem bade me ride ahead and request the hospitality of your house, my lady."

Eschiva deflated with an audible, "Oh!" while Richildis was filled with panic at the thought of such an exalted guest in the middle of all their misery. She found herself sputtering, "The Queen—oh! Agnes de Courtenay!" The last thing Richildis needed was to have her sister-in-law gloating over her failed marriage! Agnes had never brought anything but misery to the Ibelins, Richildis thought bitterly—and she would undoubtedly find it satisfying to crow over her new "royal" status.

"No, my lady: Queen Maria," the herald corrected her.

"Queen Maria?" Richildis asked, disbelieving. What on earth could the haughty Greek princess want with the likes of Ibelin or her? "But why—what—" She broke off her silly questions. How was a mere herald supposed to know the motives of his mistress? Furthermore, Richildis knew better than to think a royal herald was *requesting* hospitality; he was giving notice of what was to come. The Queen of Jerusalem had the right to the hospitality of any baron in the realm, let alone the soon-to-be-discarded wife of a baron. Richildis forced herself to focus on practical issues. "How many people are in her party?"

"The Queen is traveling with her maid, her almoner, her confessor, two squires, four grooms, and ten sergeants, my lady."

At least that wasn't overwhelming, even if it was more than they had room for at the moment. Well, the stables were all but empty, she corrected herself, and the sergeants could sleep there or in the great chamber of the keep, so it was just a matter of Eschiva and herself moving to the top floor of the keep and turning over the comfortable apartment above the solar to the Queen and her lady. The priests would have to stay with Father Vitus, she concluded. She nodded to the herald. "Of course, Sir Herald; the Queen of Jerusalem is always welcome at Ibelin."

An hour later, Richildis and Eschiva waited inside the barbican with a welcome cup for the Queen of Jerusalem as she rode in at the head of her entourage. She was wearing a deep purple velvet cloak, evidently lined with wolf. That was to be expected, of course, but Richildis was intimidated by the way she cantered into the ward, riding a gray mare so hot-blooded that she arched her neck and lifted her tail as the Queen reined her in. Richildis was afraid of horses like that.

Richildis had not seen the Queen since King Baldwin's coronation. She remembered her as an arrogant, bejeweled creature at the high table, stiff and impassive. She was startled when the Queen threw back the fur-trimmed hood of her cloak and sent her a dazzling smile. Only now did Richildis register that she had big, wide-set amber eyes in a perfectly symmetrical face, an elegant, thin nose, and soft, rose-colored lips. She was beautiful, Richildis registered—and Richildis distrusted beautiful women.

Dutifully but resentfully, Richildis sank into a deep curtsy, tugging Eschiva down with her, and rose to find that the Queen had already dismounted, turned her horse over to a squire, and was offering her hand.

"My lady of Ramla." She stopped the flustered Richildis from curtsying again. "Thank you so much for extending your hospitality in these difficult times. I know how much Ibelin has suffered, and I am here not to be a burden, but to see if there is some way I can help."

Before Richildis could recover from her astonishment at this announcement, the Queen turned and smiled at Eschiva, who was staring up at her as if she were the Queen of Heaven rather than the Queen of Jerusalem. "You must be Eschiva."

"I'm the wife of Aimery de Lusignan," Eschiva introduced herself boldly.

"Ah, Madame de Lusignan," the Queen answered, instantly recognizing Eschiva's pride in her married status, "your lord husband charged me with bringing you a kiss." The Queen at once bent forward and kissed a blushing Eschiva on the forehead.

With this little lie (for Richildis did not believe for a moment that Aimery de Lusignan had sent his wife a kiss), the Queen overwhelmed Richildis' prejudice against pretty women. The kiss made Eschiva beam with happiness, and Richildis could no longer hold back a smile of her own. As she gestured to the exterior stone steps leading up to the hall, it was with sincere warmth. "Your grace, please! Come in."

The Queen insisted on a tour of the town to see the damage for herself. The townspeople flocked to catch a glimpse of her, and she had smiles for them as well—although Richildis noted, with a resurgence of inner disapproval, that she carefully kept her distance and let her almoner distribute alms, rather than actually touch the poor.

The Queen also spent a good deal of time talking to Father Vitus, listening with bated breath to his account of what had happened during the siege. It struck Richildis as odd that the Queen showed so much interest in the role played by her brother-in-law.

Later, after a light evening meal, the ladies withdrew to the solar, leaving the rest of the household in the hall, and Eschiva performed on her harp for the Queen until she was sent to bed. At last the women were alone, Richildis with Gudrun and Maria Zoë with Rahel. "Do you wish to retire now, your grace?" Richildis asked cautiously. "Or should I put another log on the fire?"

"Oh, I'm not sleepy yet. My head is too full of imagines and thoughts. Father Vitus described the events most vividly."

"Yes, he has a way with words." Richildis sounded disapproving.

"Do you mean he exaggerated?"

"Not at all. The situation in the keep was similar. We were crowded together, conscious that we could hardly defend ourselves, and we, too, heard the screaming coming up from the city—especially the high-pitched screaming of women and girls who had fallen into the Saracens' hands." She paused then continued. "Father Vitus referred to a girl called Beth. I will tell you about her. She is a thirteen-year-old Muslim maiden, raised very strictly by her father, who owned a fruit shop near the southern gate. She claims she had never left the inside of her father's house except to go to Friday prayers and visit her uncles' houses—all within a couple of blocks. She started her monthly flux this past summer and was betrothed to marry one of her father's business associates at the start of the New Year. When the Saracens came, she and her mother were inside the women's quarters, but suddenly there were strange men there—something that should not be. The intruders were Nubians and they were clearly Muslims, but these men took one look at her and smiled in a way she knew was not decent—as she put it to me. She and her mother tried to cover themselves—because they were unveiled inside their own house—but they were roughly grabbed, and the men started to rip off their clothes. They pleaded with the men to let them alone, reciting from the Koran to prove that they were Believers, but these men were not deterred. They forced themselves on them—one after another.

"By the time we found them, the older woman was dead—she had bled to death from the wounds inflicted on her. But the thirteen-year-old was still breathing. I had her brought here to the castle, where Gudrun nursed her back from the brink of death.

"Meanwhile, of course, I made inquiries into what had become of her relatives. Her father had died defending their house, but her two uncles and her betrothed had survived. I asked them to take her home. They looked at me as if I had asked them to renounce their faith. How could I ask such a thing? Their niece/fiancée was now 'unclean,' and they wouldn't dream of taking her back into their homes to live with their still "good" wives and daughters—as if she were a whore!" Indignation rang in Richildis' voice. "The worst of it, however, was that this was exactly what the poor child expected. When I went to tell her she would be staying with us, she begged me to kill her. She said she was 'worthless' and 'filthy' and wanted only to die.

"That made me very angry," Richildis admitted, her lips drawn into a thin line. "In fact, I lost my temper. I grabbed the poor girl by her arm and dragged her from her bed. She started screaming in terror, and I think she feared I intended to kill her right there. Her cries suggested she was not as ready to die as she thought she was. In any case, I dragged her to my little chapel and forced her to kneel before the image of the Virgin Mary, and I started to tell her about Christ. I told her how he stopped people from stoning a woman caught in adultery, and I asked, 'Do you think *He* would be less forgiving of a girl who had been taken against her will? Never. He wept with you, and He still loves you,' I told her. 'Even if your uncles and your betrothed and Mohammed and Allah are too bigoted and cruel to forgive the innocent—Christ,' I told her, 'loves you. He will never turn his back on you,' I told her, 'as long as you love Him.'" Richildis fell silent, remembering the scene.

"What a beautiful thing to say!"

Richildis continued without acknowledging the Queen's remark. "Christ or his Mother or both must have been with me in that chapel, because the girl's eyes became as big as saucers and she asked breathlessly, 'Truly?' I insisted it was the case, and she asked me to tell her more. After that, Gudrun and I took turns telling her everything we knew from the life of Christ or the lives of the saints that underscored the high status of women in Christianity—not just the Virgin Mary, but the fact that Christ first appeared to women after his resurrection, the story of the woman caught in adultery, the fact that women as well as men followed Him, and that He has graced many women with sainthood since. After just over a week, she asked to be baptized in the name of Christ, taking the name of Elizabeth." Richildis crossed herself.

"That's wonderful!" the Queen exclaimed enthusiastically. "I'm sure I would have been speechless and found no better answer than to hug her and promise my protection," she admitted humbly.

"Oh, I had the words well prepared," Richildis answered coldly, with a hard look at the Queen. "You see, throughout the raid—which seemed to drag on for a lifetime—I feared that Eschiva would suffer this girl's fate—that they would break in and ravish her despite her tender age. And I kept wondering what Aimery de Lusignan would do if he found out his bride had been raped—maybe more than once—by Nubian soldiers." She paused and looked sharply at the Queen. "You know him better than I. What do you think? Would he still have honored her as his wife?"

The Queen shifted uncomfortably in her chair.

"You don't have to answer. We both know he would have found a way to set her aside—"

"But her *uncles* would never have rejected her! Not Balian!" the Queen protested.

Richildis looked piercingly at the Dowager Queen. "Balian. You always call him Balian—not Sir Balian, not the Constable of Ascalon, not 'Ramla's younger brother.' Just Balian."

The Queen blushed, and that said it all, Richildis thought, although she couldn't really fathom it. A queen in love with a landless younger son?

"But I am right," Maria Zoë insisted, trying to distract attention from her relationship to Balian. "Sir Balian would never reject Eschiva. If she had been ravished and her father had been killed and her husband had rejected her, he would be the *first* to comfort and protect her. I'm sure he would."

Richildis nodded slowly and conceded, "Perhaps—and he may yet have to."

"What do you mean?" Maria Zoë asked, astonished. "I thought they did not breach the castle walls?"

"The Saracens did not, but my lord husband is trying to divorce me—and if he succeeds, Eschiva will become a bastard and will no longer be heiress to Ramla. In which case, you can be sure, Lusignan will find a way to put her aside."

Maria Zoë could not deny that. Aimery was a landless adventurer who had come to the Holy Land to find and marry an heiress, just like Reynald de Châtillon and many before him. He would not marry a landless girl, no matter what her titles had once been and no matter how much the little girl loved him.

Before she could think of a neutral answer, Richildis continued. "It's only because of Eschiva that I refuse Barry's pressure to dissolve our marriage. You cannot think I wish to return to a man who has never been faithful and loves neither me nor our daughter," she declared bitterly—a little too bitterly, Maria Zoë thought. If she were truly indifferent to Barry, there would be less passion in her voice.

"But you were married as children—"

"It is a vile practice!" Richildis burst out angrily. "The whole concept of consent that the Church pretends to uphold is made a mockery when little girls are 'asked' to consent to that which their all-powerful parents have already decided!"

That was true enough, Maria Zoë conceded, recalling just how little choice she had had—and how frightened she had been of the 'barbarians' she was being sent to. Fortunately the man who became her confessor, Brother Anselm, had been the first Frank she had ever met, and he had been a gentle priest with smiling eyes, well suited to soothing a child's fears.

"Did you never love the Lord of Ramla, then?" Maria Zoë asked softly.

Richildis started, registering too late that her bitterness had run away with her tongue. But it was done now. "Love him?" she asked. "I don't know. I joined the Ibelin household at the age of eight, and Hugh d'Ibelin was a fine man." She smiled at the memory. "He was big and blond like Barry, but he was less taken with himself. He had a gentleness about him that only Balian shares. Barry and Henri are made of sterner stuff, more egotistical, more ambitious and grasping—more like their father, or so I've been told; I never met Barisan the Elder." She stopped and turned her penetrating eyes on Maria Zoë. "And what is Balian to you?"

Maria Zoë started, and her hand fell instinctively on her belly.

Richildis caught her breath; the Queen's belly was budding. "You're not carrying his child?" she asked, incredulous.

Maria Zoë didn't answer. She took her hand away from her belly and rested it on the arm of her chair with great dignity. She retreated within her façade and sat regal and immobile before the fire, refusing to answer.

Richildis drew a deep breath to steady herself. Even if the Queen refused to acknowledge it, Richildis felt certain it was true. That's why she's here, she concluded. It wasn't the King who had sent her to see what she could do to help Ibelin; it was Balian.

Richildis felt tears starting in her eyes. It hurt that it was her brother-in-law, rather than her husband of twenty years, who cared what became of her. She so wished that it was Barry, and in her heart she knew she loved him still, despite all he had done to her.

"Perhaps I will go to bed after all," Maria Zoë announced coolly, getting to her feet and gliding out of the room with her waiting woman silently following her, leaving Richildis alone with her misery.

The next morning Maria Zoë was sick. Richildis learned about it from her waiting woman, who came to beg for toast to help settle her lady's stomach. Richildis stared at the Egyptian woman with reproachful eyes. "It's morning sickness," she declared flatly—and the older woman smiled faintly and knowingly, but said nothing.

"Doesn't she know?" Richildis asked.

"My lady knows, but she has not yet decided what to do," Rahel conceded.

"What do you mean, 'do?'" Richildis demanded.

"There are ways of—getting rid of unwanted children," Rahel pointed out, in a calm voice that made Richildis' blood run cold. This woman might be Christian, she thought, but she had lived too long among the Muslims! "You wouldn't *really* think of killing an innocent unborn child?" she demanded—recalling that the Greeks, too, were rumored to kill unwanted children.

"There are convents where children can be born out of sight of the court and given directly to the Church," Rahel countered, without actually denying the other possibility. "You will not betray her, will you?"

"Betray her?" Richildis demanded. "To whom? Does the father know?"

"Lord Balian?" The Egyptian innocently confirmed Richildis' suspicions. "Of course not. They have not seen each other since September."

"They are both literate," Richildis pointed out sharply, annoyed by such a facile excuse.

But the Egyptian woman shook her head firmly. "My lady says he will be angry."

"Angry!" Richildis scoffed. "What right has he to be angry, if it was his doing?"

"Men are often angry about the things they do," Rahel countered calmly. "We cannot change that—only try not to arouse it."

"Dear God!" Richildis answered, remembering the Queen's fine compliments on how she had handled Beth. That had been child's play compared to this! The Dowager Queen of Jerusalem was carrying the bastard of a landless younger son who had no chance whatever of gaining the permission to marry her! What had they been thinking! Nothing, obviously. Thinking had nothing to do with lust. But who would have dreamed that this chilly, self-possessed, haughty icon could be fired with sufficient passion to take the risks she had?

Maria Zoë hated any kind of sickness. Normally robust, she resented it when her body 'betrayed' her—but this was particularly humiliating because it reminded her of her condition and, she suspected, would confirm the Lady of Ramla's suspicions. She was surprised, therefore, to find the Lady of Ramla extremely solicitous of her and urging her to stay another night.

"You don't know what it might have been, your grace," Richildis insisted as if she could not imagine the truth. "Perhaps it was something you ate—or worse, the water. With so many homeless here, I fear sanitation is not what it should be. I've ordered water boiled and will serve you nothing but that for the rest of the day—mixed with wine, of course."

"I need to be back in Jerusalem for the Christmas court," Maria Zoë protested weakly—in no particular hurry to return to a court dominated by Agnes de Courtenay.

"It's just a two-day ride," Richildis insisted. "If you leave tomorrow or even the day after, you'll still be there more than a week before Christmas. Stay here at least tonight. I thought you might like to meet Beth, the girl I was telling you about, and I know Eschiva wants to hear more about her husband. She's been badgering me with questions. She'd be so pleased if you could tell her a little more about him, and indeed about the whole court."

Maria Zoë allowed herself to be persuaded, especially when a drenching rain set in just before noon. She had no desire to get cold and wet, and so she settled into the solar for the afternoon and found herself enjoying the simplicity of her surroundings. Eschiva was as eager as her mother had predicted to learn anything about Aimery de Lusignan, and Beth was as shy and gentle as a stray kitten. She curled up at Maria Zoë's feet, her big black eyes filled with wonder as she listened in fascination to Maria Zoë's stories, translated by Gudrun, of the Court of Jerusalem. Later, Eschiva played for them on her harp. After dinner they roasted chestnuts over the fire and washed them down with hot mulled wine sweetened with sugar and spiced with cinnamon, cloves, nutmeg, and cardamom.

Richildis, Rahel, and Gudrun were stitching, and the girls resisting the heaviness of their eyelids to beg for another story from Maria Zoë, when the door slammed open and the cold and damp blew into the room. Startled, they all looked up, and Maria Zoë gasped. Balian stood in the doorway, dripping water from the nasal guard of his helmet to the hem of his cloak.

"Uncle Balian!" Eschiva exclaimed with a cry of joy, jumping up to her feet and running to him, while Beth scuttled for safety behind the tapestries, terrified of all strange men—let alone one in armor and helmet. The reaction of the girls gave Maria Zoë a chance to glance at her hostess; Richildis was not surprised, and that explained everything.

Maria Zoë was trapped, and that made her furious. She got to her feet and faced Balian.

Her anger was reflected in his face. He bent to kiss his niece absently—almost roughly—and then turned her briskly around by her shoulders and sent her to her mother, who was already calling, "Eschiva! Time for bed!"

"But Uncle Balian just—"

"You can see him in the morning."

"But—"

"That's enough!" Richildis clapped her hands and with a nod to Gudrun, who pulled Beth out from behind the tapestries, she pushed both girls into the spiral stairwell, with Gudrun—and Rahel—on her heels. The door to the stairwell thumped shut, and the high-pitched voices of the girls receded upwards.

"Why didn't you tell me?" Balian demanded, without even taking his helmet off.

"Because I knew you'd be angry," Maria Zoë retorted, her chin high and her cheeks flushed.

"Not half so angry as I am now!" Balian answered. "What the hell were you planning to do? Kill my child behind my back?"

"You didn't seem too concerned about his fate when you were making him!"

"Nor did you!"

"I asked you to marry me!" Maria Zoë countered. "If you had—"

"How in the name of Sweet Jesus Christ can I marry you when I have nothing to give you?" he shouted in his fury.

"What did Châtillon bring Princess Constance? Or Lusignan your brother?" Maria Zoë shouted back.

For a moment they stared at one another, but Balian was wet and weary and the anger was already ebbing. "We've been through all this before," he snapped, as he shoved his helmet up and off his head by the nosepiece and then yanked open the leather strap of his coif to push it off as well. He turned away from Maria Zoë and approached the fire, his numb fingers having trouble untying the cord at the neck of his cloak, but he finally managed and flung it off his shoulders. The chain mail underneath glistened wet, and Maria Zoë could see his hands were red with cold. The anger had gone out of his face, replaced by a tense expression that made him look older than his twenty-eight years.

"We must go to the King," he told her in a flat voice full of foreboding. "We must beg him to let us marry and then try to weather the storm that will follow. That is all I can think to do," he admitted, looking very glum.

Maria Zoë moved up beside him and slipped her arms around his slender waist. "I love you, Balian," she declared.

He turned and looked down into her golden eyes, and his expression softened. He bent and kissed her gently on the forehead, and then opened his left arm to enclose her in it before adding grimly, "I will not let you kill my child, nor let my child be born a bastard. If the King will not grant permission for us to marry, we must ride at once for Antioch and see if your sister can persuade Prince Bohemond to give us refuge. If he will not have us, then we must make for the Greek Empire and seek sanctuary with your great-uncle." It was clear that he dreaded this—dreaded being an outlaw and an exile.

Maria Zoë made no effort to persuade him that he might be happy in either Antioch or Constantinople, although she could imagine him being rewarded with titles and lands and living on a sunny estate in her great-uncle's empire.... Instead she laid her head on his chest and begged, "Please, Balian, try to love me—at least a little."

The plea worked. Balian remembered himself, took her into his arms properly, and kissed her warmly on the lips. "You know I love you, Zoë!" he assured her, looking her deep in the eyes. Then he kissed her again—a consuming, demanding, almost bruising kiss. "I love you too much for the good of our souls!" he gasped between kisses. "You know that!" he insisted, and they sank down onto the rugs before the fire to give testimony to that love—and to blot out the fears and the anger and uncertainty that threatened them.

Chapter 12

Jerusalem, December 1177

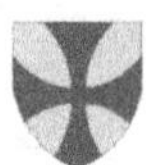

"Jerusalem has an heir!" Sibylla screamed at her brother so loudly that her voice could clearly be heard in the anteroom. "I've given Jerusalem a male heir; isn't that enough? Isn't it enough that I was chained to one rutting monster before I was hardly out of the nunnery? Do you have to sell me to the next before I've even recovered from twisting my guts out to give Jerusalem a god-damned heir?"

Balian and Maria Zoë exchanged an alarmed look; William de Montferrat might have been overbearing and self-important, but he was hardly a monster. Furthermore, Sibylla might have given birth to a son, but it was almost certain his uncle would not live long enough for the boy to grow to manhood—assuming the infant survived childhood at all. Thus, while Jerusalem might have an infant male heir, the Kingdom was still in desperate need of a grown man to wear (or at least wield the power of) the crown until such time as Sibylla's infant son was ready to defend his own Kingdom. Sibylla had to marry someone soon. The question was only a matter of whom: a western Prince selected by Flanders and his patrons, or someone closer at hand....

Meanwhile, although the King's answer had been too soft to be heard by those awaiting an audience in the antechamber, it provoked a new shriek of outrage from his sister. "I don't want to marry anyone!

I don't care whom you pick! If you really cared about me as much as you claim you do, you'd let me choose my own husband!"

Again the King's answer was inaudible, but Sibylla's response was clear. "What does the Pope know about what's good for me—Sibylla? I've done my duty for Jerusalem!" Again Balian and Zoë exchanged a look, while Sibylla continued screaming: "I'm telling you, I won't marry him! And if you bring him here and try to force me, I won't let him in my bed for all the gold in Constantinople!"

The doors to the King's inner chamber crashed open so violently that they banged loudly against the walls. Princess Sibylla stormed through the antechamber, her face red from agitation, her lips pressed firmly together in a grimace of determination, and her eyes narrowed with rage. She looked neither left nor right, and appeared not to notice the two people waiting for an audience with her brother.

Behind her, King Baldwin's old body servant hastened to close the doors to the inner chamber, and caught up with Princess Sibylla just as she reached the far exit. "My lady! My lady!" he called to her in a pleading tone. "You must understand—"

Sibylla spun around on the slave and slapped him viciously across the mouth. "How dare you tell me what I must or must not do?"

"How dare *you* behave like an alewife?" Queen Maria countered, sweeping across the room to confront her stepdaughter.

"Don't *you* try to tell me what to do, either!" Sibylla countered. "I'm the Princess of Jerusalem—"

"But you won't be *Queen* unless you learn how to behave like one."

"I will be Queen when Baldwin dies, whether you like it or not—"

"You stupid girl, this has nothing to do with what I like! The High Court of Jerusalem elects the next King, and there is more than one baron who is only looking for the excuse to declare you illegitimate! Acting and screaming like a lowborn slut will not earn you sympathy or respect!"

"Which is exactly what you want, isn't it? For your little brat Isabella to be made Queen instead of me!" Sibylla screamed back. Then she burst into tears and wailed, "Why does everyone hate me?" and ran from the room.

During this altercation, Balian had gone to Ibrahim. The old slave had been knocked backwards by Sibylla's blow, or his efforts to avoid it, and he sat on the floor holding his face in his hands. "Ibrahim! Are you hurt?"

"Hurt?" The old slave looked up at Balian with tears in his eyes. "I cannot tell you the pain I am in, my lord." His lips were quivering with emotion. "The leprosy is spreading again, and it has become ulcerous! My lord's feet are covered with running sores, and his own sister does not care! Does not even want to hear about it!"

Balian turned to stare at the closed door separating him from Baldwin, and then he reached down and helped Ibrahim to his feet. "I will go to him—"

"No, my lord! He ordered me to keep everyone away! I tried to stop Lady Sibylla, but—"

"I will go to him, Ibrahim, and he will not blame you. Zoë! Come help Ibrahim wash the blood from his lips and nose."

Maria Zoë was already taking the old slave by his elbow and leading him to one of the waiting benches, while Balian gently opened the door to the inner chamber and slipped inside.

The chamber was completely dark. Not a single candle burned here, and the only light came from a double-light window facing west, out of the city to the luminescent sky where the sun had just set. Balian stood inside the door adjusting to the dark, searching with his eyes and ears for the room's occupant. After almost a minute he realized that there was no one in sight, but the curtains to the bed were closed. Taking a deep breath, Balian moved silently to the bed and slowly drew back the curtain.

Baldwin was lying on his side, his back to Balian. His shoulder was shaking convulsively. Balian knelt with one knee on the edge of the bed and laid his hand on Baldwin's shoulder.

"Why?" Baldwin croaked, his throat cramped from suppressing his sobs. "Why does God hate me, Ibrahim?"

"He does *not* hate you, Baldwin."

"Balian! Where did you come from?" Baldwin reared up and turned around in a single gesture. He stared at his friend with wide eyes and a face streaked with tears.

"We've been waiting in the anteroom for hours, but were told you were not ready to receive us. Ibrahim tried to stop me, so don't blame him."

"Of course not! If I'd known you—Oh, Balian, have you heard? The leprosy. We thought it had stopped spreading, but it's—" Baldwin broke down again and started sobbing.

Balian sat down on the bed and pulled the young king into his arms. "Ibrahim told me."

"Why?" Baldwin cried into his breast. "Why? Why? Why? What have I done to deserve this? Why does God want to punish me? For what?"

"It is not punishment, Baldwin. Like Christ, you are suffering for *our* sins—the sins of your subjects."

"That's not fair, Balian! Other kings don't suffer for the sins of their subjects. Why me?"

"I don't know, Baldwin. I can only tell you that He has chosen you. And while you may suffer in *this* life, He will take you into His arms like a long-lost son in the next. You will go straight to Heaven, Baldwin, while the rest of us languish in our graves, in Purgatory or in Hell. He has laid upon you the suffering He reserves only for those He loves most: His Son, His saints, and His martyrs."

Baldwin drew back enough to look Balian in the face. At length he asked, "Do you really believe that?"

"I have to, your grace—or I would lose faith in God Himself."

Baldwin drew a ragged breath and then slowly straightened up, pulling out of Balian's embrace. "I don't want you to be infected," he whispered, the tears streaming down his face. Balian grabbed the bed sheets and found a corner with which to wipe the tears from his king's face. Then he held him firmly by the shoulders and looked him in the eye. "It will be as God wills, Baldwin—but it seems He does not think me worthy of your suffering."

"Or He wants to reward you in a different way," Baldwin suggested with a weak attempt at a smile. "Why are you here?"

"To ask—to ask a favor," Balian confessed.

"A favor?" Baldwin asked, frowning. "You, too?"

Balian could hear the disappointment, even anger, in the King's voice and feared the worst, but it was too late to turn back now. "I wish to take a wife, your grace."

"A wife?" Baldwin was swallowing down his tears, trying to concentrate on Balian's problems rather than his own. "Of course. Why not? Why do you need my permission?"

Balian took a deep breath. "Because I wish to marry the Dowager Queen." When he said it out loud, the audacity of his request frightened him, and he held his breath.

Baldwin did not answer right away, and his expression was so pensive that Balian began to fear that despite his affection, Baldwin would not see his way clear to approve a marriage that would surely rankle the High Court. The prospect of exile yawned like a chasm in front of him, and Balian felt his heart and stomach sinking into an abyss.

Baldwin began speaking in a soft, almost inaudible voice. "Today my mother came to me to nag me about increasing the lands and revenues of the Canons of the Holy Sepulchre. Then my uncle came to press me about more income for himself. Finally, my sister—well, no doubt you heard what my sister wanted. They all want something from me, and not one of them asked me how I felt or why I looked upset or—anything. I thought family was supposed to care about one another."

Balian felt like screaming in empathy—and like killing the Queen Mother, Edessa, and Princess Sibylla all together. Instead he answered, "Family should care, but maybe you have not been a family long enough to learn about that."

"If you marry my stepmother, then you become my stepfather, don't you?" Baldwin asked next, his face brightening. "You would certainly be my sister Isabella's stepfather, and that would make us kin." The King sounded so cheered by this thought that it left Balian at a loss for words. All he managed was a choked, "Your grace…"

"Is Tante Marie outside?" Baldwin asked. Balian was still too overcome to speak, so he nodded instead. "Don't you think we should call her in?"

"Yes," Balian agreed. "She and Ibrahim are probably very anxious."

"Ibrahim is a good man, Balian, even if he is a Muslim."

"Ibrahim is a better man than nine-tenths of your subjects, your grace."

"I set him free, you know, but he told me he was too old to go home, and asked to stay on with me. Will you do me a favor—as my new kinsman?"

"You know I will do whatever you ask of me."

"Then promise you will give Ibrahim a home when I die."

"I would be honored to give Ibrahim a home—if he lives longer than you."

"I think we can assume that," Baldwin insisted steadily. "Will you call Tante Marie in now?"

"Baldwin—" This was turning out to be so much harder than he had anticipated, albeit in a different way. "There is something else you need to know. . . ." Baldwin just looked at him expectantly. "The Queen is—carrying my child."

Baldwin smiled. "That's wonderful news! Why do you look so sheepish? It is a good thing, and shows that God favors this union as much as I do. I only hope the Greek Emperor is as favorably disposed?" Baldwin lifted an eyebrow questioningly, and his tone suggested he did not think this would be so easy.

"I've left that communication to Queen Maria," Balian confessed. Baldwin laughed, adding in astonishment as he finished: "There, you see? You have made me laugh again, Balian! For that I would give you as many brides as you like—a whole harem if you want!"

"But I ask only one."

"Bring her in."

Balian went to the door and opened it. Maria Zoë and Ibrahim were sitting nervously side by side, and both sprang to their feet at the sight of Balian. One look was enough, however, for them to break into smiles, even before Baldwin called from behind him: "Come here, Tante Marie! I want to give you my blessing personally."

Marie Zoë at once advanced into the darkness of the inner chamber and went down on her knees before the King as he sat on the edge of his bed. She bowed her head before him and said formally, "Your grace, Sir Balian and I beg your permission to marry because we love one another. We promise, if you will grant us this—"

"It's all right, Tante Marie. I'm delighted that two people I love so dearly have fallen in love with each other. I can't think of anything that would make me happier. But I understand you are in a bit of a hurry." He winked at that, but gave her no time to comment before adding, "I think we should summon the Chancellor at once so he can perform the sacrament, don't you? I will stand as witness, so none can claim I oppose this union. After that, Ibrahim," he turned to the Muslim servant, "we must celebrate!"

"Your grace, if I may," Maria Zoë begged, and Balian caught his breath at her audacity. They had asked enough of the King already, he thought. Baldwin seemed to think the same thing, for he waited for her to continue with a slight frown on his face. "If I may impose on your generosity again," Maria Zoë continued, "the only celebration I want is to dine together with you here, just the three of us—and the good Archbishop, of course, if you like?"

With relief, Balian read on the King's face that she had found exactly the right thing to say. She had given him what he craved most: the intimacy of family.

"Trapped!" the Lord of Ramla declared, as he stretched out his arm to block Princess Sibylla's escape from a window niche.

"My lord!" Sibylla exclaimed with feigned shock. "What can you want with me here?"

Barry jerked his head toward the vaulting over the niche, drawing Sibylla's attention to the sprig of mistletoe that had been secured there.

"Ah! Now I know why so many couples have been seeking out this particular niche!" Sibylla declared with a disingenuous giggle. Ramla leaned closer, and the Princess closed her eyes and raised her lips. The moment he closed his own eyes, however, she bolted out beneath his arm with an even louder giggle, and dashed back to the crowd of people dancing in the hall.

Ramla cursed under his breath and turned to watch her. Just as she joined one of the chains of dancers lacing their way around the hall, hopping and skipping to the music, she cast him a backward glance full of invitation. She wanted to be pursued, Barry thought to himself, but she was determined to give him a merry chase! Damn her!

"You're playing a dangerous game." A deep voice spoke almost directly into his ear. Ramla spun about sharply, startled and angry to be caught like this. He found himself facing his son-in-law, the Marshal of Jerusalem. Aimery de Lusignan's sharp blue eyes narrowed as he read Ramla's all-too-open face. "Very dangerous," he continued, pressing his advantage. "The King is extremely protective of his beloved sister. Do not make the mistake other men have made. His body may be disintegrating, but his will is hard as steel. He would not like to see a married man dallying with his sister. How *is* your lady wife, by the way, and *mine*?"

"They are both well," Ramla answered, tight-lipped.

"I was hoping to see them here at the Christmas court," Lusignan continued. "I wanted to reassure myself that my dear bride had not suffered in Salah ad-Din's raid on Ibelin."

"You know she did not," Ramla answered, frowning. "The Saracens were driven out before they had even laid siege to the castle."

"Yes, of course," Aimery agreed, his eyes still narrowed, "but for a child it must have been quite frightening, don't you think?"

"Undoubtedly," Ramla agreed. "Which is why her mother and she did not want to risk the trip to Jerusalem," he lied.

"Surely you could have sent an escort strong enough to overcome their fears?" Lusignan pressed him.

"They did not want to come," Ramla insisted stubbornly.

"How convenient for you," Lusignan answered, unconvinced.

"What's that supposed to mean?" Ramla tried to sound indignant, but he was too conscious of being caught red-handed to be credible.

"I mean, my lord, that I'm neither blind nor deaf. I've heard the rumors that you want to set aside your wife and disinherit mine! I can see which way the wind is blowing." He glanced toward the main hall, where Princess Sibylla was laughing a little hysterically as she wove in and out among the dancers.

And for a second time in one evening, Ramla was taken by surprise while watching Princess Sibylla. This time it was by his brother, who emerged from the hallway behind them. "The King would like to see you," he announced—adding, to the astonished looks from both men, "both of you." Then he turned and led his brother and Lusignan back along the corridor toward the King's apartments.

"What's this about?" Barry wanted to know, made nervous by Lusignan's remarks about the King's protectiveness toward his sister.

"I have no idea," Balian answered, his face on the corridor ahead, which was lit only sparsely.

"The wildest rumors are circulating about you and the Dowager Queen," Barry remarked with a glance at Lusignan—who only raised an eyebrow, but otherwise retained a closed, wary look.

"If the rumors you're referring to have to do with my marriage to the Dowager Queen," Balian responded, "they are correct. I would have preferred to tell you in more private and appropriate surroundings, but I did not find you in your chamber when I sought you out earlier this afternoon."

Barry frowned. He had been trying to find Sibylla at the time, and his guilty conscience made him lash out at his brother in a tone he might not otherwise have used. "How do you dip your wick in something that frigid without it freezing off?"

Balian just burst out laughing, remembering his lovemaking with Zoë. Then, still grinning, he quipped, "Fortunately for me, you weren't the only man to suffer from that misconception, or I would probably have had more competition."

Aimery de Lusignan snorted to himself, adding mentally that others had made a different mistake: of underestimating how fond the King was of his stepmother. He could almost regret that he had not pursued Queen Maria himself, but he had not done so badly by bedding Agnes de Courtenay. Furthermore, watching the exchange between the brothers, he thought it might not be such a bad thing that Balian had made such a brilliant match. Ramla might have inherited three baronies and be aiming even higher, but he often overestimated his talents and his worth—which was dangerous. Furthermore, he lacked subtlety and tenacity. Balian, in contrast, had consistently surprised those in power by his low-key competency, and Lusignan did not believe success was ever all luck. Last but not least, Lusignan had been impressed by how little opposition surfaced when the King announced to the entire court, smiling and proud, that he had personally sanctioned and witnessed the marriage of his stepmother to Balian d'Ibelin. There had been some lewd jokes and questions along the lines of Ramla's remarks, and some speculation about what the King hoped to gain by such a misalliance, but many more people had taken the attitude that Balian had earned the reward with his service at Montgisard—if not before. Certainly the Archbishop of Tyre had taken this line, declaring he was "delighted" to perform the service—and the Count of Tripoli had followed suit, openly and heartily congratulating first Balian and then the Dowager Queen. That spoke volumes, Lusignan thought. It was a rare man who had as few enemies as Balian d'Ibelin.

They had reached the entry to the King's apartments, and the guards brought their crossed lances upright to allow Balian and his companions to enter. The antechamber was empty, but lit by several candles. The light caught on the gilding of the lamps. No one guarded the inner door, and Balian approached and knocked once before calling through it: "Your grace, I have brought my brother and the Marshal."

Balian then opened the door and stepped back, gesturing for his brother and Lusignan to enter before him. The King awaited them, standing. He was dressed as he had been earlier for the banquet, in his full regalia with crown. Lusignan and Ramla dutifully bowed before him and murmured, "Your grace."

"My lords," Baldwin opened, "I have called you here together so that we can settle a delicate matter before the Christmas court disperses." He fixed his gaze on Ramla. "My lord, you petitioned the Patriarch of Jerusalem to dissolve your marriage—"

Aimery de Lusignan started to exclaim something, but a gesture from the King made him strangle it in his throat. Although he bottled his outrage, the look Aimery sent Ramla was one of unfettered fury. Balian was glad not to be the recipient of that look; Lusignan would make an uncomfortable enemy, he thought.

"As far as the Patriarch and I can see, my lord," the King continued, "your wife is completely blameless. She has borne you no less than six children, even if only one survives, and there has never been a hint of scandal concerning her virtue. She came to you a child bride, innocent and trusting, and she is not related to you within the prohibited degrees."

Ramla's face was reddening with every word, and Balian recognized that he, too, was working himself into a rage.

"However," the King continued, arresting the rising rage just before it exploded, "the Lady Richildis has informed us that she wishes to retire from the world and take holy orders. She is willing to consent to the dissolution of your marriage—" the King held up his hand to silence Lusignan's objections a second time— "on the condition that her surviving child, Eschiva, is recognized as the heir to Ramla and Mirabel, regardless of any issue you may have by a subsequent marriage."

Ramla started and seemed on the brink of protesting—but then he remembered that as King of Jerusalem, he would have no need for Ramla. He almost wanted to laugh, but he controlled himself. "I agree to these terms, your grace," he declared and bowed deeply.

"Good," Baldwin nodded, satisfied, but he did not smile. "That was your wife's condition. Now hear mine: I will agree to the dissolution of your marriage and consent to a new marriage with any heiress in the realm—on the condition that you cede Ibelin to your brother Balian."

Ramla spun about to look at his brother as if he'd been stabbed in the back. The look on Balian's face was so stunned, however, that Lusignan laughed. He did not know if Balian were bluffing or truly surprised, but either way, this reinforced his earlier assessment: Balian had a gift for advancing without appearing to be grasping. He was a man to watch.

Ramla frowned at Lusignan, who forestalled any comment from his father-in-law by remarking flippantly: "Not such a high price to pay for what you're hunting, is it? What does Ibelin owe? Ten? Twelve knights?" Lusignan was enjoying himself, now that he knew his heiress would not be disinherited.

Ramla swallowed the bitter medicine. He bowed deeply to King Baldwin. "As you wish, your grace."

"Good," the King said again—and now, at last, he smiled. "And, my lord, when I say *any* heiress in the Kingdom, that includes my sister Sibylla—"

All three noblemen gaped at the King.

Baldwin looked very pleased with himself as he asked with a slight tilt of his head: "Do you think my illness has dulled my wits? I know perfectly well the game you're playing, my lord of Ramla, but be sure *you* know the rules. You may marry my sister Sibylla if—and only if—you are her choice. I have agreed to let her choose her next husband. If you are that man, so be it."

Ramla bowed more deeply than before, this time in genuine gratitude. What was Ibelin compared to this? Let Balian have the scraps—and his frigid beauty. Sibylla was the real prize—Sibylla and Jerusalem.

Chapter 13

Ascalon, April 1178

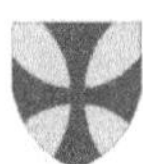

After a hard winter and a hesitant spring, it was finally warm enough to sit outside. Maria Zoë seized the opportunity to take the children onto the rooftop terrace to soak in the sun. There was a whole nursery at Ascalon now, and Maria Zoë felt a little sorry for Balian. After all, he had been catapulted into marriage and confronted with his impending fatherhood without much preparation. Yet when his sister-in-law retired to a convent, he had not hesitated to take both his niece Eschiva and the still half-mature Beth into his household as well.

Since Ibelin was now his responsibility, he had also sent Father Michael to Ibelin to assist the steward and provide him with reliable assessments of the population, revenues, and costs of rebuilding the town. More important, by offering him double his wages, Balian had induced Roger Shoreham to accept the position of Captain of the Garrison at Ibelin, and to start organizing a citizen militia along the lines he had so effectively forged in Ascalon. Maria Zoë knew Roger himself had been eager to take up the challenge (and not a little flattered by Balian's trust in him), but reluctant to go because his wife resisted leaving her friends and family. It helped, however, that young Edwin Shoreham eagerly seized the opportunity to establish his own workshop in Ibelin, where he could hope to earn the lion's share of the carpentry work that went along with rebuilding the eastern part of the town. Once her favorite son and daughter-in-law decided to move to Ibelin, Mistress Shoreham had capitulated, and she and Roger had already moved into the generous apartment over the gate to start their new life, turning over the command of Ascalon's garrison to one of his former rivals for the post.

Mathewos, too, had accepted Balian's offer to take service with him directly. That had been an easy and natural decision for the Ethiopian, as his wife was dead and his eldest son was already in Balian's service; his daughter and younger son were both unmarried and given no choice in the matter. He had been sent ahead to oversee the remodeling and expansion of the stables, which had been badly damaged by housing so many homeless over the winter.

Balian was anxious for his child to be born in Ibelin, but he had promised the King to stay in Ascalon until Pentecost, by which time the King hoped to have appointed his replacement. Maria Zoë was not entirely unhappy to remain in Ascalon while so much construction was going on in Ibelin. The costs of rebuilding the eastern part of the town were being carried by her revenues from Nablus—and since these revenues were substantial, Maria Zoë and Balian had opted to do all repairs as rapidly as possible. Balian felt this would not only restore the prosperity of Ibelin, but also help people get over the shock of what had happened.

While the town and parts of the castle were being rebuilt, Maria Zoë was given time to move her personal belongings into the castle and also make some changes of her own. From the time of its construction forty years ago, the ladies of Ibelin had not had much chance to put their mark on the place, and it remained essentially a fortress. Maria Zoë wanted to change that. She wanted a pleasure garden, for a start. She wanted two more windows in her bedchamber and another set of double-light windows in the solar. She also wanted glazing on the windows of the hall and a proper bath chamber in the northeast tower. Balian had no objections, since she was paying, but while the work was being done there would be a lot of noise, dust, and workmen. Maria Zoë was happier here in Ascalon.

Her contentment was heightened by the fact that this pregnancy seemed to be going much better than her last, and—equally important—because Isabella had taken to her new home like a duck to water. Isabella had accepted, trusted, and obeyed Balian from the moment she met him. Maria Zoë had introduced him as her "new father," and Isabella had asked if he was like her brother Baldwin.

"Well, I'm not a king," Balian had answered, amused, going down on his heels to be at her level, and Isabella had generously told him that that was all right. "There can only be one king in a kingdom at a time," she told him solemnly, and Balian had managed to keep a straight face as he agreed with her.

Isabella then shamelessly asked if he would give her a puppy, since her mother would not. Balian had told her absolutely not, until she was old enough to take care of a puppy and the dog it would become. Isabella had been somewhat baffled by this firm rejection, because her brother Baldwin never said no to her—but the look she had cast at her mother suggested she laid the blame for Balian's answer squarely at her mother's feet.

Since then, however, Maria Zoë had observed the way Isabella watched alertly when Balian gave orders to the garrison and his household. She noted that people did what he told them to do, and when the next spat came and she wanted something she couldn't have, she accepted Balian's "no" with no more than a frown and indignant muttering to herself.

It also helped that both Eschiva and Beth mothered Isabella as only two growing girls with a new, live doll can. Of the older girls, Eschiva generally took the lead, simply because she had been raised in freedom and the expectation of inheriting a fortune. Beth, while rapidly learning French under Eschiva's tuition, had yet to overcome her instilled timidity and passivity, which rendered her incapable of initiative—except when it came to caring for smaller children. Maria Zoë suspected that she had cared for young siblings in her father's home, but these had apparently died or been adopted by the same uncles who left her to die.

As they stepped out onto the terrace, Isabella started running around "inspecting" the potted plants for buds.

"Don't touch!" Eschiva admonished when Isabella reached out to grasp a hibiscus plant in her plump hand.

Isabella looked over at her cousin, astonished. Then she intentionally and provocatively did exactly what she had been told not to do. Eschiva frowned and stormed after her cousin, but Beth intervened. She raised her hand to signal for Eschiva to hold back and went to stand behind Isabella. Bending over her and stroking her hand, she urged, "Softly, Isabella, softly." Then, taking the younger girl's hand in hers, she explained patiently: "You don't want to break the stems." Isabella looked up at the native girl with wide eyes. Beth was still caressing Isabella's hand, making it relax in hers. Smiling, she started to reach out to the hibiscus with her other hand. "Look! Like this," she demonstrated.

Then the sound of a man wailing the call to prayers shattered the scene.

Beth started violently and looked around her with so much terror that Isabella became alarmed and started crying. Eschiva put her hands over her ears and closed her eyes.

Maria Zoë pulled herself to her feet and went to put an arm around the terrified Beth. "It's nothing to be afraid of," she assured the girl.

"But, but…"

"It's coming from right inside the house!" Eschiva protested, opening her eyes but keeping her ears covered.

Maria Zoë gave Beth a last hug and then left her to go to the railing and look into the kitchen courtyard. Sure enough, three turbaned men were kneeling on the cobbles, their hands on their thighs. One of them led the group in prayer and they all bowed their heads down to the ground. They stood, bowed with their hands on their knees, and then went down on their knees again and put their heads to the ground.

So these were Balian's prisoners, Maria Zoë registered. He had reported the capture of three men at the Battle of Montgisard in the hasty letter he wrote her immediately following the battle. At the time of their marriage, he had been in high hopes of receiving substantial ransom payments, but since then the negotiations had dragged on inconclusively. She had known they were being held somewhere in Ascalon, but until today she had not actually seen them.

As they sat upright on their heels, Maria Zoë could clearly see that one of them had a smashed nose over a disfigured lip. Balian had told her that one of his captives had lost three and a half teeth to Gladiator's hoof. The man with the broken shoulder, however, had healed enough so that she could not be sure which one of the men below went by the name of Rashid. She guessed, however, that it was the man on the far left, since he seemed the oldest of the three prisoners. Balian had told her Rashid was the oldest and most reasonable of his captives.

The youth, in contrast, was a "hothead," Balian claimed, but also the most valuable of the captives: the son of a powerful official at Salah ad-Din's court in Damascus and a scion of one of the leading Seljuk families in Syria. Balian was naturally frustrated by the lack of progress in the ransom negotiations, but today another messenger had ridden in from Damascus, and Balian was meeting with him now. Maria Zoë suspected the prisoners had heard about this messenger and had asked to come out, ostensibly to pray, but actually in hopes of encountering him.

The prisoners had finished their prayers and stood chatting together, glancing frequently toward the exit. Maria Zoë tensed slightly, but then she realized that at least a dozen of Balian's men were also in the courtyard, watching the captives attentively.

Maria Zoë had heard the Bishop complain to Balian that he was treating the prisoners too well. The Bishop had heard that Balian served his prisoners the same meals as the rest of the household, kept them in a room with a window, and let them sleep in beds with straw bedding. What the Bishop objected to most, however, was that Balian allowed them to visit the baths (under guard) and allowed them to pray.

Balian had shrugged off the criticism, remarking that the roles could easily be reversed, and that he had no desire to suffer Reynald de Châtillon's fate. The Bishop countered by noting that his good treatment of the captives would not guarantee good treatment should he become a captive.

The youngest of the captives caught sight of Maria Zoë and called the attention of the others to her. They all looked up, and an eruption of Arabic was followed by grins and laughter. Maria Zoë instinctively sensed that the comments were insulting, and she started to back away from the railing, but she was not quite fast enough.

From directly under her, Balian sprang on the youth who had drawn attention to Maria Zoë, knocking him onto his back and pinning him to the ground with his sword at his throat. The other two captives yelped protests, but Balian's soldiers had instantly drawn their swords and closed in around the unarmed prisoners. Balian snarled in Arabic at the youth he was threatening. Without easing the threat of his sword, he raised his voice and ordered his guards: "Seize them all, bind their hands behind their backs, and shackle them in the cellars—separated. From now on, they don't see the light of day—or each other—until their ransom is paid!"

Maria Zoë gasped, but no one in the courtyard heard her, because the guards sprang to obey Balian's orders and the prisoners were protesting more loudly than ever. She could only watch apprehensively as two of the guards grabbed the youth at the tip of Balian's sword and dragged him to his feet, while Balian's blade followed the hollow of his throat every inch of the way. The youth flung something at him in Arabic, and Balian flicked his wrist so rapidly that Maria Zoë did not even see the motion—only the sudden stripe of red on the side of the youth's face—and the terror and pain in his widened eyes.

The evidence of Balian's fury and his ability to hurt a defenseless prisoner left Maria Zoë almost as frightened as the victim.

"Take them away!" Balian ordered.

"That will leave a scar, my lord, if it isn't bound," someone protested from under Maria Zoë's feet.

"It's supposed to," Balian answered coldly. "I don't want him to forget what I just told him." He added something in Arabic, directed at the youth. Then he put his sword away and stormed out of the courtyard without waiting to see his orders carried out.

Maria Zoë backed away and looked hastily over at the three girls to see if they, too, had witnessed this scene. Fortunately they were standing too far back to have been able to see down into the courtyard, but they were holding each other in obvious fear, and Beth's eyes were huge.

"There's nothing to be afraid of," Maria Zoë told them automatically—despite her own misgivings, reinforced by the sound of clattering hooves in the street beside the residence. "My lord husband's prisoners were in the courtyard saying their prayers." She tried to ignore what had followed, but the way Beth was looking at her suggested she had understood more of what had happened than Maria Zoë herself. Beth looked down, her hands fumbling with the front of her dress.

Maria Zoë shivered. Clouds were gathering over the ocean and blocking the sun, which was slipping down the sky. The temperature had dropped noticeably, too, aided by a strong wind that sprang up as if a storm was in the offing. It had whipped the sea into racing, white-capped waves. "It's time to go in." Maria Zoë announced. "It's getting cold."

No one protested. Silently Rahel put her needlework away in her basket, and—still subdued into utter silence—the girls filed through the open door and Balian's chambers to the apartment they shared on the far side of the gallery. Maria Zoë found herself chattering about silly things like going for a boat ride tomorrow and needing new bed curtains for the girls' bed, while all the while she kept an ear cocked for the sound of Balian's return. But he did not come back.

Maria Zoë sent for the girls' evening meal, and sat with them as they ate. Then she helped Isabella undress and brushed out her fine chestnut hair, while Beth helped Eschiva. When the girls were ready for bed, Maria Zoë led them in prayer, kneeling side by side in front of the big bed.

First they said the Lord's Prayer in unison, and then Maria Zoë asked God's grace and protection for King Baldwin and the Kingdom of Jerusalem, for the Emperor and Patriarch in Constantinople, and finally for Balian, Ibelin, and the city of Ascalon.

"And for my father and husband," Eschiva chimed in.

So they prayed for the Lord of Ramla and the Aimery de Lusignan.

"And for Madame!" Beth whispered, referring to Richildis, whom she (rightly, Maria Zoë thought) revered.

"And for Gladiator," Isabella piped up, not willing to be outdone, it seemed. She was very concerned that Balian's gallant stallion was still lame from the wound he'd taken at Montgisard.

Maria Zoë hesitated, unsure if it was appropriate to pray for an animal—but then, remembering how Balian had credited the stallion with saving his life, she nodded, and ended their prayers with an appeal to Christ "for a full recovery of my lord husband's stallion Gladiator."

At last Maria Zoë could haul herself up off her knees, with solicitous help from Rahel. Meanwhile, Eschiva had thrown back the covers and shooed Beth and Isabella inside before clambering into the bed herself. Zoë pulled the blankets over the girls, then bent and kissed Eschiva on the cheek, Isabella on the nose, and patted Beth's cheek because she was shy about kisses. "Sleep well, sweethearts."

"Isn't Uncle Balian going to come to say good night?" Isabella asked. She had picked up the "uncle" from Eschiva, and neither Balian nor Zoë had felt there was any harm in it.

"Not tonight," Zoë told her. She stepped out onto the upper gallery, closing the door behind her, leaving Rahel behind to look after them.

It was dark, but light spilled from several of the downstairs rooms into the courtyard, and the murmur of male voices tumbled out of the hall as well. Whether it was for the way he'd fought at Montgisard or because he'd been made a baron, no less than seven bachelor knights had offered Balian their swords in recent months, and his household was growing.

Zoë did not know what to do next, but then a shadow separated itself from one of the columns in front of her, and Balian came towards her.

"Balian! What on earth happened?" she asked him at once, unable to keep her worries pent up inside any longer.

He took her into his arms, but he didn't answer. Despite herself, Zoë melted in the warmth of his embrace, breathing in the scent of leather, oiled chain mail, and rosemary that was distinctive to him.

Balian turned and with his arm still around her waist, guided her into their suite of chambers. Dawit was lighting the candles, while Daniel was putting pomegranates into the bowl on the table. Balian led Zoë to one of the chairs by the table and she sat down automatically, while he fetched wine and two stained glass goblets. Only after the squires had finished their duties, bowed, and withdrawn did Balian answer her question. "They have turned down my ransom demands again."

"Oh, Balian, I'm sorry. Why?"

"Rashid's father says he is too poor to pay."

"What are you asking?"

"Ten thousand bezants."

Zoë gasped. "For all of them?"

"No, apiece," Balian answered, surprised.

"Thirty thousand gold pieces?" Zoë was unable to believe her ears. "That's a fortune."

"No more than the rebuilding of Ibelin will cost me!" Balian snapped back.

Zoë was stunned into silence. She registered that he might be accepting her revenues because the rebuilding of Ibelin was so important to him, but inwardly he still wanted to pay his own way. After a moment she remarked cautiously, "I understand, Balian, but if you can't raise thirty thousand bezants, then take a little less. There will be other opportunities, surely."

"Damn them!" Balian answered, jumping to his feet and pacing to the window. "Damn them all! The only one of the whole lot whose father gives a damn about his son is the one who probably *is* too poor to pay—too poor, it seems, to have more than one wife and one son. The other two are too rich! They have four wives and countless concubines and litters of children, so that one son more or less means almost nothing to them! They accept the loss—Allah Inshallah!—and prefer their gold to their sons' lives!"

Zoë held her tongue in the face of Balian's obvious fury, but she found it hard to believe that he was right—for surely, regardless of religion and race, men loved their sons? Yet there was some logic to what he said, too; it was the nature of men to place greater value on things in short supply and lesser value on things available in abundance.

"I wrote to Ishmael's father that I would be ashamed and dishonored to offer only one thousand pieces of gold for a son, and do you know what he wrote back?"

Zoë dutifully shook her head, a little afraid of the answer. "That he would be ashamed and dishonored to have only one wife."

Zoë caught her breath at his reply, and she felt herself getting angry too. "Is that why you attacked him in the courtyard?"

Balian froze, and it was several moments before he answered.

"No. No, but the words were in my mind and no doubt added to my rage," he admitted.

"Why *did* you attack him?" Zoë persisted in a low voice; she felt she needed to better understand this man she had married.

Balian still hesitated, because he did not know Zoë well enough yet to be sure how she would react, but at length he admitted: "He called you a whore." Zoë caught her breath and remembered Beth's face: the girl had understood. Before she could even sort out her emotions, Balian continued. "He did it to insult *me*—despite the courtesy and generosity I have shown all of them. When he caught sight of you, he said, 'Look at that! These Franks are so lacking in honor, they let their wives show themselves to strange men like common whores.'"

The words sparked indignation in Zoë, and she found herself asking, "And what did you answer him?"

"Oh, I don't know exactly." Balian shrugged in embarrassment. "In my fury, my Arabic went to hell, and I probably only managed a lot of gibberish."

Zoë did not believe him entirely, but it was true that being angry in a foreign language was almost as difficult as cracking jokes in one. It had taken her years before she could be either angry or humorous in French. "What did you *try* to say?"

"Something about Franks having so *much* honor that we need not lock away our wives to protect them—since only dishonorable men would leer at another man's wife. To which Ishmael said that if a woman was so wanton as to show herself in public unveiled, a man would have to be a eunuch *not* to leer. That was when I sliced open his face, and told him the scar would remind him that Franks punished men who were so boorish as to leer at their wives. I told him he'd gotten away lightly only because he was an unarmed prisoner; otherwise he would already be dead."

Zoë took a deep breath, and then a sip of wine to steady herself. "I'm sorry to be the cause of this incident," she declared, putting her wineglass back on the table. "I shouldn't have shown myself to them."

"Why not?" Balian asked back sharply. "This is *my* palace, in *my* city, in *your* Kingdom! You have the right to go anywhere you please!

It's my prisoners who have forgotten themselves! I have been too lenient with them, but that has changed. The messenger will return to Damascus tomorrow with the news that they will be kept in chains in the darkness from now until the summer solstice. Tomorrow I will have them transported—blindfolded and in shackles on the back of an ox-cart!—to the dungeon at Ibelin. If the ransom has not been paid by the solstice, they will be sold as slaves. Maybe that will awaken some paternal feelings in their polygamous fathers!"

Ibelin, May 1178

CONSCIOUS OF HIS OWN COWARDICE, BALIAN put distance between himself and his wife's agony. Her water had burst in the night, and the contractions started soon afterwards. He had dressed at once and gone for the midwife, while Rahel and the other women took Maria Zoë to the ground-floor chamber of the northeast tower, which had the best access to the cistern. This chamber had long since been readied for her lying-in with supplies of linens, candles, a cradle, and, of course, the birthing stool.

For hours the sound of Maria Zoë's screams had been coming from that chamber, and while Balian initially kept up the pretense of checking on the work still being done on the stables and then inspecting the garrison, he had all too soon run out of things to do that did not take him away from the castle. He gave some thought to going in to Ibelin town to see how work was progressing on rebuilding the wool warehouse, but he hesitated to be so far away. Surely the ordeal would be over soon?

Balian had no experience or memories to draw on. His mother had moved away when he was an infant, and although Agnes de Courtenay had given his brother two stillborn children, he had been too little at the time to remember those births. Even as a squire, he had served in the household of Hebron after his wife was beyond childbearing age. All Balian knew was that Maria Zoë had nearly died giving birth to Isabella.

A wrenching, high-pitched scream split the early afternoon air, making Balian blanch. This wasn't a conscious scream. It was the kind of scream that was wrung from a person so racked with sharp and sudden pain that they had no will anymore. Balian had heard screams like this on the battlefield, but not from a woman—not from someone he loved.

"How much longer, did you say?" he asked Shoreham, who was standing nearby.

"Hours, my lord. If you want to ride out for a bit, I'm sure you won't miss anything."

"No." Balian couldn't do that. Instead he pounded down the stairs of the keep and entered the crypt under the first-floor chapel in the exterior wall.

The crypt was dark and cool. Balian fell onto his knees beside his brother's tomb. The effigy had been completed only two years ago and was still fresh and white, almost raw. The sculptor, a local artist who had done much of the work on the façade of St. George's, might not have the skill of the Byzantine sculptors King Amalric had invited in to renovate the Church of the Nativity, but he had known Hugh. Balian saw his brother's features in the knight lying on the top of the tomb, his legs crossed at the ankle and his hands clasping the hilt of his sword. His surcoat opened up the front to reveal his mailed legs and the garters holding up his chausses. The crosses of Ibelin dusted the stone surcoat in relief.

Balian found it intimidating to pray for the birth of a son before his brother, who had not been blessed with any live children. He bent his head and prayed instead for the repose of Hugh's soul.

His prayers were disturbed, however, by whispers coming from the chapel overhead. Irritated, Balian lifted his head to listen more closely. Stone ducts had been built to lead from behind the altar of the chapel down into the crypt so that the dead, too, would have the benefit of hearing Mass. As children, Balian and his brothers had played games seeing how softly they could speak into one of the ducts upstairs and still be understood in the crypt below. One of them would whisper something, the second would say what he heard, and the third was the judge of whether he was right or wrong.

Frowning, Balian moved toward the altar of the crypt, his head raised toward the outlet of the nearest duct.

"… She never screamed like that when I was born!" Isabella insisted in her stubborn, childish voice.

"She did, too!" Eschiva shot back. "All women do! Beth says her father's second and third wives both died in childbirth. Both of them! And the child still in them!" Eschiva sounded almost delighted to have such gruesome tales with which to frighten Isabella.

Balian was simply appalled that he had forgotten all about the children. With Rahel and Mistress Shoreham and the other women attending Zoë, the little girls had been left on their own. The measure of their fear could be judged by the very fact that they were in the chapel.

Balian left the crypt at once, and with only a single despairing glance in the direction of the "torture chamber" (as he thought of the birthing room), he climbed to the first floor and entered the chapel. He found Beth kneeling in front of the beautiful icon to the Mother of God that Maria Zoë had brought with her and had hung in a side niche. Beth was gazing up at the icon with an intense expression that bespoke doubt and fear. Eschiva and Isabella had long since lost interest in prayer, but lacking any better place to go or unwilling to abandon Beth, they were standing in the choir. Isabella was kicking one of the wooden stalls, while Eschiva slouched on the wooden rest.

At the sight of Balian, Eschiva straightened up guiltily, and Isabella looked over her shoulder to see what had made her cousin react. She looked at Balian with big golden eyes and asked simply, "When is it going to be over?"

Balian swept her up onto the crook of his arm with an honest, "I don't know, but I think it's time we all went down to check up on Gladiator, don't you?"

"Gladiator? But Tante Marie—" Eschiva protested.

"We can't help Tante Marie," Balian interrupted her, holding out his free hand. Eschiva took it obediently, and Balian started back out of the chapel. He paused behind Beth, but she pretended not to notice him. He knew she was still very reluctant to be in his—or any male—company, and supposed she was best off where she was.

Balian found both his squires down in the stables. Although he gave them a reproving look, he could hardly blame them for doing what he had wanted to do: get as far away from the screams as possible. At the sight of Balian with the girls, the squires hastily came over to be of assistance, asking whether Balian wanted the girls' ponies tacked up. Isabella said yes immediately, but Eschiva said no, and Balian decided on the middle ground. "Tack up Isabella's pony and I'll give her a lesson." Then, of course, Eschiva wanted a lesson, too, so the ponies were quickly brushed down and tacked up.

While the squires were seeing to the ponies, Mathewos came over to stand beside Balian. He didn't say anything, just stood with him, and Balian felt his sympathy; Mathewos's wife had died giving him his youngest son. Balian found himself wondering why the groom had never remarried, and then felt guilty for the thought. It was as if he were imagining Zoë already dead.

"I may have found a replacement for Gladiator," the groom spoke at last, as if to distract him.

"Really?" Although Balian had been worrying about this ever since it became clear that Gladiator was unlikely to heal enough to carry him in battle again, at the moment Balian wasn't really interested in the topic.

"Yes. He's no longer a colt. He's seven already, and he's been ill used, I suspect, although I don't know if it was the horse dealer or the previous owner."

"Ill used?" Balian tried to concentrate. "But not ruined?"

Mathewos scratched his head thoughtfully. "I think if he is well treated and comes to trust you, he will be very grateful and loyal, but we won't know unless we try. He is very cheap."

Balian looked sideways at Mathewos. Cheap had never been a criterion for buying a horse—even when he was a landless knight.

"He is so cheap that other buyers underestimate his value."

"Go ahead, buy him," Balian agreed. "We have little to lose until we find something better."

Then with a sigh, he led his stepdaughter and niece over the drawbridge and out to the tiltyard beyond the castle walls on the edge of the dunes. Here he tried to concentrate on teaching them the elements of riding, while his nerves remained on edge and his thoughts were with his wife.

"It's a lovely little girl," Mistress Shoreham declared with a wide smile as she took the infant from the midwife.

"Girl?" Maria Zoë gasped out in horrified disbelief. She had been so certain that this time she wouldn't fail; not for Balian.

The other women closed around her, helping her up off the stool and carrying, as much as leading, her to the bed. Rahel wiped the blood and other fluids off her belly and thighs with a linen cloth drenched in warm water. The midwife was busily dealing with the umbilical cord and afterbirth, and one of the younger laundresses daubed the sweat from Maria Zoë's face.

"Girl?" Maria Zoë asked again, twisting to get a look at the baby in Mistress Shoreham's ample arms, while the others tucked her in under the clean sheets, ready to receive her lord.

"A pretty little girl, just like her mama!" Mistress Shoreham agreed, wiping the red face of the infant clean with a small square of damp cotton.

"My God, no!" Maria Zoë sobbed as she curled into a ball, hiding beneath the covers in shame. It had been the birth of Isabella that had ruined her first marriage, but she hadn't cared about that so much—not like she cared about Balian. She had feared for her status, for her position at court, for her reputation—but this was different. Now she feared the loss of everything that mattered to her. What was the use of gold, jewels, or silk? What were Nablus and all her dower wealth, if she did not retain the affection of the man she loved?

Why couldn't it have been a boy? she asked wordlessly, sobbing miserably. Was God so angry just because she and Balian had known each other carnally before being married? But she had been a virgin bride for Amalric, and still He had sent a girl. Did He hate her? And even if He hated her, what had Balian ever done to deserve this? She could hardly catch any air, buried as she was in the thick comforters, and she gasped for breath, writhing in inner agony. She was so lost in her own misery that she did not hear the voices at the door, nor realize that Balian had arrived, until he reached out his hand.

"Shhh!" he urged her, his hand warm and dry on her ankle—the only part of her not covered by the sheets.

"Balian!" she gasped, but did not dare emerge from under the covers to meet his reproachful eyes. She closed hers more tightly still and tried to hide her head under her arms.

"Zoë." His warm, deep voice penetrated her sobs. "What's the matter?" he asked gently.

"It's a girl! Didn't they tell you? It's only a girl!"

"But she's healthy," Balian countered. "And the women tell me she looks like me—though I'm not sure that's a compliment, given the way she looks." He laughed, and the women laughed with him.

"Balian?" Maria Zoë tried to stop her sobs as she lifted the covers just enough to let in some air through a tunnel of linen. "You're sure you aren't angry?"

"Why should I be angry?" he asked back. "God made both men and women that they might draw comfort from one another, and He made this child of ours a girl. Should I question His wisdom in giving me a daughter? Or even if I did, why should I be angry with you?"

Maria Zoë at last ventured a peek over the edge of the covers. Balian was sitting on the side of the bed looking at her; he smiled when he saw her eyes emerge above the sheets.

Maria Zoë still couldn't believe it, but she unfolded enough to pull herself onto the pillows and sit up a little, hiccupping. "Truly? You aren't angry?"

"Zoë, as long as you are well, I am content."

Maria Zoë hiccupped and stared at him.

"Don't you want to see her?" Balian turned to the wet nurse, who placed Balian's daughter in his arms, and he then held her out to his wife. The baby was red and wrinkled with a caved-in face, a wet mouth, and a shock of wet black hair. She screamed at being taken from the wet nurse's breast, and her cry was loud and shrill.

Maria Zoë looked down at her daughter in confusion, protectiveness warring with disappointment, but she didn't take the child from Balian.

"Shall we call her after her mother?" Balian asked.

"Good heavens, no!" Maria Zoë answered. "There are far too many Marias in the world already."

"What about your mother, then?" Balian asked, realizing to his shame that he did not even know his mother-in-law's name.

"Another Maria!" she protested. "What about your mother?"

"Helvis?" Balian asked skeptically, thinking Zoë wouldn't be such a bad name.

"Yes!" Maria Zoë agreed, ending the discussion and taking the baby from him at last, her eyes now glued to her little daughter. "Helvis is a lovely name for her."

Balian wanted to protest, but the look on Zoë's face had been transformed into one of such contentment that he didn't have the heart to shatter the scene. At that moment, he beheld the most beautiful mother-and-child image he had ever seen.

Shoreham didn't like the look of the party of Muslim cavalry demanding admittance, but they came under a flag of truce—and Mathewos, who came out to translate, said they had come about the ransoms. Shoreham grumbled and gave orders to keep a good watch on them, for they had both large, curved sabers and straight swords, and they wore chain mail under their silken tunics. Their turbans were of yellow silk, and Mathewos whispered that they were from Salah ad-Din's own Mamluke guard—provoking another growl from Shoreham.

When Daniel came down to tell his father that Lord Balian would see the envoy, Shoreham pulled him aside and warned him, "Keep on your guard, Daniel. They're as likely to try to kill Lord Balian as negotiate with him."

Daniel nodded, his hand moving automatically to grip the hilt of his sword before he gestured for the Saracen spokesman to follow him. He led the Saracen across the ward to mount the exterior steps leading to the Great Chamber, where Balian had agreed to meet him. The whole time, Daniel was conscious of just how vulnerable the spot between his shoulder blades was. He wasn't wearing armor when performing household duties like this; Balian only let him put on armor for weapons practice in the morning or when they rode out on patrols. Daniel was so conscious of his own vulnerability that he didn't give a thought to what it must be like for the Saracen, alone in the heart of an enemy fortress.

The Great Chamber on the first floor of the keep was used as a courtroom, and Balian sat in the tall armed chair behind the table as he would on a day when he was hearing petitions, settling disputes, or sitting in judgment on accused criminals. He was dressed, Daniel noted with relief, in a hauberk under a surcoat, although he had not bothered with mail chausses and wore soft leather boots instead. The surcoat was yellow silk with red crosses, and each cross was outlined in gold stitching; it was one of his best, Daniel noted with approval. Balian wore no head covering, but he was wearing a large carnelian signet ring that Daniel could not remember him wearing before. He looked, to Daniel's admiring eyes, very impressive.

The Mamluke negotiator bowed ceremonially before the Christian lord, and opened with a flood of Arabic that, of course, Daniel could no more understand than Balian's lengthy answer. What he did understand was that Balian gestured for the visitor to take a seat at the end of the table—a place of honor, though not of equality—and he sent Daniel to get refreshment. "Sherbet, not wine. Our visitor abstains from alcohol."

"Ah, but, my lord," Daniel started to protest, remembering his father's warning, but Balian gave him such a reproachful look at his impertinence that he had no choice but to bob his head and back out. No sooner was he out the door, however, than he gestured furiously to some of Balian's household knights who were standing around curiously. "I have to go for refreshments," he told them, "but keep an ear on what's going on in there!"

The knights looked at one another, more amused than affronted by Daniel's impertinence. Then one of them nodded and came up the stairs to stand within easy call, while Daniel continued toward the kitchens.

Inside the Great Chamber, Balian and the messenger had finished with the opening pleasantries. The messenger had established that he was indeed sent by the Sultan himself and had come to discuss the release of Balian's prisoners—all three of them, he stressed. He was authorized to make such payments as they agreed to, but he insisted he would not begin the negotiations until he had himself seen and spoken with the prisoners and assured himself of their well-being. "The last envoy suggested that you were angry and intended to punish the captives," he noted with a cold smile.

"Did he also tell you why?" Balian shot back.

"He said there had been an unfortunate incident in which spirited young men had spoken tactlessly."

"And what would your lord call an insult to his first wife?" Balian wanted to know.

The negotiator opened his hands. "None of my lord's wives are ever seen in public! How can they provoke comment one way or another?"

"First, my own residence is not public. Second, the Dowager Queen of Jerusalem is a public figure throughout *her* Kingdom. Third, a woman who carries the blood of the Roman Emperors in her veins is more noble than I—or the Kurdish upstart who has stolen the Sultanate of Cairo and then Damascus from the rightful heirs."

The negotiator caught his breath at Balian's pointed reminder of who his master was, but did not object openly.

Balian continued, "Perhaps Ishmael did not *know* he was speaking of the Greek Emperor's niece—" Balian wanted there to be no mistake that the insult had not been to him alone, but to the most powerful imperial family in the world— "when he called my wife a whore, but calling *any* man's wife a whore is an insult in *any* country and *any* language—and even teenage boys know that. The insult was calculated and intended, born of contempt for me, my religion, my race, and my country. It has been treated as such. No more—and no less."

The negotiator bowed his head in acknowledgement, then insisted, "I wish to see the prisoners."

"By all means." Balian got to his feet, and the envoy followed suit. "You can go at once, while we wait for the sherbet." Balian went to the door and was not terribly surprised to find one of his knights there. He sent the man to fetch Shoreham with the keys to the prisoners' cells.

By the time the envoy returned from visiting the prisoners, Daniel and Dawit had brought lime-laced sherbet, pistachios, and dates. They stood discreetly in the background as Shoreham and the envoy emerged from the bowels of the keep. The envoy took his seat again, and Shoreham retreated behind the door—only a call away.

"I understand you are to be congratulated on the birth of a child—although Allah, praise to His name, saw fit to grant you only a daughter," the envoy opened.

"Did the Prophet Mohammed have a son?" Balian shot back.

"No, but that was to prevent the kind of heresy committed by followers of Ali, who falsely allege that blood ties are more important than holiness. For a secular lord, the birth of sons is necessary, and so a sign of Allah's favor."

"Did the Sultan not have a mother? Or would he get children with other men, perhaps? A world with men alone would be a sorry place—as God, in His wisdom, knew when he created the world. I do not question the will of God in creating women, nor in giving me a daughter."

"Allah created women for our pleasure—to serve us, not to rule us."

"I wonder that a man who knows the mind of God is only a slave, and not ruler of an empire," Balian shot back.

The envoy bowed his head to acknowledge his status. "And my Master wonders that a man marked by leprosy—which is surely a sign of Divine displeasure—can be master of *any* kingdom, even a Christian one."

"Is it not even *more* amazing, then," Balian countered, leaning forward onto his elbows, "that a leper youth should rout the army of the Sultan of Damascus and Cairo, and come within a lance's length of killing or capturing the Sultan himself?"

"A leper youth?" the envoy asked, his eyebrows cocked in disbelief. "Or the brothers of Ibelin? I understand your brother led the main forces at Montgisard."

Balian shook his head. "No. Not the Ibelin brothers, or the combined forces of the barons, knights, and burgesses of Jerusalem, or the Templars. Your Sultan was defeated by a leper youth with the heart of a lion and the grace of God."

"In that case," the negotiator smoothly countered, "should not the ransom go to King Baldwin?"

"My King defeated the armies of your Sultan—but your Sultan would also have been taken prisoner, if my prisoners had not come between him and me. The battle was already lost, thanks to Jerusalem and the grace of God; the Sultan's *freedom* is thanks to the courage of my prisoners."

"It is the duty of a Sultan's bodyguard to protect their lord—and if necessary, die for him—"

"As many did," Balian pointed out. "But these young men survived. Does your master blame them for it? Is gratitude alien to him? Or is he ashamed to welcome them home for fear they will cast aspersions on his own courage?"

"Of course not!" the envoy retorted, for the first time allowing emotion to show by the tone of his voice and his frown.

"Then why not pay the ransoms?"

"They are exorbitant."

"What do you think the Sultan's ransom would have been?"

"But these men are not the Sultan. They did their duty. Nothing more."

"And that is your Sultan's gratitude for his freedom?" Balian asked, leaning back in his chair. They both knew the envoy wouldn't be here at all if Salah ad-Din had not agreed to ransom the prisoners.

"The Sultan is prepared to pay five thousand bezants per prisoner, fifteen thousand total."

Balian shook his head. "No."

"You will receive nothing near that much on the slave market," the envoy pointed out reasonably.

"No, but this isn't about money, is it? I have a rich wife." Balian gestured to the furnishings around him, which were distinctly Byzantine, from the chests under the windows to the tapestries on the walls.

"Then what is this about?"

"Respect—for those who saved the Sultan from captivity, and those who nearly captured him."

The envoy absorbed this calmly, without any indication of surprise.

"I am willing to accept five thousand bezants each for Rashid and Muhammed," Balian now offered, "but I will not let Ishmael go for less than fifteen thousand bezants, because he has earned slavery through his arrogance; he would learn a great deal from it." He let this sink in, knowing that Ishmael was the highest born of all the prisoners.

Balian could see the envoy calculating, trying to guess what his master would be willing to accept. "The Sultan will pay five thousand for Rashid and Muhammed, but no more than ten thousand for Ishmael."

"Then let us settle for Rashid and Muhammed, and—if you have brought the funds—you may take them back with you."

"And Ishmael?"

Balian shrugged. "He will be sold to the Bedouins."

The envoy drew a deep breath of displeasure; the Bedouins were notoriously treacherous and often aided the Christians. "Twelve thousand for Ishmael," he countered.

Balian hesitated. He thought he might actually be able to press for the full fifteen thousand—but then again, he was tired of the whole process and anxious to be free of the prisoners. Twenty-two thousand bezants was still a fortune. He nodded, and the envoy smiled for the first time.

"We have terms," he confirmed, and they bowed to one another.

Then, for the first time, the envoy grinned. "My master has one more message for you: he told me to tell you that one day he hopes to meet you again on the battlefield."

Balian bowed his head in acknowledgment, a courteous smile on his lips, but his heart was heavy. Salah ad-Din had declared *jihad*, and he had the troops and the resources to pursue it. Since he was determined to attack, and Balian had no intention of abandoning his heritage, his people, or his God, he saw little hope that he could avoid the next confrontation. "I will be waiting for him," Balian answered simply.

Dear Reader,

If you enjoyed this book, please a take moment to write and post a review on amazon.com, Barnes and Noble, or Goodreads.

Thank you!

Helena P. Schrader

Historical Note

Balian d'Ibelin was a historical figure, and his name and deeds are depicted in the contemporary chronicles of both Christians and Muslims. Yet while his contributions to history are part of the historical record, many facts about his personal life went unrecorded. We do not know the dates of either his birth or his death, and sources (or contemporary interpretations of contradictory medieval copies of lost sources) differ on other important dates, such as the year he inherited the baronies of Ibelin and Ramla, the year his brother left the Kingdom of Jerusalem, and more. It is even a point of controversy whether Balian was the second or third son of the first or second Baron d'Ibelin.

Given these gaps and contradictions, this novel has opted for a lucid story line that is not inconsistent with key known facts and in no way violates the historical record, but condenses or simplifies some events to make the story more coherent and dramatically effective. Before focusing on the things I've changed, let me highlight the key events covered in this volume that—surprising as they may seem—are historical fact.

- Balian was a younger son of the Lord d'Ibelin, with no right to inheritance at the time of his father's death.

- The repudiation of Agnes de Courtenay was a condition of King Amalric's ascension to the throne of Jerusalem. While the technical grounds for divorce were consanguinity, this was the standard excuse used by kings to depose of unwanted wives in the period (see Louis VII and Eleanor of Aquitaine) and can be viewed as a pretext, not a cause. The real reason must lie elsewhere and, significantly, it was not dissatisfaction on the part of King Amalric, but objections from the High Court. Some sources suggest his marriage to her was bigamous, because she had been married (or betrothed) to Hugh d'Ibelin before marrying Amalric—but if this were the objection, then her children by Amalric would have been deemed illegitimate, which they were not. One key chronicle imputes immorality, claiming Agnes had affairs with Heraclius, later the Patriarch of Jerusalem, and Aimery de Lusignan, but modern historians question whether she could have had a scandalous reputation at the time of the divorce. So while the reason remains obscure, the fact is indisputable: the High Court of Jerusalem made up of the bishops and barons of the Kingdom deemed Agnes de Courtenay, despite her impeccable pedigree, unsuitable to be their queen. That is a significant condemnation, which, I believe, justifies a negative portrayal of her in the novel, and is supported by her generally negative influence on political events later in her son's reign.

- Baldwin IV really was a leper. He was diagnosed as a child, and he had already lost the use of his hands when he succeeded to the throne. Nevertheless, he was reputedly a superb horseman. For more information about leprosy in this historical period, see "Note on Leprosy" following this Historical Note.

- Baldwin IV really did bring a relief force of roughly 375 knights to Ascalon in 1177. He broke out of the encirclement with these knights to rendezvous with the Templars from Gaza. He led his army to a stunning victory over Saladin (Salah ad-Din) at Montgisard on November 25, 1177.

- According to Arab sources, both Balian d'Ibelin and his elder brother played a prominent role at the Battle of Montgisard, although Reynald de Châtillon also played a key if not decisive role.

- Despite being a landless younger son, Balian married the Byzantine princess and Dowager Queen of Jerusalem, Maria Comnena—either before or at the same time as he became a peer of the realm. Since she was independently wealthy and mature and could not have been compelled into a new marriage, this is about as close to a love match as it comes among the nobility in the late twelfth century—at least on her part. Balian's motives may indeed have been more venal.

- The marriage was, however, explicitly sanctioned by King Baldwin IV.

- Baldwin d'Ibelin (called Barisan/Barry in the novel to avoid confusion with King Baldwin) did cede the paternal Barony of Ibelin to Balian in the late 1170s, while retaining for himself the more lucrative Baronies of Ramla and Mirabel. There is nothing in the historical record to explain why. However, he repudiated his first wife of many years to marry an heiress, for which he would have needed the King's permission—hence my interpretation that the former was a condition of the latter.

Let me now turn to the features of the novel for which more literary license was necessary:

- All sources agree that the first Baron d'Ibelin had three sons who lived long enough to be considered male heirs: Hugh, Baldwin, and Balian. A Hugh d'Ibelin, apparently the second Baron d'Ibelin, furthermore played a significant role in the Kingdom of Jerusalem between 1153 and 1169 (at the siege of Ascalon, the Battle of Banias, and the expedition to Egypt of 1167), before dying in 1171. What is not clear is whether this

Hugh d'Ibelin was the older brother of the Baldwin/Barisan and Balian d'Ibelin of this novel, or—as some historians postulate—their father. The latter sources, however, suggest that the second Baron d'Ibelin also had three sons with the same names as the first, which while possible, is not entirely plausible. Alternatively, the Hugh d'Ibelin who was active between 1153 and 1169 could have been a younger brother of the first Baron d'Ibelin (since all males of the family at this time called themselves "Ibelins" without necessarily holding the barony), who was only acting as guardian for his nephews. Or—the variant I find most plausible and have made the basis of this novel—Hugh was the son of the first Baron d'Ibelin by an earlier marriage. This would explain why he was significantly older than his brothers Baldwin and Balian and was active at a time when they were still minors—and, more important, would explain why he was only Baron of Ibelin, whereas Baldwin was Baron of Ramla/Mirabel even during Hugh's lifetime, only taking the title of Lord of Ibelin after Hugh died in 1171. In other words, Hugh inherited the paternal title of Ibelin, while Baldwin (Barry), as the oldest son of the first Baron's second wife, the heiress of Ramla/Mirabel, inherited the latter titles from his (but not Hugh's) mother.

- I have dated Balian's own birth at 1149 rather than 1143, as some modern historians postulate, because the evidence for the earlier date is based on the very weak fact that he was a witness at his brother's wedding in 1158. This fact has led historians to postulate he must have been of legal age (fifteen) at the time. However, the Church viewed children over the age of seven as capable of giving consent to holy vows, including matrimony. It seems to me that if an eight-year-old could marry, he or she could also witness a wedding. The fact that Balian first plays a significant role in 1177, fighting at Montgisard and marrying Maria Zoë Comnena in an age when "adulthood" started at fifteen, makes a later date of birth than 1143 more plausible; a birth year of 1149 suited my literary purposes.

- The character of Henri d'Ibelin is completely fictional. He was invented because the Ibelin family was one of the most powerful families in the Latin Kingdom of Cyprus by the end of the twelfth century—and this under the Lusignan kings, whom Baldwin (Barry) and Balian had opposed consistently and vehemently in the Kingdom of Jerusalem. I invented a younger brother allied with the Lusignans for a novel set in 13th century Cyprus (*The Lion of Karpas*) and wanted the two series to be compatible. Since the publication of *Knight of Jerusalem,* however, my research has uncovered a historical figure to fill the role seen for the fictional brother in *The Lion of Karpas.* Since it is now too late to remove Henri, my readers will have to live with him. View him as a literary device.

- On the other hand, Baldwin (Barry) d'Ibelin had two daughters who lived to adulthood, Eschiva and Stephanie. I "killed" Stephanie off early just to help keep down the number of characters in an already complex novel.

- I have condensed the events at the time of Amalric's death from several months to a couple of weeks for dramatic effect. Historically, Oultrejourdain was appointed Seneschal and Humphrey of Toron (the elder) was appointed Constable, and they were supposed to rule jointly for Baldwin IV. Oultrejourdain either overstepped his bounds or at any rate made powerful enemies, and Tripoli was appointed Regent either just before or just after Oultrejourdain was mysteriously murdered.

- There is no evidence that Balian was Constable of Ascalon before his marriage and before his brother turned over the barony of Ibelin to him. The real Constable of Ascalon at this time was the aging Humphrey de Toron, who held a number of other titles and was not present when the town was invested. However, Balian's father had been Constable of Jaffa before being given a barony, and this was the normal means of testing an up-and-coming man's military and administrative ability. By inventing Balian's appointment to Constable of Ascalon, I created an opportunity to tell the reader a little more about the demographics of the Kingdom, provided a means to describe the dramatic (and historical) relief force that King Baldwin brought to Ascalon during Salah ad-Din's first invations, and positioned Balian to take part in the Battle of Montgisard, which historically he did.

- After bypassing Ascalon in 1177, Salah ad-Din's troops sacked Ramla and Lydda, and it was in Lydda that the population sought refuge in the fortress-like cathedral of St. George. I condensed these events and moved the venue to Ibelin, for dramatic effect and because Ibelin was more important to Balian. In the novel, Ibelin is a microcosm of the Kingdom of Jerusalem. The fact remains that one of the Ibelin towns was sacked, people did take refuge in a basilica, and both Ibelin brothers played a prominent role in the Battle of Montgisard.

- There is no historical reference to Balian's close relationship with King Baldwin IV, but there is circumstantial evidence—namely, 1) the fact that the King expressly approved his exceptionally (almost scandalously) advantageous marriage to the Byzantine princess and Dowager Queen Maria Comnena in 1177, and 2) the King chose Balian to carry his heir Baldwin V to the Church of the Holy Sepulchre in 1185. These two marks of favor are extreme, considering the fact that Ibelin was a small and comparatively insignificant barony, which owed only ten knights to the Crown. (Major baronies owed five to ten times as many knights.) Furthermore, the Prince of Antioch and the Counts of Tripoli and Edessa were all close relations of the King. While Balian's marriage *might* have been the result of maneuvering on the part of his brother, in a highly hierarchical society it would have been normal for any of the more senior barons or relatives of the King to be selected to carry the future King to the Church of the Holy Sepulchre. The fact that Balian was "exceptionally" tall does not explain Balian being given such an honor ahead of literally dozens of his peers; being a close friend of the King does.

- Although the chronicles, both Christian and Muslim, agree that Balian d'Ibelin and Salah ad-Din knew and respected one another, there is no account of how they had made one another's acquaintance. It is unclear whether they had met before the negotiations for Jerusalem, and if so, when and where, or if they knew of one another by reputation and hearsay only. The incident with the prisoners was designed to pave the way for the documented negotiations at Jerusalem in 1187 and after the Third Crusade in 1192.

- Last but not least, it may surprise some readers that I describe a lot of rain in the Kingdom of Jerusalem. However, this was the "land of milk and honey," not a desert wasteland (as some novels might have you believe), and there is a distinct rainy season, no matter how hot and arid summers—or some parts—of the Kingdom were. Ibelin lies on the fertile coastal plain, not on the Dead Sea.

The dialogue, the physical descriptions of the characters, and the supporting characters are all fiction. This is a novel—one based on historical fact, but a novel nevertheless.

Note on Leprosy

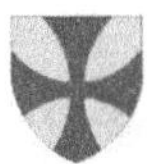

Baldwin IV of Jerusalem suffered from leprosy from the time he was a boy. He was diagnosed by his tutor William, later Archbishop of Tyre, while Baldwin was still a schoolboy, and he was recognized as a leper by contemporary society.

In writing this book, where Baldwin IV is a central character, it was important to understand both the disease as we know it today and what medieval man knew and thought about leprosy. I have relied heavily on Piers D. Mitchell's essay titled "An Evaluation of the Leprosy of King Baldwin IV of Jerusalem in the Context of the Medieval World," which appears as an appendix in Bernard Hamilton's *The Leper King and his Heirs: Baldwin IV and the Crusader Kingdom of Jerusalem*, and the excellent study of attitudes toward leprosy published by Timothy S. Miller and John W. Nesbitt, *Walking Corpses: Leprosy in Byzantium and the Medieval West.*

It was important to me that the actual evolution of the disease as depicted in this novel be consistent with both the historical record and the stages of the disease based on modern medical knowledge. For example, we know from William of Tyre that the leprosy first manifested itself as a lack of feeling in Baldwin's right hand. We know that Baldwin was an agile rider as a young adult and that he commanded his armies in person at Montgisard, on the Litani, at Le Forbelet, and even as late as the relief of Kerak in late 1183. However, his body was, in fact, decaying progressively and noticeably. William of Tyre also noted a particularly dramatic deterioration of Baldwin's health in the year 1183, and by the time he died in 1185 just short of his twenty-fourth birthday, he had gone blind and did not have the use of any of his limbs.

Based on the historical descriptions of Baldwin's initial illness, which state he had lost the feeling in his arm but that there were no other symptoms such as discoloration or ulcers, Mitchell suggests that Baldwin IV initially had primary polyneuritic tuberculoid leprosy, which deteriorated into lepromatous leprosy during puberty. There is, according to Mitchell, nothing inevitable about this deterioration—however, puberty itself can induce the deterioration, as can untended wounds (that go unnoticed due to loss of feeling) which cause ulcers to break out. Historically Baldwin led the dangerous campaign against Salah ad-Din that led to the surprise victory at Montgisard when he was in puberty, just sixteen years old. I hypothesize that it was in part because of this campaign—which required camping out in the field and going without the usual bathing of his feet and hands—that caused his disease to take a turn for the worse. According to Mitchell, children who develop lepromatous leprosy are likely to die prematurely, and so once Baldwin's leprosy had become lepromatous, it inevitably took its course through the gruesome stages of increasing incapacitation and disfigurement to an early death.

The degree to which the disease is contagious is another critical issue in this novel. Modern medical research suggests that although during an epidemic as much as 30 per cent of a population can catch the disease, once leprosy has become endemic to a population (as it was in the Levant in the twelfth century), only about 5 per cent of the population has a genetic proclivity to the disease and hence a high risk of contagion if exposed to the disease. Furthermore, if a person is susceptible to leprosy, he or she is most likely to develop it between the ages of ten and twenty—exactly the age at which Baldwin IV became ill. The adults in attendance upon him, however, such as the Archdeacon of Tyre and, in the novel, Balian, had less than a 5 per cent chance of becoming ill.

Just as important as an accurate depiction of the course of decay caused by leprosy, however, is a depiction of medieval beliefs about leprosy. We know today that less than 5 per cent of the population was likely to contract the disease if exposed, but medieval man believed the chances of contagion were much, much higher. Medieval medicine suggested at one extreme that just breathing the same air as lepers could result in infection. Yet because the disease was widespread, medieval man also knew that many men and women washed, cared for, and even kissed lepers without themselves contracting the disease. I have chosen, therefore, to have my characters subscribe to a non-scientific but plausible "enlightened" view of leprosy's contagion that is consistent with the fact that Baldwin IV was never completely isolated from society. Those closest to him evidently thought that by taking certain precautions they could remain healthy, while the majority avoided intimacy and maintained some distance without avoiding Baldwin altogether.

Medieval attitudes were not governed by the state of medical knowledge alone. Religion played a critical role. Leprosy was *not* seen as a sign of sin, but rather as a sign of Divine grace—particularly in Byzantium. Indeed, the Byzantines came to call leprosy "the holy disease," and there are a number of Greek Orthodox legends in which Christ appears as a leper. Miller and Nesbitt note that the harshest views on leprosy came from pre-Christian Germanic tribes and the Jews. Crusader Jerusalem, however, was far more heavily influenced by Byzantium than by the Germanic tribes or Judaism. This fact is underlined by the creation of the Knights of St. Lazarus in Jerusalem, probably in the second decade of the twelfth century, as an outgrowth from an earlier Byzantine or Armenian leper hospital.

In short, while the progression of the disease depicted in this novel is based on modern medical knowledge of leprosy, the attitudes and treatment provided Baldwin in the book are based on what we know of medieval remedies and attitudes toward leprosy during the twelfth century.

Glossary

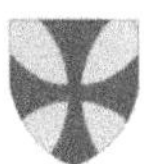

Abaya: a black garment, worn by Islamic women, that completely covers the head and body in a single, flowing, unfitted fashion so that no contours or limbs can be seen. It leaves only the face, but not the neck, visible and is often supplemented with a mask or "veil" that covers the face, leaving only a slit for the eyes between the top of the abaya (which covers the forehead) and the mask or veil across the lower half of the face.

Aketon: a padded and quilted garment, usually of linen, worn under or instead of chain mail.

Aventail: a flap of chain mail, attached to the coif, that could be secured by a leather thong to the brow band to cover the lower part of the face.

Bailli: a governor or appointed official of the Crown, but also the elected head of one of the independent commercial "communes" of the Pisans, Venetians, or Genoese.

Battlement: a low wall built on the roof of a tower or other building in a castle, fortified manor, or church, with alternating higher segments for sheltering behind and lower segments for shooting from.

Buss: a large combination oared and sailed vessel that derived from Norse cargo (not raiding) vessels. They had substantial cargo capacity but were also swift and maneuverable.

Cantle: the raised part of a saddle behind the seat; in this period it was high and strong, made of wood, to help keep a knight in the saddle even after taking a blow from a lance.

Cervelliere: an open-faced helmet that covered the skull like a close-fitting, brimless cap; usually worn over a chain-mail coif.

Chain mail (mail): flexible armor composed of interlinking riveted rings of metal. Each link passes through four others.

Chancellors: royal and baronial officials responsible for maintaining, filing, and archiving documents, particularly charters related to the transfer of property and the like. They were usually clerics, and served as advisers to their lords on legal matters.

Chausses: mail leggings to protect a knight's legs in combat.

Coif: a chain-mail hood, either separate from or attached to the hauberk.

Commune: the Italian city-states had assisted the land armies of the crusaders by blockading coastal cities and sometimes providing troops as well. In exchange, they had been granted territory in all the major coastal cities and the right to run their affairs more or less autonomously. The communes were governed by the laws of their founding city (Pisa, Venice, and so on), and had elected officials, headed by a "bailli" who represented them to the other sectors of society, particularly the feudal overlords of the territory in which they had settled.

Conroi: a medieval cavalry formation in which the riders rode stirrup to stirrup in rows that enabled a maximum number of lances to come to bear, but also massed the power of the charge.

Constable: the royal constable was the commanding general of the royal army in the absence of the king. The constable was responsible for mustering the army, ensuring it was adequately supplied, and carrying the king's standard or commanding in the absence of the king. The greater barons often had constables with similar functions, particularly mustering the vassals and securing the supplies of the baron's military entourage.

Court of the Bourgeoisie: the judicial body regulating and trying free, non-noble Frankish citizenry in the Kingdoms of Jerusalem and Cyprus.

Court of the Chain: the judicial body regulating maritime law and trying maritime cases.

Court of the Fonde: a court especially created to deal with commercial cases in market towns.

Crenel: an indentation or loophole in the top of a battlement or wall.

Crenelate: the act of adding defensive battlements to a building.

Faranj: (also sometimes Franj) the Arab term for crusaders and their descendants in Outremer.

Fief: land held on a hereditary basis from a lord in return for military service.

Fetlock: the lowest joint in a horse's leg.

Frank: the contemporary term used to describe Latin Christians (crusaders, pilgrims, and their descendants) in the Middle East, regardless of their country of origin. The Arab term "faranj" derived from this.

Destrier: a horse specially trained for mounted combat; a charger or warhorse.

Dragoman: an official of the crown or a baron responsible for representing his lord in the lord's rural domains. Although usually Franks of the sergeant class, they could be locals or knights. Their functions were very similar to English sheriffs. They were paid by their lord. The positions were not inherently hereditary, but custom favored the eldest son or a close relative of the previous dragoman.

Dromond: a large vessel with two to three lateen sails and two banks of oars. These vessels were built very strongly and were consequently slower, but offered more spacious accommodations.

Garderobe: a toilet, usually built on the exterior wall of a residence or fortification, that emptied into the surrounding ditch or moat.

Hajj: the Muslim pilgrimage to Mecca, one of the five duties of a good Muslim.

Hauberk: a chain-mail shirt, either long- or short-sleeved, that in this period reached to just above the knee.

High Court: similar to but more powerful than the English House of Lords, it was the council in which all the barons of the Kingdom (whether Jerusalem or Cyprus) sat to conduct the business of the state. The High Court was the legislature of the kingdoms, but also the chief executive body and the judiciary for the feudal elite.

The High Court elected the kings, conducted foreign policy, and tried their peers.

Iqta: a Seljuk institution similar to a fief in feudal Europe, but not hereditary. It was a gift from an overlord to a subject of land or other sources of revenue, which could be retracted at any time at the whim of the overlord.

Jihad: a Muslim holy war, usually interpreted as a war against nonbelievers to spread the faith of Islam.

Kettle helm: an open-faced helmet with a broad rim, common among infantry.

Khan: a large building built around a courtyard, often with a well, that provided temporary warehousing for goods on the ground floor and housing/lodgings on the upper stories for traveling merchants.

Lance: a cavalry weapon approximately fourteen feet long, made of wood and tipped with a steel head.

Mamlukes (also Mamelukes and Mamluks): former slaves who had been purchased or captured and then subjected to rigorous military training to make them an elite corps of fanatically loyal soldiers. Although technically freed on reaching adulthood, most generally retained a slavish devotion to their former masters and could be trusted to serve with particular selflessness. A Mamluke could, however, also be rewarded with lands and titles (e.g., a iqta) or simply valuable gifts. In 1250, the Mamlukes would revolt against their Sultan, murder him, and seize power for themselves.

Marshal: a royal or baronial official responsible for the horses of his lord's feudal host, including valuing the horses of vassals and ensuring compensation for losses.

Melee: a form of tournament in which two teams of knights face off across a large natural landscape and fight in conditions very similar to real combat, across ditches, hedges, swamps, streams, and so on. These were very popular in the late twelfth century—and very dangerous, often resulting in injuries and even deaths to both men and horses. The modern meaning of any confused, hand-to-hand fight among a large number of people derives from the medieval meaning.

Merlon: the solid part of a battlement or parapet between two openings or "crenels."

Outremer: A French term meaning "overseas," used to describe the crusader kingdoms (Kingdom of Jerusalem, County of Tripoli, County of Edessa, and Principality of Antioch) established in the Holy Land after the First Crusade.

Pommel: 1) the raised portion in front of the seat of a saddle; 2) the round portion of a sword above the hand grip.

Palfrey: a riding horse.

Parapet: A wall with crenelation built on a rampart or outer defensive work.

Quintain: a pivoted gibbet-like structure with a shield suspended from one arm and a bag of sand from the other, used to train for mounted combat.

Rampart: an earthen embankment surmounted by a parapet, encircling a castle or city as a defense against attack.

Ra'is (also Rays and Rais): in the Kingdom of Jerusalem, a native (Syrian) "head man," "chief," or "elder" recognized by the native community as a man of authority. The position was usually hereditary, and the Ra'is usually occupied a larger house and held more property or more lucrative property (such as olive orchards, mills, or wine presses) than the average peasant in the village.

Rear-Tenants: men who held land fiefs from tenants-in-chief of the crown—i.e., the vassals of vassals. Most tenants-in-chief of the crown held large territories they could not themselves manage and owed scores of knights to the feudal levee. They met their obligations by dividing up their holdings into smaller segments consisting of a few villages, or in some cases feudal privileges such as mills and bakeries, and bestowing these holdings on individual knights in exchange for rents and feudal service.

Scabbard (also **sheath**): the protective outer case of an edged weapon, particularly a sword or dagger.

Scribes: in the context of Outremer, scribes were (obviously literate) officials responsible for collecting taxes and fees within a certain domain. They were usually natives (Syrian or Greek), but they were appointed by the lord of the domain and required his trust.

They were often paid in land or payments in kind. There is no evidence that they were necessarily clerical.

Seneschal: the kings and great nobles employed this household official, who generally had responsibility for the finances of their lord—rather like the CFO of a major corporation today.

Snecka: a warship or galley that was very swift and maneuverable but had only a single bank of oars in addition to the sail, and so a low freeboard. These evolved from Viking raiding ships.

Surcoat: the loose, flowing cloth garment worn over armor; in this period it was slit up the front and back for riding and hung to mid-calf. It could be sleeveless or have short, wide elbow-length sleeves. It could be of cotton, linen, or silk and was often brightly dyed, woven, or embroidered with the wearer's coat of arms.

Tenant-in-chief: an individual holding land directly from the crown.

Turcopoles: troops drawn from the Orthodox Christian population of the crusader states. These were not, as is sometimes suggested, Muslim converts, nor were they necessarily the children of mixed marriages.

Vassal: an individual holding a fief (land) in exchange for military service.

Additional Reading

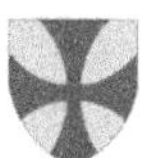

For more reading on the historical Balian d'Ibelin, Baldwin IV, the crusader states, and the crusades, I recommend the following sources:

Barber, Malcolm, *The Crusader States*, Yale University Press, 2012.

Bartlett, W.B., *Downfallof the Crusader Kingdom: The Battle of Hattin and the Loss of Jerusalem*, The History Press, 2007, 2010.

Conder, Claude Reignier, *The Latin Kingdom of Jerusalem, 1099 to 1291 A.D.*, Committee of the Palestine Exploration Fund, 1897.

Edbury, Peter W., *John of Ibelin and the Kingdom of Jerusalem*, The Boydell Press, 1997.

Edbury, Peter W., and John Gordon Rowe, *William of Tyre: Historian of the Latin East*, Cambridge University Press, 1988.

Hamilton, Bernard, *The Leper King and His Heirs: Baldwin IV and the Crusader Kingdom of Jerusalem*, Cambridge University Press, 2000.

Nicolle, David, *Hattin 1187: Saladin's Greatest Victory*, Osprey Military Campaign Series, 1193.

I also recommend the following websites/blogs:
http://defenderofjerusalem.com
http://Defendingcrusaderkingdoms.blogspot.com
http://crusades.scout.com
http://Tales-of-Chivalry.com

Also by Helena P. Schrader

Winner of the John E Weaver Excellent Reads Award for Fiction: Middle Ages

A divided kingdom,
a united enemy,
and the struggle for Jerusalem.

Book II of the Jerusalem Trilogy picks up where *Knight of Jerusalem* ends. It follows Balian to the fateful “Horns of Hattin” and on to the defense of Jerusalem against Salah ad-Din in 1187.

It was the recipient of a Feathered Quill Silver Award 2016 for Spiritual/Religious Fiction, a Readers’ Favorite Silver Award 2016 for Christian Historical Fiction, a Chaucer “First in Category” Award for Medieval Historical Fiction and was a finalist for the M.M. Bennett’s Award for Historical Fiction.

Best Biography 2017, Book Excellence Awards.
Best Christian Historical Fiction 2017, Readers' Favorites
Best Spiritual/Religious Fiction 2017, Feathered Quill
Best Biographical Fiction 2016, Pinnacle Awards

A lost kingdom,
A lionhearted king,
And the struggle to regain Jerusalem.

Balian has survived the devastating defeat of the Christian army at Hattin and walked away a free man after the surrender of Jerusalem, but he is baron of nothing in a kingdom that no longer exists. Haunted by the tens of thousands of Christians enslaved by the Saracens, he is determined to regain what has been lost. The arrival of a crusading army led by Richard the Lionheart offers hope—but also conflict as natives and crusaders clash and French and English quarrel.

The Jerusalem Trilogy is over, but follow me to Cyprus where Ibelins and Lusignans struggle to create a sustainable new kingdom in the former Byzantine provence—against armed opposition.

John d'Ibelin, son of the legendary Balian, will one day defy the most powerful monarch on earth: the Holy Roman Emperor Friedrich II Hohenstaufen. But first he must survive his apprenticeship-in-arms as the squire to a man determined to build a kingdon on an island ravaged by rebellion. The Greek insurgents have already driven the Knights Templar from the island, and now stand poised to destroy Richard the Lionheart's legacy to the Holy Land: a crusader foothold on the island of Cyprus.

CPSIA information can be obtained
at www.ICGtesting.com
Printed in the USA
BVHW04s1812040518
515201BV00002B/159/P